EPICENTER

MAJESTIC FILES - BOOK 1

ANDY BRIGGS

TANGLEBOX BOOKS

EPICENTER

Copyright © 2020 by Andy Briggs

All rights reserved. No part of this publication may be reproduced, distributed, or transmitted in any form or by any means, including photocopying, recording, or other electronic or mechanical methods, without the prior written permission of the publisher, except in the case of brief quotations embodied in critical reviews and certain other non-commercial uses permitted by copyright law.

Cover art: Shutterstock

www.andybriggsbooks.com
Twitter: @abriggswriter
Instagram: @itsandybriggs

EPICENTER
some things are best left undisturbed

ONE

VERONICA MADLE PULLED HARDER on the leash, forcing her reluctant three-year-old Labrador to follow her.

An initial hazy morning had lifted to reveal a beautiful June sky with temperatures teetering at 86° Fahrenheit, above the seasonal average for Los Angeles. A Santa Ana brought with it a welcome cooler breeze, and with it, the musky smell from the hills that most Angelenos could no longer detect. Veronica had decided to exercise her overweight pooch in Lincoln Park to savor a moment's peace before heading east for her class at California State University.

Now she was regretting it. The damn mutt had been acting oddly all morning.

She yelled louder than necessary to hear herself over the pounding rock music originating from her earbuds.

"Beano, c'mon!" She yanked the leash again.

The young canine whimpered, tail quivering between his legs, doleful eyes focused on his master, almost pleading. The animal could sense *something* no human could. An intangible fear.

Veronica's patience snapped. She pulled the leash so hard she was instantly regretful for fear that she had injured the dog.

"What the hell is wrong? I'm sorry, but you better not think I'm gonna carry your ass home—"

She was abruptly thrown to the sidewalk, as though an invisible hand had swiped the ground from beneath her feet in an elaborate conjuring trick.

At that moment, she heard a sustained basso profundo roar.

"Earthquake!" she gasped.

Most Angelenos took earth tremors in their daily stride. Veronica had experienced enough to know that this would be bigger than usual.

Around the park, people were jolted off balance. A cacophony of car alarms burst into song across the city, joining the earthly choir.

On trembling legs, Veronica raced out of the park, Beano at her heels requiring no prompting. Fine cracks spread across the sidewalk ahead of her, causing the dog to rear back, claws raking across the sidewalk.

"What is your problem now?" gasped Veronica with more than a hint of hysteria. She looked back in time to see the road violently split across the middle. One section elevated three feet into a cliff in the blink of an eye, severing sewage pipes that poured effluent across the street.

A station wagon ploughed into the raised slab of earth just yards from her, while a FedEx van approaching from the other end of the street ramped up the incline, brakes screeching. It slowed, but not enough to prevent it from tipping over the edge, crumpling the roof of the station wagon. The windshield and side windows burst as it slowly crushed the roof, trapping the screaming driver inside.

Veronica screamed and dropped the leash. Beano whined pitifully but remained rooted to the spot as his master fled. Veronica didn't even see the sidewalk part before her; it happened so swiftly. One moment she was staggering to maintain her balance, the next dropping into a fifteen-foot crevasse. Rock grazed her body as she fell, tearing open her running top and lacerating her chest and breasts, but she didn't have time to make a noise. The gap was too narrow. Her chin snagged the lip of the crevasse, her head too big to follow her body. She stopped abruptly - her own weight snapping her neck.

Beano hung his head as a powerful longitudinal shock wave slammed the sidewalk again - smashing it back together, leaving nothing more than a fine crack.

Los Angeles surfed on violent pulses of energy unleashed by the injured earth.

Roller-skaters along Venice Beach collided; two unlucky skaters clutching one another for support were struck as a Porsche careened wildly across the street, sending them high over the hood before the vehicle crashed into the already shattering glass of a vintage clothing store.

Weightlifters on the beach dropped dumbbells none too gracefully; one meathead got a whole fifty-pound weight on his exposed ankle.

Properties shook across Venice, exposing cheap materials and flagrant violations of building codes used in the construction of low rent property. One condo's foundations gave way under the punishment, and a stack of fifteen apartments collapsed into their basement, trapping everybody inside.

Walkways leading onto the *Queen Mary* writhed like rubber, spilling tourists and shoppers onto the pier below. The fifty-thousand-ton vessel rocked in her fixed moorings as angry waves lashed up across the San Pedro Bay area.

Properties across Wilmington and Long Beach took a pounding. On the corner of 7th and Ximeno, a group of hoods making a deal with kids on their way to school were busted as a streetlight swung down. The steel pole cracked open one gangbanger's skull. His companions fled as brains smattered the road.

Traffic ground to a halt at the intersection of Hollywood and North Highland, as vehicles rear-ended with the discord of twisting metal while they tried to avoid the toppling bust of a T-Rex cartwheeling from the roof of *Ripley's Believe It Or Not*.

A young girl, separated from her mother, ran into the center of the shaking road, attracted to the apparent safety of the exotic curves of Grauman's Chinese Theatre as an eighteen-wheel fuel tanker bore down. The driver spotted the flash of red from the child's romper suit, slammed on the brakes and veered with a rubber scream.

The girl's mother froze as she saw her child paralyzed in the middle of the boulevard, the truck jackknifing on the swaying asphalt. Her heart skipped as the vehicle bounced sidelong toward the child.

The little girl impulsively ducked as the tanker flipped from the ground. A quirk of physics - or a miracle - lifted the tanker just enough to sail over the child's head and collide with an empty tourist bus.

The girl was unharmed as her mother scooped her up.

The truck driver and bus driver were not so lucky in the ensuing conflagration.

Rocks and debris trickled down the Hollywood Hills. Scaffolding supporting the fifty-foot "Hollywood" sign groaned as Mount Lee buckled and writhed beneath it. For almost a century, the sign had been a symbol for the city, representing what LA stood for. Now, steel girders twisted from the repetitive violent impacts. The second 'L' dropped vertically, folding in two from the impact and was borne to the base of the hill in a cortège of rock.

Airports across the city were thrown into chaos as the alleged quake-proof airstrips developed jagged fissures. Power was completely lost in LAX as emergency generators failed to kick in. A mid-air collision between two Boeings was narrowly avoided by their vigilant pilots, who rapidly climbed from their aborted landings.

Across the hills, Burbank's Bob Hope Airport suffered tragedy as a landing Embraer private jet bounced on the cracking strip. The transverse shudder of the quake tipped the aircraft slightly to port - enough for the wing to scrape the runway, violently tearing it off. The impact buckled the port-side landing gear, and the entire plane pivoted a full one-eighty before blossoming in a ferocious fuel-injected orange fireball that covered the entire runway with burning shrapnel and avgas.

Two hundred feet below ground level, a D line Metro train shrieked along the rails as it decelerated from its fifty-five miles-per-hour cruise, stopping four hundred yards out of the Wilshire/Normandie station. Power to the third rail had been cut as outlined in the safety directives in the event of a quake of point-four magnitude or greater.

The four Italian crafted carriages were packed during the

rush hour squeeze. Six-hundred-fifty-eight bodies crammed into the train, rocking gently. Windows vibrated from the bass-heavy thunder around them.

Terrified passengers collectively held their breath, as the tunnel shook around them, unsure if it was at all safe to be seeking sanctuary underground, in the enemy's bosom.

Across the Santa Monica Mountains lay a sprawling suburbia - North Hollywood, Van Nuys, Reseda, San Fernando and Canoga Park - a desert paradise of picket fences and abandoned American dreams arranged with the beauty of graph paper.

People flocked into the streets as their homes quivered. Windows cracked and roofing joists snapped. Telephone and power cables were uprooted. Some fell onto parked vehicles, while dozens of cables sparked fires. Water pipes cracked, flooding homes and forming a web of muddy streams in the dry streets.

Fuel lines in a 76 gas station ruptured, spewing gasoline across the road: a snaking electricity cable ignited it, detonating the entire station in a deep orange fireball.

Josh Momoa was rolled off the sofa by the quake. His wife, Suzie, had the two kids cradled in her arms and was babbling incoherently. At first Josh figured Suzie had gone on another rampage, threatening to divorce unless he quit drinking. The room rolled around him, the effects of a heavy drinking spree from the wrap-party the night before. All thoughts of what he'd got up to when the grips wrapped on the movie set dissolved when the reality of the situation became apparent.

"Get under the doorjamb," he yelled.

"We're going outside," his wife screamed back, tightening the bathrobe around her waist. She held her daughter in one arm, while her son clutched her leg in fear. "This shack is a wreck!"

He grabbed Suzie around the waist, partly to stop her from going, but mostly to support himself.

"The door arch is the safest place to be! I read that someplace."

"This place was falling down before this!"

She pushed Josh away and made it into the hallway with her children close behind - just as cracks raced across the ceiling. Josh braced himself under the door arch. The two children, too young to fully appreciate their predicament, began to cry.

"Mommy!"

"C'mon sweetheart, outside," said Suzie as she urged them to the door. She turned to persuade Josh to follow, just as a section of roofing gave way. The door arch above Josh collapsed on him. Suzie could only hear his screams as he vanished in a thick cloud of plaster dust.

"Josh!"

She was about to take a step for him, but her anguished children sobered her up. They raced for the front door as the ceiling crumbled above in a cloud of choking plaster dust. She groped for the handle and pulled – but the door jammed as the wooden frame around it warped. Panic overcame her, and she tugged with animal ferocity. The door grated open as the wood split, and she raced out, scooping the children in each arm as the faint odor of gas drifted to her nostrils.

The fractured gas pipes flooded the room with invisible fumes. The aging television, still playing from when Josh crashed out in front of it, fell from the cheap wall mounts and sparked on impact.

Suzie just cleared her driveway as the house behind

erupted in a massive explosion. Windows that the quake had not shattered burst out onto terrified neighbors. The blast pitched Suzie and her children to the floor as loose mortar struck them.

She turned to watch hungry flames consume the house. Her home. Her failed dream. She started to cry.

TWO

A THIN BLACK line tore across the paper, leaving a jagged trail of peaks and troughs so dense they appeared as a solid black mass. The seismometer was bolted to the floor in the West Coast Earthquake Center (WCEC), which was just as well as the entire room rolled around it. Shelves rattled, spewing old data-filled folders and equipment across the floor.

The four scientists inside groped for the fixed desks to stabilize themselves.

"Jesus! This bitch is humping off the scale!" yelled Schofield, a ginger-haired mineralogist. His high voice was an asset when battling against the low frequency white noise generated by the shifting earth.

A fifty-something Hispanic woman jolted into him as she crossed to study the seismometer. Her brown eyes widened as she interpreted the sprawling readout. The concerned frown creasing her pretty face matched the tension in her voice. "This could be another Northridge!"

As a geologist, she'd cursed her professional bad luck for

being out of town during any quake of significant magnitude, including the devastating Northridge incident, the last big quake to rock California. However, as a person, she thanked God she'd missed it.

Fortune had smiled on Catherine Sanchez, who was visiting relatives in Morelia at the time. She quickly crossed herself, the motion causing her hand to trace a skewed path. It would have to do. Her faith was strong.

"This could be it, Trent. The Big One. Kiss your cojones boys," she yelled above the din.

Michael Trent braced himself at a computer terminal, arms and legs splayed wide to cushion the vicious motion. His blue eyes twinkled from the forty-inch screen, feeding back information from across the seismographic network.

The California Earthquake Center had its own sensors arranged across the area ranging from tiltmeters, which literally record the angle that the ground rises or is depressed, magnetometers that register the earth's magnetic field, to strainmeters registering the effect the tremor had on the surrounding rocks, and their more popular brother: seismographs.

The data flooded in from across California. Budget cuts had forced WCEC to make a deal with the California Institute of Technology to use their seismographic network to enable finely detailed analysis. Caltech Seismo Laboratory readily agreed to the collaboration, on the condition that any new research was shared with them first.

Caltech didn't realize that Michael Trent, former Caltech undergraduate seismologist, would be sharing a piece of their pie, or the answer would have been a firm "no".

Fortunately, Trent had his name conveniently omitted from WCEC's proposal, leaving the board of both establishments none the wiser to the delicate situation - WCEC knew he was on their payroll and Caltech didn't. Exactly the position Trent wanted for the moment.

For now, he could reap the data being presently collected from dozens of sensors that formed the broadband TERRAscope network, before passing it on. Individual stations housed a Streckeisen seismometer, a barograph, and a ground motion sensor. The Quanterra Q8 datalogging system was feeding a live broadcast to the lab, already rusty by today's standards. It was still a huge advancement over the days when Caltech personnel had to download the data individually from each station.

"This is incredible," breathed Trent, almost to himself. "I have seen nothing like this before. Walt?"

Trent pried his gaze away from the screen in time to see Walter Harbinson, a fifty-four-year-old fellow seismologist whose specialty was safely confined to computer modeling of quake simulations, vomit over his blue and white striped Ralph Lauren shirt. He wiped his sleeve across the white spittle clinging to his lips and shrugged apologetically when he met Trent's gaze.

"Motion sickness."

* * *

THINGS HAD BEEN GOING WELL, Alana thought as her slick palms gripped the steering wheel that squirmed against the buckling road surface. Not just well, but great. And now...

Alana Williams roared through the Los Angeles Police Department like a locomotive. Blinding ambition had pushed her to distinction. Eight long years on the street and maintaining a squeaky-clean record, despite many trying to throw dirt in her face, had won her the sought-after promotion to detective.

She glanced at her partner, who was riding shotgun. Out of shape, and six years her senior – although he looked twice that - and sweating like a sauna junkie, Ed Olmos. The ride he was now experiencing had turned his fleshy cheeks wan. The rapidly revolving red-cherry on the dash supplied the only color.

He was an unpretentious man with an innocent sense of humor, who saw Alana more as a friend than a colleague and adored his wife to the core. Alana had soon warmed to the man, who she felt was like a faithful hound. She respected his judgment and enjoyed being with him, especially in tight spots like this.

A traffic light snapped from its suspension cable and smashed onto the hood of their unmarked Saturn. The heavy box tumbled into the windshield - spiderwebbing it with a thousand fractures.

"Holy cow!" bellowed Ed as he crossed his arms over his face for protection.

Alana slewed the car around a tight corner, sliding the traffic light onto the sidewalk. The shattered windshield obscured her view, but she could still make out the plain bottle-green van ahead.

They had prepared the bust for a month. Mathias, a Greek immigrant, had been under surveillance since they'd suspected he was smuggling arms from across the border, but nothing that could be proven - until now.

Alana's team had watched the Greek receive a package from a Mexican registered vessel in San Pedro this morning. A routine Coast Guard search had turned over nothing.

Mathias had loaded his crate into the van almost immediately with help from his companion: an unknown surfer-type who had been spotted with him on several occasions.

They had been discreetly tailing the van as it conscientiously stopped at each light, indicated at every junction, precisely driven so as not to cause attention. In Alana's opinion, that was a guilty conscience, right there.

Then the earthquake struck.

Alana was born and raised in Pasadena, so tremblers were a way of life, but the sudden ferocity of this one had surprised her. Every vehicle on the road felt its fury. The target van's rusting rear doors were jarred open, spilling several automatic rifles onto the street. Alana had made out the old familiar shape of two Kalashnikov AK-47s and a Heckler & Koch MP7 before the Surfer scrambled from the passenger seat and into the back of the van to retrieve the weapons as the van screeched to a halt.

That was when he saw Alana and Ed tailing them. In plain clothes and driving a dull car, something must have screamed "cop" as he jumped back into the van, slamming the doors closed – and the vehicle then took off at speed despite the quake.

Ed had banged the dash and encouraged pursuit at the top of his lungs, but Alana's foot was already on the gas. Ed had tossed the red police light on the dash and hit the siren, which was pitifully low against the rising bellow from the earth.

And now they were speeding across a city that was crumbling around them. The van swerved into an avenue - Alana didn't know which one; she'd lost her bearings by concentrating on just keeping her vehicle on the road. She glanced at the speedo as it crept up to fifty.

"Alana! Watch it!"

Her eyes snapped up in time to see the van had taken another street as a decrepit four-story building ahead lost its corner foundations and toppled across the road - blocking it in a massive pile of rubble. The dust cloud rolled towards them.

Alana twisted the wheel and yanked the parking brake to skid the Saturn in a tight turn to follow the van. The driver's side fender glanced off a fire hydrant, which gushed a column of pressurized water twenty feet straight up. But Alana wouldn't be stopped as the Greek's van appeared dead ahead once more. A quick glance in the rearview showed nothing more than a solid wall of gray behind them. She pushed aside the thought of the lives that had been lost and focused on the ones that would be saved by stopping the weapons shipment.

Ed fought to keep his lunch down, gripping the dash so he didn't slide into Alana. This was not how he had expected the day to develop. Walking in a quake was dangerous - driving was suicidal, but it was the cop instinct that took over. If they had allowed this shipment to escape, then it was a safe bet that Mathias would jump state, maybe even the country, and vanish without a trace.

"They're going for the freeway," he warned as the van took another turn - accelerating to the Interstate 10 on-ramp.

"This is crazy," breathed Alana as they hit the ramp at speed. Ahead, the concrete stanchions supporting the freeway were swaying precariously.

"No," replied Ed. "This is crazy's twin brother: insanity."

The Interstate was chaos. Hundreds of vehicles had stopped, many of their occupants fleeing them in search of solid ground. The van careened recklessly through them, slaloming immobile automobiles and trucks.

Alana stuck close. Tires screeched as they fought for purchase on a surface that rose and fell like breaking sea waves. Ed was immediately struck by the memory of old news footage of the Golden Gate Bridge rocking like a child's swing. And now he knew what it felt like to drive along it.

Mathias felt his mind snap. The deal had been going smoothly, even ahead of schedule, for a change. His buyers were very anxious African terrorists with a passionate deadline. Politics were lost on him, but cash broke down all national and religious barriers. Then disaster: first the quake, which he could handle. Back in Greece, he had lived through many, but to discover the cops had been on his case had dissolved his calm façade.

He glanced in the mirror. Sure enough, the pig's car was practically kissing their ass. The sheer concentration needed to steer the van through an assault course of motionless traffic, just as the world turned upside down, was just too much for one man. The interstate had seemed like a fabulous idea at the time. Ten seconds later, he was deeply regretting it.

"Get those fuckers off our trail!" he yelled to the sun-bronzed beefcake bracing against the crates in the back. Cheap hire, he thought, never again.

"You mean, like, actually use this shit? Far out, man." The surfer beamed like a kid as he toyed with the MP7 he'd retrieved.

Alana suppressed a wave of panic as cracks crawled across the interstate's concrete surface, racing ahead of her. She refocused on the van as the doors swung open again. The surfer hung in the doorway, feet braced apart and one hand gripping a hand-strap welded to the van's roof, while his other hand leveled the business end of an MP7, and he squeezed the trigger.

The first wave of shots sprayed in every direction but the car. The surfer's muscles visibly tightened as he fought against the recoil and compensated for the quake, guiding the weapon just enough for the trail of bullets to chatter across Alana's hood.

Alana and Ed ducked in their seats, a pointless but instinctive move. She swerved the car away from the line of fire. Ed groped for his shoulder holster as the Surfer attempted another strafing run.

Ahead, the freeway could take no more pounding.

With a terrible crunch, support stanchions dissolved to dust - collapsing the prefabricated sections like dominos. Enormous slabs of concrete dropped - almost intact - thirty feet to the ground. People caught on the falling sections felt their stomachs lurch as they rode the freeway down like a carnival ride. The sudden impact scattered people and vehicles like bowling pins. Bones cracked and vehicles bounced into one another like children's toys.

Ed drew his Beretta 8045; despite being standard issue, it was still a firm favorite of his. The quake swayed his hand like a drunk. He fired through the windshield, punching fist-sized holes through what was left of the cracked safety glass. The van weaved erratically to evade the shots. A lucky shot capped the surfer in the knee. A splatter of blood, and the surfer's legs crumpled beneath him. The Heckler & Koch dropped as he tried to stem the seeping wound with one hand and anchor himself to the van with the other.

"Try to get closer. I'm going for his tires."

Alana stepped on the gas. Nerves jangled as the distance narrowed and she instinctively glanced in the wing mirror.

"What the hell?" she balked.

Ed glanced at her, and then at his wing mirror to see for himself. Behind them, the elevated freeway was collapsing. Slabs were dropping in rapid sequence – and the destruction was gaining on them. The sight sent a bolt of fear through them.

Alana didn't tear her gaze back to the road until she felt the impact as they rear-ended the van, which had slammed on its brakes. The surfer was flung onto the hood of the Saturn as bumpers twisted, snarling the vehicles together.

A dozen yards ahead, the Interstate had already collapsed. Mathias whispered a prayer as the impact caused his head to thump the headrest. The impact shunted the van forward, despite his foot pressing hard on the pedal. Rubber squealed – and the front wheels cleared the lip of the freeway. The van's chassis scraped the edge, drawing it to a halt. The back wheels lifted slightly as the front half tipped dangerously forward. Mathias held his breath, fearing the slightest move on his part would send him toppling down.

Alana and Ed exchanged a brief look of panic as the front half of their car was hoisted off the ground by the van's elevating rear. Their weight was all that prevented the van from slipping over.

But the vibrating road inched the van forward – pulling the Saturn with it.

The two cops jumped clear. Ed landed awkwardly, twisting his ankle. Alana landed on her feet, the sudden motion sprawling her on all fours.

She looked behind to see the collapsing freeway rush towards them - and then suddenly halt in a tremendous dust cloud. Alana breathed out hard and with it a loud laugh of pent-up relief.

The freeway had collapsed for about half a mile in either direction, leaving only their island of untouched elevated road.

The quake continued - jerking the van forward. Now she could see Mathias gripping the wheel; ashen white and not daring to move a muscle. His eyes swiveled to her with a pleading look. But he didn't even risk a cry for help.

Then the van's fender sprung loose as rust gave way. The Saturn dropped back on its wheels, the surfer still clinging to the hood for his life as his knee pumped fluid across the headlights.

Alana was helpless as she watched Mathias grope for the door in a desperate bid to escape – even as the van slipped over the edge, plummeting and inevitably crashing into the rubble below. Mathias was propelled through the windshield like a bullet. He was killed on impact and never felt the mangled vehicle accordion around him.

Alana crawled over to Ed, who, professional as ever, had his gun trained on the surfer, the barrel weaving a figure eight under the influence of the swaying freeway.

"You're under arrest, pal."

"He's not going anywhere," sighed Alana as she started trembling from the adrenaline rush comedown. "How's your leg?"

Ed kept his gun leveled. "Twisted. Not broken, I hope. Listen, don't get offended, but next time I'll drive."

Alana cracked a grin, more from a release of tension than amusement. Then she and Ed stumbled sideways. It took a moment before they realized they had been compensating for swaying ground that was now firm.

The quake had stopped.

THREE

"FORTY-TWO SECONDS," said Catherine as she dabbed a graze on her forehead, sustained when an unlocked desk draw had slid out just as she'd tripped to her knees.

Despite being fitted with the latest anti-quake architectural codes, the lab gave the appearance of being devastated but had suffered little structural damage except for one cracked windowpane. Giddy with excitement, Trent stepped over Walt, who was lodged in a corner shivering, his stomach still churning.

"What magnitude?"

Schofield hammered on the keyboard. "I'm working on it."

Unspoken anticipation filled the room as they waited for the results. Trent drummed his fingers impatiently; Catherine repetitively clicked a retractable pen to soothe her anxiety.

Walt brushed fallen papers from his vomit-stained clothes and hauled himself up, using the edge of a desk for leverage. "My stomach's telling me a six. That was heavy."

Catherine scrunched her nose as she caught an unpleasant waft from Walt. "Jesus, Walter, you smell awful!"

Walt noticed his patchy shirt, recoiled as he sniffed it, then, without a care, stripped it off, exposing his skinny ribcage, and tossed it into the trash, before sitting at his terminal.

"Who wants to lay their hard-earned cash on the Mag? Double-odds against a five pointer?" Schofield quipped.

"I'm good for fifty," said Walt as he navigated through the software menus. "Printing hard copy."

Multiple printers around the room burst to life as fan-folded sheets cascaded into already full catch-baskets.

Schofield's screen overlaid several graphs and charts; the powerful hardware number-crunched to produce high-resolution graphics of the pulsing earth visible in vivid three-dimensions. Another screen highlighted the South California area. Blue dots depicted the network of data-gathering points, while flashing red markers scattered across the quake area. Trent frowned as his finger traced the map. Most of the red was located across the city.

"Moment magnitude..." Schofield flexed his fingers in anticipation, as though he was expecting to catch a hardball. "Six point four!" He slid his wallet from his back pocket and tossed it to Walter. "Fifty's all I have. I want the leather back."

"Do we have a location?" asked Catherine.

"Looks like it was a local boy," commented Trent with ominous overtones.

Everybody's mind raced with memories of the infamous Northridge quake. All the team had experienced it, except Catherine, which was one of the most devastating tremors to rock modern day Los Angeles. Trent had been in school at the time, frozen at his desk as the other kids rushed under theirs. Northridge had been merciless and taken on a tangible form for the impressionable young boy. From that point onward, Trent became obsessed with quakes. He saw it as his destiny – study them, understand them, and figure out a way to slay the beast that kills so unexpectedly.

While there were many larger quakes around the globe – most notably the 2011 Tōhoku incident that formed the dreadful tsunami - Northridge was on his home turf. It was personal... but he had little idea just how personal his obsession would later become.

Monday, January 17th, 1994, at exactly 4:31 a.m., Pacific Standard Time an earthquake with a *Moment Magnitude* of 6.7 shook Northridge, a suburb of the San Fernando Valley. A heavily populated region of neighborhoods, apartment complexes, shopping malls, and industrial parks. All buildings were retrofitted; the newer structures included building codes to resist earthquakes after a similar earthquake in 1971.

They proved futile when the earth unleashed its wrath.

The largest known geological fault crossed the desert some 100 km east of the San Fernando Valley, the infamous San Andreas. In the three preceding weeks, aftershocks caused damage with a moment magnitude between four and five.

Official figures indicated a death toll of 57, with 1,500 seriously injured. Approximately 9,000 homes had no electricity supplies; 20,000 had no gas, and 48,500 had little or no water, all because of fractured cables and pipelines.

Thousands of people were made temporarily homeless as 12,500 structures were damaged. Freeways collapsed in approximately a 32 km radius from the quake's epicenter, trapping victims underneath double-decked carriageways. South of the Hollywood hills, destruction was harsh on older buildings and those constructed on soft soils. On buildings not fitted with earthquake codes, damage was felt as far as 47 miles from the epicenter.

Northridge was a lesson to everyone. It happened in the most earthquake-prepared area in the entire United States, yet nobody saw it coming. The S-waves - Shear Waves, slow-moving, high-amplitude shock waves that generated most of the damage - were among the strongest ever officially recorded.

The quake was caused by a previously unknown blind-thrust fault; a fault that does not extend all the way to the earth's surface. This means the ground doesn't break but bends like a rubber sheet.

Although Northridge was one of the most financially devastating natural disasters to hit California, it was, at heart, an *average* tremor.

Trent knew the math and the reality of the situation all too well. He just prayed this new trembler wasn't a reoccurrence. Contrary to popular belief, seismologists attempt to avoid earthquakes, building on their research so one day they can predict earthquakes and save lives.

A silence filled the room, disturbed only by the gentle whirring of computers as the network calculated the epicenter. Schofield's screen momentarily cleared, only to be replaced by a map centralizing on Los Angeles. Trent's heart sank as multicolored overlays, depicting various ranges of magnitude, pooled on the screen.

"It's definitely local," said Schofield.

"Radiation pattern's coming through. This is damn peculiar." Walt tapped his screen with the tip of his pen before continuing to nibble on the end. A dense red patch showed the worst of the seismographic damage as an elongated pear-shaped taper, rather than a recognizable circular epicenter.

Trent glanced at the screen. "It's a wide wave pattern. The quake has circumnavigated the harder rock," said Trent. "Just like water, taking the path of least resistance."

Catherine shook her head. "No, Mike. This is something else. The rock in this area is granite. Solid stuff. According to these readings, the quake just pushed through it from the desert."

"Are you telling me this is a new fault?"

"Maybe. What was the magnitude again?"

"Six point four."

"Right, and there are at least two hundred faults in South California which can produce that much energy, and any place around here is within thirty miles of those faults."

"Comforting thought," commented Schofield as he began filing the data into folders for further scrutiny. He'd spent most of his career in Europe, so as the newest addition to the team, he was constantly getting excited about the local geology. Something he'd long since decided not to mention on Tinder.

"The Los Angeles Basin has a lot of shit underneath it," continued Catherine. "The San Andreas has a local kink in it which, combined with the loose sediment in the basin, makes this entire area unstable. A majority of those faults are concentrated around the mountains, which are thrust up by the quakes–"

"Well, maybe not–" interrupted Trent. Catherine waved him into silence, talking over him.

"Other theories aside, the mountains move. Now locally, we have the San Gabriel range directly to the north and the

San Bernardino to the east. Now what if a minor tremor out in the desert, maybe on the San Andreas itself, caused a chain of small tremors? If they have slipped and encountered a previously unknown fault, like Northridge and Whittier Narrows, that could open it up in the pattern we see."

She pressed her hands together to demonstrate, and then slowly opened them at the palms, keeping only her fingers touching in a movement like a zipper opening.

"So, on the graph, it would look like a quake spreading in from the desert when in fact it is a fault line peeling open like a banana. Like nothing ever recorded before."

The team quietly assessed the theory. More data flooded the screen as it was downloaded.

Walt crossed to the TV. "Let's see what it's like outside."

The picture blinked to life with an aerial feed from a news chopper over the city. Columns of black smoke poured from the damaged structures below. News reporter Sarah Chong narrated the footage with a chillingly calm voice.

"... *Majority of the wreckage. We're over Van Nuys. Below, people are in the streets wandering in confusion. The stacks of smoke you can see are caused by, we think, electrical fires breaking out in buildings and spreading uncontrollably through neighborhoods. We are also getting some reports of flooding in Reseda from fractured main pipes as entire streets are swept away. We're going to take you over Sherman Oaks and into Hollywood, where we are getting a lot of damage reports...*"

Trent turned away from the television, filtering the reporter from his consciousness. The carnage from earthquakes was a factor he still couldn't get to grips with. His heart sank as a flashing image of his father came unbidden; trapped... pleading for help...

His thoughts swam... no, it was the room. He touched his forehead, noticing he'd broken into a sweat. Still, the room shook. An aftershock?

"Trent?" Catherine gently touched his arm to quell his anxiety. "Are you okay? Want to sit down?"

"I'm fine. Just felt a little nauseous," he wiped the sweat from his brow with his shirtsleeve. "I feel fine now," he lied as he tried to focus on the screen.

Catherine wasn't convinced. She stared at him a little longer.

"Thinking of Mexico?"

"Briefly. A passing thought that's out of here now," Trent assured her. He even managed a smile, although the incident in Mexico refused to be forgotten. He turned back to the computer as Schofield opened another window.

"Wow, look at this," Schofield manipulated the mouse to enlarge the window. "Massive dust plumes rose from San Bernardino eighty-four seconds *before* the shock."

"Fits the hypothesis," Catherine beamed.

"You're wasted on us, you know that?" replied Trent with a wry smile.

"I know, yet here I am with you losers."

"Can you locate the precise epicenter?"

Walt crossed to a laptop depicting a grid of constantly updating numbers. He began cross-referencing the data. Trent and Catherine watched, feeling helpless as the data was gathered. Their task was to interpret it.

"Didn't you conduct a survey of the geology Downtown?" Trent asked Catherine.

"Three years ago, but we found zip." Blind thrust faults have a telltale series of folded hills on top of them, like a crumpled blanket. A nice marker for researchers, but they had become hidden by modern construction, lurking in wait. "We discovered nothing to indicate a buried system in the area, though."

"I hope you are wrong."

"Me too, but the news doesn't look too good. And if I am wrong, then we have *another* Northridge all over again."

They glanced at the television still playing the live feed. The helicopter was now over West Hollywood. Below, fires were razing properties. Gridlocked traffic jammed the streets, blocking the emergency services.

"Guys, I've got something here!" Walt manipulated the data. "We have a hypocenter... the heart of the beast was three miles deep."

"And the epicenter?" Trent moved closer to get a better look. The screen depicted a satellite view of South California with the deep scar of the San Andreas fault highlighted by the computer. It was swiftly overlaid by another map, closer now.

"Come on... come on..." whispered Walt. "Look!"

Schofield rolled his seat over to get a better look. The chair's wheels caught on debris, almost catapulting him out. The map switched again, now an overview of Los Angeles, and the computer had added a small circle that radiated out across the city.

"There we have it," said Walt in a monotone voice.

"That's Downtown. That can't be the epicenter," said Trent, confused by the conflicting data.

Walt ran his fingers across the keyboard. He shook his head, breathing sharply out. "Well, either this computer's gone crazy, or the epicenter originated here - slam-bang under Wilshire Boulevard and I-110."

FOUR

THE LAST CROOKED step almost sent Alana sprawling. She caught her balance, her free hand capping the large brown paper grocery bag she hugged, preventing a rogue orange from escaping.

"We had men around today," commented a small, portly woman, startling Alana. She gripped the bag tighter; dug into her tight blue denim pockets and extracted her apartment keys. She eyed the old woman warily; Mrs Slovinsky owned the whole block, so it was wise to choose kind words.

"Nothing serious, I hope," she managed.

"They did some tests with some kind of machines and told me some kind of numbers. I thought they were from the IRS, but they said they weren't. Something to do with the quake this morning."

"Yes, there was one this morning. Did you feel it?" She looked meaningfully at the deep cracks coursing through the plaster walls. Her sneakers kicked little mounds of plaster dust.

"Damn right I did, missy. Shook Bobby clean off the tallboy. Animals can sense these things, I know."

"So, are we safe to live here?" She jangled the keys into the lock, did a double click to the left, and the door opened with a little help from her foot. The doorjamb must have shifted slightly. She didn't dare look inside to see if there was any damage.

"They red-tagged the shop across the street there, and the building next door. We were lucky, they said."

"That's because you had those nice young men in here last year retro fitting the place."

"I did?"

Alana sighed. Having a conversation with her landlady was like running at high altitude; you got out of breath fast. Mrs Slovinsky herself didn't seem to be able to think straight, and you could almost guarantee she would lose the conversation three or four times before she noticed. Strangely, she was remarkably good at making sure rent payments landed on time.

"Did they show you any ID?" Alana asked.

"I don't recall. Don't think so. I didn't ask."

Alana couldn't help but feel sorry for her. She had no family and kept the place in excellent working order. The rent was a little steep, but Alana could live with that. It was one of the better places on Malabar Street.

"I've told you a hundred times, don't let anybody inside without ID; it could be dangerous. Con men, thieves, hustlers…"

"Oh, don't you worry. I have Bobby to see people off. I heard something smash in there this morning, nothing desirable, I hope? I'd better go, Wheel of Fortune will be on."

Alana watched as Mrs Slovinsky crossed the passage and

disappeared into her apartment. Alana took a deep breath before daring to look in her own.

Cleaning up had taken Alana the better part of an hour, and now she was exhausted. Almost all her framed photographs had shattered as they had struck the floor. Her academy certificate had suffered a smooth glass cut through the middle, but she could patch that up with tape. The photograph of her with mom and pop had survived with a fractured frame. She made a mental note to call them as soon as the phone lines were untangled. They always worried whenever there was the slightest tremor, but Alana had repeatedly stated that they were not to call even if L.A. slipped into the ocean. Her job was dangerous enough without living with jittery parents.

But she missed them. Especially the lazy days at home in Oswego, just north of Syracuse. Both her parents had retired from their jobs in Kansas, her father handing the management of his successful crop-spraying company over to some kid straight out of business school, so he could lie back and enjoy the twilight days with his wife.

They moved near the Canadian border because dad had said the damper climate suited him. The real reason, she suspected, was the majesty of Lake Ontario to fish in, or rather its less polluted tributaries. She hadn't visited them for a while, last Christmas in fact. Maybe it was time for some leave; after today, she figured she'd earned it.

She and Ed had booked the gun-toting Surfer, who turned out to be Brian Parker, a local bum who Mathias had hired as meat. Parker needed the cash to finance a girlfriend, four-month-old daughter, and a spiraling coke habit.

Chief Bixby had found them at their cluttered desk finishing, in Alana's view, an epic report. They had waxed lyrical about their dedication in pursuing the suspects during a quake and lamented that Mathias had been pinned under the crumpled remains of his van. No bust is perfect. Ed thought that the Chief's diatribe was an attempt to congratulate them by a miserable, stubborn bastard.

They collected twenty-four rifles, ten machine guns, and three military-issue MANPADS – man-portable air-defense systems – or missile launchers to the layman, lethal enough to take down a police chopper or a passenger plane. Maybe a big enough haul to promote herself up the ladder from Detective I to Detective II... maybe Lieutenant in the next three years. Ed had warned her not to reach too far. Fine for a man with a self-proclaimed lack of ambition. He was a strident believer that she should pace her career. But Alana wanted it all *now*. Several years ahead was far too long.

She relaxed back with a lukewarm cup of chocolate powder mixed with water. She'd wanted milk but had found it had curdled; whether from the quake or the fact that the cooler had been off all day, she didn't know. She wanted to watch TV, but the cable was out, which meant the internet was down too.

Now she craved a cigarette, although she had only ever smoked one in her entire life. The stress of the day was now catching up with her nerves. Tonight was going to be a sleepless toil.

Her eyes strayed to a picture of her in better times, with Peter: a charming guy who reminded her of Tom Cruise, although nobody else could see the *vaguest* similarity. It was the only picture not to suffer damage. He was the best relationship she'd ever had, and she'd really loved him. Then again Peter really loved himself too. Let's face it, she chided herself; he was a complete bastard.

After a wonderful relationship with the maître 'd while in the academy, Alana was convinced she was ready for engagement, even confiding the fact to her mother. Three days later, he dumped her for some bitch of an accountant. Ensuing emotional turmoil almost threw Alana from graduating as she thought of nothing but revenge. The pressure of the final exams had turned out to be a cleansing factor on her soul, and a turning point as she focused single-mindedly on her career. From that moment, nothing else mattered. Her career in law enforcement had been her dream. Now it was her life, and she was going to be queen of the range. No man would ever have a look-in again. She would love, eat, and sleep her job.

She finished the bitter chocolate and stared at the empty apartment.

FIVE

A FLICKERING ORANGE flame danced on the subway tunnel's reinforced concrete wall. A pair of hobos rubbed their hands over the welcome warmth of the fire they had lit among a pile of scavenged trash they had dragged down with them. Even in LA, the temperatures outside dropped at night, and they had always found the metro to be a welcome refuge from the dangers above - particularly *other* people. They'd had a buddy who'd been burned alive by a pack of drunken frat boys, so the potential dangers underground held little real terror for them. Especially after today. In their view, the quake was just as dangerous here as in some back alley. And since the trains were still not running, a deep, calming silence smothered the darkness.

During the metro's construction, many dead end side tunnels had been cut for storage and drainage, and they provided ideal shelter.

Jack swirled a cheap half-bottle of vodka he'd found in a trash can and glanced at his companion, a stocky man in a dirty green camouflage jacket that stank of urine. He sported a forest of a beard that smothered his face, and constantly mumbled to himself in an incoherent accent that Jack assumed was Russian. Crazy from a mix of meds, alcohol abuse, and daily sunstroke, but harmless enough, and it was always good to have company.

Jack had been homeless for twelve years, since he lost his job as a baggage handler at the airport, and his wife had run off with the kids. Anybody from his old life would find him unrecognizable, with a patchy red beard and long hair that stretched between his shoulder blades in a tangled mass, solid to the touch and crawling with lice. He usually wandered the streets of Santa Monica until he'd finally taken refuge underground.

A dull rumble caused Jack to look up; his first thought was that it was another tremor. The Russian hadn't moved from gazing at the fire; he was as deaf as a post. This wasn't the constant throb he'd experienced in previous tremors, nor was it the usual background thunder of a train. There was a metallic edge to it which oscillated in pitch.

Jack frowned as he stood up. He cautiously walked to the end of the side tunnel, his toes on the line between light and the utter black void beyond. He listened. The reverberation was growing. Now it sounded like somebody was drumming heavy metallic fingers across the rails - but as loud as industrial machinery. Jack was naturally curious, and more than that, he knew that both men might have to protect their sanctuary from other marauding gangs. He moved back to the fire and plucked out a burning spar of wood; an old chair leg that he'd looted from the remains of a bungalow.

He held the torch aloft, the dancing flame holding the darkness back. Jack kicked his companion in the thigh and jerked his head toward the end of the tunnel. The Russian stopped muttering and followed, producing a rusty tire iron from under the recess of his coat. Jack nodded approvingly; perhaps his companion wasn't as mad as he made out.

They stepped into the main subway tunnel. Jack raised his burning torch aloft, but it failed to cast the light any farther. The noise was still increasing in volume. Although convinced that it wasn't a train, they kept close to the wall just in case.

"Who's there?" he croaked. With eerie timing, the clattering noise stopped. "We got guns, asshole!"

A pneumatic wheezing responded from the darkness; like that of a junkyard car crusher powering up its jaws. Jack's flame flickered as a strong breeze suddenly blasted them - then four powerful spotlights blazed to life with an audible hiss, bathing them in harsh white light. The heat from the beams was intense.

Jack dropped the burning chair leg as he fell to his knees, covering his eyes with his forearms. He felt tears involuntarily swell and roll down his cheeks. The crushing whine of servomotors continued, and Jack heard a wild battle scream from the Russian, followed by a clang of metal as his tire iron struck something solid.

Then the Slavic swearing turned into a bloody gurgle.

Jack forced his eyes open, hands shielding him from the glare. Through stinging tears, he saw a long, slender steel arm, the thickness of a palm trunk, as it swung toward the Russian. The tip of the arm burned like the sun, a mass of cracked yellow and orange swirling plasma. He watched in sheer amazement as the brandished tire iron melted like ice. Molten metal splashed on the Russian's blistering skin.

There was no time to scream.

The arm punctured through the man's chest and hoisted

him clean off the ground in a shower of red gore that fountained across the pure white spotlights.

It looked like Beelzebub himself had come to collect Jack.

He spun on his heels, but his legs had turned to jello as he attempted to run. The whirling motors changed pitch and the metallic clattering, like multiple footfalls across the rail tracks, started again. Jack felt a rush of molten hot pain across his back. Then his chest crushed, and his lungs collapsed as the blazing sun pushed through his back and out of his chest cavity.

SIX

"NO, SIR," Trent said as he pinned his cell phone between his cheek and shoulder. His hands were busy collecting a whole ream of fan-fold paper that had spilled from the printers. After a series of tech failures, they still prized hard copies.

"We were expecting *something*, but there was no indication–". He winced as the voice on the other end suddenly rose.

"*Indication my ass!*"

"There was nothing..." Trent paused, half listening to the diatribe while he scanned the sheets. "I don't believe that... Yes, sir. I will."

He caught the phone as he dropped it from his shoulder. The caller had already hung up. He tossed the paper aside and absently chewed his tongue, a habit from childhood, then ran his fingers through his short dark hair, pulling it tight to ease his tension.

"The mayor?" asked Catherine as she entered with a pair of freshly made coffees in Styrofoam cups. She handed one to Trent, keeping the other as she sat on the edge of the desk. "Cups were all smashed during the quake. Even that nice one I got from Disney. At least the Universal Studios one is made of tougher stuff," she said, picking up her precious cup. "I thought this place was supposed to be tremor resistant?"

"Just the building, not the cups." Trent sipped the coffee, savoring the warm liquid as it eased his dry throat. He hadn't realized how thirsty he was until now. Hungry, too. It was five o'clock, six hours after the initial quake, and none of the data made sense.

"The wonderful Mayor Shearer wants to know why there was no advance warning." He shook his head. "And I voted for that ass."

"Come on, he can't be serious. It's not an exact science yet. Doesn't he get that?"

"Apparently not. Looks like this is going down in history as America's second most expensive natural disaster. But if you want my money, I bet we'll catch up with Katrina real soon. So, of course, when money is involved, somebody has to be blamed."

"He can't blame *you*! He can't blame anybody," Catherine laughed at the absurdity.

Trent sucked the last drops of coffee and crushed the Styrofoam cup with a satisfying crunch. "He's going to try."

"Why us?" demanded Catherine. "Why some dumpy little research outfit in the ass end of WCEC? Caltech should have their nuts primed for not issuing a warning. They have the facilities."

"That's the problem. We are a little research outfit run by a crank. *Me*, who the rest of the academic world treats as a joke on legs."

"Mike, you can't beat yourself up. If science didn't have

people who thought outside the box, nothing would ever get discovered. We'd all still be in the box wondering if there really is anything more. So, nobody is to blame. I mean, you have to see the datasets. None of it seems right."

"What do you mean?" asked Trent, grateful for the opportunity to change conversational course.

Catherine placed her drink down and beckoned Trent to follow her to Schofield's system. Trent had sent the boys out to assess the physical damage, although really he just needed a break from their constant bickering, especially as Schofield was still stinging from losing fifty bucks.

Catherine punched up several windows of data, graphs, and maps, all an incoherent jumble to the untrained eye. "We're six hours after the tremor. That mother had a magnitude of six-point-four. So where are the aftershocks?"

"I have noticed–" Trent started, but Catherine shushed him into silence.

"Work from basics. What is an aftershock?"

Trent sighed, irritated at being treated like a kid, but he decided to oblige her; she simply couldn't shake the ex-high school teacher bottle up inside. "Most aftershocks are caused by the stress of the main shock's fault changing. If it was powerful enough, which I personally thought todays would have been a shoo-in, it should have produced aftershocks on nearby faults too."

"Right. We should have felt four or five aftershocks within the first hour, right? After that, the chance of aftershocks rapidly diminishes."

"Decrease in shock waves is proportional to the *inverse time* since the main shock," said Trent. "Read it on a bumper sticker of a really big car."

"So, the second day after the main shock has about half,

and the tenth day about one tenth the number of aftershocks of the first day; in our case, none." Trent began pacing as Catherine continued. "It's textbook. Big quakes have a lot of big aftershocks with a difference in magnitude between the original tremor at an average of one-point-two." She looked at him meaningfully.

"So, we should have had something on the scale of five-point-two ram into us virtually straight after. So, what happened?" Trent mulled over the possibilities, but no modular or theory sat with the data. As far as he knew, this was the first major quake in history not to have any follow-ups.

"I'm just presenting the facts, Trent. I don't have any answers yet. Which is why we've got to think basic."

"Even at a basic level, our data is already falling apart. Look at the epicenter, punch it up."

Catherine clicked the mouse, expanding the satellite view of South California with the rainbow radiation pattern overlaid. "For a start, this is telling us the quake moved, *moved*, under LA. Classically impossible, but let us assume our theory is sound and it is a previously unrecorded fault simultaneously cracking its length like your zipper theory. Even then, we have the problem that the epicenter is in Downtown LA with a hypocenter at three miles. That means this beast originated right under our feet."

"Not impossible."

"But not likely either. I just don't buy it. It should have been worse."

"Maybe the data's wrong? There could be a bug in the system. Instruments could be faulty. Corrupt downloads..."

Trent stopped pacing, leaned on the back of Catherine's chair to peer over her shoulder. This close, he could smell her fragrance. He didn't know what, but it smelled feminine and soothing to his nerves. For a moment, pangs of desire to be with a woman surged through him. He focused on the task at hand, suppressing his long dormant sexual energy.

"Blaming it on the equipment is the easy way out," he cautioned, "although Walt should run a diagnostic check through it to be sure. But for now, let's assume the numbers are right."

Catherine circled the epicenter with the mouse pointer. "The rupture cannot travel faster than the speed of sound in rock, which is about two miles per hour. So, this entire fault must have opened simultaneously." She clicked a measurement icon and drew a line running the length of the projected hypocenter; a number appeared over it. "That's fifty miles of fault line which has just run *through* the Northridge and San Gabriel faults to name just two, without triggering them."

"It was a pretty severe jolt," mused Trent. "Low frequency waves die off rapidly with distance, right? If we were a reasonable distance from the epicenter, then it would have been more of a rolling motion."

He moved his hands to show gentle ocean waves. Catherine smiled at his inner child, trying to disrupt the adult's stern facade, but Trent was lost in a turbulent whirl of thoughts. Everything was contradictory. Nothing fitted into the regular picture. He could taste that they were on the verge of a major revelation in seismology. The concept was taunting them, teasing on the periphery of their mental grasp. Trent could feel this was big. He just didn't know why.

"We had a lot of eyewitness reports of swaying buildings.

I mean, anything over twenty stories was affected," said Catherine.

Trent walked through the facts in his mind. "Taller buildings are more responsive to low frequencies, which means the epicenter couldn't have been that far. But we had a lot of small building damage too."

"Which indicates high frequencies. Like you said, this sucker was a sharp jolt, not just a rolling quake. We experienced everything together. The data can't be screwy. Just the facts."

"What about the soil conditions?"

"How would you like it?" Catherine was used to Trent's irritating habit of pacing the lab, but now he increased his strides, a true sign of deep concentration. It's about time, she thought.

"Dummy's Guide."

Trent subscribed to a Buddhist principle. Situations often seem more complicated than they really are due to emotional entanglements and illogical approaches people project on them, especially with professionals who often miss the simplest explanation due to their own shortsightedness. The trick was to break a problem down. Eradicate all the extraneous information and study the heart.

"Okay, if the waves pass from solid rock to loose soil, they slow down, but their amplitude increases, so you would get a more intense shaking on loose soil than on hard rock." This lesson was won during the 1989 Loma Prieta earthquake in San Francisco. The epicenter was located some sixty miles from the city. Most of the Bay Area escaped serious damage; about what was expected for the magnitude. Unfortunately, some sites in the Bay had been constructed on unconsolidated landfill and soft solids, not really because of bad planning, but to the unexplored effects of amplification. The Marina district and Oakland experienced ground motion some ten times greater than neighboring sites situated on rock. Following that tragedy, funding into quake research was given a little boost, the silver lining in Catherine's opinion. Trent didn't need the history lesson, so she didn't give it.

"A majority of the Los Angeles Basin, San Fernando Valley, and San Gabriel Valley is on loose soil."

They lapsed into silence for a moment. Trent stopped walking, unwilling to be disturbed by the noise of his own footfall. He steepled his fingers over his mouth as though in prayer. He scanned the room for nothing in particular, then locked on to Catherine. "Punch up Schofield's map of the radiation pattern," he said.

Catherine selected a window, ran the cursor down the list of stored data and stopped on one labeled with Schofield's usual shorthand "Rad Pat". Double clicking it produced the map moments later, the distinctive pear-shaped red blotch running across the city.

"What about its directivity?" Trent asked as he pointed to the screen, leaving a greasy smudge. "Let's assume that the rupture surface moved along the fault's orientation, and that it was a blind-thrust. It ran from northeast to southwest, so it must have focused energy in this direction. Out into the sea."

"So, we should have expected a tsunami," Catherine said cautiously. Tsunami, literally Japanese for *harbor-wave*. Tidal waves were a development Catherine had not yet encountered firsthand. The world saw the human misery of such disasters in 2004 when a tsunami rolled across the Indian Ocean that claimed countless lives.

"An automatic warning went out, but nothing was picked

up." Trent flopped back in a chair, feeling exhausted. He ruffled his hair to soothe his mind.

"What does all this mean?" Catherine's face lit up with the possibility of discoveries to be made.

Trent met her gaze, and a smile tugged at the corner of his mouth as they both burst into laughter. "I have no idea!"

Their laughter increased through fatigue and the absurdity of it all. Trent's eyes watered as Walter rushed back into the room. His grave expression instantly subdued them both.

"Folks, I think you better watch this," he said, riffling through the TV channels.

Schofield caught up, out of breath. "Jeez," he gasped, "the city is trashed. And there are *still* no parking spaces."

"Listen up," shouted Walter as he backed away from the television to give Trent and Catherine a good view.

It was a live press conference. On-stage was the ruddy face of Mayor Shearer standing at a microphone-studded podium that bore the *City of Los Angeles* seal. William Shearer was two hundred and sixty pounds of pure anger, dressed in an immaculate suit. He gripped the podium like a life preserver as he faced a bank of microphones and cameras. A gaggle of city councilors stood grimly behind him, clutching tablets and case files. He cleared his throat, and Trent was hit by a surprisingly vitriolic hope that the man would choke on his own spittle... but no such wish was forthcoming.

"Ladies and gentlemen," Shearer spoke in a distinctive smooth baritone that got him re-elected for his second term as Mayor of Los Angeles. "A terrible calamity has hit our beloved city today. While we must grieve for those who died and lost loved ones, we must also be cautious to prevent further casualties. If a property is damaged, then do not re-enter until an official has examined it. Local assessment teams have been hard at work since this morning. Maintenance crews are working flat out to restore power, water, and gas. Please give them time and do not tie up the phone network by reporting such outages; you may be preventing a genuine emergency call from coming through."

"Who writes this crap?" cried Schofield. He lapsed back into silence when it became apparent his audience wasn't listening.

Shearer continued. "After a call with the Governor, the President officially declared The City of Los Angeles a major disaster zone. Members of the Federal Emergency Management Agency, FEMA, have been deployed across the area to coordinate emergency responses. Raymond Faber, the Governor of California, will broadcast a message later this afternoon with more information; he's currently in Washington, where he has been since yesterday. In a moment, Henry Williams will tell you about emergency accommodation and food banks that are being set up." Shearer bowed his head to an official for a moment's subdued conversation away from the mics, before returning to face the cameras with an apologetic smile. "Well, he will be here, but he's tied up in traffic at the moment." Laughter trickled through the assembly hall.

"Guy's a real laugh riot, isn't he?" muttered Trent.

"So, while we are waiting," continued Shearer flawlessly like a true showman, "Ben Chapman from Caltech's seismology unit will explain the technical details of today's event."

Trent blanched as a thin, sandy-haired Ben Chapman replaced Shearer at the podium. He clutched several crumpled notes in his fist, which was visibly shaking. He pushed his glasses up the bridge of his nose using his thumb and looked uneasily at the cameras.

He reminded Trent of Bill Gates, although without the looks or charm. Trent felt like throwing a dart at the screen in the hope it would induce a bizarre voodoo-like death in him, but that would be a waste of a good Sony. Chapman was responsible for throwing Trent out of the California Institute of Technology. It boiled down to funding; Chapman, being the greedy bastard he was, wanted the whole pie. He guided the Board of Trustees to think of Trent as a crank. His theories seldom fitted convention and had often been a source of ridicule to some of his peers. Thinkers on the periphery were always the first to be jettisoned when budget cuts came snipping, especially ones that could tarnish the proud name of Caltech. Trent retaliated that no theory could be dismissed unless proven otherwise. This was his first experience with the blank wall of belief that surrounds the scientific community, the inability to embrace and explore something that doesn't fit their well-established theories. *Theories*.

"Today's quake," began Chapman in a voice reminiscent of fingernails scraping a chalkboard, "was of a magnitude of six-point four. The exaggerated amount of damage caused across the city was because of an irregular pattern the earthquake followed."

"I'd love to know what your theory is," said Trent. The others remained silent, well-aware of his strained relationship with both Shearer and Chapman.

Chapman stared at his notes for some time as though assimilating the words before daring to speak. "Pardon me if this gets a little too technical. The notorious San Andreas fault has an irregular kink in the local vicinity that can complicate the rupture surface of a slipping fault. A series of unusual coincidental complications gave rise to today's disaster. At eight-fourteen this morning, a quake with a magnitude of six-point-four was generated eighty miles from Los Angeles in the San Andreas. The rupture surface moved roughly ninety degrees against the fault's orientation. The directivity of the fault was pushed out, roughly westward. However, due to circumstances we don't yet understand, the energy from the quake skipped across two adjacent fault lines, triggering them to quiver violently like a guitar string. They were the Northridge and Chatsworth faults, which combined forces to drop Los Angeles to its knees today. We can only postulate that the lack of aftershocks is because of the two fault lines... cancelling themselves out, for want of a better phrase."

Everybody was shouting at the screen as Trent bolted from his chair. "What a pile of shit!"

Even Schofield was ruffled. "That's not what the data says!"

"Christ," barked Catherine, "can they get away with this?"

"And they threw *you* out because they thought your theories were crazy," said Walter, shaking his head gently.

Trent stabbed a finger at the screen. "They don't know. They don't know and are too proud to admit it, the bunch of pompous..."

"Ssssh! He's not through yet," Schofield said, catching Trent's arm and angling him back to the screen.

Chapman put his notes down and, after a sip from a water bottle, looked more confident as he went into sales patter. "This brings to light the urgent need for research into earthquake mechanics. Research costs money, and today proves that more professional research is needed to forewarn us of these events. That is why Caltech is joining with other research groups, NGL and SWCEC, to develop a broad sweeping and cooperative research program. Funding will be withdrawn from fringe research groups, such as Professor Michael Trent at WCEC, who is wasting valuable finances and resources which may have been necessary to predict today's disaster."

Trent blinked in surprise. Chapman abusing him to his face was one thing, but over national television was a new low, for even him. "I'm going to sue that jerk! How can they lay the blame on anybody? He even just said research isn't that far advanced! I bet Shearer has his dirty little oar in this somewhere, someone ought to excavate some shit on his past."

Now spittle was spraying from Trent's lips. He wiped them clean with the back of his hand, gripped a bench for support. His shoulders felt like solid rock, muscles ready to snap, but he knew it would either be a long vacation or a vast quantity of alcohol that would limber him up.

"We've had this discussion," Catherine said calmly. "It's just hot air, Trent. Let them blow their thermals off."

Trent shook his head, not wanting to answer. She was right; she had to be. Walter pulled out a cigarette carton, slid the penultimate smoke from the pack, and lit up. He took a long drag, offering the last to Trent, who refused with a sharp shake of the head.

"They can't blame you...us. It wouldn't stand." Smoke escaped from his nostrils as he studied Trent. Then he shrugged. "But it looks like they're sure as hell gonna try."

SEVEN

THE SANDY PEANUT husk split in two as it pinged off a half-full Budweiser bottle. Trent had stormed from his lab two hours ago and made his way straight to a traditional Irish bar in the Angels' heart. *The Pumphouse* had suffered minor damage to the windows and to several bottles of spirits on the wall. Trent glanced at his unshaven features in a fractured mirror, but other than a little broken glass, it was hard to spot any effects from the quake. Surrounding buildings had suffered much greater damage. Luck of the Irish, he thought.

Before leaving the lab, Trent had Schofield issue a press release about the data they had gathered. Not that it would help very much. Chapman had already branded their unit crazy, and the publicity machine had a habit of believing his every word. Catherine had warned him not to publish any release until they'd had time to assess it, but he'd ignored her. In retrospect he probably just helped fuel the *crazy seismologist* rumor by issuing contradictory information.

Feeling guilty for not listening to her, he had sent Catherine home earlier than the guys after her fiancé had called from the hospital, his arm now set in plaster. A careless driver had broadsided him, and the crumpled door had fractured his left arm in two places. Catherine had been fretting all afternoon, wondering if she even had a home to return to, so the news of Jack's accident put her focus completely off work. Trent assured her she was better off skipping the rest of the evening. Maybe a chill out period would do them all good.

That's what he said, but his thoughts were dark.

Just after Catherine left, a researcher for Anna King, a Pulitzer Prize winning TV host who had a daily slot on a new CBS lunchtime news show, called, wanting to know if Trent was available to discuss both the quake and Caltech's opinion of him on a slot tomorrow. He said he'd call back after thinking about it. Fifteen minutes later, he redialed and agreed to come on. They arranged the time, and after the peppy researcher had given him directions, he left the lab with the intention of getting completely hammered.

Harry Fennell ran the cloth over the chipped imitation oak finish on the bar, wiping the pool of slops and peanuts that had accumulated around Trent's bottle.

"You plannin' to look like a rat's arse tonight?" Harry asked in a thick Irish brogue Trent always suspected he put on for the punters.

"Tonight, Harry, you're going to be a rich man. I am going to drink every alcoholic substance in this place before moving on." His gaze darted between Harry's ample jowls and a screen behind the bar, playing news coverage with the volume low.

"Will you now? A man who can drink that much will have bigger problems in the mornin'. Not that I mind you spendin' all your cash in me establishment. But if there's somethin' on your brain, then I'd rather you spit it out now than throw your guts out over me nice clean bar."

"I take it you have seen the news? I mean, it's on right behind you," Trent said with accusing tones.

"I tuned out after repeated images of mass destruction grew boring. An' I don't recall seein' any crazed idiots prancin' around the screen. Least, none that looked like you anyways." Harry grinned, twisting the top off another Bud and putting it down as Trent knocked the other back in a single gulp. Trent's bottle hit the bar with some force, and he glared at Harry. The barman's face remained pleasant, unblinking.

At fifty-something, his face was weathered with deeply etched laughter lines. The good humor ran all the way around his waistline that permanently hung over his faded denims. They'd known each other for about seven years since Harry first took over The Pumphouse, which was a convenient staggering distance from Trent's personal grief-pit. Their relationship was on a more professional barman-drunkard level, although Trent told him everything, and in return, Harry pulled occasional favors. He was a remarkably well-connected man. It occurred to Trent that Harry knew *everything* about him. He listened to his theories with a layman's ears and was always there to offer constructive support. Harry was a whole charity on legs, but Trent only had a vague idea about his friend's own personal history.

Originally from Galway in Ireland, but brought up somewhere in England, Trent didn't know where. He moved back to Ireland to take over a family business, something to do with shoes. Several years after that, Harry moved over to New York with his brother Sam, who became sick with... some kind of problem Trent couldn't recall. Harry married, had a kid, and divorced - all within five years of running a small bar in New Jersey. He left that job and traveled west to the sun and waves, eventually finding his way here. Trent was sure there was more to the story, but he couldn't recall any other past conversations.

"Here's how I see it," Trent said as he took a mouthful of cool Bud. "Shearer has a national disaster on his hands. The polls look bad for him, so he figures he has to deflect the blame that would no doubt follow his pitiful disaster management. He pulls some heavy strings at Caltech, and they lay the pressure in my direction."

"Sounds plausible, only why would Shearer bother goin' to all that trouble? No offense, but you are of no consequence to a man like that. And I'd hardly call you a well-known public figure."

"Bad history. You remember Janet?"

"Janet, Janet," as he thought, Harry's gaze strayed to the bar's only other occupants, an elderly couple arguing in the corner who had barely touched their drinks. "Janet... got it. The redhead who jibbed you for that movie actor."

"He was an extra," Trent fumed. "He couldn't act to save his worthless life."

"Nice to see no bitterness remains."

That was just over a year ago. Trent had been in love, madly and deeply. Janet was everything he had fantasized about since college. A petite redhead with copper curls that hung around her breasts. Soft gray eyes, wide with innocence, concealed the sensual tiger that prowled inside. God, she was good in bed, the best. Unstoppable; insatiable. For four years they had dated, and the prospects of solidifying their vows loomed close by. Maybe that's what scared her off. He never found out. He suspected that she'd been having an affair for several months but lacked evidence. It was a hunch, but Trent had an excellent track record with hunches. Janet was a smart girl, devious too. One day, when they were both at Caltech, she sent a text message to tell him it was all over.

Just like that.

His entire life crumbled around him; the logical strata of consciousness groped in the darkness for a valid reason. Maybe she'd had an affair, but Trent felt he could forgive her if she came back - he might have to do some serious kneecapping to the bastard who touched her, but he would forgive her for one more chance. It never came. Phone calls were never returned, and when he arrived at her apartment, she'd vacated without leaving a forwarding address.

Trent felt the whole relationship had been one long ghost ride, her beautiful smile and warm lithe body nothing but a spectral fantasy. But the pain he felt was very real, every limb restrained by heavy invisible chains, the physical feeling of his heart shattering. Tears he thought had been vanquished in his teenage years, returned with a vengeance. It was hard to get back into a routine, or rather, a routine without her. But he did and found himself loveless and jobless within the same month.

Oddly, leaving his job had been the catalyst to suppress his depression and fight back. A few choice words and carefully edited references landed him the job at the West Coast Earthquake Center that offered him more freedom and, ironically, a higher salary than at Caltech.

He immersed himself in his work. Thoughts of Janet receded to a distant memory - only to be savagely roused when a friend-of-a-friend reported she'd heard from her. The bitch had moved in with Tony Ferrino, a useless so-called-actor whom Trent had known casually. They were living somewhere in Venice, and Trent hoped their home was - at least partially - destroyed in this morning's disaster. Sometimes bitterness was the perfect remedy for loneliness.

"What about her?" prompted Harry, pulling Trent from his reverie.

Trent tilted his Bud, watching as the liquid slid dangerously close to the bottle's mouth. He balanced it on the edge. "Politics. She graduated from UCLA and landed a job posing political dilemmas in some crappy little newspaper. I can't remember the name." He thought hard, but the name remained elusive. The only memory was of how proud he felt that Janet had landed the column just months after graduating. "Anyway, Shearer was running for office. Janet found a little backstory on him, uncovering a little alleged date-rape incident when the old man was a teenager. No charges were brought forth, of course, but she highlighted the story, which went viral online. Personally? I think it landed Shearer the job. He got the sympathy vote. But he never forgot that it was Janet who originated the story, and it bugged him. We met him a few times, and he always barbed the conversation with threats. Career threats, nothing more substantial than a whisper. Janet switched careers when she jumped out of my life. But articles soon appeared concerning the wacky professor at Caltech with his contracting earth theories: The media likened that to little green men and Bigfoot. Of course, Caltech gave me the boot." Trent took a long haul on his drink, finishing it to the last liquid sediments at the bottom of the bottle, 'the spit,' Janet had always called it. "I think Shearer was behind those stories and the unprovoked media interest."

"And I bet you couldn't keep your mouth shut about your theories?"

"You know me, expresser of public opinion, especially the ones they don't wanna hear. I shouted my mouth off about the asshole and things really turned bad for me. Who'd a thought it. My peers thought I was a quack, and Shearer kept his house clean by muzzling me with as much pressure as the bastard could muster, which wasn't too difficult since we're talking about the scientific community here. Janet got clean away with the whole thing."

Trent contemplated that fact. How a well-turned phrase can be deflected with a literary ventriloquist trick, to land the wrong person up the proverbial creek, without the necessary paddle.

Harry took the bottle from Trent and threw it into the bottle bank with a satisfying clink of glass-on-glass. "Many's a word said in the heat of the moment that would land you in trouble later. But it shouldn't hound your life forever. Sometimes you should just go home, contemplate life. Then wake up a completely new, wholesome person with no grudges or ghosts. Life's what you make of it, not what you think of it."

Twenty minutes later, Trent left the bar and crashed home in his downtown loft apartment. He ignored the fact that three shelves had collapsed in a domino effect, scattering papers and books across the lounge: tipping a withering yucca plant on its side, spreading dry soil across a cheap rug. He fell on the bed and stared at the cracked ceiling. The ceiling had always been cracked, and if there were any more channels after the quake, then they had blended in perfectly.

He closed his eyes with thoughts of purifying himself from rage and bitterness and awakening to a fresh Californian day that would bless him with a drive for life.

But in the darkness, he knew nothing would change.

EIGHT

ALANA FELT as if she were going berserk. She'd picked Ed up from his house at seven this morning and was forced to watch the display of affection between him and his wife, Helen. She thought the world of Helen, but some part of her envied both her relationship and her children.

Making it to the precinct on East 6th Street from the Valley had been a long slog, even by Los Angeles' notorious traffic standards. The media gave constant feeds of areas to avoid due to damage, but that did not seem to prevent people from venturing there. In fact, the only strand of good news for the two cops stuck in a tailback was that the Dodgers' game was still scheduled for play the day after tomorrow - although it was currently being set up as a soup kitchen by FEMA officials.

The morning had been spent examining and filing the arsenal of weapons recovered from their bust the previous morning, so that an accurate listing could be included in their final report. Alana felt the walls closing in as monotony played its hand. A takeout lunch had been their only salvation from the paperwork, and a chance to mix with the other officers.

Quake stories were still coming in. A seventy-year-old woman was found alive and well despite having the top floor of an apartment block collapse on her, burying her alive for twenty-six hours before rescuers cleared a hole in the masonry. Even now, fires were still burning, and the switchboard was jammed with calls of looting from the worst hit areas. The force was stretched to capacity with all leave canceled until the disaster zone was clear.

It was by chance that Alana and Ed were the only two officers available on non-essential duty when the call came in for a disturbance in 7th Street Metro Center. MTA Transit Police were already on the scene, but the suspected homicide was out of their jurisdiction. Chief Bixby had hesitated over freeing them but gave in to Alana's demands in the face of logic.

All entrances to Metro Station were already sealed with yellow OSHA tape and harassed looking MTA Transit Cops keeping the public and news crews at bay.

Ed parked across the street, and they pushed their way through the crowd. A black MTA officer barred their path.

"This station is closed, sir."

Ed flashed his badge, Alana following suit. The cop grunted noncommittally and stepped aside so they could descend the stationary escalator steps into the station.

"I love plain clothes detail," Ed commented as they descended. "Feels like we're always undercover."

"I don't know, I like a man in uniform."

"That is the root of all your problems. Maybe you should go for the average Joe?"

"Ed! Are you making a hit on a senior officer?" laughed Alana.

He waved the fingers on his left hand, promoting his band of gold. "I'm a happily married man!" he protested.

They reached the platform to find it crawling with cops and a white-suited CSI team setting up portable evidence tables, laptops, and lights. There was a lot of activity on the line, but their view was obscured as a skinny transit cop approached them. He flashed a crooked smile at Alana and shook Ed's hand. "Detective Williams?"

Ed cocked a thumb at Alana. "Wrong one."

The cop looked surprised as he turned to Alana. He took in her shoulder length dark brown hair that framed her high cheekbones and deep chocolate eyes. Her shirt was open just enough for him to get excited, and her black denim jeans hugged the curves of her legs with planned precision. He blushed a deep crimson that highlighted his acne and stammered apologetically.

"Sorry, ma'am, I just didn't expect... ya know..."

"A woman?"

"I didn't mean..."

Alana judged he couldn't be over twenty, a fresher. His badge declared him to be Officer Prendergast. She silenced him with a dismissive wave of the hand and pushed past him toward the platform edge.

Uniformed LAPD offers stood at the mouth of the tunnel talking animatedly to their MTA counterparts. They didn't venture beyond the power cables snaking into the eastbound running tunnel.

"We've been here a whole thirty seconds, and you still haven't briefed us on the situation, Prendergast. Are they teaching lethargy at the Academy these days?"

Prendergast followed like a reprimanded puppy determined to act the professional. "Sorry, ma'am. We have two bodies on the line. An engineering team discovered them while they were inspecting the tunnel for quake damage."

"Hit by a train?" asked Ed as he sat on the edge of the platform to ease himself down onto the low tracks. He hesitated for a moment until he noticed a white-jacketed forensic guy stumble on the third rail. "I take it the power's off?"

"Yes, sir. No, a train didn't hit them, as far as we can tell. Bodies tend to get mashed up by a train impact. These still have faces." His juvenile grin dropped at Alana's unamused expression.

"How far down are they?"

"About three hundred yards."

Alana slipped Prendergast's flashlight from his belt loop and jumped down to follow Ed onto the track. She flicked the stud on the flashlight, turning on the beam, almost blinding Prendergast.

"We'll take a look. You wait here."

Ed was passed a flashlight from a forensic woman kneeling on the platform, keying information into a PDA.

Side by side, they entered the dark running tunnel, following the cables. After a hundred yards, the shaft bent to the left almost imperceptibly at first, then quite firmly. The harsh white flashlight beams fell onto black, dirt encrusted walls. Their footsteps echoed from the curved tunnel walls. The faint sound of scurrying rodents pattered in front of them, the occasional large rat cutting past the beam.

"You know they have alligators in the New York sewers?" Ed muttered.

"You read that on the internet?"

"Uh-huh. What do you figure we have on the West Coast?"

"Maybe has-been actors?"

The tunnel straightened again. Ahead, the cables ended with several tripod-mounted lights parting the darkness, allowing five forensic officers to work on the scene. One turned to the detectives and tugged a protective surgical mask from his mouth. He nodded a greeting when Alana flipped her badge.

"Heck of a situation here, detective." He used his sleeve to mop the perspiration from his brow; the tunnels were becoming very humid. "Two bodies; male Caucasian. Probably transients." He indicated two human forms under clinically white sheets; the edges were black with grime from their brief contact with the ground.

"Time of death?" said Alana, her nose involuntarily wrinkling as she became aware of the rank odor of flesh.

"About six hours. Well, after the quake. They have run no trains since yesterday morning. They needed a watertight inspection of the system. Power has been off too. 750 volts can do a lot to a body, but this..." he trailed off. Alana was accustomed to the unflappable nature of CSI teams, but something was bothering this guy. "The MTA is going nuts; this was the last stretch of line, and they wanted the metro running again by this evening."

Ed kneeled at the bodies while Alana kept discreetly back. Death was a part of the job, and she'd seen enough horrors to take things in her stride. However, it was always the stench that turned her stomach. Here, there was something more. Another odor hidden under the putrid. A hint of burning.

The floodlights provided enough illumination, but some

stark shadows around the bodies required Ed to fill in with his flashlight. "Probable cause?"

The forensic man's grin was devoid of humor as he stopped and whipped back both body sheets theatrically. "Loss of vital organs is a favorite right now."

Ed recoiled. Alana grimaced and sucked a deep breath before kneeling at the corpses.

Light reflected from dead eyes, staring at the world in a last vision of terror. Rigor mortis held their arms in position. One lay on his back, arms crossed over his face as though blinded. The other lay several feet away, face down, with his head at an awkward angle.

But the horror came with a twelve-inch circular hole in their torsos. Through flesh, bones, and clothing. A perfect circle through which they could see the glint of the metal rail under them.

"Jesus Christ!" gasped Ed as he recovered himself.

"This has to be an accident," said Alana as she peered closer, breathing shallowly through her mouth to avoid inhaling that repugnant smell. She held her flashlight close to the wound; the forensic guy passed her a small stainless-steel pointer. She gently tried to move the victim's sweatshirt around the wound. It didn't budge. Closer inspection revealed the fibers along the circular edge were charred. "The shirt has fused to the body."

"Yup. And that takes some intense heat."

Ed suddenly realized what was missing. "There's no blood on the ground." He scanned his light around. "None anywhere. They must have been dumped here."

Alana looked between the corpses and shook her head. "No, look. This guy was shielding his face from the attacker while this one turned and tried to run. I'm guessing he was struck from behind."

The forensic knelt with them and retrieved the pointer from Alana. He indicated the inside rim of the wound where the flesh had tapered into the torso.

"The wound has cauterized almost instantaneously. That's why there's no blood and why the clothes are fused to the wound. This has all the hallmarks of severe burning. I'm talking about an industrial accident."

"But how can they be so precise?" asked Alana, standing and stepping back from the body. Her gaze momentarily met the corpse's.

"That's the real mystery, isn't it?"

Ed shook his head and examined the other body. The wounds were a carbon copy. "It's like a poker has pushed clean through them."

"But to generate that kind of heat, that's a mother poker, if you pardon my French," said the forensic.

"Why were they down here, anyway?" asked Alana.

"We got a lot of this kind of thing in New York," Ed said. "Bums sheltering in the subway where it was warm and safe from the elements. There are stories of entire communities down there. I can believe that."

Alana looked thoughtful as her flashlight caressed the subway walls in search of the clue that would solve the puzzle. "They're still extending this line, right?"

"I heard they're pushing through to La Cienega and down to Century City," said Ed.

"What equipment do they use?"

"Not sure. Drilling machines?"

"Anything that would generate the sort of heat to puncture through a man?"

"I doubt it. I think they're all boring tools, sharp drill bits, that kind of thing. Worth checking out, though."

"Okay, I'll get on it. I want you to run a check on missing persons. Try to give these guys names." Alana felt the familiar rush of confidence that accompanied a new case. She didn't know all the facts, but already had the steps of the case planned out. "And we need a list of all personnel who have access to this station."

The CSI guy carefully draped the sheets back over the bodies. "If you think a drilling tool did this damage, then you are looking for a piece of machinery weighing about five hundred pounds, attached to a massive power generator, like the size of a truck, and capable of being wielded by a single person as they *ran* after these guys."

Alana stopped in her tracks and wheeled to face him, her thoughts suddenly derailing. "What?"

He shrugged apologetically. "It's just as I see it. But if you're seriously going to follow that line of investigation, then you better put an APB on the Incredible Hulk."

NINE

TRENT SAT behind the wheel of his Prius, tapping in time to a grunge revival band on the only radio station not broadcasting quake reports.

Despite the tragedy and increasing death toll, the human aspect of the disaster was showing its face. The top story that kept LA's worn spirits up was the fact that the big ball game was still going ahead.

An irritating pain was swirling around Trent's temples, aggravated by the morning's elevated heat. The hangover; the aftershock of a good night's drinking.

Aftershock.

The word tolled in his head. There had been no aftershocks... at least, not yet. Trent hypothesized the worst case could be that yesterday's quake was a *foreshock* - a precursor to an even bigger tremor...

He shook those thoughts away. Schofield had come around early that morning with the latest satellite images of the damage. They showed a great rut cutting through the ground from the north, straight into Downtown, following the path of the bizarrely elongated epicenter. It was a *graben*, a narrow block of earth that had slipped between faults. It stretched fifty miles, possibly the result of a previously unknown cavern system collapsing along its length. At least that was the only postulation Schofield could come up with.

Caltech was still spewing their San Andreas kink theory, and the public was drowning in jargon and technical explanations that made no sense at the heart yet sounded great on the surface. Trent was still wound up about the whole bullshit campaign and personal jibes that he threw down the dregs of his coffee, intending to bulldoze his way over to Pasadena, into Caltech – and straight into Chapman's face. He'd been so wound up that he'd forgotten about his appointment with Anna King until Schofield jogged his memory.

Now, after a quick change, he was on his way to the CBS studios in the Valley, unaware of the growth of stubble that clung to his cheeks like moss.

A teenage stagehand introduced himself, but Trent immediately forgot his name - Josh, Scott, Tod... everybody in this town was called one of those. He was guided through throngs of technicians and runners that inhabited the studio corridors and constantly reminded to relax and be himself. Another assistant tugged at his jacket as she attached a radio microphone. As far as Trent could tell, nobody was above mid-twenties and regarded him more as *Exhibit-A* than a guest.

He was deposited in a comfortable chair on the set that was nothing more than painted plywood nailed together by wooden spars, looking far cheaper than it appeared on TV. Around him, people buzzed with purpose. Cameras wheeled around to focus on him; stage lights clunked on to flood the set with a rejuvenating life that made it sparkle expensively.

A leggy blonde woman in a tight-fitting gray suit click-clacked over to Trent, teetering on her heels. He recognized her instantly as Anna King despite the sour face and vape, which she pocketed halfway across the set. Her sour complexion vanished when she smiled at Trent; her grip was vice-like when she shook his hand.

"Michael Trent? Pleased to meet ya."

"Thank you, the same goes for me," stammered Trent, irritated by how star-struck he was acting. She was only a lunchtime anchorwoman, but in person, she oozed an attractive confidence. She adjusted her perfectly set hair before pulling an iPad from under the chair.

"Has anyone told you what'll be happening?" she asked, her native LA accent spilling out.

"Nobody's said anything about that. I haven't even been offered a drink yet," he added hopefully.

"Somebody get this guy a drink. What are we, crimping on the budget here? Anyway, Michael... I'll call you Professor Trent, is that okay?"

Trent shrugged. "Whatever you like."

The activity became a little more fluid. A technician called for everybody to standby. Anna glanced at the narrow Gucci on her wrist.

"We're on in a second. Okay, Mike. I'll ask you a few questions about yesterday, you fire back some answers. Keep it clear and concise and don't drown the audience in too much technical mumbo-jumbo. They need easy to digest sound bites. I want the real you. Your theories about these events."

"Okay, people, we're on in... five, four..." the stage manager counted the rest down on his fingers and pointed at Anna.

Trent heard the familiar news jingle echo through the studios. The red tally lights flicked on the two-camera set up, burning accusingly at him. He felt hot and a little dizzy. Where was that drink? But it was too late for refreshments as he heard Anna introduce him, so he concentrated on putting on a smile and looking straight at her.

"We're joined by Professor Trent, from the West Coast Earthquake Center, an independent geological survey that was, until yesterday, a Caltech affiliate. Professor Trent, what can you tell us about the events we're all so familiar with?"

"Yesterday, we were struck by a quake which was one of, if not *the* most, powerful to hit Los Angeles. Those people who should know better are blaming the event on a trigger effect caused by a kink in the San Andreas fault. However, I have seen no evidence to substantiate these claims."

"Are you saying it is not San Andreas related?"

"The San Andreas has a terrible reputation, when in fact a high percentage of recorded quakes come from the thousands of other small fault lines scattered across California."

"You mean the quake was generated by a smaller fault line? Like the Northridge incident in ninety-four?"

"The evidence I've gathered from Caltech's very own TERRAscope network suggests that an unusual combination of tremors along minor faults produced yesterday's devastation."

"I would hardly call the damage minor," Anna quickly retorted with a calculating smile.

"The damage wasn't. But if several minor fault lines reacted, then they would produce the damage we see around us. In Southern California, there are over two hundred known faults long enough to produce earthquakes as large as magnitude six. And thousands of minor fractures along the

LA basin, so it is safe to presume there are ones we don't know about, which is what happened at Northridge. Seismologists didn't know the fault was there."

"What evidence have you seen to contradict Caltech, a rather prestigious authority on any scientific matter, one would think?"

Trent was on a roll. "The data we received was unusual. There was no precise hypocenter, the heart of the quake. The whole epicenter region runs out from the desert, straight into Downtown. I must admit, I've seen nothing like it before. Satellite images show the earth has physically sunk in a graben - like a valley - along this epicenter track. I speculate that it's the result of a subterranean cavern system collapsing from the shock waves."

"So why would Caltech's Professor Chapman say it is something else?"

Trent shifted, uncomfortable again. His peripheral vision caught sight of a camera shifting position as it subtly closed in on him. Anna arched an eyebrow to encourage him to respond.

"I haven't got a clear answer to that. Maybe to increase funding opportunities?" Trent knew publicly badmouthing his rival would have repercussions, but he had no way out now.

"An awful lot of funding goes into researching quake activity, some six million a year, I believe. Many people think that money could be used for other purposes. Communities, the homeless. What is it being used for, exactly? Or is it all being swallowed up by the earth?"

"Earthquake detection is an important science, as yesterday proved to us, and six million dollars' worth of funding into something so vital is, frankly, ridiculous. There is still so much we don't know. And we're increasing our knowledge each year. The goal is to ultimately provide a sound prediction theory to prevent loss of life."

"I believe that's why you got into quake prediction to begin with? You lost both your parents in an earthquake in Mexico?"

Trent shifted uncomfortably. "That's right. When things get personal, it's a wonderful motivator. That's why I've been pursuing an advanced warning theory my entire career."

"So where is this theory?"

"Not here yet," grinned Trent, although Anna's cool gaze was now far from comforting. He sensed the question was bait but couldn't resist biting. "The scientific community is divided on the actual mechanism that causes quakes."

Anna looked surprised, even making a pretense of looking at her notes. "But I thought, and I'm sure most of the viewers do, that tremors were caused by shifting tectonic plates. Isn't that what they teach in elementary school?"

"Yeah, and without doubt, the tectonic plate theory is correct to a certain degree. But what causes the plates to move in the first place? Some people say they are floating on a molten liquid core like a boat on the ocean. To me, and some others, that seems a little unusual. I favor the contracting earth principle." Before Anna seized on his pause, Trent rattled on. "Because of that moniker, it has been given a 'fringe-science' label. But then again, anything that threatens established scientific beliefs is frowned upon, and those scientists involved are branded as heretics."

"You must agree a *contracting earth* sounds like something from a science-fiction movie?"

"Scientists agree that when the earth was formed, it was nothing more than a smoldering mass of super-hot rock.

Millions of years cooled the mass down until it could bear life. Also, nobody would argue that the center of the earth comprises a molten rock held around a dense iron core. The cooling of the earth is far from over, and as it cools, the planet contracts." He demonstrated with his hands, as though holding an invisible ball, rapidly deflating. Out of the corner of his eye, he noticed a stagehand cueing Anna to wrap up. "And as it cools, the tectonic plates are pushed against one another, fractionally. When this happens, we get quakes."

"A fascinating theory, Professor Trent, and one that could be strongly argued. But there are also, as you say, *fringe scientists* who favor a hollow earth theory. Once again, who can ultimately be proven correct?"

Before Trent could react, Anna swiveled to beam at the camera. "After the break: news on the relief work being carried out in Dodger Stadium."

She paused for the break music to swell up before dropping the smile. Trent was already out of his seat, marching across the soundstage, angrily yanking off his clip-mic, which he threw to the floor.

"Michael, hold on a minute."

"I didn't think you were going for the lunatic angle. Thanks a heap. You timed it so I couldn't even deny it."

Anna caught up to him. "Hey, don't take it personally. That's just the slant the producers had in mind. If it makes you feel any better, we'll be grilling Chapman, too."

"No. Actually, it doesn't make me feel any better–"

Suddenly, the ground rattled. Wails of alarm filled the studio, combined with the screech of twisted steel as the overhead lighting rigs danced in their mountings.

"Aftershock!" roared Trent. Anna was pitched to the

floor, savagely twisting her ankle as one of her stilettos sheared.

Trent fought to keep his balance like a surfer cresting a wave. The laser-smoothed studio floor cracked. The set toppled over as spars snapped. Studio cameras rolled across the floor.

A crack like a steel whip drew Trent's attention above him. One of the two cables suspending a heavy studio light snapped. The light precariously spun thirty feet directly over the stunned Anna King. The surviving cable grated across a roofing girder, each swing severing the steel threads.

Adrenaline flooded Trent. His senses became razor sharp - just as the light pulled free from the redundant cable.

Trent's arms slipped around Anna's waist, and using his full body weight, dragged her several feet aside before tumbling to the ground himself. The light smashed where Anna was seconds before. White-hot glass fragments showered the area. The light's hot barn-doors sprung away – one glancing across Trent's forehead. He only noticed as a trickle of blood stung his eye, forcing it closed.

Then the tremor stopped.

Anna King gaped at Trent; all her arrogance evaporated. Then, unexpectedly, she wept tears of relief.

TEN

ALANA STARED DESPONDENTLY at the stack of paperwork that had been tossed to the floor and smothered by her spilled coffee during the aftershock. She knelt and began collecting the work together. Ed hustled across with a folder under his arm.

"Fact, I've just learned that the restroom is definitely the safest place to be. I just saved my underwear from a fate worse than death. I got some theories on the transient murders. Want to hear?"

"Will it get me out of this office?" asked Alana, with a pleading note in her voice.

"The MTA confirmed all boring machinery operates on a drill-bit basis. There is no heating machinery capable of cutting through rock. Nothing on their site could inflict the wounds we saw. Forensics confirms that."

"Strike that off the list."

"I dug out a list of employees, past and present, for the MTA. The usual mix. Except one, Harold O'Reilly. The guy might as well put *disgruntled employee* on his résumé. A thorough track record of being fired from everything he's ever tried - including working on the new running tunnels. He'd had some sort of altercation and allegedly stabbed a colleague in the leg with a screwdriver. Nothing was proven, no charges were brought about."

Alana took the report and glanced through it. "Nice guy. Is there an address in here?"

"No. I left that in the car. Figured we'd be using it."

Alana dropped the stack of damp papers on her chair and led the way out of the office. "Superb policing, Ed."

"One last thing; two years ago, he was taken in for a psychiatric evaluation. Seems he suffers from mild schizophrenia."

The possibility that the case might be an easy crack gave Alana a brief wave of disappointment. Punishing the bad guys was satisfaction enough, but sometimes a challenge was welcome.

The temperature soared as the unmarked car drew into Sommerfield Avenue. Telegraph poles had crashed on to some automobiles, and debris and spilled garbage littered the sidewalk. Alana checked the address on her GPS again, and then gestured to a shabby house across the street. A scarred oak tree had been uprooted in the tremor, crushing the garage and strewing trashcans across the overgrown lawn.

"The quake gave this place a makeover," quipped Ed as they climbed out. His hand unconsciously felt beneath his jacket. The hilt of his Beretta nestled in his shoulder holster was reassuring.

Alana scrutinized the peeling paintwork and boarded windows. "Just your average psychopath's residence."

Closer inspection found the door was off its hinges and

was propped against the jamb, held in place by a brick. Alana tentatively rapped on the wood.

"Anybody home? LAPD. We're coming in."

Without waiting for a response, Alana took the weight of the door and slid it aside, reasoning that it was already technically open. Lances of sunlight pierced the gloom inside. Her boot caught a trash bag just behind the door, dozens more populating the hallway. Bile rose in her throat as a rotten stench hit her. Ed followed close behind and physically reeled from the foul stench.

"Something died."

Alana's automatic found its way into her hand as she edged toward a door. "LAPD!"

The floorboard under Ed's foot groaned with his weight. He flashed an apologetic grin to Alana and then positioned himself at the side of the door opposite her. He mouthed a countdown, then turned and booted the door open with his full weight. A hole smashed open in the cheap wood, almost swallowing his foot as the door swung open with enough force to dent the wall behind it. Ed's Beretta swept the room, offering Alana cover to dart inside. By the numbers, her weapon swept the blind spots behind and above the door.

Several steps in, Alana lost her balance over more torn trash bags. Rats scurried for cover in the ankle-deep household waste: fast-food containers, soda cans, and microwave dinners. Congealed slop coated it all, giving the odious stench.

"This place ought to be condemned. I'll hazard a guess that we won't find him here."

Alana breathed into her sleeve in an attempt to filter the smell.

Ed raised his jacket over his mouth to avoid taking a

lungful of fetid air. He noticed a pile of books on the dresser. "Check these out."

Using the tip of his gun to avoid physical contact, Ed pushed a stack of yellowed, dog-eared books on their side, all by one author.

"H. P. Lovecraft. Our boy is into his horror."

He swept through a few pages, all of them covered in urgent pencil notations. He reached for another, *At the Mountains of Madness*. Again, every page was hastily covered in scribbling.

"A literature critic."

"There's more stuff over here," said Alana, reaching for a pile of notes, crumpled magazines, and Internet printouts: all with the same theme:

"Occult... mysteries... UFOs. Our boy's a real conspiracy whack job. And there are reams of printouts from the Internet. All the same crap."

As their eyes became accustomed to the gloom, more stacks of notes became apparent. The smell of rotten trash faded as their sense of smell shut itself down in self-preservation. They moved into the next room, a hovel of a kitchen. Mysterious stains covered the work surfaces, sporadic mold growing on abandoned food.

The ground-floor bedroom offered the biggest clue.

"Alana, come see this," hollered Ed as he entered. Alana poked her head around, instantly registering the massive construction blueprints on the wall, schematics for the LA Metro.

"This guy was into stealing the office stationery in a big way," said Ed. "What do you think? Maybe those bums got in the way of O'Reilly's own private terrorist campaign?"

Alana's vibrating cell interrupted their musings. She

retrieved the sleek iPhone from her jacket and answered. From across the room, Ed couldn't hear the voice on the other end, but looked up sharply as Alana spoke.

"The 7th Street Subway?" She met Ed's gaze, and he could tell from the rising pitch of her voice they had another lead in the case. "We'll head right over." She hung up and looked back at the blueprints.

"Another body?"

"No," she broke into a smile. Picked up a dog-eared Lovecraft novel and stared at the grotesque monster depicted on the cover. "You won't believe it."

ELEVEN

AUTOMOBILES SAT fender to fender in the usual LA conga. Twisted buildings and rubble stacks on the sidewalk added an apocalyptic feel to the city, but nothing Angelenos couldn't take in their daily routine.

Trent gripped the wheel of his Prius so tightly his knuckles whitened. His stomach churned from the cocktail of anger and subsequent adrenaline overdose at the studio. A pickup next to him blared an oppressive wall of sound that vaguely resembled rap music. Trent cranked the knob of his radio up to compensate. It played some unidentifiable teenage pop sensation.

The aftershock had jarred him both physically and mentally. His handle on the situation had become even more fragmented. Not that *an* aftershock was anything unusual: he'd expected one. Only not this long after the initial tremor. And not as powerful. Immediately after leaving the television studio, which was scrambling to get back on air, he called Catherine at the lab. Walt was on the case, tracing the hypocenter and calculating the magnitude.

Trent was still smarting from the interview, although Anna King had profusely apologized about her heavy-handed tactics after Trent had saved her life. But the damage was done, the bad press out. An incoming call from the lab derailed his train of thought.

"Hi, Catherine. What have you got?"

"Nothing on the aftershock yet," replied the filtered voice. "But, first, you're a hero."

"Hero? What have I done now?"

"Anna King? You never told me you saved the life of a celebrity."

"Big deal. In fact, I'm regretting it. How did you know?"

"Ms King came back on air and sang your praises sky high. Told the world what a fabulous seismologist you really are and regretted her leading choice of questions. And lucky for you, one camera was still recording during the tremor. They got the whole thing on tape. Real ratings boost for that show. You're trending on Twitter."

"Fabulous," he said dryly. "If you tell me there's going to be a cash reward, I may even smile."

Catherine laughed. "Fat chance, Trent. But you got the booby prize. A call from the MTA. Must've seen you on TV."

"Tell them I know nothing about trains."

"They've got a problem on the subway, and they need our help."

Trent shook his head. Building a subway right through a geologically unstable area smacked of stupidity. "They have their own team for that, don't they?"

"They need some professional advice on site, and immediately. I told them you were free."

Trent tried to think of an excuse but came up empty-handed.

"Okay, fine. Tell me where, but one thing, you're coming with me."

Brief directions and equipment lists followed. Trent hung up and took the next right out of the jam, heading for Wilshire and Normandie.

A waiting MTA transit cop stepped from the shade offered by the subway's entrance and guided Trent inside. Several press photographers snapped away, none recognizing the newly minted television hero.

The cop didn't speak a word as he led Trent down static escalators and onto the main platform. A CSI team was hauling equipment from the running tunnel. Power cables zigzagged across the track connected to floodlights dotted down the subway. The darkness ate their intense light.

Four people waited on the edge of the platform. One was Catherine, wearing casual jeans and an extremely jazzy top that hurt the eyes. A bespectacled man in a dark suit approached and vigorously shook Trent's hand.

"Michael Trent, pleasure to meet you. My name is Steven Howards, Director of Services for the MTA. Your assistant here brought down some equipment." He indicated the other man and woman with him. "This is Detectives Olmos and Williams from the LAPD."

Trent shook their hands, a boyish grin turning the corners of his mouth as he locked eyes with Alana.

"Pleasure," he said.

She unconsciously brushed a stray lock of dark brown hair from her eyes. Trent was momentarily transfixed, only a gentle nudge from Catherine breaking his reverie. She thrust a horn shaped box in his hand.

"Your Nose, Trent."

The nose was a complicated array of sensors that constantly sampled the air, checking for dangerous gas build-ups.

"Why the police? What's happened?"

Steven Howards thrust a hardhat in Trent's free hand as the group moved toward the running tunnel entrance.

Alana half turned to Trent. "This morning, we found a pair of transients killed on the subway line. We're not too sure what they died of, but it was unusual, to say the least. We're here in case you find any evidence to help us."

"Evidence? From what?"

Alana jumped down onto the track. "From whatever we find down here. Watch out for the third rail. It's now live."

Ed helped Catherine and Howards by lending a supporting arm. Uneasy with the height of the platform, Trent sat on the edge and lowered his legs down. He didn't notice Alana's smirk. Trent stared at his grime-covered hands, looked for something to wipe them on, and then settled to wipe them across his jeans, leaving black stains. They entered the running tunnel.

"Keep to the side," advised Howards.

Trent piped up, his voice echoing loudly. "What has happened down here? I thought the MTA had their own team for quake inspection?"

"We do," said Howards. "And I'm proud to say we finished our survey an hour ago. No damage at all, so the trains are running again."

"When?" asked Trent with a tinge of concern. But the question had already been answered. The rail next to him began to gently quiver, then a sound like a dozen nails across a blackboard as a light appeared from the murky depths. Howards gently, but firmly, pushed Trent against the wall.

"Is this safe?" asked Catherine. Even in dim light, Trent could see the concern in her eyes.

"Not to worry. They're running slow. Control knows we're on the line."

Seconds later, six thirty-foot long carriages glided past with a low rumble. Pressed against the wall, Trent caught strobe-like images of people on the train staring into the blackness or reading newspapers as a steady warm breeze blew his hair.

He glanced to see how Catherine was coping and noticed Howards kept a pace from the wall. Trent misjudged the distance from the train as it lumbered past; there was a good two-foot clearance from where he stood. But he didn't like to take chances, even though he now knew his back was stained with grime.

The train passed with a slight sucking effect that almost caused Trent to lose his balance. As they pressed onward, Howards resumed his narration.

"The aftershock caused more problems than the main quake. Part of a tunnel wall collapsed, away from the track thankfully, revealing some kind of cavern system beyond."

"Surely that would have shown up on a geo survey during construction?"

"You'd have thought so." Howards shrugged. "They did a complete geological survey before construction, found no sign of it then."

"That's not an uncommon event," said Catherine. "Some narrow fissures can run undetected mere feet away from a construction. There have been cases of construction workers having to extend foundations of a building because of a previously undetected fissure system. Some are even as big as five feet across."

Howards looked bemused. "Five feet, huh? Here it is."

He passed Trent a flashlight. Ed activated his and trained the thick white beam across the smooth tunnel wall. It fell into a void some twenty feet in diameter. A perfect circle.

"There's no detritus," said Catherine, surprised as she scanned the floor. Not a stone out of place. Trent scanned his light into the gloom beyond.

"No rubble inside, either. Check out the edge here." He ran the beam around the circumference. "Glazed."

Alana touched the rounded edge. "Feels like glass. What kind of heat could cause this?"

Trent shook his head. "Intense. I mean, we're talking volcanic levels to do this kind of work. I'm no volcanologist, though." He thumbed a button on the electronic nose and made wide, circling gestures with it as he took samples of air.

Alana combed the surrounding area with her flashlight. Her expression turned incredulous as the light fell across the white chalk markers that showed where the murdered transients were found only a dozen feet away.

"Burn holes in the wall and in the victims. Any thoughts?" asked Ed.

"Maybe this isn't a murder case after all. Maybe it's a geological phenomenon?"

Trent studied the small screen on the electronic nose. Each detected chemical had been identified in the search for anything lethal. "Canary's in the green. No sign of any harmful gases."

"Professor Trent..." began Alana.

"Call me Mike, or Trent," grinned Trent. Catherine rolled her eyes. She recognized *that* tone in his voice.

"What kind of geological event could cause this?"

"A gas pocket could have been disturbed by the aftershock and blown out, but you would expect residual gas readings and debris."

"Perhaps ball lightning?" said Catherine.

Ed frowned. "I thought that was just science fiction?"

Trent shook his head. "Mainstream science doesn't like bringing ball lightning into the equation. It's been photographed and results to reproduce it in the lab have had varied success. Problem is to maintain research grants, most scientists stick to conventional wisdom."

Catherine shook her head. "Ball lightning has been spotted by hundreds of people during quakes, so it is not something we should readily ignore."

"But nobody knows what it really is?" asked Alana. Trent shook his head.

"Could it kill?" asked Ed, who had been scrutinizing the fused edge of the opening.

Trent shook his head. "There are no recorded cases to my knowledge."

"But for example, theoretically, could it burn a hole with a diameter of about a foot through a person?"

Trent latched on to the line of questioning. "You're talking about the murders here this morning? Both of them?"

Alana shot a sharp glance between Trent and Catherine that reminded them this was business, and she was the law. "What we talk about here, all this, is confidential until this case is under lock and key."

Trent nodded keenly; armchair intrigue was his vice.

Both he and Catherine listened as Alana described the bodies they found this morning and the web of hypotheses around them. Alarm bells rang in Catherine's mind as Detective Williams recalled searching through O'Reilly's apartment.

"Do you think there may be a madman down here? Ready to kill us?" she asked with a tremble in her voice.

Ed grinned, pulled his automatic more for show than necessity. "That's why I'm here. To serve and protect."

"Okay then," said Trent, "I can buy the madman story, but not the cause of death and certainly not this." He expanded his hands to take in the hole's size.

"But you must admit it seems a little coincidental?"

"I think the ball lightning theory is our strongest contender right now."

"Maybe, but let's face it, the most obvious place to look is down that hole. Are you coming?" said Alana.

Trent looked at the rails as they quivered again from the faintest reverberations of an approaching train. Alana stepped into the portal, her flashlight reflecting slightly off the walls within. Trent leaned close to Catherine. Her wide eyes told of the doubt in her mind.

"Do you want to wait here?"

She blinked away the doubt, as though it were a figment of Trent's imagination. "Are you kidding? Miss a chance to explore some weird geology?"

She followed Alana through. Trent suddenly felt like he was holding the party back until Howards coughed apologetically.

"I will wait here. Some engineers will be down soon."

He edged against the wall; his face cloaked in shadows. He was scared down here: piss-his-pants scared. The knowledge made Trent feel a lot braver, and he stepped through the gap as another train slowly rolled past. Glancing back, he mused the passing carriages looked more like a sliding wall, penning him inside this tunnel forever.

Alana stroked the walls with her hand as she walked. They were cool and glassy. The incline dropped sharply, almost a full thirty-degrees.

Catherine closely inspected it. "Obsidian. The rock has been turned to glass. This is typical of volcanic movement."

Trent swept air with the sniffer. "Nada. Air clean."

"What were you hoping to pick up on that thing? FM radio?" chirped Ed.

Alana glanced over at her partner, detecting a trace of fear in his voice.

"It's what I don't want to pick up. Methane, sulfur, anything connected to volcanic activity."

Ed was already sweating. "You guys keep mentioning volcanic activity. I thought L.A. was nowhere near that kind of thing?"

"Molten rock's part of the Earth's mantle. It's never that far away–"

Alana suddenly gave a yelp as her foot slipped on the glazed surface. She slumped on her ass and cascaded into Catherine - who also lost her balance from the impact. With a shriek, they both slid down the incline together, sneakers and boots squeaking against the smooth surface as they fought for purchase.

"Hold on!"

Ed reached out and lunged for them. With no grip underfoot, he dropped to his knees and fell flat on his chest, knocking the wind out of him. He slid headfirst after them, flashlight leading the way.

Trent made the mistake of running forward, intent on catching Catherine as she fell. The floor was as slick as ice. He slipped, knocking the breath from him as he landed on his side. His flashlight tumbled ahead of him as he slid into the Stygian darkness ahead...

TWELVE

CATHERINE HIT a mineral column with her shoulder, bringing her to an abrupt stop. Any faster and she would have dislocated it. Before she could move, Alana careened into her – both gasping as the wind was knocked from them.

They hadn't been traveling quickly, but Alana estimated they must have slid over sixty feet. She got to her feet in time to sidestep Ed, his welcome flashlight illuminating the surroundings a little. Trent rolled after him, slamming straight into a wall. She rushed to his side.

"Trent, are you okay?" Alana retrieved her flashlight that had rolled several feet away and scanned him with the beam.

"Fine...no problem." Trent sat up, a crunching sound drawing his attention to the smashed sniffer gizmo that had broken against the wall.

Catherine helped Ed stand, using his flashlight to check the big man was okay before turning the light on the chamber they stood in.

The smooth, glass-like walls had given way to a natural cave. Stone columns supported the roof some fifteen feet above. Several smooth passageways continued at various angles in the wall.

"It's like a hive," Alana whispered, her voice echoing.

"Now this is getting odd," Catherine said as she examined the walls. "There's no sign of fusion on these rocks." She wagged the light across the chamber's jagged walls. "If magma was responsible for carving out those tunnels, then this cave should be affected." Ed didn't understand. "Lava is essentially a liquid. It flows like water. This cave would have to have been flooded, building enough pressure to form the tunnel we just slid down. The surface of these walls would have melted just like in the tunnel. But they're rough. Natural."

Alana retrieved her own flashlight and focused on the deep silence. The silence was absolute, nothing from the outside. No train noises or sounds from the busy streets above. Not even a steady dripping she associated with caves... but there was *something* else.

Alana's senses isolated the sound from the background chatter. She slowly turned in a circle to pinpoint it. Whatever it was, it seemed to come from a nondescript passageway opposite.

She crossed over. Training and instinct guided her hand, connecting it with her Beretta holstered on her belt - just as there was a flurry of movement in front of her.

Trent spun around. The shot rang out so loud it made his ears ring. Catherine screamed next to him. For the second time that day, his adrenaline turned events into a slow-motion ballet.

At a run, a disheveled man careened into Alana, pitching them both to the ground. Her gun and flashlight dropped -

the strobing light creating long dancing shadows that threw the entire scene out of perspective.

The attacker grunted as he pinned her to the floor. His sunken cheeks were matted with stubble, and hot saliva dripped from his lips as one hand gripped Alana's throat. There was a glint of steel in his other hand.

Trent's own heartbeat roared in his ears as he surged forward. He slammed into the man from the side, dragging him off Alana and sending him crashing against the wall. Trent's momentum rolled him to his feet in time to avoid the wild man's slashing blade.

Catherine ran to help, years of karate training after-school resurfacing from her memory. "Trent! Watch out!"

With feral speed, their attacker lunged again with a wild swing. Trent ducked. The blade sparked as it struck the rock just above his head. The maniac's return swing sliced clean across Catherine's thigh as she closed in from the side. A smooth red incision stained her jeans, and she staggered against the wall.

Another shot thundered in the cave. The blood-stained knife dropped from the man's grasp and a crimson patch blossomed across his shoulder. He staggered before shock took away his legs and he collapsed in a heap.

Ed kept his weapon trained on the man. "LAPD, Mr O'Reilly. You're under arrest."

Alana retrieved her sidearm and flashlight and then joined Trent at Catherine's side. She whimpered as she clutched her bleeding leg. Her fingers were already bloody from attempting to clamp the wound.

"Are you hurt anywhere else?" asked Alana.

Catherine shook her head. Alana pulled at the inside lining of her own jacket and tore a long strip off. She twisted the cloth lengthwise and tied a tourniquet around just above the wound.

"This isn't ideal, but you're going to be okay," Alana assured her. "Looks like the blade missed any arteries." Catherine winced, her eyes watering as Alana pulled the tourniquet tight.

"Keep relieving the pressure," Alana warned. She turned to Trent. "And what about you? Are you hurt?"

Trent nodded, still partially deafened from the gunshot and more than impressed at Alana's cool headedness in handling a murder attempt in a cave, a hundred feet underground in an earthquake zone. Alana treated him to a warm smile. "Thanks for helping me out."

O'Reilly rolled onto his back and crawled against the wall, clutching his shoulder. Blood seeped through his fingers, staining his already damp and dirty shirt. He panted heavily, muttering to himself just too quietly to understand.

Alana carefully approached him with hands raised in a non-threatening gesture. "I have to take a look at that wound, okay?"

O'Reilly ignored her, continuing his incomprehensible murmuring.

"I've got him covered," said Ed, repositioning himself for a clear shot. Then for O'Reilly's benefit he added, "Do anything freaky and I will shoot you again. This time, it won't be a warning."

"Do you understand that you've been arrested?" Alana ventured closer. "Don't resist or we will use force. Is that clear?" He looked beyond her, his eyes focusing on some inner nightmare. Alana crouched and slowly reached for O'Reilly's wound. "I just need to see how bad it is."

His hand snapped out and clamped blood slick fingers

around Alana's wrist, pulling her closer to his rank breath. She held up her free hand to Ed, indicating for him to hold his fire. Ed's aim didn't waver.

Alana struggled, but even with slick fingers, O'Reilly's grip was too tight, but he made no further move to harm her.

"They're here." Through cracked lips, his voice was barely a whisper.

"Who is?"

O'Reilly coughed violently. "From the deep..."

"Who? Is there somebody else here?"

"*Dero...*" spluttered O'Reilly, repeating it like a mantra. He suddenly released Alana, his hand clamping back over his wound. His piercing green eyes focused on her, reflecting primal fear.

"They are coming," he spluttered. "The Dark Lord has arrived..." Alana resisted the urge to pull away from the man as his voice dropped to a hoarse whisper. "Save yourself." The look of stark terror on his face chilled Alana. "Run."

Alana looked at Ed for advice. He shrugged. "Crazy talk."

Alana motioned to his shoulder. "Let me see."

O'Reilly suddenly became rigid, his head cocked as he listened. Alana froze.

Trent suddenly spoke up, "Listen!"

His voice echoed, soaking into the deep silence. Alana held her breath. Then she heard it, a dull rumble like the approach of a freight train.

"The subway..." whispered Ed.

Trent shook his head. "It's getting louder."

"Aftershock?" Catherine checked the roof of the cave, figuring this could be the worst possible place to be.

Ed looked at her in alarm. "How safe are we here?" The

look on her face was the chilling answer he didn't want to hear.

Trent wiped the sweat from his palms. "It's definitely getting louder."

"Or closer," breathed Alana, glancing at O'Reilly, who was now frozen with fear. She sprang to her feet and slowly turned as she tried to pinpoint the source.

"Too late..." O'Reilly breathed just loud enough for Alana to hear. He pressed fearfully against the wall and closed his eyes in anticipation.

"Let's get going," snapped Ed.

Trent pulled Catherine to her feet. She hooked an arm over his shoulder and winced as her leg took her weight. They both swayed unsteadily. She reached out to support herself against the wall and felt a tingle charging beneath her fingertips.

"The wall's vibrating," she said.

Trent gingerly touched the rock. Sure enough, it gently trembled. "I second the vote to get out of here, right now."

Ed rushed over to O'Reilly and hauled the unresisting man to his feet, then hesitated as he sensed something. He slowly pushed the flat of his hand toward the wall. "Is the wall supposed to be hot?"

Now they could all hear a sound like sizzling bacon. "Get away from that wall!" bellowed Trent.

The rock emitted a faint glow. O'Reilly shook himself free from Ed's grip, shoving the cop to the ground as the wall exploded in rock fragments and dust.

Trent pinned Catherine behind a natural pillar as fragments impacted around them. A small chunk glanced off Alana's brow, drawing blood.

Everybody tore their gaze back to the wall as the dust

cloud as it thinned out - revealing O'Reilly suspended several feet in the air. Arms and legs swinging like a useless marionette. A slowly revolving, foot-long drill-bit had punctured through his chest. Tendrils of his gut still whirled in the grooves of the bit.

Alana fired a shot at whatever was behind him. As the dust thinned, four spotlights pierced the gloom with an intense, focused light that searched for each of the group in turn.

"Go! Go!!" shouted Ed, squinting against the light as he fired. The shot was answered with a metallic ricochet.

O'Reilly's body swayed as the thing moved behind him. A pair of slender metal arachnid-like legs stepped through the hole in the wall. Ed's flashlight glinted from a huge metal body some nine feet high. His jaw slackened as the machine slowly entered the cave, accompanied by a whine of servos.

Eight spindly metallic legs propelled the machine over rubble. The body was encased in an elliptical housing that reflected cobalt blue under the flashlights. A segmented torso reared up like a mechanical insectoid centaur. Two small multi-joined arms wielded spinning drill bits, some three feet long – one of which held O'Reilly, who was shaken free like a rag doll. Another set of larger servo-assisted arms sat above the drill-arms. These were much thicker, hinged and criss-crossed with chunky segmented pipes. They ended in huge half-spheres. The mottled pattern on the surfaces glowed cherry-red. Globs of liquid rock dripped from the plasma-arms, hitting the floor with a hiss and rapidly turning black as it solidified. A sleek, featureless hawk-like head swiveled to face the humans, the four independently mounted shoulder lights moving in unison.

Ed rang out another shot that pinged from the torso. Trent pulled Catherine toward the exit, the pain in her leg forgotten. Alana sprinted for the slope, Ed walking backwards as he followed, not daring to take his eyes off the monster.

Trent reached the slope first, his feet skidding on the treacherously smooth surface. Reaching them, Alana slung Catherine's other arm around her shoulder, and they pressed upwards, feet constantly slipping and squeaking.

The mechanical horror inspected O'Reilly's mashed body, its head cocking one way, then the other, with a semblance of curiosity. It brought Ed enough time to reach the others.

Catherine was slowing them down. Trent opted to move behind her and physically push her up the gentle slope. His shoes nearly gave out on the floor, but he maintained his balance. That gave Alana the opportunity to move forward, lighting the path ahead. She risked a glance behind. The tunnel curved, and she lost sight of the machine - but its four ominous spears of light traversed the passage as the walls shook with the sound of multiple footfalls.

Lagging behind, Ed holstered his gun and dropped to all-fours to make the ascent. His face was red with exertion, and he was already fighting for breath.

Alana yelled back, "C'mon Eddie! Move your fat ass!"

He didn't hear her. All he could hear was the sound of his labored breathing and the approaching rumble behind him. Then that was drowned out by the voice of his beautiful wife telling him to be careful and not get home too late because the kids will miss him. The thought of never seeing his family again churned a knot in his stomach.

Then he slipped and began sliding backwards. His hands pressed against the obsidian surface to increase his grip, but his slick palms offered little grip.

Trent pushed Catherine into Alana as she turned and abruptly stopped to bellow at Ed.

"EDDIE!"

She motioned to double-back, but Trent stopped her as the spider-machine raced around the corner and almost trampled Ed as he slid beneath it. The bulky machine gave an agile dance as it suddenly stopped and turned to watch his descent. A drill arm lunged out; piercing Ed clean through the chest. It effortlessly hauled him off the floor and toward its head. Once more, the head jerked as it studied the flailing man. The impulses were purely random nerve impulses. The sheer weight of pain had dulled his senses. Ed's gurgling cry was choked as blood rushed to flood his throat, seeping from his nose and lips.

"Eddie! No!" Alana drew her piece and fired indiscriminately at the machine – one shot smashing a spotlight, the others bouncing harmlessly off and doing little to distract it from its kill.

Trent pushed Alana's arm aside, blocking her view of the horror. "We must go. *Right now.*" Alana resisted, but Trent used more force to get her moving again. "We need you right now."

Without looking back, they turned and fled as fast as possible up the incline.

Ed was still conscious, unable to control the spasms racking his body. A plasma-arm slowly angled toward him, and he was dimly aware of the heat prickling his skin. There was the briefest buzz, like a million angry hornets as the orbs' tip glowed brighter.

Trent glanced back in time to see Detective Edward Olmos annihilated in the blink of an eye under the unimaginable column of heat. A rational part of his mind refused to accept what he saw. It wasn't horrific – the man was there one moment, the next he'd simply gone like some hellish conjuring trick.

Then a curve in the passage interrupted his view. Thankfully, the passage leveled off, and they were able to increase their speed. The opening into the subway tunnel lay ahead, heralded by the welcoming glow from the service lights. They sprinted from the portal full speed, straight onto the subway line. Alana yanked Trent back - preventing him from pulling Catherine over the live rail.

Howards was still waiting for them, standing in a recess across the track, looking at his phone. His inquisitive smile turned into a frown when he saw the grief on Alana's face.

"What's down there?"

Anger welled in Alana as she recalled the machine callously spearing Ed. Only Catherine's petrified voice brought her back to the situation at hand.

"There's a train!"

A single light blazed from the end of the tunnel. The rail Trent was standing on vibrated through the sole of his shoe. With Alana's help, he helped Catherine over the electrified third rail. Although traveling no more than ten miles an hour, Trent only just jumped onto the opposite track just as it rolled by.

Howards looked between the pale faces. "Where is the other detective? What did you find down there?"

"I think you're going to find out," whimpered Catherine, as the ground shook beneath their feet.

The sound of tortured, twisting metal filled the tunnel,

and the train rocked violently as a great force smashed it from the side. The jarring impact shattered the windows along the carriages. Emergency brakes locked, spitting out a shower of sparks as the wheels ground against the track.

Commuters inside flailed for something to hold on to as the metro rocked. Lights flickered, then plunged the carriage into darkness. A wave of confused cries flowed through the train.

Helpless, Trent hunkered in the shadows with Catherine and Alana. Howards stepped forward as the now stationary train rocked again, his confusion overwhelming any fear he felt inside.

Three spotlights combed the side of the train, briefly falling on the scurrying occupants inside.

One boy pressed his face against the fragmented window as the machine strode past, its featureless beak head peering in for closer inspection.

Alana ejected the magazine from her automatic and thrust a fresh one in. Trent laid an outstretched hand on the barrel as Alana raised it.

"That didn't work last time. Don't move and keep quiet, and we might just get out of here."

Panic rippled through the passengers as they realized the danger was not an earthquake, but something entirely new. Five Hispanic hoodlums, who moments before had been causing consternation amongst the other passengers with their loud shouting and threats, now sweated heavily in the corner of one carriage, as the machine stopped outside, its search lights slowly combing toward them.

The machine used the side of its plasma-arm to experimentally rock the carriage. Once more, it seemed to study the response, giving every indication this was something new to it. The abrupt jolt caused passengers to scream louder. Several cell phones shot up to capture every terrifying moment.

One hoodlum lost it. The darkness was bringing on a severe bout of claustrophobia and any shred of fearless gangster was shed as he ran down the length of the carriage. The trio of searchlights immediately fixed onto him.

He drew a revolver from the front of his jeans. His first shot shattered what was left of the window - sending shards of safety glass across a woman with her child, sitting close by, and took out one of the three searchlights.

From the darkness of the tunnel, Alana and Trent saw the muzzle flashes. Trent shook his head in disbelief. "Now it's pissed."

The machine reared back, the broken light swinging limply from hydraulic cables that spat yellow fluid across the train. Like a praying mantis, the mechanical terror extended both its plasma-arms through a smashed window – forcing the fleeing gangster back the way he came.

The arms savagely drew apart, peeling the carriage wall apart like a can. Cowering passengers turned to run, trampling over one another in their bid to escape. The entire carriage rocked as the spider machine forced its way inside, sweeping its four arms, tearing bolted chairs from the floor like toys.

The hoodlums backed into a corner. Another four shots emptied the revolver - but did nothing to halt the machine's advance...

Howards watched, open-mouthed, as half a carriage was vaporized in a flash as bright as the sun. He looked away, but it still took several moments for his eyes to readjust. The entire side of one carriage was missing. The metal on the remaining edges bubbled and hissed as it rapidly cooled. Everybody who had been trapped inside hadn't stood a chance.

The remaining passengers poured onto the tracks from broken windows or levered-open doors. Their screams had died down to an almost eerie silence as they focused on survival.

Alana shoved Trent's restraining hand away and darted forward, waving her flashlight. "Stay off the middle rail! It's electrified!"

A young couple didn't listen as they ran hand-in-hand, the man stepping onto the third rail. 720 volts surged through them both, causing body hair to singe and their eyeballs to pop as they crashed to the floor.

The mechanoid surged forward through the center of the train. The carriages rocked violently as it peeled the walls apart like a sardine can. A low burst from the plasma-arms and the remaining half of the carriage caught fire.

People bumped into Alana as she tried to guide the exodus from the tunnel, as cloying black smoke obscured the train behind them. A child's cry caught her attention. Smoke was starting to obscure everything. She hunkered low to avoid inhaling it. Already her eyes were stinging.

"Mommy!"

It came from the train. Alana pushed against the thinning tide of people to get closer. She ran the length of the burning train as the child cried out again.

The Dero machine cleaved another carriage in two as it turned in her direction to advance back down the length of the train, back toward the cave from which it had emerged.

Alana tore her gaze from the approaching monster and saw the grubby face of a little girl sheltering under the greasy wheels of the train, dangerously close to the third rail. She crouched and reached for the girl.

"Hey there," Alana was amazed by her own calm voice. "What's say we both get out of here."

The child had her arms around her knees and was visibly shaking. Above her, the carriage rocked as the Dero closed in. Alana leaned forward and took the girl's wrists. She urgently pulled, but the girl resisted.

"Please, we have to go."

"I'm scared!"

"I am too, honey, but it's dangerous here and your mommy is waiting for us."

The girl looked at her with wide, innocent eyes. "Are we going to die?"

Alana looked up to see the monster upon them. *Yes*, flashed through her mind in a silent answer. This close, the machine looked even more lethal.

Alana darted under the train for cover and clasped the little girl. The train shook around them as the machine passed overhead. Multiple clattering footfalls sounding like golf ball sized hailstones striking a roof. Alana held her breath as she clutched the child, waiting for white-hot death.

But it didn't come.

In a burst of speed, the mechanoid gracefully leaped from the train and disappeared back through its hole. Alana opened her eyes – stunned that she was still alive, as was the girl who was trembling in her arms, eyes tightly closed.

A hand shook her shoulder, making her flinch. It was Trent.

"Williams, it's gone. I suggest we don't hang around

either." He looked at the girl and flashed the smile of somebody uneasy around children. "Hey sweetheart, why don't you come with us?" He'd helped Alana crawl out because the girl refused to let go and clung to her for dear life while making sobbing demands to see her mom.

THIRTEEN

SHE HAD CRIED fat tears that stained her white cotton blouse. Now silence bled through the house, and Alana was inwardly relieved that Helen Olmos had finally excused herself to grieve in private. Only now, calmed by the soothing gurgle of an eight-foot aquarium tank, Ed's most cherished possession, could Alana process what had happened.

Wilshire had been chaos, but the MTA cops there handled the situation competently, sealing off the area and ensuring the terrified passengers were met with medical aid and councilors. Bixby appeared on the scene as Alana got her cuts cleaned by a paramedic. The sting from the antiseptic did little to focus her mind away from a million tumbling thoughts.

What the hell had just happened? What was that machine? And how can Ed be dead? Murdered.

Bixby ordered an immediate press blackout, all the survivors whisked away under armed guard, and cell phones confiscated - although the captured images showed very little recognizable beyond blinding searchlights and blurry dark images. Trent had insisted on swapping numbers with Alana before escaping from the scene with Catherine. Both looked haunted by what they had experienced.

Bixby had ordered an emergency meeting with Mayor Shearer tonight and she fought to attend, but he shot her down and insisted she take some leave to cope with her loss. Alana haggled her way in. After all, she'd seen the attack firsthand.

The department shrink had tried to make Alana go home and rest, but that wasn't her style. She was restless. Afraid that if she stopped long enough, her thoughts and emotions would catch up and overwhelm her. The first task at hand was to break the news to Ed's wife – no, *widow*.

The word sounded hollow, unnatural; but there was no shaking it away. She sat for fifteen minutes outside Ed's house, drumming up the courage to push the bell and make the announcement that would shatter Helen's world.

Sixth sense, body language, or sheer woman's intuition, Alana didn't know - but Helen's reaction was muted, as though she'd expected to never see her husband again.

She calmly invited Alana in for a coffee as she told her story. Bixby had ordered her not to reveal any details, but Alana was beyond caring. Helen listened gravely, without interruption. The bizarre nature of his death didn't even provoke a twitch of skepticism from her. Alana was the first to crack as emotions welled inside her. That was the catalyst for Helen. Both women hugged, and she felt Helen sag as if every bone in her body had been removed. Alana felt awash with selfishness and guilt – she had no right to cry now. Helen had lost more than she could ever conceive.

Luckily, the children were out for the night, staying over

at their respective pals for a twenty-four-hour gaming marathon, blissfully unaware of their loss.

Alana knew she should stay with Helen, but the desire to seek revenge on whatever had killed her partner meant she should be in the thick of things. She waited until Helen's mother arrived before hastily making excuses to leave and making it Downtown to City Hall in record time.

She traveled in silence. Painfully aware she was alone. The empty seat beside her felt almost sacrilegious.

* * *

TRENT DROPPED Catherine outside her apartment. The aftershock had hit her street pretty badly as it shook already weakened buildings down to their knees. They had spoken little on the drive. Catherine absently touched her leg where the paramedics had stitched the knife wound and bandaged it tightly. The hospitals were overflowing with quake victims, so there had been no suggestion of visiting the ER.

Catherine hugged Trent tight as they stopped outside her apartment. Tears filled both their eyes from the horror they had just witnessed. Trent found his own hand shaking, so he gripped the steering wheel tightly. Catherine mumbled something about seeing him at the lab later, but he was not really listening, instead lost in theories about today.

What was that thing? A science experiment gone awry? A foreign power on the verge of invasion? The creation of some mad engineer? Perhaps a previously undiscovered subterranean race? They were all as unlikely as each other.

Already he could see his career coming to an abrupt halt if he was ever to air those thoughts. Hell, he was even ridiculing *himself* for thinking about them. But whatever it was, the felon the cops were chasing seemed to know about it. During the walk back to their vehicles, Alana had quickly filled Trent in on the investigation...

The jolt of the passenger door closing brought Trent back to the present. Catherine was already halfway up the steps of her apartment. Trent sighed, shifted the car into drive and pulled away, nearly broadsiding an Uber that honked its horn irritably. He rubbed his eyes, resolving to pay more attention to the road.

Thirty minutes of random driving found him on the highway heading toward Caltech. This stretch had suffered no quake damage, and Trent saw it as some sort of sign. He wanted answers, and Caltech seemed the sensible choice. With all their irrational quake theories, maybe they knew more than they were letting on.

Ben Chapman in particular.

Built in 1917 by Bertram Goodhue, the distinctive Spanish Mission-style white buildings that formed Caltech's Geological and Planetary Science Division reflected the overhead sun, adding vibrancy to the site. Scientists, students, and technicians milled about the campus as Trent pulled into a visitor's slot in the parking lot. He slid his Maui Jim shades off and climbed from his car. Cramp shot through his legs, and his hand was still trembling. He sucked in a deep breath to pull himself together.

The striking buildings shielded the campus from the usual L.A. hubbub, creating an almost serene atmosphere. He made his way across the grounds, noting that nothing had changed since he was last here. In fact, the last time he'd traversed this path had been in shame and anger. Well, at least he still had the anger.

He cut across a quadrangle toward the refectory. Ben

Chapman was as regular as clockwork. The city might be bowing on its knees, but Chapman would be in there five-thirty prompt to feed his ugly pigface.

Chapman oversaw Caltech's various earthquake research programs and had a habit of interfering so much that he practically ran each of them. During his stint here, Trent and Chapman had a personality clash the size of the Titanic. Trent could still recall the gummy smile as Chapman expelled him from the campus. He also had a hand in Mayor Shearer's pocket - anything for that little extra funding - so Trent wasn't expecting a warm greeting. But at this moment he had only one question: what did Chapman really know?

As Trent emerged from the welcome air conditioning into the searing hot air, he noticed a huge black Escalade parked close to the entrance. He stopped in his tracks as a pair of towering, black-suited men strode from the building with Ben Chapman pinned between them. Trent took a pace back behind the cover of a sculpted hedge to make sure they hadn't seen him.

The suits efficiently ushered Chapman into the back of the Escalade before climbing in on either side, effectively blocking him in. The vehicle sped away before they had time to fully close the door.

Trent suppressed a shudder; these bozos had *Government Agent* written all over them. He'd watched enough bad movies to recognize the drill. He lost sight of the car behind a spinney of trees. There was no use in lingering around much longer; he had seen enough to confirm his suspicions.

Chapman knew more than he wanted to admit.

He wheeled around and headed back to his car, thinking about his next move. Probably a cold shower; maybe a drink. He remembered Detective Williams telling him the Mayor and Chief of Police were meeting to discuss the situation. Trent considered getting himself invited to that. He stuck a hand in his pocket and fingered his phone. He'd keyed in Alana's telephone number. Maybe he should call her? Between the two of them, they could start demanding some transparency to proceedings.

A sixth sense suddenly kicked in, drawing his gaze across the parking lot. The black Escalade was idling across the way, a passenger window lowered and a shade wearing man gazing at him. Trent had only a moment to register this before the car took off with a sharp screech of rubber.

FOURTEEN

WALT TOOK another bite from his lukewarm In-N-Out burger, and his tastebuds thanked him for it. His eyes shot across the computer enhanced readouts on the monitor in front of him. The mouse idly toured the screen as he attempted to extract meaningful answers to the unconventional recent quake activity.

His eyes were strained from both concentration and lack of sleep. Trent had asked him and Schofield to draw some rapid conclusions, but the data were conflicting with every theory he could throw at it. It was frustrating. He cranked the volume up on his laptop speakers, filling the room with the soothing tones of Mozart.

He wondered why Trent hadn't called in and then cast his eyes across to the landline. Since Trent's morning show antics, the phones had been going crazy. Schofield had taken them all off the hook for a moment's peace.

Schofield entered, pushing the door open with his back as he carried two large Styrofoam coffee cups and a greasy bag of doughnuts. He dropped them on the table and lowered the music to a more tolerable level.

"Dessert," he said as he fished a cinnamon doughnut from the bag. "Any new leads?"

"No joy," sighed Walt as he peeled back the plastic lid from the coffee. "I keep running filters and pattern analysis across this thing, and every time I get something different. Maybe this isn't a quake after all."

Schofield looked dumbly at him. "I think you better look out the window. Billions of dollars in damages, hundreds killed from wobbling earth. I'd class that as a quake. A freakin' serious one."

He always gave a few seconds' silence before launching an offensive at Schofield.

"Good detective work, Holmes. Yes, we have had a quake, but it doesn't bear the same characteristics as Northridge. Another lifetime ago, well before I joined this kooky outfit, I did some work on a government operation."

"You're a regular James Bond." Schofield spun a chair around, using the backrest to support his coffee hand. Despite himself, he was intrigued by Walt's latest revelation.

Walt swilled a mouthful of coffee around his mouth and looked thoughtful as he continued. "They were testing the effects of nuclear bomb blasts. Out at sea, in the desert, and so on. My section had to report on how the ground is affected during a blast. Readouts there showed tremors that seemed to appear just like quakes, but they were, in fact, just blast signatures. The main discovery was the anomalies in an artificially induced quake, such as rolling epicenter readouts. Just like we have here."

Schofield looked Walt squarely in the eyes, then broke into a broad grin. "You are a crazy fruit loop, my friend. I know the gangs in this town are tough mothers, but I think even they would just stop short of pulling nuclear warheads on each other!"

Walt shook his head. It was always an uphill struggle to get Schofield to take anything seriously. "I just tell it like I see it."

Schofield's grin dropped. "What about terrorism? Al-Qaeda?"

"That's a massive stretch, but I guess we can't rule it out."

Schofield raised a hand to silence him. He cocked his head to listen to something. Walt looked at him questioningly as Schofield slowly rose from the chair to look around the room.

"What? What's up?" asked Walt.

"Listen!"

They both strained – nothing but Mozart. Walt leaned backward and paused the laptop. Silence descended for several seconds... then a soft scratching sound broke it.

They darted across the room to the seismograph housed in Plexiglas and mounted on industrial shock-dampers to stop unwanted vibrations from the lab. The pens gently zigzagged across the paper as it was automatically threaded through, folding neatly into capture baskets on the floor.

Schofield opened the case and leafed through the slowly mounting pile of paper until he found sections with a straight line indicating no activity.

"Started just minutes ago. Another aftershock?"

Walt stared at the jagged ink lines; the troughs and peaks spaced apart to show a gentle rhythmic tremor.

"This is no aftershock. It's been happening far too long. This is something else."

"What?"

"I'm not sure. But something's happening. *Something* is moving down there."

* * *

A FLOCK of reporters had descended outside City Hall, now chasing the scent that a cop was killed during a subway blaze. Quakes were already old news, and the metro disaster provided fresh meat, made even more intriguing because of the press blackout. But as these things do, word of a fire had leaked out.

Alana flashed her badge to get inside, but her mood darkened as Mayor Shearer's personal security hassled her before they reluctantly allowed her into the inner sanctum.

Passing through the grand vaulted hall, she was finally led to a smaller room bedecked in garish yellow wallpaper and dark mahogany paneling. A sturdy stained oak table dominated the space. Chief Bixby sat at one end; silver framed glasses perched on his nose as he read through a typed report sheet detailing the events of the last few hours. Three men and two women sat beside him, bureaucrats from the Mayor's office.

Out of place amongst them was a good-looking blond man whose muscular frame was almost bursting from his black one-piece jumpsuit. He looked up from reading his own report and flashed Alana a reproachful look. She vaguely recognized him but couldn't place from where.

A team of kitchen staff fed them snacks and drinks. Alana gratefully took a black coffee; the sweet aroma gave her a boost. She felt hot and dirty, suddenly aware of her matted hair and the black streaks marring her face and hands, since she hadn't had time to clean or eat since leaving the subway.

Bixby rose and greeted her in a hushed voice. "How is Helen?"

"In shock. Her mom's with her now."

"Department's sending over a bouquet, and our condolences."

Alana looked at him as if he were crazy - as if flowers would help! His soft frown soothed her; quite a difference from his usual formal grimace. He meant well; the concern was deeply embedded in every line, as was the stress. Alana thought if she looked long enough, she'd even see his hair turn gray.

Bixby offered her a report. "This is a chain of key events since the earthquake yesterday, right up to the subway."

Alana didn't even give it a cursory glance as she threw it back onto the table. "Where's the Mayor?"

"Held up. We need to decide a course of action that is going to resolve whatever happened in the Metro before the shutterbugs out there get their hands on it."

"You have a couple of hundred eyewitnesses and a pile of bodies to corroborate my story."

Bixby held up his hand, encouraging her to lower her voice. "Whatever it was, we need a lid on the truth right now. If that went public, we'd have a stampede on our hands."

Alana raised an eyebrow. "The truth? I don't even know what the truth is. Has anybody figured out what we saw down there?"

"No. The tunnel has been sealed off, and the train hasn't been inspected. Nobody is going down until we figure things out. What about this guy, O'Reilly? What's the connection?"

"He was our key suspect for the transients murdered

down there. But now I just think he was at the wrong time, and definitely the wrong place. He probably saw that thing and it threw him over the edge."

"What we have is a tragedy with an assailant of unknown origin, and no evidence for any of it. Nobody is calling out the National Guard just yet until we have some hard proof of what we are dealing with."

"They can't send people down there. Ed and I both shot at that thing, the bullets just bounced off!"

"Then we'll send a reconnaissance team with serious firepower. That's why we have Special Weapons and Tactics." Bixby pointed to the blond beefcake. Alana's memory was sparked.

"SWAT? Chief, I don't think that's such a great idea..."

Bixby became aware they were now talking louder and held up his hand to silence her. Several people around the table glanced across. He dropped his voice to a deep whisper. "Remember, this is also City Hall politics. Let's see what the Mayor has to say." He returned to his seat, adjusted his glasses, and then continued reading the report.

Alana released a heart-felt sigh and moved toward the large paned windows. Through the triple-glazing, she could see reporters huddled at the base of the steps. A barrage of flashbulbs popped as the Mayor's Mercedes turned the corner and rolled to a halt outside.

Whatever the outcome was tonight, Alana knew she wouldn't like it.

***

HARRY FENNELL UNCAPPED another four bottles of Coors Light for the noisy crowd at the end of the bar and swiped the tips tossed carelessly in a patch of spilled beer. Their loud banter merged with the background noise. Business was better than usual, probably because most people were trying to avoid going back home to make repairs. He was so rushed off his feet it left little room for conversation. He tried to spare a moment, for Trent sat at the other end of the bar, next to a bearded trucker who was wrapped in his own thoughts.

He passed Trent a Budweiser and leaned across the bar, practically screaming to be heard over the jukebox as it kicked in with yet another U2 song.

"You look like a man desperately in need of cheering up, Michael. What would be bitin' you today?"

"I can't begin to explain."

"Hold on," said Harry as he moved to serve two middle-aged women. Harry had three other staff on, dressed in tight *Pump it at the Pumphouse* T-shirts that accented their figures. Harry had thought it a good idea, and Trent had to agree. He watched as the women playfully flirted with Harry – which always made the Irishman feel uncomfortable. On a normal day, it amused Trent. Tonight, however, he was far from entertained. Even the cool beer in his mouth tasted of nothing.

"They'll be hangin' around at closing, I bet." Trent didn't respond. A frown creased Harry's face. "Michael, are you with me tonight? You're not all there, are you? I was just tellin' you a tale."

Trent unpeeled the label of the beer bottle into tiny pieces. "If something happens that you can't explain, what are you supposed to do about it?"

"What kind of question is that?" laughed Harry, but his smile faded under Trent's doleful look. "Jeez, I guess you search for an answer and don't stop until you find 'em. I thought that's what scientific men like yourself do."

Trent nodded reluctantly. "I suppose so. But is that what *you* would do?"

Harry's eyes twinkled as he leaned close. He slid an envelope from his pocket. "Personally, I would accept this ticket for tomorrow night's Dodgers game and come with your old mate, Harry. Got 'em off a man in the know. A very good pal of mine. They're terrific seats."

Trent stared at the envelope; normally he would snatch a chance like this.

Normally.

"Thanks, Harry. Appreciate it. But I can't. I really can't."

"It's *Dem Bums!*" Harry regarded him with surprise. His son had let him down at the last moment, and he knew Trent was an enormous Dodgers fan. "I'm sure you'll figure it out," he said as he vanished to serve another group along the bar.

Thirty minutes later, Trent found his way back to his apartment. He applied all his weight to shove the door open just enough to slip in sideways. The aftershock had caused a small wooden cabinet to dance across the hall and lodge itself neatly behind the door. He hadn't tidied the place since the main tremor, but the effects of the aftershock were noticeable.

He didn't turn the lights on when he relieved himself in the latrine. Zipping up, he moved into the lounge, stumbling on *something* that crunched underfoot. He fumbled for the table lamp, only to find it smashed in two where it had leaped off the table. He took out his cell and used the flashlight function. Only then did he notice he had voicemail. He accessed it, switching to the speaker.

"Professor Trent? This is Detective Alana Williams.

Ah... the Mayor has just finished the meeting and they're going crazy down here. You should have come; it would have been nice to have an ally. I need you to meet me outside the Metro as soon as you get this. Call my cell. They don't know what they're doing. They're sending the SWAT down there."

Fifteen

Police lines cordoned off several blocks of Wilshire and the surrounding streets. A throng of curious spectators and eager press were held at bay by OSHA tape and a wall of police vehicles, their red-and-blue strobes pulsing.

Trent was met by Alana, and she led him past the police lines, toward the entrance. He shielded his eyes from banks of powerful spotlights that had been set up *facing away from the station* to dazzle prying eyes and overexpose the curious lenses of the media. A police chopper circled overhead, keeping the eyes-in-the-sky at bay.

Trent and Alana did not speak until they had penetrated the wall of light, and then Trent was stunned by the activity around the subway entrance.

A line of men wearing black one-piece suits formed a chain from the back of an unmarked van, passing metal flight cases into the station. Black cloth Velcro tabs on their uniforms disguised the bold white SWAT acronym. Dozens of technicians and uniformed cops milled around a spaghetti-snarl of wiring leading from the subway into a windowless mobile control room on the back of a truck.

"What's in the cases?" asked Trent.

"Weapons. The Mayor thinks brute force is going to stop that thing down there."

"But your gun had no effect."

"Mr Mayor claimed we didn't use big enough guns. The asshole speaks, and the PD obeys."

She ushered Trent up a flight of steps leading into the side of the command room. Trent was suitably impressed by the interior. Every spare inch was taken up with server racks, monitors, and vision mixing desks – an entire TV eco-system in one. The monitors currently showed nothing but a live feed of the metro entrance.

Alana drew up a seat for Trent and sat with him just behind a middle-aged woman operating the mixing desk. She flashed a quick smile at Trent, who caught her name badge: *Reynolds*.

Alana nodded to the monitors. "Each member of Weapons has a body cam. A few have cameras mounted on their rifles." She saw Trent's frown. "Originally developed so they could see around corners without being lobotomized. All transmissions are broadcast back to Moco here."

"Moco?"

"Mobile Operations Command."

"So, what theories has Shearer conjured up about the death machine down there?"

"The list is long and dumb, ranging from an experimental Chinese or North Korean reconnaissance drone to a combined effort by the Mexican cartels to dig a tunnel to LA to pipe drugs in secret. Either way, the Mayor wants to keep wraps on the whole thing, so when they destroy it, he'll look like the national hero who saved the country."

"Jesus, that guy's riding his ego all the way to insanity."

A screen suddenly popped to life with a clear night-enhanced image of the subway tunnel. Three people walked steadily in front of the camera. Then the other monitors came to life in a domino effect, showing each of the body cams from the seven-strong squad.

Reynolds adjusted a wireless microphone headset,

angling the thin microphone closer to her lips. "Okay Deep Con, I have visual. Relay audio check."

The muscular blond guy Alana met at City Hall turned to a camera and gave a thumb-up. "Sergeant Horvath: reading you loud and clear, Moco. Squad, call in."

Trent didn't register the names as they checked in. He was fixed to the screens, tense from anticipating an attack that was sure to come. The displays danced and weaved until they all showed the deserted Metro platform and the ominous the running tunnel ahead.

"Why didn't they send in a remote camera?"

Alana shrugged. "I brought it up. Suggested they fly a drone down there, but..."

They sat in silence as the team moved into the running tunnel, cameras straining in the low light. But as their night vision kicked in, and details came into sharp relief.

Sergeant Horvath gave a short commentary as they proceeded in, and it wasn't long before the burnt husk of the train carriages came into view. Metal and fiberglass had fused into distorted lumps. The night vision cameras, assisted by UV light, highlighted human forms twisted among the wreckage. Arms raised to fend off an unstoppable terror - all viewed on the screen in eerie gray and green.

Sergeant Horvath's voice came through with a tremor. "Are you getting this, Moco?"

"We see it, Sergeant."

Horvath approached one body that was hanging from a shattered window. His gun-camera inched closer to a prone figure. Cheekbones poked from charred, sunken flesh. Eyeballs had melted like jello down the face.

"Victim looks to have been burned to death by intense heat." Sergeant Horvath narrated with the cold detachment of somebody who had seen too many horrific sights. "Visual ID is impossible. The hand is fused to the train..."

"Sarge!" cried an alarmed female voice. Trent could not identify which monitor to look at until Alana pointed to number five. The image showed the subway train peeled back like paper.

"This must have been where the machine got into the carriage," continued the female trooper. "Man, it must have been huge."

Alana tapped Reynolds on the shoulder. "The tunnel entrance should be in the wall just behind the train."

Reynolds relayed the information to the squad. Sergeant Horvath moved around the carriage, fragments of the windows crunching underfoot. As the camera perspective shifted, the gap in the wall came into view. A black portal that night vision couldn't penetrate.

Horvath continued his clinical narration. "I see it, Moco. Okay, squad two-by-two. I'll take point. Follow my lead."

Alana tore her gaze from the monitors and looked away. Trent caught her deep sigh, and without taking his eyes off the monitor, he placed a placating hand on her shoulder. She tensed, then sagged, imperceptibly leaning against him for comfort.

* * *

THEY MADE excellent progress down the incline before Sergeant Horvath's steel-toed boot lost traction on the polished floor. He only caught his balance by flailing his arms. The other troops around him tensed until he raised his hand to show all was well. Since entering the tunnel, nobody had spoken above a whisper.

Taking extra care, the team descended the incline without incident, the slow curve of the corridor constantly concealing what horrors lay ahead.

Near the bottom of the slope, Horvath raised his fist to stop the party. He knelt to examine the tunnel floor. His gloved fingers combed across the glassy surface before tracing over a large patch of dried blood that streamed downhill, disappearing around the curve.

He slowly stood, listening to the darkness. Ahead wasn't just silence, it was the complete absence of noise. Something so deep, all he could hear was his own heartbeat. Another hand gesture resumed the unit's descent.

They followed the blood trail, which bore all the hallmarks of a body dragged from a crime scene. As the passage straightened and became level, he saw a lump in the path ahead. It was a bloody mass. Occasional grizzly lumps poked from dried incarnadine pools, but there was nothing recognizable in the twenty-foot or so pool of minced flesh and blood. The stench hit Horvath, and he gagged. Behind him, another member of the team vomited across the wall.

"Moco, we have found..." He sucked in his breath. "I think they're human remains, but I can't be sure..." He felt his stomach lurch again.

A young trooper edged forward, braving the gore. Freeman, a youthful, over-enthusiastic member of the team. She poked her rifle muzzle at something that immediately clung to the metal as she lifted it into view.

"Sir, we have some residual fabric. Clothing presumably." Her eyes widened with a cocktail of fear and excitement. "What kind of weapon could do this?"

Horvath didn't want to give that question much thought.

Instead, he rallied his troops to continue. It was several yards before he heard a distorted voice over the headphones.

"Sergeant. This is Professor Mike Trent," the voice lost its distortion as the Professor pulled the microphone away from his lips. "The wall on your left. Can one of you move closer?" Horvath complied. The air was becoming increasingly humid, and now his hands were sweating in their protective gloves. "There," said Trent, "can you see it?"

Sergeant Horvath frowned at first as he studied the wall. Then, like an optical illusion, it became clear what he was looking at. He took a step backward. What he had assumed was a natural blemish was a huge scrape mark on the otherwise smooth surface. A swirling pattern became apparent, pivoting to a central point in which fragments of cloth had fused with the wall.

"It looks like a massive bore hole."

"The machine we saw had a pair of huge drill-arms. Bits the size of your head. You wanted to know what killed that detective? Imagine your entire body being corkscrewed inside-out in the space of a second."

A chill ran down Horvath's spine and he noticed the concern on his troops' faces. He rallied himself.

"Thanks for the heads-up, Professor, but we're not a Haunted House ride. With all due respect, sir, I would appreciate it if you wouldn't scare the bejesus out of my squad," snapped Horvath. "People fall in! What we are facing here is a tangible enemy. That means it can be destroyed. The people down here did not have the training or firepower at our disposal. Always keep that in mind."

Without a further word, the group reassembled and continued their cautious advance down the tunnel.

Trent threw down his headset in response to Reynolds'

vitriolic glare. "Sir, you are here as a scientific liaison. Keep your *opinions* to yourself."

Trent's brow furrowed. "What have you told them was down there?"

"They were briefed on the situation," replied Reynolds, her back to Trent.

Trent and Alana exchanged a look. She shrugged; she was just as much out of the picture as he was.

"With all due respect, I call bullshit. Me and Detective Williams saw that thing firsthand. Why were we not asked to attend the briefings?" He looked at Alana for support. She cocked her head, silently agreeing with Trent, but not daring to voice her opinion.

Reynolds' silence fueled Trent's anger. "You didn't tell them jack, did you? They don't know what to expect."

Reynolds wheeled in her chair to face Trent, angling the microphone away from her mouth. "Sergeant Horvath was briefed. What he told his team is his business. We need to operate according to facts. *With all due respect,* not the overemotional views of survivors..."

Trent tossed his headset to the floor and grabbed her chair to swing her farther around, so they were nose-to-nose. "People died down there!"

Reynolds swiftly batted Trent aside with her forearm and kicked back in her seat. "Interfere again and you will be arrested. Do you understand?"

Alana interceded as Trent lunged forward again. "Trent! This isn't helping," she warned. Her anguish from the trauma of the last few hours was enough to calm Trent.

Reynolds glared at him defiantly. "If you have no valuable input, then I suggest you leave."

Trent snatched his headset from the floor. "I have no

intention of leaving. Your people need me. They have to have *somebody* they can trust."

* * *

"MORE SIGNS OF A SKIRMISH, SIR."

Sergeant Horvath moved across the cavern they had just entered. A trail of blood led to a dismembered hand amid some rubble. Horvath's flashlight continued to follow the trail around the base of a stalagmite on which a man had been impaled. The man's arms and legs had been bent backward at acute angles, bones rupturing the skin. His entire chest cavity had been removed, and the body hooked on the stalagmite.

Horvath's foot kicked empty shell cases on the floor. He swung the flashlight over the face of the impaled man. Dried blood clung to his cheeks and open eyes focused on infinity with a look of unimaginable agony.

"Moco, we have located missing Detective Ed Olmos."

There was a pregnant pause, then a subdued reply. "Affirmative, Sergeant."

"There are several other tunnels branching out from here. Please advise, Moco?"

Horvath frowned, pushed the headset closer to his ear, unsure if he really could hear muffled arguing. Moments passed before receiving a response.

"There is a rubble stack at the back of the cave. The passageway continues beyond that. Please investigate."

"Roger, Moco."

Horvath motioned his troops forward. He could tell from their expressions that this was not quite the scenario they had been briefed on. He noticed Freeman and Brady, the youngest guy on the team, exchange flash grenades from their belt clips. Horvath turned a blind eye. He couldn't afford morale slipping. He eyed the rubble-strewn ground lining the new passage they were about to enter.

Reynolds' cool voice came over his headset. "Be advised to go in with wet noses."

"Wet nose. Copy." He flicked the safety on his rifle. He made a series of hand-gestures to his team: stay silent, prime their weapons, and be vigilant. Then they advanced over the detritus and into the new tunnel.

* * *

TRENT LEANED across to look at a computer monitor displaying several readouts. He tapped the screen.

"Are these from the sensors your team is carrying?"

"That's right. Don't worry, Professor, if there is anything dangerous, then the system'll let us know."

"Then why has nothing been triggered? Look at this methane readout. Those kinds of levels in that enclosed environment are dangerous."

Reynolds' smirk wavered as she keyed the microphone. "Horvath, how're you feeling down there?"

"Fine, MOCO. The air tastes a little stale, but clear."

Trent rubbed his temples, smiling to himself. "Jesus. The gas is odorless. The stuff pumped to your home has an odor added for safety. It's not natural."

"They feel fine, Professor."

"That's my point. They won't feel anything until they drop."

"Then what do you suggest they do?"

"Do they have masks?"

Alana nodded. "Regulation gas masks that protect from tear gas. Will that be good enough?"

"Temporarily. Unless they run out of air. They just better not start firing down there," he added ominously.

Reynolds turned to Trent with an expression that could kill. "You can't seriously expect them not to defend themselves? This is a seek and destroy mission, not a ramble in the hills."

"I'm not the one who sent them down unprepared. If you want them to survive, then I suggest you extract them *immediately*. If they shoot down there, then they're as good as dead."

"MOCO!" The urgency in Sergeant Horvath's voice was unmistakable.

"Copy, Sergeant."

"We have a light ahead. Have we cut across another metro tunnel?"

Alana scrambled for the paper schematic maps of the subway. The squad's route was marked with red ink. "No. No tunnels at your height or in that direction. And they're deeper than any sewage or utility passages."

"Sergeant, be advised that is *not* a subway. We don't know what it is, so proceed with extreme caution."

"Roger that."

Reynolds caught Trent's fierce look out of the corner of her eye. With a deep sigh, she keyed the microphone again.

"And Horvath, there are potentially dangerous gas deposits where you currently are. Use your masks and safe your weapons. Do not fire. Repeat, do not fire."

She turned to Trent.

"You happy now?"

"No. Not while they're still down there."

* * *

ONLY RIGOROUS TRAINING prevented the squad from open rebellion.

"Don't fire? That's crazy!" Freeman looked at her companions to back her up. "You saw those people back there!"

Horvath was staring ahead. The light was still there, a steady faint glow. He unfurled his safety hood, bringing the breathing apparatus to his mouth. "You heard the orders. Mask up."

He slid the mask on, pressing the plate firmly against his face to ensure an airtight seal. He tugged the three restraining straps for a tight fit. The radio link was suddenly filled with deep grunts and rasping breaths as everybody's masks were secured.

"Follow my lead," commanded Horvath. "Let's go!"

With each step, the passageway became wider, transforming from a circular to an ovoid shape, the curved walls now blending perfectly with the ceiling and ground in one fluid arc. It gave Horvath the creepy feeling of walking through a super-sized artery.

The pale glow ahead seemed to change intensity. Horvath stopped the team with a raised fist. He squinted at the light.

"Does anybody else think that light is *moving*?"

Sure enough, it slowly bobbed and shimmied like a candle flame.

"Affirmative," murmured Freeman. "Maybe it's a fire?"

Brady wiped his visor with his sleeve, and then gently touched the smooth floor. "I don't think it's a fire," he said quietly, "and I think it's moving this way."

Horvath's eyes widened with comprehension. His fingers traced the wall, picking up the faint vibration. He barely had time for profanities as a rising growl filled the passageway. Four blinding spotlights pinned them from the end of the tunnel, caught like roadkill in the path of a juggernaut.

"Stun grenades!!"

Sergeant Horvath hadn't recognized the sound of his own voice, but felt his hand tug a condensation-covered cylinder loose from his bandolier. He unhooked the pin, the spring-loaded clip spinning away as he hurled the grenade.

Four stun grenades exploded in unison as the steel behemoth lumbered from the shadows on slender arachnid legs. The sudden flashes and ensuing smoke screen were enough to distract the machine from its victims for a few precious moments.

The machine reared in front of Horvath. His fingers automatically squeezed the trigger. The muzzle flash was a foot from his masked face, but he didn't care. Ricochet sparks danced across the monster. A segmented pipe on its plasma-arm ruptured, fluid spraying across the walls.

The machine's four arms failed ineffectively under the hailstorm. The tip of one drill arm speared through one trooper's mask, his head churning into sludge.

Horvath emptied an entire magazine, only partially aware of Reynolds screaming in his ear. Brady's mag ran dry. He plucked a stun grenade from his belt and hurled it with precision before swiftly reloading.

The grenade deflected from the Dero's torso and struck Horvath in his Kevlar-padded chest. It exploded with enough force to crack his reinforced faceplate and hurl him clean off his feet. He slammed into the curved wall, sliding down in a daze, vaguely aware his rifle was now yards away.

The Dero's plasma-arm glowed diabolically crimson as it discharged a wave of super-heated air down the passageway, instantly vaporizing three of the SWAT team into greasy pools.

Freeman had enough presence of mind to charge headlong at the machine, the blast passing overhead and searing her back. She landed hard on her side, oblivious to the crunch as her forearm fractured. The pool of fluid that escaped from the ruptured pipe on the machine's now redundant second plasma-arm acted like grease, carrying her under the mechanoid.

Now behind, she could see a pair of symmetrical sunken vents low on the machine's chassis. Freeman pulled a grenade from her utility belt. She paused only to check it was an explosive rather than a stun grenade, before pitching it with her fractured arm.

Only by the grace of God, and years of playing ball with her dad, did the explosive hit home inside the elliptical vent half a second before exploding.

The machine buckled as an entire flank erupted in flame, cascading shrapnel into the wall. Green flame poured from the rupture – igniting a layer of gas at ceiling height.

Horvath, Freeman, and Brady – the only surviving members of the team - were thrown to the ground by the shock wave. Like a perversely inverted ocean, blue flames rolled across the ceiling with skin-blistering heat.

The Dero thrashed fitfully – then seized in position. Flames that poured from its chassis died as though smothered by an invisible extinguisher. After a flamboyant debut, the pyrotechnics on the ceiling burned themselves out, plunging the passage into darkness.

* * *

REYNOLDS STARED BLANKLY at the monitors as they rolled static. Alana sat back in her seat, fingers covering her mouth. Trent wiped tears from his eyes with shaking hands.

"Sergeant Horvath, this is Moco, do you copy?"

The crunch of static.

"Deep Con, this is Moco. Please come in. We have lost visual."

Still nothing.

"Did you record that?" asked Trent as he finally found his voice.

"Got it all," said Reynolds as she checked the radio frequency. "Deep-Con–"

"Moco, this is Deep Con, we read you," came a garbled voice.

"What is your situation, Deep-Con?"

"Ah, this is Freeman," the voice sounded confused for a moment. "The team is down. I have the Sarge with me. Pulse is strong, but he's not conscious. One other survivor, Brady. No other survivors. None."

For a moment, Reynolds didn't know what to say. "What is your assessment on the target?"

There came a bout of coughing from Freeman before she responded. "Target is eliminated. It took a grenade up the ass-pipe to stop it."

"Are there any markings on the machine? Decals? Letters?"

"Ah, standby."

Tensions slowly mounted as silence filled the truck. Alana rose from her seat and anxiously paced.

"Negative on markings," came the reply twenty seconds

later. "We are just trying to get some illumination. There appears to be something inside... JESUS!"

Alana jumped in her seat at the sudden exclamation.

Reynolds thumbed the microphone. "Deep-Con, come in."

"Moco... there appears to be a... it's organic. There's something... this thing... carcass is badly burned. It's... *Jeez*, I haven't seen... before."

"Say again," said Reynolds as she attempted to clean the signal.

Trent's face flushed with excitement. "Tell her to get a sample and picture. Anything."

Freeman's voice crackled over the PA. "Ah, what is that? Standby."

Reynolds felt herself panicking. "What is *what*? Deep Con. Freeman?"

Nothing.

Then a monitor flickered to life, the name displaying "Roberts". Obviously, somebody had found the trooper's gun. Freeman appeared in the picture and walked toward what appeared to be a wall of light.

"Freeman, we have visual. What is happening? Where is the machine?"

"Moco, we are penetrating the tunnel. We just heard something... I don't know..." static garbled her words, "... and a light."

Alana looked questioningly at Trent. "What does that mean?"

"There appears..." a blast of static, followed by "...feel a breeze," Freeman's voice drifted over the speakers. "The noise... some activity..."

The video feed suddenly over-exposed – dark shapes milling out of focus. Trent leaned close. "What is that?"

"SHIT!" cried Freeman, "Moco, Moco! Be advised–"

The audio cut as the gun camera swung on Freeman, her petrified face and haunted eyes staring into the lens as she mouthed silently.

Static rolled as the audio and video were lost.

"Freeman? Come in. Brady, do you copy?" Reynolds thumbed the microphone repeatedly.

Trent jolted from his chair and broke from the stuffy truck, gulping at the fresh air outside. Alana joined him, but both felt their legs buckle, forcing them to sit on the steps for support.

"What just happened?" Alana asked numbly.

Trent fought his racing heartbeat and increasing nausea.

"Trent?" said Alana, her voice almost slurred with fatigue, "What did they see?"

Trent shook his head, too confused and scared to speak. One thing was clear, there were more of them down there.

FIFTEEN

THE SATISFYING SOUND of a hardball hitting the ash wood bat was washed out as the local crowd roared their approval, and the scattering of hard Seattle Mariners fans booed. The batter's feet dug deep into the sand as he powered toward first base, the discarded bat arcing through the air behind him.

Harry Fennell cheered the Dodgers' newest hitter, Charlie Lemur, as he circled for a home run. Around him, the crowd was on their feet, but Harry did not dare dislodge the beer and hot dog nestled on his lap. He'd come to the game alone, selling the ticket he'd reserved for Trent at the entrance for just over double what it was worth.

FEMA officials had done marvels for the ground, transforming it back from a soup kitchen to a sports venue in half a day. Along the sidelines, Harry noticed many FEMA jackets, enjoying a brief respite from the chaos. He didn't blame them. The current mood in LA meant everybody was looking for some light and release. He entrusted running the bar to his head barmaid, and swiftly departed without looking back, determined to enjoy himself and not think about how the world was collapsing around them.

Situated in Elysian Park, Dodger Stadium had suffered only a few rattling lights during the tremors as the whole park sat on solid rock. Just out from the stadium, the Pasadena Freeway had suffered some brutal damage and was still closed. Despite the difficulty in attending the game, people had taken surface streets and arrived early. Some had even walked a dozen blocks from parking their automobiles - an unheard occurrence in Los Angeles.

The scoreboard danced and flashed as Lemur made a home run. The crowd was ecstatic. Even the Mariners' fans took the match with good grace. After all, most of them had suffered major travel delays in getting here, so they were determined to have a good time. Harry figured that natural disasters brought out the best in people.

Two hundred feet above the stadium, a Miller Beer blimp cruised into view, neon lights dancing across the logo. The floating advertisement also offered a home to the sky-cam that allowed television viewers some extraordinary aerial views of the game. Since the quake, the use of drones had been reserved for emergency services.

The crowd settled as José Ramos paced from the bunker, experimentally swinging his bat through the air like a practiced fencer. The Mariners' pitcher felt the weight of the ball and exchanged rapid hand signals with the catcher, partly to confuse the batter, but also to warn which slick move was up next.

The two warriors faced each other. The pitcher reworked the dirt on the mound to balance his footing. A tremor of excitement circulated across the stadium as he wound up and pitched. The ball dipped under the bat and into the catcher's mitt.

The crowd cheered as "Strike!" was called.

Harry crammed the last sliver of a hot dog in his mouth as the video screens switched to a close-up of the pitcher's face. José Ramos smirked, playfully trying to ignore the trash talk only he could hear. The pitcher stretched, wound up the shot, and –

A dull boom of compressed air echoed through the stadium. It was so powerful the pitch soared wide and thudded into the grass. A twelve-foot steam plume punctured through the earth just past third base, scattering the fielders.

A rising murmur washed around the stadium as another plume erupted through the turf across from the diamond, this time catching a retreating Mariners' fielder and hurling him twelve feet across the grass.

Cameras around the stadium swung to capture the plumes. The scoreboard switched to the sky-cam view. Around the stadium, people clambered uncertainly to their feet. Harry remained seated, slowly chewing the remains of the hot dog.

Near third base, two players took a brave step forward as both plumes suddenly glowed with a light of their own.

Then, with the force of a Herculean jack-in-the-box, a huge mass bounded from the hole. The players backpedaled in alarm. Cameras racked-focus to capture the bulky Dero emerge - its two plasma-arms still cherry-red from the recent boring. Its hawk- head surveyed the stadium as another clambered from the second opening, the four utility arms pulling it from the shaft.

Across the stadium, a third Dero clambered from the steam vent, closely followed by a fourth.

Now a tide of screaming terror flowed through the stadium, as spectators understood this was not an elaborate part of the show. Thousands of bodies rushed to the exits. People fell underfoot, trampled with no regard from others who were more focused on their own survival.

The sudden activity startled the Deros. They spread across the pitch, watching the flow of people. One machine leveled its plasma-arms at the bleachers - and let rip. The super-heated blast ignited a pair of FEMA officials as it struck amid the crowd of spectators. Those caught fully by the beam vaporized in the blink of an eye: as did the benches and two feet of solid concrete. Skin blistered and boiled on those close by; the wave of heat igniting clothes and hair.

The players took flight across the pitch. One Dero pounced after the nearest man like a lion on a killing spree. The arachnid legs powered it across the ground at over thirty miles per hour. Its torso hunkered low as it speared its hapless victim with a drill arm.

After being poleaxed, Harry finally dropped his meal and fell onto all fours, sheltering behind a stanchion. Another Dero fired its heat-ray across the opposite side of the stadium. From his vantage, Harry could see people caught in the blast. Some were instantly disintegrated, while others burst into flame. Their screams of agony washed across the field like the soundtrack to his worst nightmare.

José Ramos rolled for cover just as the entrance to the bunker he was heading for exploded in a shower of masonry that swallowed his screaming manager. He felt his kneecaps jar from the impact, but terror overrode the pain when the killer Dero rounded to face him.

Its head cocked as it slowly approached. Jose rolled onto his back and scuttled toward the boundary wall. The machine stopped. Its plasma-arms locked backward as the drill arms buzzed forward. The revolving bits sparkled in the remaining floodlights.

José pushed against the wall. The Dero took a menacing step, in no rush to dispatch its trapped prey. José used the wall to rise to his feet – then he suddenly sidestepped and snatched a bat from the rack standing just feet away. He waved it menacingly.

"Come on!" he screamed. "Try me now, you bastard!"

Putting all his weight into a swing, he struck the Dero's torso, making a noise like striking a steel drum. The crazed batter had time for two more ineffective blows before the Dero thrust out the whirling drill-bit.

Twenty yards away, Harry watched as José Ramos was callously hoisted above the machine's head, his thrashing body revolving around the drill; spraying gore like a macabre garden sprinkler before it split in two.

Harry tore his gaze away, searching for the nearest escape route. A mass of people blocked several exits close by. Others had collapsed into piles of rubble.

A pair of Deros marched side by side across the field, stopping in the center of the diamond. Harry watched as the rear-legs of one machine splayed out, the front body upward to compensate for its head's limited vertical movement. It used its drill-arms for balance as it aimed the plasma-guns skyward.

Harry's incomprehension soon faded as he followed the weapons' path to the blimp that had remained over the stadium.

The Dero rocked from the recoil as it fired a pulse of

heated plasma at the aircraft. The first shot narrowly missed, leaving a black scorch stain across the Miller logo. A second blast hit home: tearing into the blimp's cradle and melting a huge hole in the craft's side. The helium blimp rolled with the finesse of a whale. Fortunately, the gas was nonflammable, but the fabric caught fire, spewing glowing embers across the stadium as the airship nose-dived.

For a split-second, Harry was convinced the blimp would land directly on top of him as he rolled into a fetal position. But, realizing he was not dead yet, he risked a glance from behind his folded arms as the blimp careened into the bleacher's roof. Lights sheared off and the metal roof folded like paper under the blimp's weight. The aircraft scraped along the structure before toppling off the stadium and crashing in the parking lot beyond, crushing dozens of vehicles and several people as they spilled from the stadium.

Harry clambered to his feet. The exits may be blocked, but he didn't want to stay in the stadium any longer. Fleeting memories of a movie flashed into his mind in which defenseless Christians were flung to half-starved lions. He rushed up the nearest steps, vaulting over the seats to join the tail end of a crowd shoving through a narrow fire escape. Harry's ankle twisted as he stumbled on the uneven ground. Looking down, he was horrified to see they were trampling over dozens of people, some still moving.

The four Deros spread across the stadium and began taking out the massive floodlights with their heat rays. Metal buckled and twisted as the hundred-foot lighting towers collapsed.

At the last second, Harry noticed the tower above was swinging in his direction - seconds before the lighting rig crushed him.

SIXTEEN

WALT STILL HAD a nacho frozen halfway to his mouth as he watched the carnage on television. The camera was positioned a little way from Dodger Stadium, capturing the tide of people pouring from the structure. One half of the stadium was well ablaze; curling orange flames fingered the night sky. Helicopters had kept their distance as a Channel Nine chopper flew low over the stadium and was liquified, molten metal splashing down into the stadium.

Walt took off his glasses and turned to the rest of the group; words failing him for the first time in his life. Trent had called his team together just forty minutes earlier to discuss the situation.

Schofield had different channels playing on whatever screens were available. Catherine watched with a solemn expression; her tired brown eyes hidden behind an uncombed fringe. Trent and Alana stood at the back of the room; pale and shaking, as if reliving their own personal nightmare.

Walt couldn't stand the tension anymore. He tossed his food aside and cradled his head. "Okay, what the hell is going on? What am I watching? Anybody?" He looked hopefully at the others with the expression of a schoolboy who thinks he is the only one not in on the joke. "Trent?"

Trent puffed his cheeks, letting out a long sigh. For a moment, it looked as though he was ignoring Walt.

Schofield spoke up. "C'mon, Boss. You didn't want us here just to discuss the game, did ya?"

Trent nodded slowly. He folded his arms to prevent the others from seeing his shaking hands. "In answer to your question, Walt, we don't know *what* is going on," he indicated himself and Alana. "We had a run-in with one of these this morning." He glanced at Catherine, who refused to make eye contact with anybody. "What we have here is a puzzle."

"Puzzles," echoed Walt with a tinge of hysteria. "I like puzzles. I'm good at them; I can handle them. But the rest of that," he waved dismissively at the screens, "is just too surreal for my tastes."

Trent tried to resume his briefing, but the words wouldn't come. Alana placed a reassuring hand on his shoulder and stood up. "Here's what we have. Yesterday, my partner and I were called to the Metro at Wilshire and Normandie." Her voice cracked slightly, but she took a sip from a Coke can on the desk and continued. "Two transients were killed. Their chest cavities ripped out. After the aftershock this morning, technicians found a hole in the wall of the running tunnel. Trent and Catherine were called to see if it was geological."

Catherine shook her head, still staring at the screens. "It wasn't natural. The rock had fused under intense heat and pressure. The only thing I ever saw like that was volcanic. We went down with the detectives and..." she tailed off as she met Alana's gaze, unable to continue.

Trent wagged a finger at a screen showing the Deros emerging from their chutes. "We ran into one of those down there. It murdered Alana's partner. It nearly killed us."

Walt's eyes widened. "Do you know what these things are?"

Alana shook her head. "It was a machine. We don't know where it came from. It followed us out and attacked a subway train. Killing more people."

"Holy cow," chimed Schofield. "This is next generation craziness."

"Oh, it gets worse." Trent leaned forward in his chair. "The Mayor ordered a SWAT team to go down and destroy the machine. They went. None of them came back. That's when I called you guys. And now, this."

The silence that filled the lab was peppered only by multiple news stations replaying the stadium attack from different angles.

Walt licked his lips. "How many of them are there? The SWAT destroyed one? There are four in the stadium. So that gives us five robots that suddenly turn up?"

Trent stood up and walked to the TV, which showed a perfect freeze-frame of a Dero. "You keep saying robots. I don't think they are. When the SWAT destroyed one, they mentioned organic matter inside. That was about as detailed as the report got."

Schofield joined Trent at the TV. "They're an insect-like design. Four arms, two drills, and a pair of laser cannons or whatever they are."

"Some kind of rock melting device," said Catherine. "That's what they used to carve out those tunnels. The rock was as smooth as glass, and I've only seen that with volcanoes. The heat they generate must be intense."

Alana frowned. "Do we even have that technology? Just to melt rock like butter?"

"The short answer is we don't," said Walt, his eyes fixed on the reruns of the stadium carnage. "Unless, of course, you mean *we* in the military sense of the word. In that case, who knows what they have got?"

Catherine brushed her hair behind her ears as her shock was slowly replaced by scientific curiosity. Trent smiled inwardly. This was more like the old Catherine. "Trent, have you been to Caltech?"

Walt jumped to his feet at the mention of the name and dashed over to a table where seismograph printouts and maps lay. Trent ignored him.

"I went there after dropping you off to see if I could find out why they are spewing the kink in the San Andreas theory."

"And?"

"I got to Ben Chapman's office in time to see him being marshaled into an unmarked black car by a bunch of heavies."

"Kidnapped?"

"They looked like your playbook Government goons. Black car, black suits, designer shades."

"Why would the Government kidnap Ben Chapman?" asked Schofield. "I find it a little insulting that they didn't kidnap me."

"Got it!" Walt waved the printouts above his head like a triumphant student.

"Yesterday's quake moved from the desert and *into* the city. It wasn't a fault zipping open - it was them excavating through the earth. They straddle a couple of fault lines and triggered the quake. That's why it had the signatures of a moving target."

Catherine nodded. "I think you're right."

"I don't think five of those things could shift enough mass quickly enough to cause a quake of that magnitude," remarked Schofield as he crossed for a fresh look at the data.

"Unless there are more of them," said Alana dryly.

Schofield laughed. "More? I think you would need a couple of hundred to make an impact that wide."

He suddenly noticed the tight silence that enveloped the room. He looked up and blanched as he realized the implication of his statement.

"A hundred... at least. But that's impossible..."

Alana pulled her cell out. Trent turned to stop her.

"Who are you calling?"

"We have to tell the Mayor about this."

"Tell him what? We don't have proof, just speculation. The last thing they're going to do is listen to me, especially when they have Chapman telling them whatever they want to hear. Give me time, okay?"

Their eyes met, and Alana complied, slipping her phone away.

"But if you're convinced about this, then so am I," she said.

Trent picked up an iPad and called up a local map. He circled the Wilshire subway and Dodger Stadium. "Okay, we have incidents with the machines here and here. The two places are not exactly close."

"That's not quite right, Trent." Catherine took the iPad

and zoomed. "The D line terminates at Union Station. That's within spitting distance if you're traveling underground. And we don't know how far their tunnels run."

"But why the stadium?" said Alana. "Just to kill people? It makes little sense. They could have hit the streets at any time."

"You're talking as if this is an act of terrorism," said Walt dismissively.

"That's exactly my point. If this isn't some sort of statement, then why come up at all?"

"Ventilation," said Schofield, surprising himself.

Trent looked at him. "What do you mean?"

"You're digging down deep in mother earth's lap, melting rock and generally poking holes into natural gas reserves. I don't care how high-tech you are. If you don't clear that out, then two things will happen. Either you'll suffocate and die, or you'll blow yourself apart. Either way is a zero-sum game. They needed to clear the tunnels, pure and simple."

Trent felt a twinge in his temples, the forewarning of a stress migraine. Walt retrieved a box-file of printouts and scattered them over a table.

Alana watched the TV. A frightened young man was openly weeping as he recounted his story to an eager Sarah Chong. Schofield had killed the volume, but in Alana's mind, she could hear the terror in the man's voice. In the space of a day, her world had been turned upside down, then ripped apart. She should be feeling sad or scared. Instead, she was angry. Perhaps a reaction to her grief, but she needed decisive answers.

"Any ideas where they come from? I mean, if there is somebody inside... a pilot..."

Schofield looked up from his monitor and waved a finger. "North Korea, Russia, Iran, or China, they're your culprits. North Korea, they don't have the tech. Which leaves Iran, Russia, or China."

Alana circled her finger to encourage him to keep thinking. "So why attack like this? Why attack at all?"

Schofield shrugged. "Because it's an accident." Alana raised an eyebrow and shook her head. Schofield sighed. "Okay. New Cold War, Russia is back to buzzing our airspace and territorial waters, to study how we react. We do the same." He indicated his screen. "So, these guys are some prototypes for covert subterranean warfare, dreamed up by whoever the Chinese or Russki Elon Musk is. They're sent *under* us. They hit a problem, accidentally trigger a quake, things go wrong. Gases, fault lines, heck, we even have tar pits out here. They figured they need to come up for air and - boom - they find themselves in the middle of a Dodgers game and on national TV. They panic and get trigger-happy."

"I think I have a bearing on these things," said Walt, waving a sheet of data.

For the first time in days, Trent felt a glimmer of hope. "Walt, you're a genius."

"Simple detective work. I backtracked on the data. Remember, I told you the initial readings seemed to come from out of the desert? Bingo, I looked at sensors further afield and trace it all the way to Nevada."

Alana frowned. "Nevada?"

Walt pulled his glasses off and massaged the bridge of his nose. "Only the biggest military test ground in the world. Groom Lake, Area 51, White Sands – whatever you want to call a piece of the United States the size of Switzerland and dedicated purely to top secret Government research."

"That can't be right."

"Detective, I'm telling you what the data is telling me. Whatever these machines are, they appear to be our very own."

SEVENTEEN

EVERY SPARE POLICE unit had been assembled to seal off Elysian Park and the neighborhoods directly surrounding the stadium. It was no mean feat, as the Police Academy and Barlow Sanatorium had been used to temporarily move the soup kitchens and emergency shelters from the stadium. Now they had to find a new location, and space was at a premium. A sea of headlights heralded the arrival of light armored vehicles that were usually deployed for riot situations. They set up position on the ring road around the stadium.

The fires had extinguished inside the stadium, leaving the whole structure resembling a crumbling Coliseum bathed in darkness. Nothing stirred beyond the armored vehicles and heavily armed police except litter, gently rolling in the breeze and caught in the powerful floodlights surrounding the stadium. Every flat square inch of Elysian Park was now home to all available aerial units the police had at their disposal, including several seconded civilian choppers. East LA had been declared a no-fly zone for commercial traffic, and police warned news crews to keep to the periphery of the security perimeter. The few drones that had been flown over had been shot down with pinpoint accuracy, so all attempts had been abandoned.

An expectant calm had fallen across the city. Anticipated riots and looting failed to materialize. As the cold fingers of fear had gripped the heart of the city and squeezed with a vice-like grip, it seemed Angelenos found solace in supporting each other.

Police units from around California had been drafted to patrol the danger zone, but none had yet met the machines face-to-face.

Chief Bixby stood on the steps of a mobile communications post and stared at the silhouette of the stadium. It was a welcome break. The air-conditioning in the communications vehicle had broken about an hour ago, and now the truck was like an oven in the dry Californian night.

Bixby was a man of ambition and considered himself a champion for any minority, a reputation that had dogged his career and undoubtedly slowed it down. He recognized the same passion in Alana, although he would never admit it to her face. Left to his own devices, she would be the first female police chief in the LAPD.

But right now, that seemed more of a curse than an accomplishment.

Everything he could see was at his command, and it made his stomach twinge with the birth of an ulcer. The situation was unprecedented and required a lot of manpower. Bixby seriously doubted there was enough available. The Mayor had been playing the phones all afternoon demanding answers and had since been whisked away to yet another press conference.

"Chief, we're online," said a technician from the depths of the vehicle. Bixby slackened his shirt collar to cool himself down before entering the sickeningly hot room.

Banks of monitors replayed feeds from many cameras around the stadium. An older techie, who looked as if he'd been dragged from a rock tour, sat at a computer cycling through the images. The younger technician was up to his elbows in cables as he jammed them into HDMI sockets, routing vivid thermal images.

"They managed cranes around the stadium, just about peeking over the walls to give us a fix on what's going on in there." The tech inserted the final cable and slid the mixing desk back into position as he took his seat. Bixby leaned over his shoulder as his fingers clattered across the keyboard.

Bathed in gray and white, the images were ultra-sharp despite them coming from utter darkness. The four machines were visible, blanched white from overexposure because of the heat they were producing. They stood motionless, three on the field next to the chutes they had excavated, and one halfway up the bleachers. The mass of bodies carpeting the ground was disturbing. From the forty-two thousand attendees, the media estimated only ten percent had made it out.

"What are they waiting for?" asked Bixby, almost to himself. His cell suddenly vibrated, scattering his thoughts. He answered without looking at the caller ID. "Bixby."

"Chief, I need to see you now."

"Alana?" He doubled-checked the name on the screen.

"I'm with Professor Trent from WCEC. We have information about those machines that you need to hear."

"Go ahead."

There was an uncomfortable pause, and Alana's voice dropped. "It has to be in person."

Bixby sighed. He didn't have time for theatrics, but he also didn't have time to argue. "You'll have to get over to the stadium. I can't budge from here."

"We're on our way." Alana abruptly hung up.

Bixby held the phone to his ear for a few seconds, unaware they'd been cut off, as he stared at the motionless killers on screen. He was only vaguely aware of being told the Mayor's press conference was about to begin.

*** * ***

A MAKEUP ARTIST swabbed the perspiration from Mayor Shearer's brow. He didn't notice; he was staring at the wad of cue cards in his hand, all rapidly scribbled by the same spin-doctor. No time for slick teleprompter spiel. He'd have to improvise, which wasn't his strongest suit, especially considering the decisions that had just been made behind closed doors.

Doubt nagged him. He knew what he must do, but the implications were beyond anything his spin-doctors could smooth over. Staring at the podium outside City Hall, beyond which stood a phalanx of cameras and journalists, he felt like a condemned man about to ascend the gallows. This was nothing short of political suicide. No, not suicide, *murder*... political murder. The future had been taken out of his hands.

The Mayor did not speak as he walked toward the large double-doors. He resolutely refused to make eye contact with the party around him, instead staring solemnly at his own feet. His aide stood behind and just to one side, now oddly silent, a far cry from the usual last second briefing notes that usually preceded press conferences. Even the ceaseless background noise of traffic was missing, something he never thought he'd miss in LA.

City Hall's door swung open, and Shearer quickly walked several yards to the podium. The crowd was silent, collectively wondering what possible new announcement could be made.

Shearer took position behind the bank of microphones and coughed as he laid his cue cards down. With a trembling hand, he poured water from a bottle into a glass and took a sip. He glanced around for a familiar reporter, eager for a friendly face, but the lights blinded him. Instead, he gripped both edges of the podium with white knuckles.

"Ladies and Gentlemen. People of the City of Los Angeles, I stand before you as your elected Mayor in my solemn duty to protect and serve you all to the very best of my abilities. As you know, rescue services are stretched far beyond breaking point just to cope with the earthquake damage. Despite several assurances, National Guard units are only just being mobilized." He marshaled his thoughts. "Now a new danger faces us: these new killers. What are they? Where do they come from? And why are they attacking us?"

He paused again to catch his breath, unaware of the dramatic effect it had on the crowd. "These questions deserve answers. I want those answers, but I cannot give them to you. LAPD has performed miracles in securing Elysian Park from any further attacks. But that is not enough. To fight these merciless killers, we need a stronger arm. That is why, effective immediately..." His throat dried up. He took a sip of water from the glass before he continued. "Effective immediately, complete control of the city will be handed to the United States Military under the command of General Carver. As of this moment, Los

Angeles and the surrounding districts are under martial law."

A ripple of disbelief circulated as Shearer stood back and a uniformed General, who emerged from City Hall during his speech, took his place. Although his uniform was impeccable, General Carver sported a fresh crimson scar running around his ear and down the side of his neck.

"Thank you, Mayor." Carver's voice carried an unflinching air of confidence. "We haven't ascertained the motives or origin of this new threat. We believe it to be a covert operation by a foreign national to undermine the Government of the United States. No nation has claimed responsibility. So, effective immediately by order of the President of the United States, I declare this city under military command. Every citizen of downtown LA is to obey a curfew as of midnight tonight. Thereafter, anybody on the streets between eighteen hundred hours and six hundred hours will be arrested." His steely gaze defied the murmurs that spread through the crowd. "This is not house arrest. This is not politically or racially motivated. This is a matter of utmost National Security, and anybody not willing to assist his or her country will be tried as a traitor to the United States."

"As I speak, military units are being deployed across the city. Their primary task is to prevent these machines from harming any more civilians. Downtown will be evacuated, and access blocked with armed units who will patrol the streets. Once our scientific advisors are on the scene to assess the situation, we will use any force deemed necessary to stop this threat. Air Force, Marine, Army, Navy, National Guard, police, and fire departments now fall directly under my command, as authorized by the President. As will those of all other government offices, including FEMA teams operating inside the restricted area. On a personal note, I know how this sounds in our democracy. These are hard times for everybody, but rest assured, I will do everything in my power to make this city, this state, our country... a safe place. You media folk will be informed of progress through regular conferences, but any further information will be embargoed until we have a better handle on the nature of the threat. Thank you for your attention."

Carver spun on a dime and headed back inside City Hall as every reporter in the area bellowed out a question. Mayor Shearer focused on the tip of his shoes as he followed the General. Never had he suffered a more crushing blow than now, and he suspected the military knew far more than they were revealing.

EIGHTEEN

ALANA AND TRENT reached the stadium command post at the same time military trucks were arriving, spitting diesel fumes into the night air. M1 Abrams tanks, accompanied by a dozen Stryker armored personnel carriers, and LAV-25 light armored vehicles prowled through the streets with the confidence of an occupying force.

Bixby looked wan as he intercepted Alana and Trent heading toward the command post. He urgently grabbed Alana's elbow, slowing her pace. She thought his hair was a little grayer, the lines on his face deeper.

"When they ask, you are my second in command and the Prof has been drafted in for official advice as a direct request from the Governor. They're going to do everything they can to shaft us off on this. I take it you've heard the news about Uncle Sam?"

"National Security. Heard it on the radio. Is that him?" Alana nodded at General Carver, who was leaning on the hood of a jeep, studying plans of the area with a colonel.

"That's him. He's a real piece of work."

"Do I have to salute?" asked Trent sarcastically.

"You have my full permission to flip him the bird," snarled Bixby. "You're a civilian, so you might just get away with it. Everybody else around here is jumping at his shadow."

He led them over. Carver's eyes studied the newcomers as he listened to his colonel's briefing.

"General Carver, this is Detective Alana Williams who has been on this case since the first incident. She was the one who found the transient victims in the subway. She is in charge of the investigation. And Professor Michael Trent from WCEC has been working closely with us on the scientific implications of the events. They were the first to witness the machines."

Carver didn't even acknowledge them. They could have easily been insects. Instead, he fixed his steely gaze back on Bixby.

"This is a military matter now, Chief. Your forces have been redirected under my control. There is no *case*, as you put it. And we have the very best scientific advisors analyzing the situation."

Bixby was just too hardened to take any crap. "You may be in charge of all this, but as we have an unconfirmed number of people murdered by these things, that still puts it in our jurisdiction. I read the press release, General. You're not here to replace us; we are here to *assist* you. Least ways, that's how your boss put it." He took some small pleasure in seeing a flicker of annoyance. "That includes giving you access to people who have had firsthand encounters with the enemy. How many of your men can boast that?"

The muscles in Carver's jaw bulged, his brow creasing as a vehement reply swelled in his throat. Alana snorted with disgust at the male bonding session and stepped between the two men, redirecting Carver's rage.

"Testosterone aside, General, one of those bastards killed my partner right in front of me." The details were vividly fresh in her mind, although it now felt like a lifetime ago. "I saw how it moves. Saw what those weapons can do. I saw people atomized right in front of me. You show me any of your staff who are more experienced than either of us." She laid a hand on Trent's arm. "I don't care about politics, General. The situation is bigger than that. Bigger than you or me."

Carver's eyes narrowed, but Alana continued undaunted. "Professor Trent and his team have reason to believe there are many more of these things underground and have evidence that they caused the earthquakes." The flick of Carver's eyes to his colonel wasn't lost on either Alana or Trent. "What kind of leader ignores the experts?"

Carver bit his words, fazed by the direct approach Alana employed. After years of ass-kissing in the Pentagon, it was a refreshing change to meet somebody so arrogant. Carver waved his hand to a knot of people emerging from the command truck.

"Your views are quite frank. And as much as it pains me, you are also correct. The situation is colossal. I want you to brief both myself and my science advisor."

Trent's ears perked up. "Science advisor? General, let me assure you, you'll find nobody more qualified for the job than me."

Carver slowly turned and sized Trent up. "Professor Trent. Until this morning, I didn't know who the hell you were. Then suddenly I hear a lot about your work, and your, let us say, *unorthodox* theories."

"Pleased to hear my reputation precedes me." He wasn't expecting Carver to smile. In Trent's experience, that was never a promising reaction.

"Oh, it does. I believe you know my lead advisor. Professor Ben Chapman."

Trent's stomach tightened as Ben Chapman detached himself from the knot and joined them. Behind Chapman's square glasses, his eyes narrowed at the sight of Trent. His normally thin face seemed sunken around the cheeks, his eyes black from lack of sleep. As he repositioned his glasses, Trent noticed his hands trembling. He'd expected a snarky comment or a degrading one-liner. Instead, Chapman remained silent and merely nodded.

Alana sensed the instant drop in temperature between the men, but she was getting used to all this male one-upmanship and it was, frankly, getting tiresome. However, there was something about Trent she admired. Perhaps it was his resilience to defy the odds. From what she knew about him, stubbornness was the only reason he still had a career. Or perhaps it was the glint of amusement that tugged his lips during his arguments. It was somehow comforting; giving his opponent the sense he knew something they didn't. It was almost charming.

***

THE LIGHTS RAISED as the hastily edited video ended abruptly. The stoic faces of General Carver and Ben Chapman, along with several other unnamed uniformed officers, all swapped uncertain looks. Trent clutched the slide clicker to quell his anxiety. His presentation had gone well, and the lack of questions or counter-analysis of his data surprised him. Standing at the back of the room, he saw Alana was just as surprised by the muted reaction.

Eventually, Carver reclined a little in his chair and rubbed the flat of his palms against his knees.

"A well put together presentation, Professor Trent. Your analysis concurs with our own, and I have to say," he cast a scathing glance at Ben Chapman, "that sometimes surpassed that of our own team. You say the origins came out of the desert. What are your theories there?"

Trent felt his cheeks flush. He'd refrained from mentioning the ideas about wayward military projects.

"Well, sir... the data is *inconclusive* at this time."

"But surely you have some ideas?" Carver's gaze was unflinching.

Alana flashed a small smile at Trent but offered little advice. He involuntarily chewed his lip, gathering the resolve to speak.

"If you want my frank opinion, data suggests it came from the covert military establishment at Groom Lake, Nevada. We... I theorized it could be a military experiment gone awry."

Murmurs rose from the officers at the back of the room. Trent felt his ears burn as an old General waved his hand dismissively.

"You can't seriously believe the United States Military would *lose* a project and then threaten to destroy its own cities to cover it up?"

Trent stood his ground as the atmosphere in the room turned distinctly hostile. "You wanted my assessment, General. And, right or wrong, if I read the data that way, then you can be sure others have too. In China, Iran, even across Europe, I'd be surprised if similar conclusions aren't reached."

Carver stood sharply, causing Trent to flinch. For a moment, he was convinced he was about to be ejected from the room, or worse, arrested under some arcane law. The General slowly circled the table until he stood by Trent's side. He was a muscular figure who effortlessly intimidated Trent. Carver stared at him, boring into his soul, before he gave a single nod and turned to the room.

"People, I must stress the sensitivity of what has been stated today and what you're about to hear. This information stands at Majestic level."

Alana raised a finger. "What does that mean?"

"It's a security level so high you're not even aware it exists." A trace of humor flashed across Carver's face. Trent almost jolted when Carver placed a huge hand on his shoulder. "Professor Trent is in the ballpark with his ideas and theories, although they're not as accurate as he may believe. At the beginning of this week, tests were carried out at the Groom Lake facility on a new missile designed to penetrate the earth's surface. Project Excalibur succeeded and unleashed a simulated subterranean nuclear blast two miles down. The blast apparently disturbed a massive, submerged *anomaly*. The anomaly rose to the surface as if the ground was water," he used his hand to show the movement, "before heading laterally through the ground, right in this direction. Soon afterward, the quake struck. And you know the rest of the story."

Silence engulfed the room. Trent became aware he was sitting on the edge of the desk, his jaw slack. None of the assembled officers dared speak. Alana moved closer, thoughtfully combing her hair around her ears.

"If these machines are not rogue projects of yours, then what *is* your theory about what was disturbed?"

Carver folded his hands behind his back and straightened his already ramrod posture. "An excellent question, Detective. Obviously, it is the primer to this whole enigma. What if I told you we didn't know?"

Alana circled the table and stood next to Trent. It gave her a modicum of comfort and reminded her of the trusted partner she had lost just hours earlier. The very thought filled her with rancor. "Then I would have to disbelieve you, sir."

Carver nodded in agreement. "As civilians, you, the Prof here, and Professor Chapman are not normally privy to the information you are about to hear. If you so much as hinted to another person what I am to tell you – well, I'll be blunt. It will be a treasonous offense. And the Government isn't beyond execution to protect National Security."

Chapman reacted violently, springing to his feet. "Executed? This is America, for Christ's sake!"

"This information is so sensitive that it is on a need-to-know basis. Hell, even as we speak, the President himself is being briefed for the first time. Make no mistake, we will stop at nothing to preserve this secret for as long as it takes. That you must understand."

Resigned to his fate, Chapman sighed heavily as he pulled a small pink bottle of Pepto-Bismol from his jacket and chugged it down like liquor.

"You've all heard rumors about *little gray men* and *flying saucers*. Well, every officer in this room is attached to some kind of project to deal with, spy on, or reverse engineer such technologies."

Trent was stunned. He took some comfort in seeing Chapman's brow creasing.

"And we're in a race with a dozen other countries around the world to crack those secrets." As if the admission was an enormous weight off his shoulder, Carver sat on the edge of the nearest desk, his shoulders minutely slumping. "During the sixties, another mystery came to light. The Cold War fueled the need for underground bases and cities, just in case the Russkis started getting antsy. The Cuban Missile Crisis put the paranoia needle off the chart." Trent and Alana slowly became aware this speech was for the benefit of the whole room. The other officers looked as mystified as they were. "The Pentagon spent an inordinate portion of their budget on creating entire subterranean communities that would thrive if a nuclear holocaust came to pass. As these structures were being built, we discovered a network of tunnels under the ground. Just from their formation, scientists could tell they were not natural. They were not only artificial, but ancient too."

"We didn't know what caused them. Cultures around the world, from across history, believed in subterranean civilizations. The Vikings spoke about a Hollow Earth, a thought that was carried forward by the Nazis who constructed huge underground facilities. Liaising with Nazi scientists taken during Operation Paperclip revealed an intriguing story."

Carver lapsed into silence and gazed at the floor as he assembled his thoughts. Nobody dared speak. Even the background noise outside seemed to take a moment's respite.

"In the last years of the war, the Nazis began work on a base located in the Antarctic. The thinking was to build a place of solitude where the Aryans could lick their wounds, rally their forces, and one day take the world by storm. Thousands of construction engineers and Jewish slaves were used to build this city deep beneath the ice. But something happened. Details are sketchy, but it seemed that a boring hole unearthed some kind of ship. Not under the ice, but under the actual Antarctic landmass, burrowed in rock strata beneath ice that was millions of years old."

Alana could scarcely believe the General was serious. She half expected a punchline at any moment.

"Whatever the Nazis did appeared to have activated it. The vessel suddenly powered up and took off through the ground. But not before destroying the base. At the end of the war, when we discovered the remnants, all that was left were a handful of survivors and the empty half-built city."

Trent glanced across the room. The Generals seemed calm and composed. In contrast, Ben Chapman was sweating heavily, a dark V-shaped stain forming on the front of his shirt. Alana was almost serene. Beautiful and composed despite the weight on her shoulders. He marveled that she wasn't freaking out; he could barely hold his thoughts together. This was too big. Way out there.

"Since then, various Government operations found tunnels networked around the globe. Kennedy was in power when the decision was to send a task force down them to investigate. One tunnel complex was located under Texas. The team headed west." He paused and smiled at Alana, like an old uncle imparting a family secret. "You've only seen the smaller tunnels. They can be quite a size. The team used regular issue jeeps and soon requested refueling trucks; lots of them. This tunnel, ignoring the offshoots, ran all the way to China."

"No way," barked Trent with disbelief. "That's what? Nine thousand miles under the Pacific!"

"The team encountered those machines." He gestured in the stadium's direction. "And so did the PLA. China's People's Liberation Army. The resulting firefight ended with the deaths of all but two of our unit, and a hundred Chinese Soldiers vaporized. All fighting together. All fighting this one threat. The encounter ended with a powerful earthquake that destroyed a small village community in the *Lianhua Shantou* region. The machines escaped without a trace. And until now, they'd simply fallen off the map. A joint Sino-US group dubbed them *Deros*, a quaint abbreviation for *Detrimental Robots*. You can blame the Chinese for that moniker. But it fits. The machines don't seem too friendly and haven't tried to communicate."

"They just stay out of our way," Trent said quietly. Then pointedly added, "Until somebody goes and gives them a hell of a wake-up call."

Another uneasy silence gripped the room. Alana felt her heart pounding through her shirt and checked everybody's reaction. Collected military brass were subdued as they assessed the implications. Like a masterful stage performer, Carver allowed the silence to build until the pressure was almost tangible.

"So, gentlemen, ladies, our options are as limited as our time. Our hands are firmly tied behind our backs on this one. We gotta decide what to do."

A white-haired Army general plucked an unlit cigar from his mouth, which he used as a prop to deflect his tension. He stabbed it in Carver's direction. "I thought the answer to that was obvious, Dan. We blow the shit out of them. Way below where nobody will notice. No repercussions to the surface, and then LA can continue with its crazy life."

"I wish it was that easy. What you have seen are only the drones."

"Drones?" Alana was alarmed.

Carver nodded. "Like worker ants. They always seem to accompany a larger craft, the one we disturbed under Nevada. These larger craft vessels always remained on the edge of detection. And now we have one right under our feet."

"And how big is *big*?" asked the cigar-toting general.

"About a mile and a half long. That's an estimate. We don't know exactly how many of the Deros are down there. The situation is an intelligence white-out. Men don't stand a chance."

A thin-faced and relatively young Marine Lieutenant General, with his hair forming a perfect widow's peak, leaned forward. "You mentioned the development of a burrowing missile, Project Excalibur. Can we use that?"

Trent laughed aloud in disbelief. "A nuclear blast? Under Los Angeles? Think of the network of fault lines under our feet. *Thousands* of minor lines, and many that have yet to be identified. Trigger those with a nuclear detonation, and it could start a chain reaction along *every* fault line from here to San Francisco. And that's just to start. Have you heard of the Ring of Fire?"

"Of course–" the Marine started, but Trent talked over him.

"A series of tectonic faults right around the Pacific Ocean. Imagine them all triggered in unison. You're talking about sinking the Western Seaboard with a single blast, then taking out most of Asia with it."

"A gross exaggeration, Michael." Ben Chapman climbed

to his feet, mopping his brow. So far, he'd been brooding quietly, but now professional jealousy was superseding his anxiety. He scowled in Trent's direction as he continued. "Hundreds of underground explosions have been carried out next to fault lines to explore such effects, and no evidence has *ever* surfaced that a nuclear detonation could trigger an earthquake. Now, I must admit I'm having some difficulty accepting this... wild... situation. But using Excalibur seems the most sensible course of action."

"You're talking about a blast in a major fault line area. No experiments have been conducted in a zone like this. What about surface destruction?"

"We can use a high-yield neutron bomb," said Chapman with a tremble in his voice. "It will deliver a powerful punch, but the radiation will dissipate quickly. The surrounding rock will fuse, ensuring none will seep to the surface or into the water table."

Trent felt the value of his opinions rapidly devaluing as heads nodded around the room. He was under no illusion that if they didn't need him, his time at the head of the table was over. He pushed past Ben Chapman. "General, use a little common sense. The ground LA is built on is as fragile as glass. It simply can't take any punishment!"

Carver's brow knitted together. "Professor Trent, your opinion has been noted, but we don't have time to field academic discussions. We need an action plan we can deliver, and this is it."

"At what cost?" He stabbed a finger at Chapman. "What he's proposing is suicide! What about a non-nuclear payload you can plant down the tunnels? Something with just enough punch to destroy the main craft?"

"Nothing can be mounted on the Excalibur. We'd have to walk something like that down. That really would be suicide." Carver drew to his full height to address the rest of the room, making it painfully clear that the conversation with Trent was over. "Gentlemen, I want this operation planned and ready to roll in two hours with the help of Professor Chapman. Professor Trent, I would like you to stick around as an observer. Your opinions are welcome."

Trent stood dumbfounded as the room swiftly cleared as chairs rolled across the floor and a low sea of voices rose as various secure cell phones contacted the relevant departments. Chapman smirked as Trent caught his arm to stop him from leaving.

"Ben, you can't seriously believe there will be no chain reaction?"

Chapman shucked him off. "Data is clear, Trent. No proven correlation between a nuclear blast and a quake. *Real* scientists put a lot of effort into that study. You've heard about genuine science, haven't you?"

"Only from people like you. Pompous, career-minded fascists. That's just based on my own research, of course."

Chapman appraised Trent with a tinge of sorrow. Trent could swear his eyes flashed a haunted look before the stubbornness returned. "Feel free to stick around and observe. You may learn something." He hurried out to join a waiting general, taking care to slam the door behind him. Trent sat on the edge of the desk, bewildered by events.

"That's reassuring," said Alana, as she sat next to him. "That every profession is populated with career idiots." Folding her arms, she stared far away. "I should've gone to visit my parents."

"Why didn't you?"

"Because I convinced myself I hate fly-fishing. My dad, he loves it. Moved up to a little town that's not on any map. Looks right across the Canadian border. It's always damp. Not like here. And I thought I could be doing good right here."

"You're a regular Debbie Do-Right." He was pleased to see he'd inflicted a smile. "What about a husband... or partner?" He inwardly cringed when she looked at him with a curious frown.

"Never had time. Ed was like a brother. That's all I thought I needed. Now I see that is so wrong. We all need something else to fall back on. What about you? Family?"

Trent had never been a lady's man or even the school charmer. He'd been told he was handsome, often enough, but at his core self-doubt always nagged him. Flirting was something that happened to other people. So now, with Alana's thighs gently pressed against his, and her head tilted almost on his shoulder, his internal dash was flashing warning lights he was incapable of translating. He couldn't figure out whether she needed comforting or was simply unaware how close they were. She struck him as a woman who was completely unaware of the affect she had on men. He forced himself back into the conversation.

"No family." It came out a little harsher than he'd wanted.

Alana playfully nudged him with her shoulder, her brown eyes widening with intrigue. "It seems we have a choice. We can get the hell out of here and let my dad lecture us on fishing lures, or we sit here while we're being groomed to take the fall when the Western Seaboard turns into Atlantis."

That was exactly what Trent had concluded. Carver had

no interest in his opinions. He just needed a scapegoat. The question was, what could they do to stop a catastrophic mistake?

NINETEEN

THE CHEAP FORMICA dented as Schofield slammed another metal storage case onto the desk. His nervous fingers unlatched both catches, and he swung the reinforced metal lid open, revealing the carefully filed folders inside. His hand slid across the tabs, creating a sound like cards being shuffled.

"No, nothing here either," he said after a rapid search. He slammed the lid closed and hoisted the three by two case onto a stack of five others. The tower represented the team's sum total of data analysis and research that stretched back before efficient computer storage systems. Schofield hadn't gotten around to digitizing most of it, using the flimsiest of excuses not to. Now he was paying for it.

Catherine hunched over a computer, clicking through files as she chased any data on nuclear-induced earthquakes. She hastily created a bot to find links between reported tests anywhere in the world and subsequent quakes. A lit cigarette burned in the ashtray next to her, practically untouched as she concentrated.

Trent had headed straight for the lab, leaving Alana at

the stadium to report on any fresh developments. He woke Schofield, Catherine, and Walt from their beds to demand they get back to the lab for the third time in twenty-four hours. Schofield had arrived before Trent, even though he hadn't been briefed on the nature of the situation; he knew Trent well enough not to ask. Plus, Trent's news was now easy to guess.

Grinning wildly, he said, "They're going to nuke those machines, aren't they?"

Trent had only taken two steps into the room. If only Schofield knew the true nature of the enemy.

Catherine snorted, "Like they'd drop a bomb on Downtown. If the Government was willing to do that, then they would have nuked the riots long ago."

Trent didn't have time for conversation. "Where's Walt?"

Schofield hadn't heard. He was already fantasizing about the pending detonation. "Can we watch it?"

"I'm sure you'd see it, even if you were asleep at the time. Just before you died."

Schofield's grin didn't flinch as he let out a low whistle of dread. Walt entered, a long coat thrown over his dressing gown, his feet comforted by tartan slippers, and sporting an expression like an insomniac roused after the best sleep of his life.

"Whatever your excuse for yanking me out of bed at 3:00 a.m. is, then you better explain to my wife before she develops an interest in DIY castration on both of us."

"I need you to skim every file you can on data connected to the effects of nuclear detonation along fault lines. I need something within an hour. Schofield's doing the papers, and Kate's searching recent records. What about the archives?"

"You made me drive here along a freeway belonging to a

Mad Max movie, just to ask me that? I could have told her how to access the files over the phone!"

With a hint of anger, but a flourish that indicated Walt enjoyed being of use, he slid into a chair next to Catherine and gently ushered her aside, pulling the keyboard away from her fingers.

"I've already written a bot to–"

"No bot'll find this," he said dismissively as he typed. "I worked on Government-funded research to analyze nuke-quake relations. Since then, I've been working on a computer model of those effects, since the last French Polynesian Atoll tests. Remember the furor about eco-damage? Well, that got me thinking about the movement of submerged tectonic plates and the use of nuclear detonations as a possible trigger." His fingers danced across the keyboard, opening hidden files he'd password protected.

"To *move* tectonic plates?"

Walt nodded. "Think of it as a flight of fancy, but what if you could shift a plate to, I don't know, raise a mountain range under Moscow?"

"Geological terraforming?"

"I mean, practically, even an elevation of a couple of inches could be catastrophic."

"That would be playing God."

Walt grinned. "Oh yeah. And it feels excellent."

Schofield shook his head, "All this time Walt's been concocting his own games, and he's been giving me a hard time about playing *Call of Duty* over the network!"

"It's not a game," huffed Walt.

"No, it's weaponizing earthquakes," Catherine shot back.

Walt stopped typing and shook his head with just enough sarcasm to make her angry. "No, my dear. It's a scientific model, based on the energy unleashed in previous quakes and their effect on neighboring fault lines."

Catherine snatched her cigarette. "You're a dick. And if you call me *my dear* again, your wife will be too late to castrate you."

"Promises, promises," he breathed as he found the file he wanted, and double-clicked. On screen, a map of peaks and valleys appeared, resembling the Rockies. Colorful fault lines crisscrossed the surface.

Walt gestured proudly to it. "This is a simulation of the ocean floor. Wherever I click on this map, it will simulate a nuclear detonation above the surface. Like so."

A click of the mouse caused an expanding red circle to appear on the screen. Moments later, a noticeable shift occurred on the map as several of the peaks crumbled away in a cloud of pixels.

"This is like nostalgic 8-bit joy," Schofield said.

"Forgive the graphics; the budget didn't stretch to a special effects team. But as you can see, the peaks have eroded, and the plates shifted, causing a simulated quake of..." he rolled the mouse to a number at the top of the screen. "7.2 on the scale. Hot stuff. Now, do you mind telling me the gross importance of this right now?"

Trent studied the screen. "Can you apply this to any fault line pattern?"

Walt shrugged. "Sure. If we have accurate geographic surveys, I just need to import the data maps and run the program. But I better tell you, I cheated a little. I deliberately placed my warhead on a strain along the fault. If it was just simply nearby, the result wouldn't have been as impressive. Can I guess where you want this simulation running?"

"California. I want you to run this simulation on our

most complete map. Target it on our current hypocenter and epicenter."

Walt spun in his chair. "Hey, this is really far-out hypothetical terrorist stuff. If you're thinking about assassinating the Mayor, I can think of more discreet methods than a nuke."

"The military is planning to launch a nuclear device on those machines."

"A tad extreme, wouldn't you say?"

"Can you do it?" pressed Trent.

"Sure, but it will take about half an hour to reconfigure the code. It's crazy, but I can do it. What kind of nuke? Low yield on the surface?"

"Low-yield neutron bomb detonated 3 miles down."

"Jesus," spat Catherine in disbelief. "That is beyond crazy. What the hell is down there?"

Trent wanted to tell them but knew Carver's threat wasn't just bluster. During the drive here, Trent had convinced himself he was being followed. "I can't tell you." His eyes met Catherine's. "But I think Harold O'Reilly was definitely on the right track."

* * *

MAYOR WILLIAM SHEARER rubbed his temples, achieving little more than aggravating the throbbing veins beneath his skin. His aide had left with an army captain and said he would be notified the moment a decision was made. To add insult, every military attachment who answered his calls was a lower rank than the last. It was clear he was outside the loop, looking in.

He could taste the bile in the back of his throat rising.

He'd been proud of the speed with which his profile had been lifted to martyr during the initial quake response. Just the day before it struck, he'd been feeling the pressure from the City's bureaucratic cesspool that was eager to see him out of office. Before his aide departed, they had just received leaked information from an opinion poll cast before the quake. The City thought far less of him than he thought of the brainless imbeciles to whom he spoon-fed his campaign fodder. The low ranking in the poll had tumbled him from despair into darker ether. Saving the city had been the re-election gift he needed.

Another benefit of the natural disaster was that he could spend more legitimate time away from home - in particular, away from his money-grabbing wife, Martha - and spend it with his secretary. Not the most original move, but Shearer never had much imagination. But now it seemed Martha had sniffed a scent of the affair. In fact, she had pictorial evidence and threatened to hang his balls from City Hall.

Throb-throb-throb pulsed the vein on his forehead, slowly powering the migraine beneath his brow.

And now *this* cluster fuck.

Indecision from a nervous governor, who was at loggerheads with the President because of the ongoing lack of help combating wildfires and the dwindling water table, had resulted in a delayed request for National Guard assistance. Yet that had been superseded by the mass military migration. It had been so rapid and fluid that it almost seemed like a pre-planned operation. The news that they were going to bomb the city had been the moment he knew his career was over. There would be no comeback despite assurances that the damage would be practically zero.

Practically zero? What the hell was that supposed to

mean? The General had informed him that it was a series of *adaptive measures* to destroy the *foreign infiltration*.

Just what foreign body was being destroyed was never answered. Shearer's insistence that he should tell the people the truth was killed with sharp-tongued threats under the guise of *National Security*.

Shearer was helpless but resolved not to give the public, the military, his political backstabbers, or his loathsome wife, the pleasure of seeing him crumble in the eyes of the world. His hand slid into the desk drawer and pushed documents aside until his fingers coiled around the warm handle of his Colt automatic. He slid it out without a glance and pressed the smooth barrel tip against the offending throbbing vein.

This is the way to immortality, he thought. He wouldn't be a victim. He would remain a martyr. People would put up statues to honor his sacrifice, ensuring they would never forget him. Like he ever cared for them, anyway.

* * *

THE AIR CONDITIONING inside the truck felt as if it was pumping out warm air and made General Carver nauseous, but he still refused to slacken his shirt collar. One hand toyed with an ice-cold Coke can while he scrolled through a tablet. He sat reading a series of specifications detailing the Excalibur Missile.

A sharp rap at the door broke his thoughts and a lean-faced lieutenant stepped in. "Sir, Nellis reports a shadow flight is fueled and awaiting final confirmation."

Carver looked back at the tablet, wondering if they were making the correct move, but blighted by the lack of answers.

"Tell them to wait. I will give the execution order directly."

A smart salute, and the officer quickly exited. Carver let out a long sigh and stretched his shoulders back, the joints cracking, and turned back to the tablet for one last appraisal of the weapon he was about to unleash.

The MOP - Massive Ordnance Penetrator - was very different in deployment from the more traditional *bunker busters*. He was familiar with Boeing's GBU-57. The high-explosive warhead could spear through the earth to a depth of 200 feet before exploding. Useful when fighting the Taliban, but not this new threat. Previous prototype earth-penetrating weapons had suffered development problems because they relied on detonating a nuclear explosion to tear the ground apart; something that went against international law and every nuclear proliferation treaty.

This one was different. He had been at the first test out in Nevada just days ago. The first tests that had unleashed the beast beneath their feet...

A PROLOGUE

Spiraling cones of dust drifted from an unmarked, desert-camouflaged Oshkosh Joint Light Tactical Vehicle as it crossed the dry Nevada lakebed. There was no road; that would be a clear sign for prying spy satellites.

Inside, the khaki-clad soldier at the wheel peered through the dust-encrusted windshield at tire marks carved in the parched earth. He gripped the wheel, adjusting to follow the fresh tracks that stretched into the distance.

The installation was ultra-secret. Most of those who funded it didn't know of its existence. When an official visit was expected, the Facility would drive a truck out into the desert. The heavy prints it left behind formed a temporary path that would be swept away by the dry breeze a few hours later.

General Carver tried to relax in the vehicle's cool interior, but the lack of sleep had made him irritable. Twelve hours earlier, he'd been enjoying an illicit margarita and the flirtatious attentions of his secretary back in his Pentagon office.

He was called to an impromptu meeting over concerns

that Congress was looking to cut the military's Black-Budget - an eyes-only document that governed how the military spent its money on secret development projects.

Carver had drawn the short straw, and here he was shipped out into the middle of the goddamn Mojave Desert to witness the testing of... Christ knows what kind of missile.

The Learjet flight had been uncomfortable, the desert heat intolerable. At least he had the satisfaction that the next hour or two would involve scientists and administrators attached to the mystery project clamoring to kiss his ass.

He glanced once more at the dossier in hand labeled: PROJECT EXCALIBUR - MAJESTIC CLEARANCE.

Sensitive information escalated the levels of security from "confidential", "secret" to "top-secret". Certain levels were compartmentalized on a need-to-know basis to prevent information being given to all and sundry, with mere top-secret clearance.

Even the President himself didn't have access to certain compartmentalized subjects. "Majestic" was one stage higher than top secret, and he knew for sure the President knew jack about this project.

"Straight ahead, sir."

The driver broke Carver's chain of thought. The tracks they were following led down a gully, sheltered under the shadow of a looming limestone edifice poking from the desert floor like a warning finger. They ended before a massive matte-steel door. The rocky overhang prevented the entrance being spotted from the air, aided by the door obliquely angled toward the ground like a "V" to enhance the camouflage.

Hidden cameras assessed the vehicle and its occupants. The door rumbled to life, slowly lowering into the ground with a fluid movement. Path clear, the driver sped up into a sloping concrete tunnel lit periodically by spotlights that did little more than define the road several yards ahead.

Carver glanced back as the colossal door elevated back into position. Another, even thicker door rolled aside as they passed, locking behind them with a boom of finality. Carver was used to airtight levels of security in the paranoid world of Government operations, but this was one of the tightest he'd seen.

They pulled up in a subterranean parking lot housing two-dozen vehicles: a mix of unmarked jeeps, trucks, and a black bus with armored windows, all meticulously cleaned and serviced. Three men waited to greet them at a single door that beckoned them deeper into the complex.

A fair-haired man in Levi's and a garish Hawaiian shirt opened the vehicle for the General. Carver recognized him from his picture in the dossier; the name came shortly afterward.

"Ben Williams?" asked Carver, shaking the man's hand. No saluting civilians.

"That's correct, General. I'm the administrator of Project Excalibur. Welcome to our sanctuary."

Carver was surprised to find he was shivering. The complex's air-conditioning must be running flat out. He strengthened his grip to hide his shiver.

Ben motioned to the other men. "I'd like you to meet the key members of my team. Professor Murray and Professor Heinzel."

Carver shook hands and exchanged terse nods with the two scientists, both distinctive in their impeccable white lab coats. Murray was balding and energetic. Heinzel was older, with comely looks, more fitting to an actor than a scientist, Carver thought.

"Please, follow me," said Ben, escorting Carver and the scientists through the door. "With Congress whining, I've had to fast-track today's demonstration. Now that's a waste of money if you want my humble opinion."

"I don't want your opinion. I just want some results I can wave in their faces." They entered a long corridor lined with white doors on both sides, marked only by numbers. The whole atmosphere was sterile. "But I won't bullshit you guys," said Carver. "Congress is baying for cutbacks and your project was short-listed."

"Political pay-raise time then?" quipped Ben. Carver remained silent, inwardly agreeing.

"The bottom line is if you can't convince me that this research is important to the well-being of the United States, then funding will be terminated. There will be no appeal." Carver noted the worried exchange between the scientists, but they remained silent. Ben grinned further, nonplussed.

"General, I will convince you that Excalibur is essential." They reached another solid door. His fingers danced over a raised keypad, and the door rapidly slid aside. "And who knows, you may then want to increase our budget?"

They entered a large command bunker, walls bedecked with rows of computer monitoring stations and walls covered in ultra-high-definition screens showing a dozen angles of the desert outside. It gave the illusion of a grand panoramic window if it was not for the environmental data overlays. Carver assumed the feed was live.

"This is where it all happens." Ben grinned. He raised his voice to get the attention of the team inside. "People, this is General Carver. You're here to impress the hell out of him."

The eight gathered technicians briefly glanced from their

posts and nodded, eyeing him with nervous mistrust, before resuming their tasks.

Ben indicated around. "I don't enjoy wasting time on small talk. If you've no objections, I wanna proceed with the demonstration."

Carver gave a single nod, already planning his time on the jet as soon as he could get out of here. Sadly, at his level, military work had become nothing more than an overwhelming assault of emails.

"The dossier was pretty thin on the ground when it came to explaining what you're doing here. Care to elaborate, Williams?" said Carver. Ben was a little too "showbiz" for Carver's liking. His tone of voice reflected that. Ben was quick on the up take, suddenly all business.

"Intelligence reports are constantly revealing new underground facilities in unfriendly countries. Chinese sub bases, Korean nuclear facilities, Iranian missile silos - even complete cities. Conventional weaponry, including nukes, cannot deal with these structures. They're just too darn inaccessible and well-protected, beyond the range of our existing weapon-set, which is primarily designed for land, sea, and air attacks. Excalibur provides a solution by penetrating straight to the heart of the problem."

Ben could see that Carver didn't grasp his allusions. Heinzel stepped in to further explain with a pronounced Dutch accent.

"Remote Viewing projects have enabled us to locate subterranean cities in Iran."

Carver's face remained neutral, although the thought of Remote Viewing projects sent a chill down his spine. It belonged to the arcane and, in Carver's view, the fringe study of psychic powers. A 'viewer' would sit in a dark room and calmly describe places and events on the other side of the world with uncanny accuracy. Despite Carver's dislike for such things, the U.S. Government's Black Budget funded such activities - especially as whispers in the Pentagon still maintained that Remote Viewing was how they found Bin Laden and Saddam Hussein. Carver had to admit, the chances of one soldier stumbling across a small, camouflaged hole were highly improbable without some kind of intelligence, but his Christian upbringing made him frown at the reliance on anything vaguely supernatural.

Ben continued. "Facilities like these also exist all over. They not only house entire battalions but weapons, ammunition, and food to keep an army alive for years without surfacing. In the event of war, they could prove to be a surprise in subdued countries. Think on a much larger scale than the Taliban in Afghanistan. In China, technological advancements are being made in these subterranean facilities, very much like our own Groom Lake."

Carver laughed inwardly. Groom Lake or Area-51 was the best publicity stunt the Government had pulled. Located north of this facility, it was originally established as a Majestic Level research center. But the public started snooping and media coverage made many in the Defense Department nervous. They moved the research and development base a little farther west, using Groom Lake to attract the conspiracists, thus successfully focusing prying eyes away from the real testing grounds.

"If these facilities are deep beneath the ground," said Carver, "then even a high-energy missile could not penetrate far enough down."

"Exactly," chimed Murray. "The current scenario is to storm these facilities with troops. With such a direct approach,

the loss to our forces would be unacceptably high. Futile, probably. Excalibur eliminates all of this."

Carver's curiosity was roused, although he tried to hide it. "How?"

Ben eased back into the conversation; his whole manner suggested a persuasive used-car salesman.

"Since the sixties, the Los Alamos National Laboratory has been developing underground boring machines. They pioneered the Kerf Melter tunneling machines capable of tearing through rock at a walking pace, practically liquefying the earth with their nuclear-powered cutters. This enabled debris to be easily cleared from the tunnels."

"I am aware of the Kerfs, Williams. Hell, every classified underground establishment in the United States was created with those."

"What we've done is advance that technology," said Heinzel. "By constructing a compact Kerf, and then amplifying its output. The resulting product was then integrated into a specially designed missile. The Excalibur can tear through the earth at up to fifty miles per hour, for three miles."

Carver reacted. The possibilities of such an efficient killing tool raced through his mind. Ben could see they had nearly won the vote. All it needed was a little kick.

"Look at that." He pointed to a screen relaying a three-dimensional radar image. A small blip with the radar signature of a pigeon was headed their way.

"What you see is a B2 stealth-bomber on approach. The aircraft will deploy the Excalibur missile from a height of five-hundred feet in the desert out there." Ben moved to a set of computer displays. One monitor showed a shimmering swirl of colors and dark blocks. Another rendered the fuzzy image into a side-on display of a submerged bunker, with various *passageways leading from it. Carver felt as if he was looking at a colorful but oddly angular ultrasound womb scan.*

"That bunker is the size of your average suburban home and is located a mile beneath the center of the lakebed you crossed. The branching passageways are T-tunnels that'll collect data from the blast-site in less than a millionth of a second. This other display," he gestured to the swirling colors on the monitor, "depicts a live sonar feed from the site. A slightly pimped-up version of what paleontologists are using these days. These babies are positioned every hundred feet beneath the ground in a sphere around the bunker. We've effectively got a three-sixty vision around the target."

Carver nodded, although his attention was primarily on the B2 as it drew closer.

"In addition, we have our eye-in-the-sky. A satellite equipped with long-wave ground-penetrating synthetic-aperture radar, allowing us to see right into the heart of the blast-zone."

Ben traced his finger across the touch screen to highlight the bunker amid the colored swirls. The resolution slowly adjusted like a magic-eye picture. As Carver tuned into the data, the images came into sharp relief.

"This will give us a live view of the subterranean detonation?" he asked.

Ben couldn't suppress a smug smile. "You're watching a live broadcast from a mile underground. From any angle."

Carver whistled appreciatively under his breath. Murray and Heinzel's body language eased for the first time, now sensing the atmosphere was taking a positive spin.

"Sir, K-flight has started its run." said a female technician hunched across a communications set. "Permission to launch?"

Ben nodded. "Granted. General Carver, keep watching."

Everybody focused on the images of the desert outside. The blue sky didn't betray the presence of the approaching stealth. Carver felt a twinge of excitement as a technician began the countdown from ten. He'd been out of action too long; one too many cocktails in political parties. The hair on the back of his neck prickled when he noticed the black smudge on-screen weaving through the valleys.

"There she is," he whispered.

Ben glanced at the animated general, suddenly assured the project was safe.

The blotch on the screen morphed from a speck to a portentous bat-shaped shadow as it zoomed toward the camera. The view changed to that from a high peak, looking down on the lakebed as the shadow serenely banked through jagged peaks.

"Missile deployed!" called the technician.

The B2 banked sharply, eating altitude as it cleared the blast zone as the smudge of the released missile hurtled earthward.

The screen image flicked to a close-up of the impact point – as the missile stabbed into the earth with deadly grace. A fountain of dust rose some fifteen feet, the missile leaving nothing more than a four-foot crater in its wake.

Carver watched the sonar display. A pencil-thin line bored swiftly in the direction of the bunker.

"An onboard computer corrects the missile's trajectory depending upon the soil-type it encounters."

"I hate to be premature, Williams, but you're impressing the Hell out of me." said Carver, his eyes glued to the display.

"Sixty seconds to impact!"

Anticipation for the 'kill' flooded through Carver.

Subterranean facilities have always been a deadly conjuncture in war. His own memories of sending young soldiers down narrow tunnels in Afghanistan, to face unknown perils, still chilled him. One time, a young, overly keen private had volunteered to flush the crack. They dragged his body out just as the Taliban had finished carving the boy's face from the muscle layer beneath. Nuking that dust hole from the face of the earth had never been an option. Pity, thought Carver.

"*Fifteen seconds.*"

The Excalibur missile's course had held true, characterized by a Bugs Bunny style burrow left in its wake. The technician began a countdown as Carver watched the action play out.

"*Impact.*"

A screen displaying seismic shock graphs peaked red. Carver watched as a dark blotch erupted across the scans of the bunker complex. The ground trembled as the nuclear shock wave reached them. Just as suddenly, the dark spot condensed to the size of a tennis ball as the atoms that formed the bunker and surrounding earth tightly fused into a solidified clump. All eyes flicked to the external monitor in time to see the desert floor drop some fifteen feet in a circular crater a quarter mile in diameter: the typical signature of an underground nuclear detonation as the ground sank to fill the sudden void below.

Ben checked the monitors, satisfied. "*Target destroyed. Minimal surface disruption. No radiation contamination topside and zero friendly casualties.*"

Carver vigorously shook Ben's hand. "*Congratulations, Project Excalibur has my full support.*" *He turned to the scientists keeping a discreet distance. In their experience, science and the military were entities that didn't mix.* "You have done some mighty fine work here. Keep it up."

"I took the liberty of pre-arranging a celebratory lunch for you, General," said Ben, flashing his winning smile. *Carver felt no longer in a rush to get back to the office. In the last five minutes, his opinion of the man had pivoted a clean one-eighty.*

"That's just what—"

"Sir, I think you better look at this."

Carver and Ben pressed around a technician who was bent over her terminal, brow tightly knit as she read the puzzling data rapidly scrolling down the screen.

"Maybe it's a glitch?" said Ben.

The tech shook her head. "No, sir. Diagnostics ran fine."

"What's the problem?" *Carver asked. Murray and Heinzel edged their way between the men and scrutinized the data.*

"We've upset something." *commented Murray.* "It appears to be some sort of aftershock. It's gaining intensity."

"An earthquake?" *asked Carver.*

"This whole area is tectonically safe for nuclear testing," *Ben rebuffed, although his words fell flat as he sensed something. The faintest of vibrations penetrated his Nike sneakers.*

Then they all felt it.

The reinforced floor shook beneath their feet. Styrofoam cups spilled from desks. Those standing had to support themselves against the control desks that were bolted to the floor.

"What's happening?" *demanded Carver.*

"Shit!" *Ben was staring at the sonar monitor, mouth agape. Carver joined him and almost lost his footing as a technician collided with him.*

The bottom of the screen was black. His first impression

was that it was a tech glitch. But as he watched the darkness rise through the earth like a surfacing whale, engulfing the area of detonation, he knew it was something more than instrument failure.

"Are we losing sonar?" asked Carver.

"Everything's running fine." Ben could barely speak as perspiration beaded across his brow. He tapped the screen. "That's a physical anomaly." He could barely believe his own assessment as it engulfed the screen, heading straight up.

A technician duly altered the controls. The sonar image expanded to reveal the entire lakebed - including a submerged facility with dark shapes moving inside, too small to define. Carver realized he was watching the very bunker he was standing in, and suddenly felt detached, as though the experience was nothing more than a simulator.

A dark speck dwarfed the complex above it, rising steadily with a rib-shaking bass. Unlike the Excalibur missile, this object did not leave a trail behind it. Instead, it seemed to glide through the liquified earth around it.

"Heinzel!" Ben shouted as the room shuddered even more. "What is it? Gas pocket?"

"No, sir. It seems solid. There's no earth displacement. It's a solid object under its own propulsion. I have never seen--"

The room violently jolted from the sudden impact. Carver caught the images on the screen in time to see the collision.

The reinforced walls and floor sprung wide cracks as though made from ice. Every screen and light in the facility glitched. Carver was flung several feet over a control panel, his head glancing off a wall. His probing hand felt warm blood seep over his ear. He tried to climb to his feet, but a wave of dizziness staggered him back on his ass.

The whole room began to list, pushed aside by some

titanic force beneath them. Loose items toppled from terminals and bounced toward a wall. As the angle increased, people lost their balance, sliding across the smooth floor – some off their chairs, others falling flat - to follow anything else that wasn't bolted down.

A collective yell rose in the bunker as everybody left standing gripped bolted desks to stabilize themselves. Ben lost his footing, only regaining it when he wedged himself against a desk.

Heinzel was not so lucky as the incline became more acute; he was hurled headfirst into a wall, his neck broken.

Across the desert floor, it was an incredible sight, witnessed by the last functional surveillance camera, perched on a peak a mile distant. At the foot of a mountain, the ground erupted as the previously submerged bunker was pushed to the surface at an angle, a mass of steel supports and disintegrating concrete. The growing dust across the lakebed rolled like gentle sea waves as the dirt underwent liquefaction. A bass-heavy shock wave echoed through the valley.

Ben crawled to General Carver, who had pressed himself into a corner as concrete fragments cascaded down. Their eyes locked.

"Are you okay?" shouted Ben.

Carver nodded once, then winced from the pain it caused. Ben was mere inches away. He held out his hand so Carver could pull him up the slope to avoid cascading detritus. Just as their fingers latched, a computer bank sheared its bolts from the wall. A half-ton of circuitry smashed down on Ben and effortlessly shattered his ribcage. Carver's face remained stoic as crimson fluid seeped from under the steel rack and pooled against the crazily angled wall.

The shaking abruptly stopped.

Every screen had smashed. Emergency lights swung from dangling mounts, assisted by the faint rays of sunlight that poked through gouges in the walls. Harsh cracks from severed electrical wires and the trickle of masonry were the only sounds.

Carver hauled himself upright; his pale face caked in blood.

"Where did it go?" he whispered through cracked lips.

TWENTY

FEAR BREATHED across the city as the earth once again shook with rage.

Concrete trickled off buildings, weakened by the previous quakes. A delicatessen in Chinatown was one of several buildings to slip its foundations, rapidly folding in on itself in a cloud of masonry, killing the occupants trapped inside. In the street, hastily erected power cables snapped, crashing to the road in a flurry of sparks against the night sky.

It was over in seven seconds, leaving nothing but dogs barking against the jarring squeal of a thousand car alarms.

***

CATHERINE SANCHEZ SCRAMBLED for the seismograph readout toppling from the printer. The quake had taken them all by surprise, and they were rooted to the spot as it shook the lab. Schofield's storage box tower collapsed, spilling the carefully indexed papers across the floor.

The window near Walt buckled, cracking in two. The top half slipped from the frame, shattering into a thousand razor fragments, some of which grazed his face.

"I bet it's the same locale," shouted Catherine, even though the initial rumble had subsided and left the room relatively quiet. She jotted the time on the printout with a red pen that was secured to the machine with Velcro for such emergencies.

Trent slid over to Walt, who was covering his face with a hand. Blood seeped between his fingers; he let out a stream of profanities.

"Walt, move your hand. Let me see."

Trent used a little weight to pull Walt's hand away, revealing six small incisions on the left of his face: two on the forehead, leading across to the temple, three peppering his cheek, and another on his neck - all quite small, but pumping an alarming quantity of blood. Glass crunched under Trent's boot as he shifted to get a better look at his injuries. Small shards of glass hung off his coat.

"Schofield, get the first aid kit."

"Am I gonna die?" groaned Walt.

"One day for sure. It's a lot of blood, but it looks worse than it is. Just a few scratches. I can't see any glass in the wounds."

Trent's cell sounded as Schofield tossed over the first aid kit. He flipped the box open and removed a sealed pack of medicated swabs. His phone's screen had somehow cracked, obscuring the caller's ID. He hit the speaker and placed the phone on the table.

"Hello?" He tore the pack open with his teeth.

"What caused that tremor?" It was Alana.

Trent unfolded the sterilized swab from the packet and

angled Walt's head to clean the wounds. "We don't know yet. Could be a regular aftershock. We're not able to verify that right now."

"Two of the machines have retreated back down the vents and the other two are patrolling the stadium."

"Was this before or after the quake?"

"Just after, why?"

Walt snorted as Trent pressed too hard. He pulled away, snatching the bloodied swab from Trent's hand. "That stings like crazy! I'll do it."

Trent snatched his phone and took it off speaker as he moved away from the others.

"If they're responding to the tremor, then maybe they didn't expect it. Which means things could be more unstable than we think. Tell the General that I'm on my way with a simulation he needs to see. I'm heading over now."

Trent didn't wait for Alana's response; instead, he ended the call with his thumb. He turned back to Walt, stabbed a finger at the computer screen.

"You have minutes to get your simulator running with the local geo survey."

"I'm bleeding to death here!" protested Walt.

"You're going to do much more than bleed," said Catherine with an edge to her voice.

Schofield rolled his chair next to her, glass crunching under the casters. Her screen displayed an enhanced image of the stress lines under LA. "The data is still streaming in, but it already looks bad. If this is right, then it wasn't an aftershock. Those things are on the move again. Not far, just a quarter of a mile - but a definite acute angle, turning northward."

Trent's stomach churned as he looked at the predicted

location. On its new course, it would run parallel to the San Andreas. Its movement already upset the geology of the land, so further interaction with the mother of all fault lines was unthinkable. On top of it all, the US Military was about to detonate a nuclear device right under their feet.

California was about to become history.

* * *

"GENERAL, YOU MUST LISTEN!"

"Detective, I listened, and now I am taking decisive action."

"Trent has evidence that what you are about to do won't work. It'll make matters far worse."

Alana trailed behind General Carver as he hurried to the mobile command. Aides followed in somber silence after initially trying to block Alana's access. She'd even punched one man, who roughly grabbed her shoulder. The situation only defused when she pointed out she could still arrest him. That had won an appreciative smile from Carver, and he allowed her to join him.

"I have rooms full of scientific advisors, Detective. They have access to the best data and finest research. They conclude it will work perfectly."

"What if they're wrong?"

"Are you advocating we do nothing? Just sit here and hope the problem goes away?" He looked sidelong at her. "You don't strike me as the type who sits back and lets things slide. I'd hazard you got this far by going with your gut."

Alana hated the fact he was correct, but was damned if she would give him the satisfaction of knowing.

"I work with hard evidence. Think about this logically!"

Carver stopped dead in his tracks and faced her. He towered over Alana, but she was well disposed to male authority and immune to intimidation.

"I think about what I'm doing every second, *Detective*. We're not solving crimes here. It's a completely different discipline. There are millions of lives at stake, and they don't even know what the threat is. That is the very nature of National Security. Jo Blow knows jack about the real threats that face us all every day. Why do you think Majestic-level security exists? There are plenty of ways to hide secrets, but some things even a President shouldn't know."

He looked vulnerable, the stress finally showing after a lifetime of secrets. Alana found it shocking that she suddenly thought of the General as a human, not a cliché. She knew that he really was a man concerned with his duties.

Carver's stoic mask slipped back into place. "It's too late now, anyway. The order has been given."

* * *

A BLACK BAT swept over the cloud layer at thirty-five thousand feet, with a dull roar from its four turbofan engines. The radar invisible B2 bomber leveled out and decelerated to a cruising speed of five hundred twenty miles per hour.

Powerful computer hardware took over the aircraft, allowing the pilot to release the controls and indicate to the navigator to pull their orders from a locked stowage compartment, opened only by two separate key codes known to each man.

The Navigator extracted the small phone-sized screens that only activated once their thumbs had been scanned, meaning they had to momentarily roll off their flight gloves.

The instructions were concise, designed for maximum clarity. It was a set of coordinates and an official code to authorize deploying the aircraft's payload.

Years of moving around with the military had made visualizing any area of the globe a simple task - and these coordinates seemed too close to home – he knew exactly where the target was, but just for his own reassurance he entered them into the navigation computer.

Before they had departed from the enormous hangars at Nellis Air Force Base, they had been briefed that the B2 would carry a live nuclear device designed for deep-surface penetration in a populated area. They had not been told the area, or even the country where the bomb would be deployed, never mind the reasons behind the attack. There was no war on, so there had been little reason to suspect this flight was nothing other than another training sortie.

Except the orders also instructed him to activate the aircraft's transponder. Doing so would render the B2's stealth capabilities useless, as it would be detected on any radar. It made little sense. The pilot's pulse quickened as the computer confirmed the coordinates as Downtown Los Angeles, California, USA.

Both men exchanged a look.

Not a word was said. They had been trained not to question orders, and their every word was recorded. The navigator ran the co-ordinates through the computer twice more, just to make sure.

There was always the possibility, the pilot thought, that this was just a hypothetical test run, and the aircraft contained no weapons at all.

That must be it.

The B2 rushed onward, not deviating a single inch from its flight plan.

* * *

RUSTY STEEL SUPPORTS jutting from a pile of masonry gouged the paintwork on Trent's Prius as he mounted the sidewalk. He saw Catherine in the passenger seat flinch as her door panel buckled.

The latest tremor had blocked the street with telephone poles and a traffic light that had dropped onto an unfortunate Neon automobile. Somehow, it had caught fire. The automobile still smoldered as Trent circled around it, the stretched fire services unable to deal with the new slate of calls.

Catherine was fixated on the wreckage. She wondered if the occupants were still inside, trapped, burned alive maybe? But dense black smoke blotted the potentially grisly view.

The rapid events of the last twenty-four hours had kept Trent's mind busy, but surrounded by so much destruction, he was experiencing violent flashbacks to Mexico City.

Trent, much younger, his tiny arms unable to haul the massive rock off his father. His father's hand, matted by dark blood, poked from the rubble, clenching feebly. Trent had only recognized it by the gold wedding band decorated with Mayan symbols that his wife had bought for their wedding in Yucatan Province. His familiar, deep voice was muffled as he screamed for help. Tears coursed down Trent's cheeks as he pleaded for help in freeing his father from the hotel wreckage.

People rushed around him, blurred like time-lapse photography - all unable to help. A bright flash startled him, and he turned to see the face of a Mexican reporter holding a dusty Nikon to his eye. He would later find that same picture on the cover of several newspapers that ran the story of Mexico City's worst earthquake in twenty years.

It was that quake that had snatched both of Trent's parents away - turning a much-needed vacation into a nightmare, as the hotel folded like a deck of cards. Trent had seen it all happen from the relative safety of the swimming pool, which had rocked him side-to-side as waves evenly rolled through it – much to his delight.

That was the incident that had propelled him into the world of seismology. A crusade to prevent what had happened to his parents from happening to anybody else. Quakes couldn't be prevented, but accurate predicting and early warnings would save countless lives. It was a worthy calling.

But so far, he'd failed.

"Trent?" Catherine's voice roused him back to the present. "You okay? Relax, this will work." She patted Walt's laptop on her knee.

Updating Walt's quake simulator was painstakingly slow, as he took every available opportunity to complain about his injuries, convinced there was glass in his wounds. The griping was really to mask his annoyance that his precious program kept crashing when they imported the new Southern California geo data. Rusty old coding was the fault, and other than rewriting the entire software from scratch, Walt was forced to create patches and pray.

Trent found time was against them as they crossed town, back to the stadium through new quake damage. At least when there was a clear stretch of road, he could floor the gas, confident that no traffic officers were available to stop him. He was pleased Catherine had come with him. Her firsthand encounter with a Deros could prove essential. At first, she'd been resistant to the idea of getting close to the killers again, but Trent didn't have the time to argue and had to practically force her into the car.

He glanced again at the clock on the dash. Carver's two-hour deadline was approaching, and Trent was acutely aware he'd spent half that time traveling between sites. He accelerated down the ghostly quiet street, cursing he didn't own a faster car.

***

ALANA WORRIED her thumbnail between her teeth. Since General Carver's rebuttal, she had little to do, choosing not to follow him into the command post. Instead, she sought Chief Bixby to see if he could get through the General's wall of stubbornness.

Unfortunately, Bixby was at a loss for ideas and was called away minutes later to oversee the withdrawal of his squads from the area, which was now designated a blast zone.

Alana had sat on the hood of her car to watch the columns of press vehicles and police units leaving in an orderly fashion, not long followed by the military artillery. Fortunately, Elysian Park's civilian population had already been evacuated, but as for the remaining Angelenos...

She leapt from the hood when she saw headlights approaching, ignoring the honking horns of the departing traffic. She reasoned only one person would be crazy enough to drive into a blast zone and smiled to herself when Trent climbed from the car. Catherine followed with a laptop cradled protectively in both arms.

Trent dashed over. "Where's the General?"

Alana was already heading toward the mobile command. "This way. He's already launched the strike."

Trent was incredulous. He broke into a run, Alana and Catherine following close behind. A lone guard stood outside the command post and nodded when he saw Alana.

The mood inside was somber. Most of the Top Brass had gathered, led by the four-star General Carver - whose eyes were fixed to a fifty-inch monitor screen displaying the airspace around Los Angeles. Faith in the missile's precision had kept Carver here; that and the lack of time to set up anywhere else.

General Carver didn't even look up as Trent took the laptop from Catherine and opened it. Ben Chapman stood in the far corner, eyes darting between the radar and a wall screen showing the live feed of the stadium with the two sentinels prowling the grounds. His eyes briefly met Trent's. His smugness had evaporated, replaced by the look of a condemned man.

"General, you need to see this," said Trent as he held the laptop in the General's line of vision.

"Not now, professor."

Trent raised his voice suddenly, causing everybody to face him. "Goddamn it! You said we had two hours before you committed to any course of action."

Carver's brow furrowed, his steely gray eyes not allowing his thoughts to be read. His tone was measured, as though he was undertaking nothing more than an exercise.

"You felt the latest tremor? How many more of those do you think this city can endure?"

Trent started Walt's simulation. The terrain was rendered in 3D but looked unfamiliar, with none of the identifiable manmade landmarks. Thousands of fault lines highlighted in colors to represent their status. Blue for minor through to red for major, the big mother of them all, the San Andreas running down the side of the map like a fresh surgical scar.

"You're looking at a geo-survey of LA. My team developed this simulation to predict damage from major quakes, including artificial methods of environmental damage directed on the earth's mantle - such as nuclear detonations and fracking." He looked at Chapman. "It uses the same algorithms you use, and it's all verifiable data." When he turned back to Carver, he was pleased to see he had the General's attention. "This simulation is based on hard data, not opinions. Watch. This is what's going to happen to the entire state if you don't stop this madness."

Ben Chapman edged forward to watch. Desperate to have an ally in the room, Trent angled the screen for his benefit. For a moment, nothing happened. Trent prayed Walt's coding skills were up to par.

Catherine gave him a reassuring nod. "It's an old laptop. Our budget's too tight to afford..." she trailed off.

The simulation suddenly flashed white concentric circles that spread out from the allocated detonation. Seconds later, faults around the area flashed as they were given a new lease of kinetic energy. In the blink of an eye, the lines expanded exponentially up to San Francisco and down past San Diego. Then the edge of the map dissolved.

"The timeframe is sped up, but..." Trent couldn't read the General's expression. Chapman's cheeks were bleached white, and his bottom lip twitched fitfully.

A throbbing white line shot up the San Andreas towards San Francisco as Southern California disappeared into the Pacific. Moments later, the fault lines erupted across San

Francisco's Bay Area in a flash of white, the land mass vanishing.

The Eastern Seaboard was no more, with the ocean rushing in to greet the Rockies.

"Amplify that further south, and you have just killed Mexico. A tsunami, perhaps the largest one the planet has ever seen, will carry across the ocean towards Asia. I didn't work out the figures, but now every fault line around the Ring of Fire is triggered in a race against the tsunami. One will hit moments before the other. The repercussions will continue around the globe, eventually triggering quakes in Europe. One big enough to topple the Canary Islands into the Atlantic. That alone will send a wave across the Atlantic large enough to take out New York. And those are just the fault lines we know about."

Carver's steely blue eyes softened as they focused on Trent, but Trent stole the silence before anyone could speak. His tone was flat, almost casual.

"It's not too late. A self-destruct blast at altitude would probably not initiate anything. But a detonation at the heart of the beast where the stress builds..." He trailed off, letting the weight of his words sink in. "Of course, it won't be instantaneous. It will take between forty to 60 minutes for the energy to race up to Northern California. But that doesn't matter. There is nowhere to run. The seabed data isn't factored into this, so I don't think the ocean will rush in to reclaim the Rockies. A good 60 percent of California will still be above sea level, just uninhabitable after a quake registering round 13 plus on the Richter scale."

Chapman almost choked on the news. "That's an extinction-level event! Same as the meteor strike that wiped out the dinosaurs."

A lone blip on the radar screen powered toward the target tagged as *Downtown*. It moved with the lethal grace of a bullet.

Carver finally spoke up. "A most graphic portrayal, Professor Trent. And an interesting theory. But the decision has been made on more substantial evidence."

"He could be right."

Ben Chapman felt every eye in the room swivel on him. Carver wheeled around on him like a predator. Chapman raised a finger to ward him off. "He *could* be right. Perhaps. The evidence can certainly... pivot towards that hypothesis–"

"We're not talking about a fucking textbook theory," barked the General, his forehead boiling red like a primed volcano. "You are paid for your *concrete* analysis of the situation!"

Ben Chapman took a wary step back. "It's impossible to give absolutes!"

Carver's fists clenched as he wheeled around to the radar screen, planting both hands on the desk for support, his mind whirling with possibilities.

"General, stop the bombing," said Alana with perfectly calculated soothing tones.

Carver's jaw clenched as he nodded his consent. He turned to a young bespectacled woman who had one hand on the earphone headset that connected directly to the stealth bomber.

"Put me on to the pilot–"

A methodically clipped voice interrupted as it echoed from the speakers.

"This is Shadow Flight. Package away. God help us."

TWENTY-ONE

GRAY SMOKE CURLED from the cherry-red tip of Chief Bixby's broken cigar that poked from his mouth like a crooked elbow, broken as he was jostled in the flurry of activity to evacuate the immediate area. Although the reason for the pullback had been wrapped in secrecy, rumors of an imminent counterstrike were rife. He stood at the edge of the combined military/police barricade that circled the Elysian Park district. The mere presence of an official line had drawn crowds of people who thought moving several blocks was a major evacuation. Their own safety wasn't on their minds, not if they had the opportunity to witness something macabre happen to other people. Thank the Lord for normality.

Assuming they were a safe distance away, Bixby wished his seven-year-old son could be with him to safely witness what was undoubtedly the fightback. For a kid, it would be a video game come to life, and no doubt be one of those "wish I was there" historic moments. He suddenly missed his family, whom he hadn't seen since yesterday morning at the breakfast table. He glanced at his watch – no, two days ago at breakfast. He'd kissed his wife goodbye, and she'd taken their son to school. A typical moment in time that he never thought twice about. Until now. Once this situation was packaged away, he vowed to take his family on a brief vacation to the mountains, camping maybe.

A murmur through the crowd disturbed his contemplations. One of the military jocks pointed up, "Look!"

Bixby followed and saw nothing but darkness. Then, as his eyes adjusted, he saw stars normally not visible under LA's light pollution, but with so many lights and the power grid still out, the heavens offered a rare peek.

Then he saw it - a shadow raced across the sky, visible only because the fuselage was blacker than the night sky. It soared low over the hills, only a couple of hundred feet above the buildings and sporting no running lights. Only as it banked did the bat-like silhouette become obvious.

"Jeez! Batman's about to bomb LA!" he heard some quick wit say. "Stealth Bomber" was the phrase that ran through the military contingent.

There was a small firecracker flash from the belly of the craft, and something dropped. *Must be a bomb,* thought Bixby. His thoughts were verbally confirmed by several people around him.

Moments later, gravity set the device perpendicular to the ground, and a second flash came as the rocket fired, thrusting the missile at incredible speeds towards Dodger Stadium.

Carver watched the video streams as the Excalibur's thruster kicked in. The tip of the missile glowed amber as the Kerf Melter kicked into action. It hit the ground a fraction of a second before a dull boom shook the windows of the operational vehicle.

He missed the sophisticated sonar tracking equipment used during the trial. Instead, a computer simulation marked its path as the missile melted its way through stone like a hot poker through butter. Its onboard computers corrected every slight deviation from the pre-programmed target.

"Can you abort the missile?"

The question blossomed in Carver's mind - making him acutely aware that he was concentrating on his inner monologue. He was even unaware of who'd asked, so answered without taking his eyes off the screen. "It's not a game with an on/off button. From launch, the missile was primed. We can't pull the plug."

"12 seconds to detonation," warned the bespectacled women tasked with monitoring progress.

Everybody braced themselves as the countdown continued. Carver splayed the palms of his hands on the desk to support his trembling legs.

Trent felt his chest constrict. If it was the onset of a heart attack, then he wouldn't have long to suffer. Alana's hand fell onto his and clasped tightly in the final few seconds. She looked serene, as if accepting the inevitable. Only her eyes gave away the fear inside.

"Detonation."

It felt as though the air had been sucked from the room as a wave of intense silence blanketed the command center. Ben Chapman collapsed in his seat, fumbling for an inhaler stowed in his pocket, as an asthma attack struck him with force.

Seconds passed.

The tension was finally broken as people exchanged

surprised looks across the room. They were still alive. Then, like a sudden downpour after a drought, low chuckles erupted as tension fled.

"Jesus Christ! We're still alive!" somebody chimed from across the room.

Chapman grinned despite fighting his ragged breathing. Carver closed his eyes, saying a silent prayer.

Alana punched Trent in the arm as she gave a small whoop of relief. A broad smile parted her lips, and she impulsively moved to kiss him. The gentle rustle of his facial hair rubbed against her soft cheek, the slight sound drawing them back to the reality of the situation. Her smile faltered against Trent's grave countenance.

"Trent, it's okay to be wrong. In fact, I prefer it. We're alive."

He shook his head and paced to the screen that showed an animation of the detonation three miles down. He took his phone out and scrolled through his calls.

Mixed emotions swirled through Alana. Intense relief accompanied by confusion at Trent's reaction to the situation, and confusion over her impulsive attraction to the seismologist. She knew duress could bring people together and hoped this was just such a reaction. After all, Trent was not her type.

Not *normally* her type.

Alana closed her eyes. Now she was editing her own thoughts. Sure, Trent was attractive in a serious dour kind of way; not that there had been any time to see him under a different light. She chided herself for thinking such things; they were just muddying her concentration.

Trent crossed over to the group, who were busily congratulating themselves and shaking hands. His first words were swallowed by the noisy chorus of felicitations. Carver's head turned when he caught just a few words. Other people noticed the General was staring inquisitively at Trent, and a hush descended.

"There was no detonation," repeated Trent, a little more loudly. Carver's jaw muscles danced involuntarily, but he said nothing. Trent continued, holding up his cell phone for evidence. "I just called the lab. They were monitoring. Every instrument in the region registered nothing but the initial impact. A detonation would have sent the needles off the scale. But there wasn't even a hiccup."

Carver flicked a glance at Ben Chapman, who was on his phone. He looked sidelong at the General and nodded.

A mustachioed Marine general rounded on Trent. "Then your instruments are fucked up. Million-dollar military hardware doesn't simply *not work* like a cheap Taiwanese radio."

Trent rounded on him with a scowl. He was tired of the arrogance he was forced to wade through. "Bad news, buddy, that's *exactly* what happened. Your toy went wrong somewhere down the line - and thank God it did, otherwise you and I wouldn't be having this conversation right now."

Chatter erupted as questions and accusations flew across the room. The focus of the melee fell on Chapman as the team's official scientific advisor. Trent slipped outside.

Away from the noise, he inhaled deeply - dropping the mobile in his pocket and using both hands to smooth back his hair so tightly he could feel his scalp complain. He walked across the short grass that cushioned each step until he had a clear view of the stadium. It remained dark and silent. A quick sweep of the sky revealed no sign of the stealth bomber.

He heard her footfalls and turned, the worry on his face softening into a slight smile.

She eyed him with concern. "Are you okay?"

"I'm so tired of people like them, always kissing each other's butts until it goes wrong. Bureaucratic bullshit. Trying to lay the blame when they get caught. Had to put up with it all my life."

"If it makes you feel better, it's a wall we all face. Some more than others."

"Doesn't mean I have to like it."

"In this day and age, you'd think a woman detective on the force wouldn't raise an eyebrow. It still ticks people off. Small minds hate big changes, but my mom taught me one thing - I'm in control to get me to this point. Not the people who tried to get in my way."

"Your mom sounds like a smart lady. I lost my folks when I was still a kid. On vacation in Mexico. A quake brought half our hotel down on them." He shivered as he recalled the moment. Alana's hand graced his shoulder, giving a welcoming feeling of relief.

"You are right. *You're* in control here, Trent."

"They only believe I'm right *after* the event. It's the same with quake prediction. You warn some poor hicks everything they own is about to be swallowed up by the earth, and they just look at you and laugh because it hasn't happened to them before. They don't want to believe you. But when it happens and they survive by pure luck, then they turn and say, *why didn't you make us believe?* You can scream 'quake' until you're blue in the face and still be ignored. It's only after the event those in power turn and demand to know why they were never told."

"You should tell them to clean the crap out of their ears," smiled Alana.

Trent relaxed slightly as Alana's infectious smile got to him. They held each other's gaze. Trent licked his lips, suddenly finding himself nervous and unsure what the silence between them meant.

The spell was broken as Carver exited from the Communications Centre.

"Professor Trent!" He looked around several times before spotting him, then marched over.

"We need you back inside."

"Why? I thought Chapman had all the answers."

"Obviously not," said Carver grimly. "I need your expertise in this situation. We may not have sunk California, but we still have our original problem. Those things are still down there, and if they got wind that we were trying to blow them off the face of the planet - then they might just get angry. I saw what they did in China. I don't want to see it happen again. Tell me what we need to do."

TWENTY-TWO

DAWN'S SLENDER fingers curled over the horizon. Earthquake scarring across the city had kept most people at home, which was ideal for Walt as he took every available side street to avoid hitting blocked roads. The streets were devoid of gangs or the homeless. He had to wonder where they had gone.

He'd watched the news footage of the missile launch, the B2 picked out by cameras as it dramatically soared over Downtown. Trent had been vague about the nature of the reprisal, and he suspected he knew more than he was admitting, especially about the threat. The excitement during the night had kept him alert and on the ball, aided by a can of Red Bull, but now both effects had quickly left his body, sending him crashing. The window on his Saturn was down, allowing the warm air to slap his face to keep his eyes open. He only cared about getting home to his wife and collapsing into sleep; he was *still* wearing his robe. There was no chance Trent would drag him into the lab tomorrow. His body would simply refuse to cooperate.

Catherine was in the passenger seat, already sound asleep, her head gently tapping against the window with the motion of the car. Her car had a flat tire, and she'd asked for a ride home instead of trying to find a replacement. Walt had no objections, but now he was feeling put out by the extra forty-five minutes it would add to his journey, maybe over an hour if the roads had not been cleared. Perhaps he should have slept in the office like Schofield.

The atmosphere in the lab had been a mix of jubilation and disappointment that the nuke had not detonated. The data from such an explosion would have been invaluable, ensuring their experiments would be funded for the next fifty years – provided they didn't die in the process. Schofield's first thought was that the blast might have damaged the finely calibrated sensors, but diagnostics had shown everything was working just peachy.

Rubber screeched as Walt mashed the brakes, twisting the wheel a half-turn to violently lurch around a traffic light standing in the center of the road. Catherine's head bumped the window, awakening her with a yelp. She looked around, trying to spot the danger, both hands gripping the dashboard to secure herself.

"What is it? What's happening?" She sounded a little too panicky for her own liking.

They had stopped in the middle of a crossroad where the suspended traffic lights had crashed to the ground. Two of the lights still worked, rapidly playing through the sequence. The red and green hues cast eerily on the unwashed fender of Walt's automobile.

He lifted his glasses away from his sore eyes and gently massaged them. "I must have been drifting off. Then I suddenly saw this." He waved towards the traffic lights.

"Where are we? Doesn't look too familiar."

"Good question," replied Walt, replacing his glasses on the bridge of his nose and peering around. "With all the detours around here, I must have been following them on autopilot. There's a rail depot over there."

A chain-linked fence ran parallel to the road ahead. A right turn led through a set of padlocked gates, into the yard itself, which was bathed by a lone security light playing across a small yellow and black striped diesel shunting wagon and an empty flatbed moored on a weed-riddled track.

Walt frowned, "Know any rail depots?"

"Near Wyvernwood. Guess it puts us near the river, which is completely the *wrong* way home. Navigation is not one of your strong points, huh?" She checked her phone. "No signal. Cell towers must be down. Swap. I'll drive."

The brief period of sleep seemed to have miraculously done the same job as a good eight hours in bed. The wound in her leg twinged when she put weight on it, and the bandages itched. Catherine scratched at them, despite many reprimands from her fiancé. She spotted the street sign usually attached to the traffic light had slid towards the sidewalk. She walked towards it. Then stopped.

The metal sign was vibrating on the asphalt.

"Aftershock..." Catherine said, but the words died on her lips when she saw the rolling stock was slowly trundling forward with a drawn-out, rusty squeal. Then there was a sudden bright flash that registered half a second before the diesel locomotive was lifted into the air and a shock wave pounded into Catherine.

She was carried several yards backward, smashing into the windshield of Walt's car just as it imploded.

The wall of sound pounded Walt's ears as if he'd been

punched. He was flipped over the hood of his car. The bulk of the vehicle protected him further as broken glass and debris peppered the intersection.

Dazed, he peered over the hood in time to see the burning diesel locomotive cartwheeling back to earth - crashing onto the flatbed wagon. The impact split the wagon's iron chassis in two, while huge chunks of the locomotive's engine sheared away and demolished the depot's chain-link fence. A whole section of metal fence rendered through the hood of Walt's car – forcing him to duck or be decapitated.

Walt felt something warm race down his leg and prayed he'd pissed himself, rather than being injured and bleeding. Pressed against the floor, he could see under the car. The rail yard beyond was foaming with violent orange flames. He could feel the heat singe the hairs on his arms and face.

"Kate!"

Walt could barely hear himself above the roar of the flames. He scrambled to his feet, daring to poke his head above window height. He winced as his face got a full blast of heat from the inferno, causing his eyes to smart behind his lenses. Catherine still lay on the fragmented windshield. The section of fencing had punctured her body, staining her clothes dull red. A piece of metal had shot clean through her nose, leaving a gaping hole where her pretty face used to be. Glistening flesh scattered around the body.

Walt vomited.

He became aware of movement in the flames. The rail tracks had been blasted in two, the broken sections curling upwards like an unfinished roller coaster, revealing a gaping hole beneath. A Dero clambered from the pit, flaming detritus clanging against its chassis. The four arms shook to dislodge a few pieces of scorched metal, and it stepped half across the boundary fence onto the sidewalk.

Walt had only listened to Trent and Catherine's descriptions and seen the television footage from the stadium, but none of it prepared him for the towering behemoth in front of him. The eight arachnid-like legs created ruts in the sidewalk as it stepped forward. The two razor-sharp drill-bits stabbed at him, while the pair of plasma cannons hung gunfighter-style further back, the orbs still glowing from the intense heat needed to cut through the earth.

Flames reflected from the dull cobalt blue body and torso that reminded Walt of an eight-legged centaur. The hawk-like head scanned the area as another machine followed it out of the tunnel.

The second Dero joined the first. Walt felt every muscle in his body become rigid as they approached.

They moved to either side of Catherine's body. One lowered forward, the front legs splaying like a giraffe, until the head was inches from her. A drill arm edged forward, the whirling bit spinning to a halt. It rolled her body over as though checking for vital signs.

Walt emitted a whimper when he saw the back of Catherine's head. The shrapnel entrance wound had taken out her nose, but the larger exit wound had removed most of the back of her head.

The second Dero's head shot around, detecting the sound from Walt. Both machines reacted with swift, fluid, and nearly silent movements as they circled the automobile from either side.

Walt was trapped between them.

He froze, his heartbeat hammering. "Don't..." was all he could bring himself to say.

One cocked its head inquisitively, then slowly brought one massive plasma arm up to him. Inches away, the swirling glow changed from amber to cherry-red, yet he couldn't feel any heat.

Until it unleashed a brief pulse of energy. It was less than a nanosecond in which Walt discovered what it was like to walk in the heart of the sun.

TWENTY-THREE

"FOUR MORE LOCATIONS," intoned a young female Intelligence Officer with her hair tied in a tight bun. It was already dawn, and the physical toll was already making the staff manning Mobile Command sluggish and irritable. "First in Evergreen Cemetery, a rail yard near Boyle Heights, and another in Lincoln Heights, and the last in MacArthur Park."

General Carver digested the new information as the officer overlaid the locations onto a map that now dominated the primary screen. The four new locations were south of Elysian Park and formed a perimeter around Chinatown and half of Downtown.

"What's the damage assessment?"

"Drones showed the Deros appeared to be patrolling the area. The first sign of heavy artillery sent them back down the shafts."

"Casualties?"

"Twenty-six men and five Abrams. We don't know how many civilians, but there have been reports of mass casualties. It was a massacre."

Carver hung his head. Although a hardened military man who took the loss of his men as part of the job, civilian deaths always weighed heavily on his conscience. He fixed an eye on Trent, silently asking for his assessment.

Trent stroked the bridge of his nose. The night's events had forced his mind to operate at peak performance, especially when Ben Chapman was firmly told to wait at home for any further developments. But in the light of a new day, his stamina was starting to flag like those around him. He found it difficult to focus on the information in front of him. Sometimes the words blurred, and conclusions eluded him like a tantalizing shape in the fog.

"It would be useful if the drones could get some air samples, but my guess is that we'll get some above-average gas readings, which means these are more ventilation shafts."

"But why now? Could it be related to our attack?"

Trent's thumb thoughtfully rubbed the bristles growing on his chin, and his mind jumped to the previous night's near-kiss with Alana. Had it been just a spur-of-the-moment flirtation, he wondered. He wished she was here, but she'd been ordered back to the precinct by her Chief. Now Trent missed her company and silent support.

"I can't see how the missile would require them to ventilate the area, unless there was some kind of radiation leakage. Then you have contamination seeping into the city."

Carver shook his head firmly. "Impossible. The radiation from the warhead dissipates within hours of detonation. And it didn't detonate."

"Without further details about what we're dealing with, it's all speculation." One thought that nagged him was if they were just machines, then why would they require ventilation? The organic elements they'd found in the single

Dero they'd destroyed had given no clues. It could have been some sort of pilot. Equally, Carver's scientific team had hypothesized the possibility it was a *bio-computer*. "Perhaps their excavating process is prone to combustion? There are potentially huge gas deposits underground. In theory, they could be generated during a quake, except we've never had the opportunity to be at an epicenter during a quake."

Frustrated, Trent collapsed into a chair and locked his fingers together. He knew he was in danger of falling asleep if he closed his eyes. Speculating on the nature of the marauding killers was not the job of a seismologist, and for the second time within a minute, he wished Alana was here. This was a detective's work.

Carver loosened his shirt collar and used one hand to rub the iron-hard muscles in his neck. Turning to the Intelligence Officer who watched patiently and expressionlessly, he said, "Let the PD handle the bodies. Get whatever ground-penetrating satellite images we can on each location. I want a complete breakdown, from soil content through to gas emissions. Give the results directly to Professor Trent. I want armed aerial units, airborne units sweeping the city. Every predator drone we have, I want it in the air. There is an Apache unit based at Nellis, rouse that nest."

The Intelligence Officer hurried out of the trailer to pass on the orders. General Carver moved across to a jug of filtered coffee simmering on its heated plate, poured himself a black shot into a cup with the message *As Tough as Shit,* and waved the jug in Trent's direction. "Pick-me-up?"

"Super strong and as black as hell," Trent said as he forced himself to his feet and gratefully took the cup from the General, ignoring the dirty coffee stains already etched into the side of the mug. "I had a thought, but I have no evidence to base it on."

Carver took a mouthful of coffee that instantly sharpened his senses. "Right now, I'll take anything."

Ironic, thought Trent, all throughout his entire career he'd failed to turn up solid evidence for his theories, yet here was a man who had a considerable responsibility on his hands with the lives of millions at stake, and he would take Trent's hunch as gospel.

He sipped the coffee that was just warm enough to be palatable and then knocked the rest back in a single gulp before continuing. "In the desert, during the Excalibur test, I assume you had the whole area wired with sensors?"

"Of course."

"I need the data. You said there is a larger machine that was disturbed, and something with the kind of bulk you suggest would trigger a major tremor. In order to move that kind of bulk, you would need one hell of an excavation device. Do you have pictures of the Deros?"

"Right here." Carver slid his laptop over and called up several photographs of the machines in the stadium.

Trent studied the images. He pointed to the machine's arms. "These two smaller arms are capped with these drills, which seem to act like a standard bore. But they're not suitable for rapid burrowing through rock. The other set of arms is larger, so presumably heavier load-bearers for these plasma heat-rays. It is safe to assume these cutters literally vaporize the rock, at the very least, at a walking pace. The cauterized tunnels I saw at the Metro Station prove that. The logical assumption would be that their arms are used primarily for burrowing and not as weapons."

Carver was thoughtful. "You're trying to convince me that these are not attack vehicles."

"They're dangerous, absolutely. But when they surface, they don't migrate far from the tunnels. If they're vaporizing rock, then it is safe to assume there are some pretty noxious gases being released."

"Hence the need for ventilation shafts," said Carver as he nodded. "They must be carving out a warren down there."

"Perhaps, but there is something..." Trent trailed off as his gaze switched from the screen to the table map. "I need the data from the Excalibur tests. I know you're willing to back a hunch, but for once in my life, I think I should get some facts to back me up."

"I'll have the results emailed across."

"Not here, at my lab. I need my team to help me with this."

Carver gave a curt nod. "Time is fast running out. I must consider our next move. With or without solid facts."

* * *

A BASS HUM pounded Alana's ears, forcing her to massage her temples against the growing headache. She'd felt confined like an animal when she returned to the precinct and found the entire place in disarray. The last tremor had thrown even more paperwork onto the ground, and the antique computer network had been down for over a day. If that wasn't bad enough, broad sections of air-conditioning ducts had snapped their mounts and crashed through the ceiling tiles. The few that survived now rattled with a hum that set nerves on edge and cascaded tides of plaster dust from between cracks in the ceiling.

The entire downtown area had been operating with a skeleton crew, as most units had been assigned to evacuate and patrol Elysium Park. The military presence increased by the hour, and more armored units rolled through Glendora on their way to contain the newly emerged machines.

Alana had found herself tasked with identifying victims of Dero attacks, which currently extended to her identifying who was missing from the Stadium. Calls had been coming in all day and night on the few lines that were functional.

Fatigue had hampered her decision-making ability. After a two-hour nap at her desk, she now felt invigorated, and instructed a team of four officers to trawl through gruesome television footage of the game and its subsequent massacre from multiple camera angles and try to identify victims using facial recognition; retrieving the bodies was not an option just yet.

Reports of machines surfacing elsewhere threw in additional curveballs to an already impossible task. Alana had received information on these from the military operation, which, Bixby had reminded her, was running the show. But the incidents away from the Stadium offered her the rare opportunity to slip from the office and investigate the victims on site.

Such a gruesome and mundane duty was something she'd always actively avoided. Aside from not being career fuel, she found it to soul-crushing. Alana had always strived to make a difference, not to be resigned to picking up the pieces. Returning to the station and Ed's empty desk, still covered by his untouched personal trinkets that now lay under a fine veil of plaster dust, had brought home the loss she'd kept from the forefront of her mind.

The first site was in Evergreen Cemetery, but Alana did

not relish the thought of that investigation and pondered how many bodies had died *before* the machine made an appearance. Instead, she began her examinations in Lincoln Heights. The lone drive had further compounded her growing sense of isolation. Most radio stations were off the air or playing constant news updates, so she made the journey in silence. It took almost an hour to reach a high school a few blocks from the City View Hospital where the bodies had been moved.

A military cordon surrounded the school, and Alana flashed her ID to pass beyond the APC blocking the road. The soldier in charge of the site had told her the Dero had punctured its way through the playground - and immediately launched an attack on a gang of eleven teenagers who were idling around the jungle gym. Residents had heard the commotion that lasted for only forty seconds, before the machine had returned down the shaft.

A forensic team was taking samples of the area while they nervously eyed the gaping hole in the playground. A pair of olive-colored LAV-25 light armored vehicles kept their M242 Bushmaster chain guns trained on the area, while with 20 heavily armed soldiers surrounded the abyss, fingers balanced on the triggers of their powerful M27 assault rifles.

As she joined the team, Alana speculated on what the youths were doing at the school at such an early hour. Discarded needles visible among the twisted metal debris were testament to the drug problem that plagued the city.

The edge of the hole was cauterized like the tunnels at the Metro, beveling outwards as molten earth was pushed from below. Twelve feet away, the colorfully painted jungle gym was charred and bent into a grotesque sculpture.

Alana reached the edge of the pit, noticing the young soldiers were all keeping a healthy distance back. Her boot caught loose stones that dropped silently down the fissure – and she saw the soldiers wince. Not that she expected the Dero to pop out like a jack in the box. A drone was vigilantly circling the area, primed for any sign of movement from below. As far as its camera could tell, there was no sign of the enemy.

She knelt and traced a hand over the cool melted rock. It brought memories racing back of Ed's contorted face as he ran with every ounce of strength from the pursuing giant. She closed her eyes to block the vision from her mind. But that only gave her a blank canvas on which to paint his last moments, as he scrambled on all fours, boots slipping on the smooth floor - before losing all traction and sliding under the killing machine as the slender drill arm snapped out to spear his body. Alana's mind's eye focused on the agony creasing Ed's face as blood dribbled from his mouth.

"Watch your step, ma'am." Alana's eyes flickered open to see a soldier had moved closer to her. His weather-beaten brow deepened when she did not move. "Ma'am, I said careful on the edge."

Alana nodded dumbly, looking back down the pit, which descended into utter blackness. "Have you got a light?"

"Ma'am?"

"A flashlight? Or better still, a signal flare?"

The soldier didn't look as though he'd understood the question, then reached for his belt and passed a red flare to her.

She examined the stick with a quick thank you; then twisted the end. Holding it at arm's length as a bright red flame erupted from the tip. She could feel the sudden intense heat against her face before she dropped the flare down the hole.

The soldier craned over to watch with her as the flame tumbled end-over-end into the darkness, almost vertically, before hitting a sharp curve in the tunnel far below where it skittered out of sight.

A long moment passed with both Alana and the soldier staring into the dark void. The red after-image of the flare danced on their retinas. Alana found she'd held her breath, waiting for a terrible penance for dropping the flare. But nothing happened.

"Deep mother," muttered the soldier as he returned for a cigarette with his buddies. Alana silently returned to her car, face unreadable.

Most of the youths' bodies were charred beyond recognition, and the pathologists told Alana they were still checking dental records. Two of the victims carried wallets that had fused to their clothes.

In a hospital side room, Alana donned latex gloves and manipulated a scalpel to prize them apart. One contained the driving license of an eighteen-year-old Caucasian guy. Alana passed it to a uniformed officer to notify the family. The second wallet contained no identification other than two gold Visa cards bearing different names: obviously stolen. Alana tossed it into an evidence tray and informed the pathologists to call her as soon as they had positive IDs.

The day was becoming uncomfortably warm by the time Alana arrived at the second site. It was a rail yard just north of the river.

The rail yard itself was still ablaze, as tanks full of fuel had subsequently ignited after the initial attack. Watched over by a phalanx of military, the fire department valiantly held back the flames before they had the chance to spread.

The ventilation hole had come up under a track that was broken in half. It took Alana several moments to visually untangle the wreckage of the locomotive from the flatbed wagon.

She brought her attention back to the automobile in the center of the crossroads outside the rail yard. The rear of the car had melted in a pool of metal, leaving only the front half. The CSI team swarmed around the first body pinned to the hood, eager to complete their task and get the hell out of there.

Alana steeled herself against the rank smell of burning flesh as she examined the victim. It was a woman, although most of her flesh had been seared. Fragments of metal and gravel riddled the car and the body.

A forensic woman approached Alana. She pulled off her face mask and scalp cap to reveal a shock of well-groomed blond hair.

"What a mess," she commented almost casually. "We can run a trace on the car once we can access the engine. But the guys retrieved ID from the victim." She handed Alana a sealed, transparent bag containing a rectangular brown leather purse with Aztec markings cut into it. The work ID had already been extracted and was intact. Alana saw the WCEC logo on the ID before she recognized the face, and her heart sank.

TWENTY-FOUR

THE THUNDEROUS SOUND of rotors had caused Schofield to roll off the table that doubled as his bed. He ducked under the Formica surface, anticipating another quake was about to strike. He was relieved when, through the window, he saw Trent stepping out of a Blackhawk chopper that had landed in the parking lot.

As they attempted to contact Catherine and Walter, Trent had briefed him on the situation, this time without omitting the historical first encounter with the Deros and Carver's grim threats about National Security.

Schofield eagerly downloaded the Excalibur files and felt a thrill of excitement when a *Top-Secret* warning flashed on the screen. Now he felt as if he was finally a member of the inner sanctum.

Trent hung up on his call. "Catherine's fiancé said she didn't come home last night. Neither did Walt."

Schofield wasn't really paying attention. "The swine, I didn't know he had it in him."

"They're not answering their cell phones, either."

Schofield didn't take his eyes off the screen. "You think they've eloped?"

"I don't think Walt's her type." Trent anxiously tried both their numbers again. "Straight to voicemail."

Schofield searched through the folders of data on Excalibur. "Gas emissions... whoever filed this was an idiot. Geological... ah..." He opened another folder and was greeted by a dozen more sub-folder. "Environmental..."

Trent considered calling Alana but registering them as missing persons seemed not only premature but also a desperate attempt to speak to her. He resisted trying to call the others again.

"Anything raising a flag for you?"

"Yeah, I think so. I think it happened ten seconds after the explosion." Schofield circled the mouse pointer over a color-coded timeline. "High quantities of gases not usually associated with subterranean nuking. A sixty percent raise in methane output and," his face buckled with surprise, "weird, there's super-high levels of sodium monoxide in here too."

Trent marveled at Schofield's skill in interpreting the data. "So, what would your conclusions be from this?"

A satisfied grin fell to muddled confusion in one movement. Schofield gently shook his head as he fumbled for a meaningful connection. "My only conclusion is that it's weird shit and Kate'll be able to tell you something more concrete."

Damn, thought Trent. He redialed Catherine's number and again hit her voicemail. "Does any of that correlate with emissions from any of the ventilation shafts?"

"I have the Stadium results here, and some came through from Lincoln Heights a couple of minutes ago."

"Let's see them." Trent's hopes raised when the outside

lab door loudly slammed closed. They both expected Catherine and Walt to walk in. Alana entered, looking tired and frail. The smile forming on Trent's lips didn't make it to fruition when he met her eyes.

"You look like you're going to collapse. Sit down. Schofield, get some coffee over here."

Alana accepted his guidance to a seat. As Schofield moved for the coffee, the office phone rang, and he scooped it up.

Trent gently combed Alana's hair from her eyes. "Have you slept?"

She shook her head. "Listen, Trent, I have some bad news."

Trent's expression remained neutral, but his imagination performed a ballet.

"Trent, it's General Carver's aide on the line. They need answers, fast."

Trent waved dismissively at Schofield, but he didn't reply. He noticed Alana's eyes for the first time, how green they were, shimmering like jade. Funny, he thought, last night he could have sworn they were deep brown. He forced joviality into the situation. "I hope you're not going to tell me the poor Mayor is dead?"

Alana registered surprise. "How did you know? They found him this morning with his brains blown out. Suicide."

Trent felt a brief feeling of guilt but assured himself it was only momentary.

Alana continued. "But that's not why I came. We found this at the scene of a Dero attack at a rail depot." She pulled a plastic bag containing Catherine's purse from her pocket. When Trent did not move to take it, she laid it on the workbench. "It belongs to Catherine Sanchez. On the way here, I heard they identified the car as belonging to Walt."

Trent reeled from the news like she'd struck him a physical blow. He felt himself falling backward. His hand groped for a chair and pulled it under him. Schofield cradled the phone to his chest, partly to muffle their voices from the aide on the other end, partly to feel something physical. "They're dead?"

Alana couldn't meet his gaze. She nodded somberly.

"A Dero killed them?"

"Two of them breached the surface. Just for a few minutes. They were just in the wrong place..."

Trent nodded solemnly, but tears worked through his eyes and down his cheeks. Now he wanted to. He could not bring a single image of Kate or Walt to mind. He felt Alana's hand squeeze his. Then he fell into a comforting hug as his face pushed against her shoulder, and he caught the scent of something warm, soft, and soothing.

Schofield's suddenly harsh business voice cut through his senses. "Trent, the General says they're planning to go in."

* * *

THIRTY-THREE MINUTES, and not one second of peace. Trent's stomach lurched as the military chopper made a swift banking descent into the park. Schofield had pleaded to come, but Trent insisted he stay at the lab and monitor any seismic activity, any slight movement that could signal a serious change in plans. Schofield sulked like a schoolkid at being left behind, despite the importance of the task.

Alana sat next to him, seeming more at ease with the chopper's violent motion. She had insisted on coming along with him. If the military were planning to send a team down, then her and Trent's firsthand knowledge was unrivaled. Trent was just happy to have her by his side.

He'd been theorizing about what significance the increased gas emissions had on the situation at hand, especially the high levels of sodium monoxide, which was way out of place in Los Angeles. Trent shared an idea with both Alana and Schofield. Their initial reaction was naturally skeptical, but they had to admit there was a plausibility to the idea.

Trent hadn't had a moment to grieve for the loss of his two friends. His first instinct was to call Catherine's fiancé, but Alana had assured him uniformed officers were more adept at delivering bad news. She made the call to the precinct to make sure a bereavement counselor was sent to Walt's family as soon as a positive ID had been made through dental records. Trent forced their loss from his mind as other matters overwhelmed him.

General Carver had instructed Trent to return. He'd received orders made by the only other person above him in the food chain - an Executive Order to destroy the Deros immediately. That meant sending a team down to deal with the rats, and everybody's memory was fresh with the SWAT team's slaughter.

The chopper's door was drawn open by a ground crewman. The downdraft from the rotors buffeted Trent as he was helped, his laptop clutched tightly to his chest. He swept his gaze across the operation camp before helping Alana climb down. The crewman motioned them to follow him across the field to the now-familiar set of trailers, his voice lost in the helicopter's roar.

Inside, General Carver and the usual assembly of lower

ranks were gathered around, armed with tablets and laptops displaying maps and videos of the ventilation tunnels. Trent noticed Carver had even had time to change into a fresh uniform and felt self-conscious in the clothes he'd worn for the last few days without so much as a cold shower.

Carver glanced at them, and with no preamble, launched into his speech. "Most of you know Detective Williams and Professor Trent." He seemed to be addressing two power-suited people standing prominently at the head of the table. A strong-jawed man with flecks of gray hair and thick eyebrows that made his face look predatory. A tweed-suited woman stood at his side. Her hair was held in a tight bun, and her face covered in makeup carefully applied to heighten her angular features. "If we have any authority on the Deros, then these two are it. They have been down the tunnels and have faced the machines, which is more than anybody else in this operation can claim."

The suits walked around the table and shook both their hands firmly. There was something about the man that seemed familiar to Alana.

"It's a pleasure to meet you both. Your role here is immeasurable." He curtly turned back to Carver. "Now that everybody is here, the President requires a plan that we can implement immediately. Something he's going to feel confident about telling the Nation. I don't want to remind you about the political stakes here."

Alana glanced at Trent and rolled her eyes. More political interference.

The suit continued, "The entire world is watching. So further mistakes are not an option. We've already had to spin any comments about the missile you sent down being nuclear. If it got out that we have lost an unexploded warhead underneath Los Angeles, then those machines will very much be a secondary problem to deal with. That warhead must be retrieved, and the machines stopped. Other nations have offered their aid, but that would just look like we can't handle affairs in our own backyard. So please, give me something to work with."

Carver cleared his throat. "Before we discuss the military options, Mr Spontain, I believe Professor Trent has some important news for us."

Spontain, of course, thought Alana. Doug Spontain was the new Secretary of Homeland Security. Suddenly Alana felt, more than ever, that her career was riding on the outcome of the next few hours. Trent didn't react to Spontain's presence. Maybe he didn't recognize him, or maybe he was beyond caring.

Trent put his laptop on the desk and opened it, turning the screen so they could all see. "It's not so much news as speculation, although I have some evidence. I will be the first to admit the idea is a little... unusual."

Spontain's eyebrows arched, but he didn't comment. Trent pulled up several graphs with chemical elements along the x-axis and units running up. A jagged line peaked and troughed along the graph, and Spontain made a pretense of studying it. Trent was sure the man didn't understand a single pixel. Eventually, Spontain admitted as much.

"What exactly am I looking at here?"

Alana suppressed a smile and coughed gently into her hand.

Trent pointed to the wavey line. "This is the analysis of emissions from the Excalibur's desert tests and those from the ventilation tunnels right here in LA. Geographically, both regions have different rock and soil composition, but the same gas emissions. Gases which shouldn't be there naturally but have been detected in both instances."

Spontain rubbed his chin, nodding. His aide whispered something in his ear, prompting him to speak. "So, the connection is the Deros?"

"I wasn't thinking of the machines directly. These readings are high, more than I would estimate even a couple of hundred of those machines could emit. I was thinking of their base, the mother ship that the military's sensors picked up. That was the craft that settled under our feet and caused the first tremor."

"So, these gases come from the main craft?"

Trent collected his thoughts. "Yes. Specifically, I think these gases come from the *drive* of the main craft." Blank looks all around, so he continued. "You know, the engine? Melting the rock in front of you is one thing, but *something* has to propel the craft forward." He tapped the laptop's screen again. "These gases are not caused by the rock melting; it *must* be something else. Therefore, by deduction, it must be the main drive. And according to this data, it is a *colossal* machine."

Murmurs circulated the room. Carver's brow furrowed, and he glanced at the Spontain, who was lost for words, Carver spoke the question.

"What kind of power source would release those gases? Nuclear?"

Trent shrugged. "I don't have enough data to speculate about that. Judging by what I've seen, I bet it's not technology we're familiar with." He held up a finger in warning. "Remember, this is an educated guess, but it is the only thing that seems to fit. No radiation traces have been detected above background norms, so perhaps it is some kind of chemical source? The Deros might mine the elements needed to power it."

"An interesting speculation, Professor," said Spontain. "And I'm sure useful from a scientific standpoint. Of course, it is a relief that the thing isn't nuclear powered, but I can't see how that nugget will affect our decision." He stared levelly at Trent as though daring him to comment.

Trent felt a tide of anger rush through him. Darn it, this was just like dueling with Shearer. Maybe all politicians went to jerk school? Spontain opened his mouth to address the Generals, but Trent beat him to it.

"You obviously haven't made the connection. The desert reading was taken just before the craft surfaced. They were not present in the Metro when we first investigated, but now they are, and the Deros seem intent on excavating holes to ventilate it. Ask yourself why."

Spontain drew himself up to his full six-foot-three height and stared down at Trent, obviously not used to being so flagrantly interrupted, and Trent knew he'd irked the man. He never had much truck with politicians.

"Why don't I ask you, Professor Trent?"

"The craft is powering up. It's getting ready to move again."

For a moment, the news didn't sink in.

Then the trailer was full of raised voices vying for attention. Carver's rose above them all, pleading for calm once again, but with little luck until he slammed a palm on the desk.

"ENOUGH!"

Trent glanced at Alana, who indicated with a flick of her eyes to Spontain. He was grinning widely, rubbing his hands together. When the room became calm again, he spoke.

"Now I understand, that is excellent news."

Trent was taken aback. "Excellent?"

"If you're correct, then we can assume it's getting the hell out of here. It is no longer our problem."

"You can't be serious? They may go to another country and ravage that."

"And the United States Government will be more than happy to lend any aid it can–"

"Or," interrupted Trent vehemently, "it could move further inland, which means crossing the San Andreas to the west or triggering fault activity north or south. Remember, the last tremor was the ship repositioning northward. We're talking at least another seven-pointer, *minimum*. I'd say that'd climb to nine, in a city that's already on its knees. The damn nuke might well have exploded anyway, because if that thing moves again, then it really will be the end."

TWENTY-FIVE

MAJOR JOSEPH ADAMS had been roused from his bed by urgent tones on the telephone. At first, he'd thought he was back in the barracks, until the comforting hand of his wife gently massaging his back assured him that he was still at home. But they both knew a call during leave meant a serious matter to attend to.

Joseph hadn't been told where he was going, only that his unit was being assembled at Fort Meade for essential duty. He pushed a strand of loose blonde hair from his wife's deep blue eyes and gently kissed her. Business, he said. That was enough. Used to the cloak-and-dagger lifestyle, she forced a smile and wrapped herself in a flannel robe to help him pack his kit bag.

He woke his two sleeping daughters with a gentle kiss. He'd long learned that they wanted to know when he was going, rather than have him slip out of the door for weeks on end. The last sight of his wife in his Mustang's rearview mirror, as she waved from the door of their new home, strengthened his resolve to quit Special Ops, particularly his very specialist niche in Majestic Ops. He loved the job, and God knows he'd seen some seriously weird shit. However, every time he was called out, he vowed it would be his last. But this time, the thought rang true as he pulled away.

Fort Meade was busier than ever as the country was placed on a war-footing. Everything might have been happening in LA, but that didn't stop the rest of the country from worrying that the ground was about to open under their feet.

Joseph was ushered into a briefing room where two members of his crew had already arrived, and they sat waiting for the remaining five. General White, kitted in his field combats, connected a laptop to a data projector. He seemed to have some difficulty getting the display on the screen.

Lieutenant Blake, a wily, eager-to-please, and indispensable member of the team, toggled through the projector's control commands until a cheesy-looking PowerPoint display appeared. Joseph smiled to himself. You could always judge how long an operation had been in planning by the poor quality of graphics used in the brief. And right now, he was generously estimating a whole ten minutes of planning.

Lieutenant Douglas - with his trademark thick mustache clinging to his lip like a rare caterpillar - mumbled a few words of greeting but seemed immersed in the battered novel held in one huge hand, the page bent so far back that the cover was obscured, and the spine cracked. He met Joseph's inquiring look and gave him a flash of the cover, Homer's *Odyssey*.

Three more members of the team arrived with news that the other remaining two members of the team were currently *en route* to the target area from Las Vegas and

Cancun, Mexico, respectively, and would be briefed on the flight.

It took thirty-three minutes to be briefed, and when the team filed out of the room, they were all unusually sober. They had faced unusual situations before; hiking through Venezuela jungles to retrieve crashed *aircraft* of dubious origin before enemy units located them, or tracking down fringe terrorists who had far more exotic beliefs than merely which god should be worshipped. The team never spoke about their duties outside the strong bond between the eight of them; besides, nobody would believe them. Now they were facing danger again in a situation that resided beyond the realms of normality, and this time it carried with it a very clear and present danger.

Somehow, that was worse than the unknown.

As they filed onto a waiting private Gulfstream jet, it was Blake who spoke first with his mid-western drawl.

"This is a little closer to Hell than I would have liked to have gotten, sire."

Blake often swapped the formal tag of "sir" for "sire" as a nod to Joseph's rank, but even his joviality seemed forced today.

Joseph nodded and took a last look around the base as he climbed the steps into the jet. For a moment, he wished his wife was in his arms to see him off, but then thought she would spend the following nights unable to sleep if she saw the look that now haunted his eyes.

* * *

ON THEIR APPROACH to Burbank Airport, Joseph had

been surprised that the quake damage was been so vivid. On closer inspection, he was appalled.

Sections of freeways had toppled; buildings were sucked into the ground, forming a bizarre Escher landscape. The most notable was the trench leading into the city like a cancerous scar. A *graben,* he remembered from his technical brief, caused as the earth beneath the city sunk. Christ knows how they would patch that mess up. On the streets and freeways that had been cleared, long columns of traffic stood in a gridlock so dense it would take a decent quantum mathematician several days to untangle it. Burbank Airport itself seemed structurally sound, despite the blackened fuselage of an aircraft that had crashed on landing.

They had traveled in silence, doing what soldiers do: snatching sleep at every available opportunity as if it would be their last. A Blackhawk was waiting to transfer them to the Stadium, and Blake seemed uncharacteristically rattled by the sight of an Apache Gunship escorting them in. They all remembered the footage of the Dero's heat weapon plucking the airship and choppers from over the Stadium. Who knew if they'd be next? At least on the ground, they'd have a fighting chance of survival.

The flight was over in moments as the dark shape of Dodger Stadium loomed into view, with its walls now blackened from fires. The chopper set down on the edge of the park, amongst a network of military green trailers and support vehicles.

Even from the window, Joseph could make out the grinning Lieutenant Mitchell standing with his arms crossed over his barrel-chest. Snatching him from Las Vegas had been a blessing that had saved him from his losing streak, which was becoming his normal vacation pastime.

Joseph already had the door open before the chopper landed with a solid thump. He ran out, punching Mitchell on the shoulder like bears playing. Lieutenant Ryder was the last of the team to arrive, not too happy about ending his sun-kissed vacation in Puerto Vallarta.

They were all escorted to a narrow trailer and briefed on the Excalibur missile and the warhead it carried. Mitchell was the explosives guru, even though they were all cross-trained to minimize mission failure should one of them be killed. But even Mitchell didn't relish the prospect of disarming a nuke.

Further maps were presented to help guide them to the heart of the beast, the massive mother ship itself. What perils they would face inside - if there were some other intelligence controlling the Deros - and the geography of the craft itself were all classified as *unknowns*.

The real tombstone had been the news that they'd be carrying *new technologies* to complete the mission.

They'd often been called upon in situations to drop into enemy territory and test-drive new weapons; - from railguns to *exotic particles* - but those were always quick in-and-out missions - Afghanistan, Iraq, and the like - with heavy support from standard military units. To go into uncharted hostile territory, with a bunch of tech that was, for all intents and purposes, untested, was crazy.

The room was silent after the briefing. The lack of usual ribaldry was a sign of the uncertainty ahead. Lieutenant Douglas nervously toyed with a button on his fatigues and studied the rest of the crew. All were somber, except Lieutenant Rodgers. The youngest on the team; with a forehead that, rather than recede, was *ascending* down his head. The general consensus was that his hairline would merge with his eyebrows by the time he was forty. Rodgers glanced around the room with a sparkle in his eyes and a wry comment on his lips, although he knew better than to mouth off when he saw his colleagues' grim expressions.

Joseph was well aware of the macho image the Special Forces portrayed in Hollywood movies. Every one of them had dined out with a hot date on exactly that. But the reality was very different. Special Forces training had been a living nightmare for all involved. It was some of the toughest training in the world, and Joseph felt sympathy for any gung-ho kid who thought they could dance through that shit storm. But that was the point, to be prepared for anything, anywhere. A kick-ass boy scout.

"Questions?"

Mitchell raised a hand as if he was still in school, but talked immediately before Joseph could give him a nod. "I'm a little uncomfortable going all that way, to use explosive material I've never played with."

"I questioned this with the General, and they rallied back with the fact we have been ordered to use *anything* in Uncle Sam's armory, and some bright honcho decided the Beluga would serve that purpose."

No one had heard of Beluga until the briefing, when they had seen stills of the device. It lived up to its name, taken from the beleaguered whale, referring to the size of the bomb. Some seven-foot long and wider than a man, it had to travel on its own set of caterpillar tracks and used AI to follow whoever was controlling it.

Lieutenant Mitchell had blanched during both briefings, all dreams of a good old sack of C-4 obliterated. Beluga had a non-nuclear yield, but just as powerful a punch. Once primed, they had thirty minutes to get out of blast range before the quantum bomb *imploded*. The technical specifications had been a little over-the-top, but the gist was, once primed, the core of the bomb would become super-dense, causing it to crush in on itself. The immediate vacuum would generate such jarring force it would take out everything else within half a mile.

Mitchell wasn't pleased with Joseph's answer, so Joseph added. "They've assured me that it's push-and-go tech. So simple, Lieutenant Rodgers here could manage not to screw it up."

Rodgers flipped him off as the others sniggered, raising the atmosphere in the trailer a little. Mitchell still wasn't happy, but didn't push it. It was out of his hands.

"We will carry some serious firepower of our own. We're taking FN-SCARS with uranium-tipped ammunition, which should penetrate the Dero's hides. We will be allowed flash and smoke grenades but no standard explosives. In addition, we will have a whole new toy to play with, and I hand that over to Richards. Congratulations, you're our point-man."

Lieutenant Richards' lean face registered curiosity. He'd been the last to join the team after they lost a man during an accident on a clandestine jaunt through Indonesia. Richards soon established himself as a precious part of the group, despite Blake holding a grudge because he was replacing a friend. He was gifted at implementing new technology, but this was the first time Joseph had entrusted him with something so important as point duty. In all essence, he would lead them down - or at least take the first steps.

Joseph unveiled a piece of kit from under a heavy tarpaulin. It was a rifle, at least in first appearance. It was an extra half-length and slightly bulkier than an M27, and the barrel section seemed to pivot away a full ninety degrees from the stock on a complex gimbal arrangement. Five lens-like tubes surrounded the barrel itself, with sheathed wires running from the back of them, into the gun's stock. The stock was heavily padded, with a harness that crossed over the shoulders and chest.

To further add to the unconventional appearance, the wires running along the weapon met and twisted like an umbilical cord, running into a set of VR goggles.

Richards rose from his seat and ran an admiring hand along the weapon before picking it up to feel the weight. It was surprisingly light.

"This baby is the latest generation of around-the-corner firepower – the Panoramic Servo-Assisted rifle, model thirteen, PSA-13 for all you acronym freaks. Servo-adjustable barrel with nightscopes, thermal imaging, laser rangefinders, and live video feed including optical zoom targeting."

The team gave an assortment of low appreciative whistles at the specifications. Richards looped his arm around the shoulder harness and bore the weight of the weapon. Joseph helped him tighten the harness, securing it with carbon fiber buckles. He then picked up the visor and spread the strap with the outstretched fingers of one hand.

"The HUD is projected on a light-enhancing visor." He placed the visor over Richards' face. "Just power her up with the toggle."

Richards' thumb found the small joystick mounted obliquely from the stock. The slight pressure activated the weapon with the faintest of hums. Joseph was amused as Richards' voice rose excitedly as he looked around the room.

"Night vision?"

"Yep, but better than active illumination. It's almost day for night. Move your thumb."

"Now my Head-Up Display is active. I see ammunition status, wind speed and a set of what look like elevation controls." The excitement never lost his voice as his thumb made a gentle circle with the joystick. Immediately, the barrel of the gun rotated in a gentle upward arc. "Wild. This thing can even shoot up?"

"Full on-hundred-eighty-degree arc along the horizontal with a fifty-degree vertical. Have you got the sight up?"

"Roger. A smaller window just in front of me. It's got... a zoom."

"Four times twenty-four magnification," Joseph recalled the technical specs he'd digested. "There should be on-screen options on the right-hand side."

"I see them," Richards said as he swung the weapon towards his fellow teammates. They all could see it was unloaded, but they instinctively dodged aside. "Thermal. Neat."

"You have two hours to get used to it. Have a blast."

There was a genuine buzz when it came to fielding new equipment, and it was partly that thrill which set Joseph's Special Ops Unit out of the usual loop. Keeping the buzz was important. It took the edge off the fact it hadn't actually been tested operationally.

The hardware was cleared before the final briefing. He introduced Trent and Alana, then waited patiently as the professor fumbled setting up his laptop presentation. Joseph was surprised that the man was a professor with his stubble-clad chin and youthful appearance. He'd been expecting a gray-haired geek. Beyond that, there was nothing physically remarkable about him, yet he'd somehow survived a close encounter with a Dero.

He was accompanied by Alana, who didn't look like any

cop he'd met before. The dark circles under her eyes betrayed the lack of sleep, and she wore a no-nonsense frown. Again, whatever hidden qualities she possessed must be remarkable to survive facing a Dero.

Trent turned to the team and took a moment to find his words. "You must excuse me. I'm used to either talking to a room full of geeks or soulless politicians. I've been told you're fully briefed. But I think you should know whatever they've told you is mostly based on guesswork."

Joseph nodded and took a seat with the rest of his team. "Sounds about right."

Trent nervously cleared his throat, casting a quick glance at the Detective. Joseph sensed there was something there; a connection, or just resignation about what they had been through?

"I'm here to give you the science behind it all, so you may find some of this repetitive and probably very dull, but it might save your lives. We have just come back from an analysis of the craft they disturbed under the Mojave. Nobody has seen it. All we have to go on are seismic readings and some ground-penetrating radar stations. However, we now estimate the craft right under our feet – the one you are going to destroy – is approximately one and a half miles long."

The team exchanged surprised looks but remained silent as Trent continued.

"It's capable of gliding through the earth just like a submarine through water at speeds of up to eighty miles an hour. We don't know exactly what process drives it, but I guess it is the same method employed by the Deros, which I will explain more about in a moment."

Trent took a mouthful of water from a bottle, and

glanced at his audience, all rapt with attention. They were being sent to hell, and he was giving them directions.

"There is reason to believe the mother ship's engine emits gasses not common in its environment. We detected these just prior to its sudden movement in the desert, and we're picking up traces now. We think that means there is a possibility it's gearing up to move again."

Joseph glanced at the reaction of his men. This was news to them, and, obviously from the professor's look, he was surprised they didn't know.

Rogers spoke up first. "Moving where?"

"Obviously your brief was just that: *brief*. The arrival of the craft, plowing through hundreds, perhaps thousands of fault lines, under LA triggered the initial quake and subsequent tremors. The last tremor was caused by the craft repositioning towards the San Andreas."

He flicked through the chart showing a simple drawing of California state with red crisscrossed lines representing faults.

"Right now, the ground is settling after the initial quake. Stresses between rocks will slowly build again, and new fissures will already have formed. If that ship powers up and moves out, it will trigger another series of shocks. This town won't survive that, and neither will you. If there is a tremor while you are underground, passages can collapse. If you're lucky enough to avoid being crushed, then you may find your only exit route has been blocked. There is zero chance a rescue team could drill miles down, on the off chance of finding you alive."

Joseph always hated it when somebody tried to strike fear into his men. They knew the risks, now they needed the facts. They didn't need somebody else's imagination filling in the blanks. However, he could see Trent's comments came from a place of concern.

"You have been told about the Beluga you will be taking down there, and the only thing I can add to that is that when you arm it, get the hell out of there as fast as possible. Do not stop. The aftershock alone could bring the entire system down on your heads."

"Excuse me, sir," Blake raised his hand, a look of extreme trepidation on his face. Trent gave him a nod to continue. "Is there an alternative method?"

"They weighed up the alternatives. C4 might not put a dent in the mother ship, and an outward-blasting nuclear payload would trigger a devastating series of quakes. As much as I hate it, this new super-dense bomb is our best, in fact, *only* option."

Lieutenant Douglas' hand reluctantly snaked halfway up. "What is our survival rate on this sojourn?"

Joseph felt Trent's eyes turn to him, as if seeking confirmation to continue. Joseph gave a curt nod. His men deserved the truth, no matter how slim the odds.

Trent's Adam's apple bobbed furiously as he studied the men. "If you have a clear line out, and can move fast enough, with no Deros in your path, then I'd estimate about sixty-five percent."

Silence prevailed in the room as the gravity of the situation took effect.

Lieutenant Mitchell broke the silence with a sickly grin. "Hell, I was always told that there was a fifty percent chance of being killed by anything. Either I will or I won't. I guess these are better odds."

Ryder turned to him, slapping his own forehead to indicate how dumb Mitchell was. "Are you kidding? That's why you always lose in Vegas. You don't understand odds!" Tension snapped as laughter flowed through the room. Mitchell gave a heavy Dutch rub across Ryder's cropped hair, almost forcing his head to his knees.

"You're one crazy sonofabitch!"

The team broke into riotous laughter like bulldogs roaring. A smile formed at the corner of Joseph's mouth, but didn't make it to his eyes when he saw the pitying expressions crossed between Trent and Alana. They obviously didn't understand that laughter was the best weapon against fear. Joseph knew he would laugh heartily all the way down.

TWENTY-SIX

TRENT HAD FURTHER BRIEFED the team on the Deros' abilities, and that had done little more than seed a further cloud of doubt about the operation. Official estimates stated there were approximately ten machines lurking below. Estimates that Trent thought were dubious at best.

No matter how slim the intel, there was no stopping Joseph's team from starting their descent. From the mobile command unit, Trent watched as two Apache Gunships flanked the single Dero guarding the stadium. Both choppers had spat a volley of Hellfire missiles. The Dero had turned with a violent twitch, the plasma-arms discharging a split-second before it was decimated across the scarred baseball diamond. The heat blast scorched one Apache, which combusted into a fiery hulk as it crashed onto the bleachers.

Trent had watched it all from the mobile command unit. Carver and the assembled top brass had no time to lament as Joseph's Special Ops squadron deployed from the back of an APC. Storming the stadium and taking up positions around the tunnel in a minute flat.

Radio communication had been slick and thin as the team zip-lined down the hundred-foot vertical shaft before the passage curved level. A Huey had then flown in low, lowering the Beluga package down the tunnel.

The atmosphere in the command room was thick with tension. Spontain wore a permanent scowl since, moments before he was due to set foot aboard his jet, destined for the distant safety of the Capitol, the President had instructed him to oversee the operation in person: a task that Spontain was *happy* to do.

Alana had been sent back to her precinct, depriving Trent not only of an ally but of a critical expert. Even Carver spoke up for her, but Spontain didn't care. She wasn't military; she wasn't security cleared. In his eyes, she was superfluous. Within minutes, Carver's authority had been effortlessly superseded, and Trent silently positioned as chief scientific pecker, and the first to take the fall when things went wrong. For a fleeting moment, Trent wished Shearer was still alive so he could kick up a stink, which would conceivably get Trent out of the mire he now found himself in.

Now all he could do was sit back and watch as the computer generated a three-dimensional map of the tunnel complex as the team's LIDAR sensors picked up every twist and change in elevation.

The mission clock continued to tick up. Not a single word was exchanged in the room or with the team. Trent sensed the atmosphere in the room was as thick, and potentially poisonous, as the one beneath his feet.

* * *

A SMALL WHINE of servomotors turned the gun barrel a full fifty-degrees around the tunnel bend, bathing the passage with infrared light. Spread flat on the ground, Richards studied the blank tunnel through his goggle's imaging screen, before grunting into his throat mic: "Clear ahead."

Spread thirty feet behind, the rest of the squad rose from their crouched positions. Joseph motioned to his team to move forward. Each member of the team wore compact night vision goggles that sharply rendered the tunnels in bleak greens and grays. State-of-the-art they might be, but already Joseph felt a migraine forming as his eyes tried to focus on the screen an inch from his eye.

He waited for the team to take positions, slowly advancing down the new bend in the passage. Speed was an issue here. They couldn't go charging ahead as they had to remain close to Lieutenant Mitchell in the rearguard who was guiding the Beluga Bomb.

The Beluga itself resembled a seven-foot-long tank cradle with the missile strapped between the tracks like a miniature Scud. Two spotlights stood raised on the vehicle, one covering the area in IR rays, the other a powerful spotlight ready to be deployed in an emergency. Like a loyal dog, the Beluga followed Mitchell, its onboard AI cameras recognizing hand signals, so he could stop or signal it to follow with a gesture.

A thirty-foot cable dragged behind the Beluga like a rat's tail. It formed the essential part of the communication with the surface, relayed via a heavy transmitter mounted on Lieutenant Blake's back that transmitted the signal into the surrounding bedrock using ultra-low frequency (ULF) waves that could be picked up by a ground penetrating satellite miles in orbit.

Even traveling downhill, progress had been slow through the initial stages as they first encountered the smooth sloping corridors. Their first few steps into the tunnels had more in common with the Marx Brothers than a group of elite commandos as they slid across the smooth floor. The Beluga's tracks caused the bomb to dangerously slew sideways at each turn.

But overall, Joseph thought, the equipment was performing well since it had all been custom designed within the last few hours. Some pieces of gear were still held together by cheap solder and gaffer tape.

"Sir?" The urgency in Richards' voice stabbed through Joseph's earpiece. "I'm sure I heard something up ahead."

"All silent. Mitchell, hang back," whispered Joseph. He edged past his men as they tried to flatten themselves against the curving sides of the tunnel. He joined Richards on the edge of a lip that marked the tunnel's path into a steeper descent. The lieutenant had a greater visual range with the rifle, so Joseph waited for him to speak as he surveyed the inky darkness.

"Can't see anything, but I'm damned well sure I heard movement."

Joseph had long learned to take heed of his men. They were not the type to get jittery over a few rats or dripping water.

"Sir, we have incoming on ULF," said Lieutenant Gordon.

"Patch it through."

Gordon adjusted the controls using a small wrist mounted screen. Seconds later, everybody heard a rapid clicking - like a cicada concert - pitted with a stuttered, throaty vocalization that resembled a bronchial cough.

Joseph frowned. "What is that?"

"Could be a bad transmission," said Gordon, doubting his own words, "Or maybe interference."

"An attempt to jam our comms?"

"I doubt it. It's on a different frequency."

In the command unit, Trent leaned forward in his chair, fingers massaging the side of his nose as he listened to the nervous voices over the communications channels. The odd sound continued, reminding him more of a wambling stomach than any form of communication.

"Some sort of geological interference?" Carver asked.

Trent shook his head and was painfully reminded about the limits of his knowledge. Catherine would've been the expert on that. Something was niggling the back of Trent's mind, but the idea slipped his conscious grasp every time he fumbled for it.

Joseph's low voice rose through the control room. "I heard it. Up ahead. Possible movement."

Then the thought landed in Trent's lap and made his stomach turn. He clamped on a pair of headphones and switched channels to focus on the unusual signal.

"There's structure in that signal!" he bellowed across the control room, unaware of the volume of his own voice. Spontain glared at him, but Carver indicated Trent still had the cans on and nodded for him to continue when Trent tossed them excitedly on the desk.

"It's not interference. It's a code or a language."

The Secretary of Homeland Security burst into laughter. "Son, that's like no language on this goddamn earth."

Trent could see the faces of operators across the room as

the implications set in. Spontain was the last to understand. Carver wheeled around to emphasize his point. "We don't know where the hell those things came from. Trent?"

"Obviously, the machines communicate. And no matter how good their technology is, they're going to hit the same problems as us. Standard frequencies just don't work underground. They've been using Ultra or Extremely Low Frequencies right under our noses. We should have been listening for them because I bet they've been listening in on us from the very beginning."

"Holy shit..." Carver blanched.

"General," Spontain took the General's arm to turn him around. "You can't seriously be saying we're dealing with Martians now?"

Carver narrowed his eyes. "What? You think they're Chinese? Or a last Nazi defensive from the War? Get your head out of your political ass and start looking at the facts."

A voice suddenly yelled over the PA: "Jesus Christ!" The rest of the chatter drowned out by deafening gunfire. One word surfaced above the cacophony:

"Dero!"

TWENTY-SEVEN

WHAT RICHARDS initially thought was a smudge on the camera resolved itself into a mechanical behemoth bearing down on them so fast the screen couldn't display the image as anything other than a blur.

He fired; the uranium-tipped bullets slammed into the Dero's torso, releasing a fountain of fluid. The spider legs moved with such swiftness the machine sounded like a highly tuned electric race car.

The smaller drill arms were held forward, the bits spinning menacingly. Richards thought he was dead as the Dero barreled past him. He felt a crushing weight on his back and was pushed hard against the wall. It took a moment for him to realize the weight was Major Adams, who had rolled on top of him, saving him from being trampled to death.

The Dero's target was behind them.

Lieutenant Rodgers stood his ground in the center of the tunnel, unleashing a whole magazine of ammunition into the beast. Blurred through his night-vision goggles, the Dero appeared to cross the open space between them like a ghost.

A drill arm punctured clean through his chest, spinning his blood across all the soldiers and coating the tunnel with guts. Rodgers' body twitched as he was lifted into the air and violently hurled against the wall, forcing Joseph to duck.

Joseph rolled to his feet, firing from the hip, his muzzle flash almost blinding through his goggles.

Richards rolled to his feet, hoisting the rifle around. Luckily, the body harness took most of the weight, allowing him to adjust the automatic targeting with the thumb toggle and unleash a hail of deadly fire. The weapon's recoil slid him several paces across the smooth floor, but he watched in satisfaction as chunks of metal fell from the Dero's hide. The rest of the team opened fire, tracer bullets crisscrossing as they pounded the target. One leg joint was blasted off, but the machine limped on.

Joseph expected the machine to take out the new threat, but instead it continued pushing towards the back of the group. It was zeroing in on the Beluga. How it knew about the threat he couldn't imagine, but the Dero pushed through the enfilade with all the determination of a suicide bomber.

"Mitchell! Fall back! Fall back!"

At the back of the line, Mitchell rose to his feet. He didn't fire, fearing hitting his own men. Now the Dero was fifty feet away and closing in, and it sent a shiver down his spine as the hawk-like head turned with deadly grace towards him. He emptied a whole magazine as he backed away, walking into the Beluga. The bomb's AI system was having difficulty processing the Dero's shape, and the curtain of bullets was further confusing it. The unit uselessly turned one way, then the other, before finally locking onto Mitchell and pivoting to follow him.

Mitchell glanced back to see Lieutenant Ryder try to

assault the Dero from the side. A drill arm snapped out, the length of the spinning cone grazing his face. Ryder staggered backward, both hands clutching his bloody cheek. Mitchell was relieved his night-vision goggles couldn't pick out the detail as the skin stripped from his face.

"Flash!" cried Douglas as he hurled a grenade at the Dero.

Everybody turned, shielding their eyes, except Lieutenant Gordon, who looked up - just as the white-hot magnesium flash-grenade detonated twelve feet in front of him. His goggles shorted with an electric crack, but not before Gordon's retinas were scarred by the blinding light. He dropped, fingers clawing at the pain in his eyes.

The Dero reeled backwards, buying Joseph time to eject his rifle's magazine and slide a new one in. A move he'd practiced countless times with his eyes closed was now a lifesaver in the dark. He squeezed the trigger with venom. More gunfire erupted all around as the soldiers circled the Dero. Chunks of chassis were blown away and bounced off the tunnel's curved ceiling.

Only Richards' keen sense of hearing caused him to wheel around to see a second Dero barreling down the tunnel like a subway train.

"Incoming!" he yelled, turning on the new adversary. Pockmarks dented the Dero's armor until Richards' gun suddenly ran dry with a chilling click.

The furious Dero was upon him. He felt his legs buckle, dropping him to the floor as it roared *over him* - the spider legs clattering on either side. He felt something catch his leg, but didn't stop to check. Instead, he dragged himself to the wall, becoming lightheaded with every second. He knew he must be bleeding out.

Joseph pressed against the wall as the new Dero thundered past, its plasma-arms locking forward as it fixed on Mitchell and the sluggish Beluga.

"Flash it!" yelled Joseph as his fingers curled around the cylinder on his belt.

He depressed the grenade's trigger and flicked the pin out with his thumb before hurling it. Just beyond the Dero he could see the others tossing grenades.

The cavern was filled with a blistering light that was visible even through closed eyes. Then a blast of heat washed over him, singing the hairs on his face.

Joseph opened his eyes and blinked away the afterimage until he saw the Dero staggering away from the burst of lights. He hammered the Dero with the rest of his magazine. More gunfire joined in. The Deros staggered, lashing out with the powerful drill arms. Everybody kept their distance as pneumatic pipes ruptured and the machine's armor ripped apart under the onslaught. Smoke rose from multiple penetration points, and with it, a foul smell as the machine finally became immobile and silent.

"Cease fire!" bellowed Joseph. The cordierite smell of ammunition hung thick in the air thankfully masking the stench coming from the machines.

The two Deros stood side by side, heads and weapons hanging limp. Moments passed in silence. The intensive firepower had cracked the machines like plastic, rather than metal. Joseph slid his hand from the gloves and ran his fingers across the surface. It was warm and smooth, definitely not metallic. Fluid trickled from the bullet holes and with it, a vile scent of sewage.

He looked around and saw some of his men lying on the

ground. Thoughts of the machine vanquished as his attention focused on them.

"Get some light in here."

Somebody fired up a chemlight that filled the tunnel with stark white illumination. The first things Joseph noticed, as his eyes grew accustomed to the light, were crimson channels of blood sliding down the tunnel's obsidian walls. The next was the burning husk of the Beluga. What remained of its tracks was melted to the floor. He recalled the burning sensation as the Dero's heat guns had fired, and now he felt his heart sink.

Their sole weapon to defeat the enemy was destroyed.

The control room was deathly quiet. They had heard the screams and the gunshots before comms were lost. On the map, everybody watched in despair as the blips representing each of the Special Ops team vanished altogether.

Trent looked questioningly at Carver's ashen face, but the General ignored him completely. Time stretched seconds into minutes as the implications of what had happened percolated.

Then a radio squelch distorted the speakers. A faint warble came through, sending a pair of technicians rushing to enhance and clean the signal.

Then Major Joseph Adams' voice crackled across the room, distant and faint, but recognizable. "Ops, do you read?"

General Carver snapped up a headset. "Go ahead, Major."

"Situation's under control. Two Deros destroyed. We've lost Rodgers and Ryder. Gordon appears to have been blinded, and Richards has a broken leg. We've salvaged the ULF but won't be able to proceed with mobile communication. The Beluga has been destroyed. Awaiting orders."

The control room was plunged into chaos as the military leaders shouted over one another. Trent lost track of the conversation, but noticed the grave look on Spontain's face as he spoke to General Carver. A brief altercation, then Carver appeared to resign himself, holding his hand up for silence. He raised the headset to his lips.

"Major Adams, what is the status of Lieutenant Mitchell?"

"Mitchell has minor burns but is combat ready, sir."

Carver looked unblinkingly at Trent as he continued. "Is the Beluga irreparable?"

"Affirmative."

"Then we must proceed with Alternative Two. Do you copy?"

"Confirm: that's Alternative Two. Copy. We won't have radio contact from this point out."

"Copy that, Major. And may God walk with you. Out."

The line became a hiss of static. Carver flopped wearily in his chair; the room once again silent. Trent rose from his desk and approached the General. Spontain was talking in low, urgent tones into a secure phone.

"General, you asked me to be a scientific watchdog on this operation, and I think it is my responsibility to advise you to pull those men out. They don't stand a chance."

"They have a mission, Professor, and they know their objective far outweighs any one man."

"But with no bomb, they can't continue the mission. If Alternative Two is Lieutenant Blake trying to blast the craft with C_4, then I can tell you, it's a complete waste of time."

"I agree with you, Professor Trent."

"Then what's Alternative Two?" Trent turned to Spontain as he hung up the phone. "What's going on?"

Spontain stared at the map on the screen before finally speaking. "Alternative Two is a backup plan. In the event we lost the Beluga, the secondary priority to locate and destroy the nuclear missile we popped down there - suddenly changes into a *recovery* operation. Once the missile is located, it is to be re-armed and detonated directly under the main craft. Have you any objection to that, Professor Trent?"

"Yes. An infinite amount! That puts us right back at where we began!"

Spontain cut him off. "Your view has been noted, Professor."

"This is crazy," pressed Trent. "If you detonate that thing, then we all die."

Spontain wheeled around. "And if we don't, even more people could die. Your tenure as Scientific Advisor is over. Please accept our escort *off* this military site."

A pair of armed guards materialized and flanked Trent. They gripped his elbow and guided him to the door. The last thing he saw as he was escorted out was General Carver hanging his head in shame.

TWENTY-EIGHT

TRENT ACCEPTED a chopper ride back to his WCEC lab. The gnarled freeways below were still laden with traffic, and he was thankful he didn't have to meander through it. Time was now critical, and the brief journey allowed him to cycle through plans ranging from the bizarre to the ludicrous.

Bringing public pressure to bear was out of the question. It was impossible to inform the populace of what was happening under their feet in time to stop it. Plus, the Mayor was dead, depriving him of the only media coverage he could expect to get. He knew that mouthing off to the public would be a breach of National Security, ensuring he only had a future scrubbing dirty linen in Guantanamo, but right now that wasn't much of a threat, as he'd be most assuredly dead.

The only person he could rely on was Alana, and he was certain she would talk him down from his wild, cavalier plan. It was the only idea that made any sense... and it was the craziest of the lot.

Grief slowed Schofield's every motion, and he felt barely

able to function. It didn't help that he'd been left alone in the lab that was filled with Walt and Katherine's personal possessions. From Walt's family pictures, to Katherine, Walt, and himself soaked at Universal Studios and her unwashed coffee cup still on her desk - it was the little things that made the biggest waves.

So lost in reminiscing, Schofield didn't hear Trent return. He looked apprehensive when Trent saw sound frequency graphics on his monitor and asked what he'd been doing.

"Eavesdropping," Schofield replied with a nervous smile. "I know it's kind of illegal, but how was I to know the military would use ULF frequencies down there?"

Trent grinned, suddenly remembering the network of sensors at Schofield's disposal. Earth resonance prior to earthquakes was something Trent thought they should investigate and had lobbied WCEC to give him a grant for a dozen sophisticated listening posts around the area. A bolt of hope struck him.

"Could we use the array to transmit down there?"

"One-way traffic only, I'm afraid. Give me a couple of bongo drums and maybe we could generate the frequencies needed."

Trent sighed. Transmitting a signal to order the Special Ops team back to the surface would have been perfect. Hopes dashed, he had no choice other than to go with his crazy plan.

He dialed Alana's cell and paced as it rang. She answered moments later and from her tone, she was relieved to hear from him. She'd been told to go home and rest, but unable to sleep, Alana had been clawing at the walls in her apartment. Trent didn't want to talk over the phone but stressed that they needed to meet. Urgently.

Thirty minutes later, Alana arrived at the lab, the cherry on her car's dash, blinking as it had been all the way here. Trent briefed her and Schofield on the situation, all thoughts of National Security abandoned, which meant he had to keep cutting off Schofield as he tried to lever in questions about the Dero's origins.

"Trent, I don't know what we can do about this."

"I have a solution, but it's a very long shot. And exceptionally... insane." Alana's brown eyes widened with anticipation. "We go down and stop them from using the nuke and find some other way of destroying that ship."

Alana broke into a shocked laugh.

Schofield drummed his fingers on the desk. "Let me get this straight. You want to go down and stop a bunch of Special Forces guys from achieving their mission. Then battle your way through half a dozen of those machines, before trying to figure out a way of blowing up a mile-and-a-half long ship?"

Trent shrugged. "If the ship fires up and leaves, then there is a chance, a slim chance, that we will survive the aftershocks. If they launch the nuclear device down there, then it's certain we won't."

"It's suicide, Trent. I want to kill those bastards as much as anyone else, but you can't walk into the lion's den without serious firepower."

A smirk tugged at Alana's mouth. "We have that."

Schofield looked at her in surprise. "Excuse me, detective? You're supposed to be talking him *out* of this."

"Congratulations, Prof, you've talked me into coming with you." He raised his hand to object, but she cut him off. "I have access to exactly the firepower we need."

While he knew he couldn't do it alone, he had no intention of asking anybody to come with him. Alana tilted her head defiantly, leaving no doubt it was a prerequisite, not an offer.

Schofield shook his head, fingers scratching his scalp, frustrated that his words would only fuel their desire to continue with the plan.

"Hell, you've got to die someday. Why not today?"

Trent's uncertainty was replaced with relief and a kamikaze feeling that they were about to do some good, even if the probability of survival would be left to the flick of a coin.

***

A MUFFLED curse hissed through the tunnel, making Major Joseph Adams wince. Even though Lieutenant Richards had ingested more than enough morphine, he still griped about his leg. The bloodied flaps of skin had been more cosmetic than dangerous and easily stapled down, but the broken bone was all too real. The Dero must have trampled him during the attack, and if that was the case, Joseph was amazed he was still alive.

The diminished group had said very little since the attack. They hid the bodies of their companions behind rock outcrops, hoping there would be a time later to give them a proper burial.

Richards had been relieved from point duty by Lieutenant Douglas, who scowled at the mere thought of using the latest piece of smart weaponry. He was old school and had constantly grumbled as Richards briefed him on the weapon's characteristics, particularly the powerful recoil. He showed him the bruise on his side that was swelling to a nasty purple shade as a result.

Lieutenant Blake had suffered burns to his left cheek and beard from the Dero's heat-ray. The skin was blistered and would undoubtedly require plastic surgery if he had the luxury to survive, but considered himself more than fit for duty.

They continued steadily down the new sharp incline. A network of corridors branched off like a honeycomb, and if it wasn't for the location data stored on Gordon's wrist-mounted tracker, their new task of finding the Excalibur missile would have been all but impossible.

Lieutenant Gordon stumbled on with Mitchell as a guide. The velvet darkness meant there was no way of knowing if his eyesight was returning, so he wore night vision headset. After forty minutes, he started claiming that he could see blurred flashes of color.

Failure hadn't been part of Joseph's lexicon. Plenty of missions had turned south. It was the very nature of Majestic operations, but he'd never sustained such casualties. Two men. Two friends. That was unheard of. The blow to his own morale was shocking. He resolved to get out of Majestic after this to spend more time with his family. All he had to do was live long enough, and right now that seemed to be a rapidly diminishing chance.

Joseph checked the screen on his wrist. A graphic display acted as a rangefinder, and a few gizmos that plugged into the device's com-ports picked up the stray missile's homing beacon.

"Target ahead, fifty feet."

Joseph had felt his ears pop but couldn't say how long

ago. The missile was approximately a mile down, the sort of depths miners called deep. The craft itself was almost another mile down at the fringes where gold miners feared to tread.

"Movement ahead." Douglas's measured warning had them scurrying for cover against the smooth, impenetrable walls. Joseph tried not to guess how many tons of rock hung above their heads. One tremor, one misplaced blast, and it could all come down on them. He concentrated on peering into the gloom.

Douglas edged forward, pressing every inch of his body flat against the floor, his night-vision scope focused on the insectoid form of a Dero.

Joseph crawled forward until the shape resolved itself in his goggles. The Dero was inert. The shaft of what he presumed to be the Excalibur missile poked through the roof of the tunnel, spearing the machine clean through its body.

"Mitchell, light it up."

Mitchell ignited a chemical stick, bathing the tunnel in crisp light. Douglas stood, his gun never wavering from the machine. He edged cautiously forward, around the Dero. The Kerf spearhead had melted through the rock above and straight into the machine. The chassis was pocked with blisters as the interior superheated as the missile speared through its underside before stopping against the floor.

"Hey, I can see light," exclaimed Lieutenant Gordon, extending his hand experimentally. "Some basic shapes are coming back."

Mitchell patted him on the shoulder and helped him sit against the tunnel wall. "Stay here and use your ears. We want nothing creeping up behind us." Gordon nodded, grateful for the break, and gently massaged his eyes with the balls of his palms, hoping to rub the sight back in.

Mitchell joined Joseph at the stricken Dero. He covered his mouth to stop inhaling the odious smell coming from the cracks in the machine. A thick liquid had dribbled out, pooling like bile at the machine's feet before it had solidified. He crouched to examine the Excalibur. The missile's tip was embedded an inch into the rock. The heat had liquefied the stone, but it had soon cooled and hardened, ensuring the missile was firmly planted in the bedrock.

Joseph knelt, careful not to touch the crystalized ichor. He took a thumb-sized flashlight from his belt and circled it over the missile cap, revealing a six-inch panel riveted to the side of the missile and awkwardly angled towards the tunnel wall.

"We need to open that hatch to disengage the warhead from the missile. Means lying in the crap on the floor."

"What is it?"

Joseph poked it with his gloved finger. "Cooling fluid? Whatever it is, I don't advise rolling around in that stuff."

Mitchell unfastened his utility belt, unrolling pouches of tools he would need. He slid under the Dero, looking more like an automobile mechanic than somebody about to extract a nuclear warhead.

Joseph moved out of Mitchell's way. He checked Richards was acting as lookout before turning his attention back to the Dero. On closer inspection, he could see the segmented armor was held together with a structure resembling a cross between a beehive and a concertina, allowing maximum flexibility. Something glistened within the folds of the material.

His flashlight revealed the nook was where two seams

came together, leaving a slight gap. It reminded him of the door panel on his Mustang. He slipped his fingers in the gap and pulled. It fractionally moved, but there was definite resistance. He adjusted his stance and inserted the fingers of both hands into the gap. He hauled back, using his full body weight. There was a sudden hiss of gas, and the weight was suddenly taken from his hands as the Dero's front torso slowly fell forward. At the same time, the rear *centaur-*section peeled in half with a massive hiss of air that sent him reeling back and gagging for breath from the stench within.

Everybody edged backwards, weapons raised, as the Dero unfolded like an exotic origami model.

Still underneath, Mitchell rolled aside, fearing the Dero was powering up. He saw the canopy open above him and swiftly drew his automatic. His first instinct was to release four shots into the atrocity before him. Only Major Joseph Adams' words, which sounded far away even over his earpiece, prevented him from emptying the magazine.

"It's already dead!" cried Joseph, pushing Mitchell's firearm aside. Mitchell stood and backed toward Gordon.

Richards and Blake appeared in the circle of light at a run, weapons ready, but they were brought up short at the sight before them.

Richards heaved from the stench. "What the fuck is it?"

Lieutenant Gordon clambered to his feet, feeling with outstretched arms. "What's happening? What is that stench?"

Mitchell grabbed Gordon's arm to root him to the spot and growled, "You don't want to know."

Inside the Dero, a pile of glistening body fluids bore the evidence of a once-living pilot. The missile had skewered the corpse, rupturing most of the creature inside out. No identifiable trace of limbs or a head could be seen; the missile impact had taken care of that. Cracked display panels and twisted bars that resembled Hieronymus Bosch-designed joysticks covered the inside surfaces.

"What am I looking at?" Blake asked, his face contorted with both disgust and fascination, unable to keep his eyes away - like watching a bad road accident from the safety offered by distance.

"The pilot," sighed Joseph. "I had a hunch these damn things are alive. Not robotic. Not cybernetic, but, well, they sure ain't human."

Richards wiped his nose on his sleeve, attempting not to breathe in the fetid odor. They had all seen enough strange things to absorb this revelation without reaction, but the confirmation that they were dealing with another intelligence was still disarming. "If these things are just some kind of guard, then what about the rest of the creatures?"

"What do you mean?" asked Blake.

"Are there more of those creatures around, you know, not in these exo-suits. Just walking around?" He tried to identify legs but failed.

Joseph killed the notion before it could settle with everybody else. "Okay, people, we have a job to do. Richards, Blake, get back to position. We don't want any of these things sneaking up on us. Gordon, stay with Blake until you get your sight back. Mitchell, open this can up. I want the warhead out and prepped in fifteen minutes. Let's go, boys."

His team rallied into position but couldn't mask the increased uneasiness they now felt, but years of following orders to the core propelled them on.

Joseph's mind threw up the images of Rodgers and Ryder, killed by monstrosities such as the one perched amid the exo-suits. He felt a surge of anger. That wasn't the right emotion to feel right now. He had to stay calm and in control. He forced himself to think of his wife's beautiful green eyes. It wasn't enough to stop a new nagging thought. What the hell did the creature look like before the missile speared it? The thought sent a chill down his spine. He hoped they wouldn't come face to face with a live one.

TWENTY-NINE

IT WAS SURPRISINGLY EASY, almost worryingly so, to break into the police station and steal a truckload of lethal weapons.

Trent was sick to the pit of his stomach as Alana flashed her badge and strode confidently across the loading bay entrance to the fortified gate of the police storage facility. She slipped some documentation to the guard on duty, who exchanged some small talk when he recognized her. He gave the papers a courtesy glance before throwing the switch to open the gate. Once the double steel gates had rolled back on their sunken rails, Trent drove the unmarked white van into the courtyard. He reversed it towards the loading bay, watching Alana wave him backwards in the rearview mirror. She held up her hand as a signal to stop. Trent killed the engine and climbed from the cab. He adjusted the blue overalls Alana had provided so he blended in with the rest of the staff.

Alana projected casual confidence as she walked into the

evidence storage room. The guard gave her a brief nod from behind his bulletproof window.

Trent thumbed the green, rubber-covered button on the truck's tailgate to lower it. He released it as the metal tail came to a halt, gently grating steel against the raised concrete loading bay. His heart was racing. He reminded himself to act casual and angled his black baseball cap just enough to mask the guilt on his face. Here he was, a thief in a police station.

The clatter of shutters startled Trent from his reverie as a set of secure loading shutters automatically rolled up, revealing Alana pulling a red manual pallet jack carrying a pallet covered in heavy green webbing that stood some two feet taller than her. She wheeled the jack around and smoothly guided the package into the truck.

"That's it." Alana gave Trent a thumbs-up as she trundled the jack back into the warehouse.

Trent's hands were shaking as he thumbed the tailgate controls, sealing it up. It seemed to take forever for Alana to return. He climbed back in the cab and saw Alana in his rearview mirror, exchanging a joke with the guard, before joining Trent.

As they pulled out, she whispered, "Take it slow." She nodded to the security at the gate, who showed minimal interest as they passed through.

And that was it. They were on the street and heading towards Wilshire Metro Station with enough firepower to start a small skirmish.

Nothing more was said until they pulled into a side alley half a block from the Metro. The road was just wide enough for Trent and Alana to climb from the vehicle and squeeze around to the back. They opened the rear doors and climbed inside.

An overhead fluorescent flickered epileptically as it filled the van with a dirty yellow light. Alana ran a packing knife across the cargo net restraints. As she bent over, Trent's eyes automatically ran along her tight denims that accentuated her body. When he met her eyes, she was staring straight at him. Guilty, he quickly averted his gaze to the rusty metal wall. He didn't see her smile as she hacked off the rest of the webbing.

"I can't believe it was so easy," said Trent, searching for anything to banish the awkward silence.

"Me and Ed made the bust the other day. According to the system, it's still my evidence pending further investigation. And with most of the computer network still down, nobody is in the mood to trawl through paperwork."

She slashed the final restraint, and Trent helped her pull back the heavy netting, revealing a dozen unmarked wooden crates. She opened a red toolbox at the back of the van, found a pry bar that fitted neatly in a sliver under the crate lid, and shoved it down as hard as she could.

The lid opened with a crack that was too loud in the dark street. Trent kept watch from the back of the truck, nervously waiting for the ever-present gang or police patrol. But the streets were deserted.

When he turned back to Alana, he reacted, almost falling out of the truck as she pointed the business end of a FIM-92 Stinger missile launcher at him.

"Jesus Christ!"

"What do you think?"

"I think we'll be going down there better armed than that Special Ops unit. What is that?"

Alana held the five-foot tube at an angle so Trent could see the handgrip, ergonomically curved to fit the hand, and the padded shoulder rest. "Stinger surface-to-air missile, designed to take out fast-moving airborne targets." She flipped up two crosshair sights positioned at the middle and end of the launcher. "Just point and squeeze. Works well on ground-based targets like trucks or tanks. I'm not too sure about the safety tips for using them in confined spaces though."

"We'll take them. What else have we got?"

The red LED of an e-cigarette lit Officer Prendergast's face as he inhaled deeply and blew out an expansive cloud of strawberry-scented smoke. He sat back in the uncomfortable seat of his MTA car and cast a baneful eye toward the Metro Station.

With everything going on, he would rather be back home, or better, out of the city. Instead, he'd been assigned the night shift, making sure nobody entered. That was easy. Nobody was around. He was more concerned about what might come *out*. The only thing that had changed in the last five hours was the lighting; now the entrance was bathed in shadows that smothered the eerily quiet street. Since the first quake, the streetlights had been off, normally a cue for looters to go to work. But with the latest events, things had been unerringly quiet and amazingly boring.

His department still treated him like the new kid, even though he'd been there for six months already, and he knew that's why he landed the job nobody wanted. Resources were stretched so thin that his relief wasn't due for another six hours, and there was no chance to sneak away for a coffee. Besides, the military had cordoned off the area, so who would...

Something moved in the shadows at the end of the street. A trick of the light, surely?

Prendergast peered into the darkness and fought a deep yawn. Only when he'd fully inhaled a lungful of smoke did he see there definitely was something moving down the street. A car, rolling silently forward with the lights off. It stopped thirty yards from the subway entrance and oozed suspicion.

Prendergast felt his neck muscles bunch. He was all alone out here, possibly with a gang of crooks about to cause trouble. He turned his vape off and tossed it on the passenger seat as he reached into the footwell and felt for the Benelli M4 shotgun clipped there. But he didn't pull it. His eyes were accustomed to the dark, and he could just make out a lone occupant in the vehicle. His relief was only transitory. Who would come here in a designated no-go zone? A fleeting hope that he was being relieved early was doused when he couldn't discern any MTA insignia on the car. It was too dark to even determine the color of the vehicle.

A moment's deliberation won over the urge to investigate the vehicle. After all, that's why he was here. He snapped the shotgun from the clips and climbed from the car, closing the door as silently as possible. He kept to the shadow, the shotgun firmly pressed across his chest with the barrel angled toward the sky. He kept his fingers clenched to avoid squeezing the trigger through nerves.

Twenty feet from the car, the occupant still hadn't seen him and was nervously drumming the wheel. Then he flicked on the interior light, holding up a sheet of paper to read. The dim light gave Prendergast just enough detail to see it was a Caucasian male with short red hair, dressed in plain clothes and looking extremely twitchy.

Prendergast pumped the shotgun. The ominous *click-clack* served as a warning that he was armed, and it had the desired effect. The newcomer looked up in alarm and slammed both sweaty palms against the windshield.

"Don't shoot! I'm unarmed!"

"This is a restricted area, bozo. Get out of the vehicle."

For a moment, the driver seemed not to respond, and Prendergast thought of shouting again at the dummy, but then the man got out, keeping both visibly shaking hands in view.

"This area is off-limits," yelled Prendergast, leveling the gun.

"Waiting for some friends," came the man's frightened reply.

Prendergast glanced beyond the man, just in case anybody else showed up. "And who exactly would that be?"

"That would be us, Officer." Prendergast whirled around, almost letting off a shot. He stumbled backwards at the sight of two people carrying so much ammunition and weaponry strung to every available niche that they belonged in a movie rather than on the streets. He tripped on a raised sidewalk slab and landed hard on his ass.

"It's Detective Williams. You remember me from the other day?"

Prendergast waved the shotgun uncertainly. The woman pointed a flashlight at her own face, and he instantly recognized her. Then he felt ashamed of his pratfall in front of somebody he found attractive. She extended a hand that Prendergast reluctantly accepted.

"Sorry, ma'am but I wasn't told that you'd be down here."

"That's because this is a classified operation. You've seen the news, right? These things are moving fast all over. How are you feeling, officer...?" her eyes strayed to his name badge, "Prendergast?"

Feeling like a fool, Prendergast mumbled "Okay". He glanced at the other two men, who seemed to be in deep conversation and examining equipment on the car's rear seat. Prendergast angled for a better view, but Detective Williams stepped in his way, still speaking to him.

"I'm sorry, ma'am, what did you say?"

"I said I'm glad to find you on this shift. It's always good to see a friendly face." She winked, and Prendergast felt a thrill of flirting. "You're reliable. Somebody I can trust."

Under her sparkling dark eyes, he couldn't stop a smile creeping across his face. "Thank you, ma'am."

"At least I can tell you what is going on here. As you know, we're currently under military authorization, so everything you hear is secret. They have sent a team down the tunnel system under the stadium. In order to establish communications, we have to set up a relay system where the tunnel network meets the Metro Line. That's what's in this vehicle you were astutely about to check."

"You're going down there?"

"That's what the weaponry is for. We've been tasked to monitor communications from the lip of the tunnel."

The thought of escaping the drudgery of watch duty gave him a spark of hope. "Can I come with you? As backup?"

"Afraid not. I need a man topside. Somebody I can rely on. Remember, this is a restricted operation. No cops, no regular soldiers, and definitely no civilians. If things go well, then your name will be mentioned in all the right places. I'll make sure of that."

A chance at promotion sounded priceless. Anything to land him off the detail nobody else wanted. The night was unfolding well, thought Prendergast as he returned to his car. By the time he'd retrieved his e-cigarette, the detective and the two men had already hauled equipment from the car and ducked through the spider's web of OSHA tape that covered the Metro entrance.

He inhaled deeply. The cute way the detective had winked at him assured him this would be the one to change his career.

After tonight, nothing would be the same.

THIRTY

MITCHELL GRUNTED as he swung the weight of the depleted uranium warhead into a shielded backpack. The heavy pack was woven with lead threads, and the warhead, a device not much bigger than a softball, almost tripled the weight. Contrary to popular belief, radiation from the warhead was at a safe level until activated - and then the sheer energy produced would be phenomenal.

Ready to go, and refreshed from their momentary break, the Special Ops team pressed onward into the darkness.

"Just hit two miles," whispered Joseph over the headsets.

Over the last ninety minutes, the temperature had increased, and air tasted metallic. Sensors on their belts that checked for toxic gases read negatively, which had given rise to some concern that the equipment was malfunctioning. Blake ran a diagnostic check and assured everybody it was all A-okay, and reasoned the stale air was probably because of the lack of circulation deep down here.

Time lost all meaning in the eerie green wash offered by

the night-vision goggles. Gordon's vision had improved enough to see pale blotches that floated ghost-like in front of him, but details were still a blur. Blake had assured him that if he could see absolute blackness - then his vision had returned to normal.

Blake felt his ears pop again as they advanced down the steep incline. And something gentle passed across his face. It was a faint breeze.

Lieutenant Douglas' worried voice cracked over the intercom. "I have something ahead!"

Joseph's command barked straight afterwards over their headsets, although Blake could hear the hushed command echo through the tunnel. "Hold positions."

"Looks like a large space beyond," Douglas reported.

"Check it out," said Joseph.

They were all spaced so far apart that Blake could only discern Major Joseph's body shape hugging the wall. Douglas was beyond his range.

"OK... I see a ledge about twenty feet in front. Looks like the whole tunnel just ends in a cliff. Wow... standby."

His lapse into silence put Blake on edge. They had seen several branching tunnels joining this one, but the Major had insisted they follow the incline down. Had they taken the wrong turn into a dead end?

Douglas's voice came over the airwaves again. This time, he was talking quickly. "I see... oh, man..." he faltered in awe. "It's a cavern. I mean a massive space. You could fit the stadium in here several times over. I can just make out the far wall with the gunsight. It's deep too. Christ almighty..."

Douglas felt his palms become clammy. Nobody dared talk.

"You won't believe what I'm seeing... oh, shit!"

His startled voice was so loud, Douglas realized he had not only heard it over the headset, but also aloud. Through his goggles, he saw a figure approach him.

It was Lieutenant Douglas, and he was moving *fast*.

* * *

FLASHLIGHT BEAMS BOBBED over the smooth tunnel walls. The entrance looked exactly as they remembered it. The gutted, derailed train carriage hadn't been moved, neither had the remains of the victims inside. The sickening burning smell still filled the tunnel.

Trent tried to breathe through his mouth. He heard Alana inhale sharply next to him. In the pale illumination, he caught her expression. This is where her friend was killed, and now she was going back.

"Are you sure you want to do this?" he asked.

Alana nodded grimly.

Trent shifted the weight of the backpack containing the equipment Schofield had rounded up at short notice. The cumbersome M27 rifle was heavy and and unfamiliar in Trent's hands. He duct-taped a flashlight to the barrel to free his hands and tried not to think that he'd never fired a gun in his life. It certainly wasn't the time to mention it to Alana.

Alana also carried an M27 with a similarly taped flashlight. An arsenal of weaponry and ammunition hung from her belts and a bandolier that made her look like a trendy bandit.

Determined, she stepped into the Dero's tunnel. Trent followed close behind. Ahead, the tunnel curved down, and Alana didn't hesitate.

"Careful," said Trent, quickening his pace to keep up with her.

"We've been here before. I know what's ahead."

That's what worried Trent, and within thirty-seconds, they had stumbled across Ed's body. Alana briefly shone the flashlight across the corpse, but Trent gently nudged the light aside, shaking his head.

"Don't."

But it was too late. The brief glimpse of the pulverized body looped over a stalagmite and the ripple of movement from dozens of rats chewing the decomposing flesh had burned heavily on their minds. Trent felt a wave of nausea. He reached out for the wall but misjudged the distance, and staggered, throwing up against the curved surface. His stomach heaved several times, and his throat stung from the burning bile.

"Can you walk?"

Trent nodded, strength returning to his limbs. "I don't have the stomach for this. I hate horror movies. Medical shows make me ill. And real life... well, that sucks."

"The Marines have a head start. We haven't got time to dawdle around." Alana pulled half a packet of breath mints from her pocket and offered the pack. "Take these. Try not to be ill again."

Trent took them, wiping his sleeve across his mouth. Some hero he was turning out to be. Alana continued down the tunnel and didn't look back. After several minutes, they entered the larger cave where O'Reilly's body lay mercifully hidden behind a rocky outcrop. Only the Irishman's legs were visible, bent at obtuse angles.

The cave extended further than Trent had estimated; the flashlights doing little to unmask the shadows beyond.

Trent produced a small gas detector and took a sample. "Levels are clear, but from now on, I keep this thing on. If you hear a constant beep, then it has detected unsafe gas levels." He hooked the device to a loop on his belt.

"How unsafe?"

"Minutes before you turn green and asphyxiate."

Alana combed her flashlight around the cave, revealing several other branching passageways angling down towards hell.

"Which way?"

Trent tossed the rifle off his shoulder and checked the compass on his phone. They didn't have the Special Ops' digital mapping kit, but he was confident enough with a compass and the digital clinometer. He'd been part of many speleology groups in the past to feel confident enough to locate the mothership. Besides, he had a sneaking suspicion all the tunnels lead to the same source.

He wagged a finger towards the tunnel opposite the one they'd entered through. "If we keep heading that way and down - we can't go wrong." He was about to add some dumb, hard-hearted remark when he heard a roar like a freight train. A rush of air swept through his hair, and he half turned as a Dero rushed from a side tunnel.

Instinct took over. He slammed into Alana, pulling her behind a huge rock as a heat-blast liquefied the floor where they'd been standing moments earlier.

The Dero hurtled past like a charging knight before it could slow enough to turn. As it passed, Trent saw the scorch marks on its side and the two smashed spotlights. It was the same machine that had killed Ed and O'Reilly.

The Dero's legs did a complex shuffle as it arced around

to face them. Terror rooted Trent to the spot as the Dero raised its plasma cutters, the tips flaring to life.

A blow struck Trent in the side, and he felt a rush of searing air singe the hairs on his left cheek. Through a veil of smoke, Trent watched - in adrenalin-induced slow motion - as a line of fire severed the Dero mid-chest. The explosion was deafening as the shock wave bowled Trent across the cave.

With a pounding head, Trent fought the lulling urge to pass out. When he dared look again, the Dero had been destroyed. All that was left were fragments of burning chassis and five legs reaching in the air, twitching spasmodically.

"What...?" Trent muttered, climbing to his feet. Alana stood gunslinger-stance, the smoking Stinger missile launcher across her shoulder.

"Next time, try not to get your face scorched off by the rocket exhaust. Are you okay?"

Trent nodded, despite still feeling dazed. Alana softened and ran a gentle hand down his blistered, red cheek.

"You'll live. That's a bonus." She lowered the launcher, sliding the two halves compactly back together. "This is probably the most user-friendly thing ever made. Makes shooting down airplanes easier than making espresso. It even has instructions on it."

She pointed to three colorful cartoon-like panels on the side of the launcher depicting the stages of preparation. It reminded Trent of the Sunday morning funnies.

"You're like an underground Rambo."

Alana's forehead creased. "You could have tried to get a few shots off with that popgun of yours," she teased. She shouldered the launcher as she circled the burning hulk. "If it stayed here, then I figure it's some sort of sentry guarding the way in."

"Let's hope it's the only one."

"Let's find out."

THIRTY-ONE

LIEUTENANT DOUGLAS HAD RETREATED a hundred yards before dropping to his knees. When the rest of the team caught up with him, he still could scarcely form a coherent sentence despite years of military training.

Joseph calmly talked him down, assisted by a small shot of morphine to ease his anxiety. He confirmed the passage abruptly ended in a cliff extending down into a massive cavern that could engulf a small town. At the bottom lay the colossal mothership. Swarming around, he estimated there were about a hundred Deros guarding the site.

Overwhelming opposition was something they had faced many times before, but this was something different. Their mission was beyond impossible.

Joseph took the PSA-13 and ordered Lieutenant Douglas to stay back and calm down. Joseph put the goggles on and made sure the umbilical cord of wires from the gun did not interfere with his movements. The weight was an added complication, and he marveled that Douglas had brought it this far without complaint.

Ordering everybody to stay put, Joseph scrambled on all fours to the end of the corridor, noticing a constant breeze and light ahead. The tunnel abruptly ended in a cavern. From his vantage point just below roof height, he could see that Douglas had possibly underestimated the size.

The cavern stretched away for at least two miles and was lit by powerful spotlights lining the ship's hull. The craft ran the length of the space like a colossal smooth pebble, tapered towards the nose and broader towards the rear and approximately half as wide as its length. Its nose was surrounded by a massive circular collar from which smoke or steam rose, but Joseph's position only offered him a limited view. The rounded aft section had four massive cylinders poking from beneath the skin, reminiscent of a cross between Saturn 5 boosters and something out of Star Wars. A dull blue light pulsed from irregular slats along the length of what he assumed to be the engines. Behind, a huge tunnel curved away behind it, a dark testament to the craft's progress.

Joseph nudged his thumb over the gun's joystick, manipulating options in his goggles. He enhanced the zoom on the gun's camera and angled the barrel so he could get a better view while remaining hidden.

The length of the craft had several ramped hatches towards the rear, opening into the depths of the craft. He watched as a Dero raced down the ramp and across the cavern. He tracked its progress with the camera. Once it reached the wall, its drill arms pushed into the rock. The surrounding surface was pockmarked with bored holes.

Joseph frowned and widened the zoom a little, noticing another Dero alongside, then another and another.

He pulled back hard on the control to see a line of some

two-dozen machines against the wall carving pits large enough to swallow them.

"*Sonofabitch*," he muttered to himself.

Lieutenant Douglas' voice came back online, reminding Joseph that the mics were constantly active. "What d'you see, Major?"

"They're mining the wall. There must be about twenty-five...no more."

After a few minutes, a Dero would leave its place against the wall and return to the ship, presumably to unload its ore. It reminded him of busy worker ants, and as the analogy hit, he noticed that there was a chain of machines running between the craft and the walls. Widening the image even further, he could see the walls themselves comprised hundreds of tunnels, like a slab of Swiss cheese. The scale of the operation was immense.

"There are hundreds of them."

Using the joystick, he rotated the gun barrel around to peer straight down the incline without his needing to move. The barrel twisted a full fifty-degrees, revealing a sheer drop along the irregular surface. The only possible way down would be to rappel. Fortunately, there were no Deros on their side of the cavern. They were occupied on the opposite wall. He gave the area one last sweep with the camera before retreating down the tunnel, desperately trying to figure out how to navigate his team safely through this new nightmare.

* * *

"STOP!" hissed Alana, as she pulled Trent down against the lee side of the wall.

Trent heard the all too familiar noise of an approaching Dero. "Maybe it won't come up here?"

But Alana had already unslung the Stinger launcher off her shoulder and was rapidly assembling the unit. Her M27 lay on the floor, so the flashlight fell on the instructions on the side of the weapon. She pulled the launcher to its full length by holding one end between her feet and yanking up, then became aware the sound of the approaching Dero had changed.

It was moving faster.

Alana had already assembled her launcher and slid a heavy missile into the pipe. She looked up at Trent, who was struggling to slot the handgrip into the brackets on the launcher. She snatched it from him and locked the grip in place in one fluid motion, but in doing so, fumbled with her own launcher.

"Dammit!" The Stinger clattered noisily on the floor and slid ten feet down the corridor. She moved to follow but stopped as a Dero filled the beam of her flashlight. It charged towards her with *another* close behind.

"Shoot it!" screamed Alana as she pushed the missile launcher into Trent's hands, darting forward to reclaim her own.

Trent acted on impulse alone and raised the Stinger wildly – not bothering to sight down the length or steady his footing, he fired.

The recoil pushed him hard against the wall as the missile smoked away, exploding *under* the lead Dero. The machine staggered and lurched as two of its legs were shattered in a mass of mechanical fluid. Shards of rock and shrapnel punctured the Dero's exposed underbelly, and the Dero lurched to a halt. The whole machine shook erratically.

Meanwhile, Alana slid along the floor and snatched her weapon. She took a beat to line up the second Dero that had raised its heat-ray weapons to fire. She didn't wait for the locking tone and squeezed the trigger. The missile loped the short distance and impacted the Dero head-on. Alana ducked low as the fierce conflagration hurled debris that rained around her and Trent. A secondary explosion severed the first Dero's right-hand cannon in a colorful burst of sparks.

Trent looked up from the rock he'd taken cover behind. One Dero was nothing more than a few burning pieces of metal on top of buckled legs. The other continued shaking violently as servo fluid dripped from the severed plasma-arm.

Alana lay on her back several feet away, staring at the machines with wide eyes and a Cheshire Cat grin. Trent carefully laid his Stinger on the floor and rushed to help her stand, feeling a dull throb in his left shoulder as he took her weight.

"Great shootin', Tex," he said, pulling her up.

"Two of them down! We're better than the U.S. Marines, huh?"

"Did anybody ever tell you that you're one violent woman, Detective Williams? Ow!" He almost bit his lip as pain jolted his shoulder. He could barely feel Alana's fingers as she squeezed the dull throb.

"Does it hurt here?" Trent nodded and her fingers moved. "What about here?" He shook his head. "Okay, I think you have dislocated it when you fell. Stand straight."

Trent tried to wave her off.

"I'll be–"

CRACK. Blue flashes passed in front of Trent's eyes, and he felt himself flush as pain flashed through his shoulder, then subsided, leaving only the desire to scream. He experimentally flexed it, now finding it fully mobile.

"Thanks," he managed as his eyes streamed, "but next time, let me suffer."

He leaned against Alana to catch his breath, and his head lolled against her bosom. Her heart was beating quickly beneath her leather jacket. Masked by the scent of sweat and the burning Deros, he could just make out a warm feminine smell, reminding him how long it had been since he was last with anybody. Work had consumed him, and now it was literally going to do so with a fatal finality.

Alana gently lifted his head, so they were nose-to-nose.

"Are you okay?"

He let her eyes search his. "I read stressful situations can throw people together in impossible relationships." He inwardly kicked himself for the nerd-worthy comment.

Alana smiled and brushed her fingers through his hair. "I guess it's the rush of still being alive."

She inched closer...

Then they both sharply turned as the quivering Dero moved with a torturous sound of twisted metal. Alana pushed Trent away and swung the Stinger around before remembering it needed reloading.

The Dero opened like a complex flower, revealing the seething mass inside.

Alana reached into her backpack, which was notably lighter. Only two missiles remained. She looked up as the mass took shape as it moved. She was never one to scream in fright. Not a single horror film had invoked a sound. She had been at the briefing, known about the Deros' potted history, and yet had still half expected human intelligence behind them. What she was looking at, however, was beyond anything she'd mentally prepared herself for. Stark terror seized her, and she wanted to scream the nightmare away. But no sound would come from her parched throat.

The pulsing gray mass inside looked like an eight-foot-long tapering slug. Pus oozed from deep wrinkles on the skin - whether or not they were wounded, she couldn't tell – but the creature stank like an open sewer. The front half of the body was slightly less slug-like, and the torso curled upwards some seven-foot tall and was capped with a bulbous head that had dozens of glistening black eyes peering in every direction. Six massive tentacles, two tipped with dangerous-looking barbs, the others capped with three slender flexible fingers, unfolded with the sound of wet flesh ripping.

The entire torso of the creature was split with a vertical mouth, lined with hundreds of sharp hooked teeth. The gaping maul widened, letting out a piercing chittering sound that carried through the tunnel.

Trent's legs buckled at the sight, convinced that such an abomination should not exist. He forced himself to pick up his M27 from where he'd propped it against the wall but felt as though he was walking through molasses.

The two front legs of the machine splayed wide as it lowered, allowing the creature to slide into the tunnel, leaving a thick trail of slime. Another spine-chilling scream, and the creature charged with surprising swiftness, the flailing tentacles whipping some five feet ahead.

Trent now had the rifle ready and squeezed the trigger. Time took on an artificial slowness as bullets tore across the wall and the exosuit before finding the creature.

Skin undulated from each bullet impact, but it did not slow. Trent was fixed to the spot as the creature bore down on him. The fanged maw gaped wide, filling his vision.

Tentacles wrapped around the M27's barrel, and the weapon was plucked from his hand.

The beast reared back with a chittering cry, raising itself several feet. Trent felt the beast's fetid breath and closed his eyes against the inevitable.

A violent force struck him full in the chest. His hands and face were splattered with fluid, and he felt a blast of heat burn his face. As he slid down the wall, the last thing he saw was Alana rushing towards him, tossing the smoking Stinger launcher to the floor.

THIRTY-TWO

A PERFECT ORANGE ball balanced delicately on the horizon, and General Carver couldn't help but speculate if it would be his last sunrise.

He'd taken the chance to slip from the claustrophobic control unit to watch the new dawn. Fatigue had long set in as the team stared at blank monitors and listened to silent radios. Now the fresh air cleansed his senses and revitalized his mind.

Since losing contact with the team, they had heard nothing. Not a whisper. Seismographs were put on-screen so they could search for any hint of a successful mission. When nothing came through, he felt almost as isolated on the surface as his men were deep underground.

Time was against them. The mission would have to be deemed a failure soon.

Strike two. Failure was one option he detested. However, right now he was struggling with something else military planning had ingrained in him: never green light an operation without a *three-fold* backup plan.

For the last hour, he'd attempted to buy time with Spontain before they employed their third and final option. Now Carver had squeezed every last drop of time from his allowance and had no choice but to move to the tertiary plan: the remote detonation of the Excalibur warhead.

The planning team had taken into account that if the Special Ops team had been eliminated, then it was hoped they were close enough to the enemy for the nuclear warhead to be effective. A remote pulse from a ULF signal would be enough to trigger detonation.

Professor Trent's warning about detonating the warhead rang in Carver's mind, but the decision had been made before Professor Trent's evaluation. The President, advised by Chapman and Spontain, thought the risk was acceptable.

In the last ten minutes, seismographs had detected minor shifts from the craft parked under the city. Analysts had concluded the craft was about to make a move, which they all agreed would level Los Angeles - if not also causing Trent's apocalyptic scenario to unfold. And if the craft moved across to the East Coast, under Washington... hell, the entire country would collapse. At least this way they may only lose Hollywood.

Trent's dark warnings about a tidal wave that would destroy most of Asia and send shock waves three times around the globe were almost too much to comprehend. The President had the safety of the nation to consider. Everything else was unfortunately moot.

"General?"

Carver turned to see a young technician at the control center door. She couldn't be over twenty-four and had such a keen air about her that Carver wondered if the army had done a superb job of desensitizing her.

"You're needed in the hub, sir."

Carver nodded. His mouth was too dry to reply. He took a last look at the perfect sunrise, then entered the dark nerve center, the young woman closing the door behind him, killing the light.

* * *

THE COATED NYLON line was silent as it unfurled two hundred forty feet to the dead blackness of the cavern floor below.

Lieutenant Douglas was on point again, so he had to descend first. An automatic retarding harness was fastened around his body, and he reclaimed the PSA-13 from the Major. It was firmly strapped across his chest so he could perform a free-fall headfirst and be able to operate the weapon if necessary.

The drop was a walk in the park, something he'd done countless times, and it was more of a pleasant distraction considering the situation. He retarded his fall several feet from the ground, all the while keeping a vigilant eye on the Deros across the cavern. Releasing the line from his harness with his balled fist, Douglas landed like a cat and sprinted for cover behind an enormous pinnacle rock of five jagged columns projecting up from the ground like claws. By the time he'd taken position, Blake had made it down.

Joseph had formulated the bones of the plan in minutes, but his options were severely compromised because of the condition of his men.

Lieutenant Gordon had gained his vision just enough to see blurs through the night-vision goggles. As long as he could tell the difference between a man and a Dero, he was useful. He felt a firm tug as the line was attached to his harness. A brief confirmation from Joseph and a firm push sent him over the edge.

Unable to rely on visual cues to arrest his fall, Gordon had counted as the others had made the plunge. He'd gotten to four and a half before they had jammed the brake on. He coolly counted against the velvety swish of the line feeding through the harness. One second either way could leave him an open target for a Dero, or a wet patch on the ground. Luck was with him. His feet hit the floor hard, but he stopped short of crunching into the rock. He felt Blake's hand grab his arm, and the cable detached.

"You almost disintegrated up on reentry, pal," whispered Blake.

"I shouldn't have used you to time my own fall. You've put on some pounds, you fat bastard." He heard the mock-offended snort as Blake led him over to join Douglas.

Lieutenant Mitchell was next, securing the warhead to an extra harness around his waist. The added weight meant a freefall was out of the question, and that meant he would be more of a target on the way down.

Major Joseph took the weight of the rope, belaying it around his waist. Lieutenant Richards, nursing his broken leg, anchored the line, using a rock as a capstan.

Joseph gave two firm thumps on Mitchell's back as he lowered himself over the edge. Below, Douglas was the only one able to provide cover if the Deros spotted the hanging target. If that were to happen, then there was no doubt the mission would end suddenly and painfully.

Forty feet down and Richards grunted from the strain, readjusting his position. Joseph saw the man's face was screwed in concentration. Evidently the pain in his leg was more than he cared to show. He also knew that Richards would endure any pain to keep his team safe. His thoughts were sidetracked by a dull bleep that echoed across the chamber. Then Mitchell's voice crackled over the intercom. "Major!"

Joseph silently cursed. He'd ordered radio silence in case the Deros were monitoring communications. For Mitchell to disobey an order, something must be seriously wrong. He halted Mitchell's descent and peered over the edge, assured that the Deros hadn't responded, before looking down the line to see what the problem was.

Mitchell was adjusting the cradle under his body that housed the warhead. He looked up at Joseph and spoke with incredible calm. "The warhead just came online."

"Say again?" Joseph watched as he rotated the warhead to examine it. A pair of LEDs flashed nonchalantly on the warhead.

"It looks like the warhead has been armed. There ain't no fancy countdown, but a pair of blinking lights which should be off."

"Did you touch anything?"

"No sir, it was hanging like a baby - then it lit up like Christmas."

"Can you disarm it?"

"Can't say right now. And definitely not from here."

"How long have we got?"

"Incoming!" warned Douglas.

All heads snapped up to see one of the Deros break from the rock face and scurry around the craft. Until now, they'd observed a regimental chain, obediently moving between the rock face and the craft, but now one had strayed from the pack and was heading their way.

* * *

"HOW MANY TIMES do I have to save your ass in one day?"

Trent grimaced as he wiped the slime from his skin. He experienced a faint burning sensation and tried not to think about what the creature's guts were doing to his skin.

"That's why I pay those tax dollars. You work for me."

They both had edged away from the puddle of smoldering flesh and had no desire to investigate any closer.

"How are you feeling?" asked Alana, eyeing him with concern.

"Surprisingly okay." He held up his hand. "Although this stuff burns."

They spent the next few minutes cleaning the ooze off him. Alana took off her leather jacket and used it to wipe him down. Using a small Swiss Army knife she'd stowed in her kit, she fashioned a pair of leather strips to wrap around his hands.

"Better?"

Trent flexed his fingers. They felt sore, but he didn't want to complain. "Fine."

"Good. That means your vacation is over." Alana thrust his M27 into his hand. They wordlessly gathered the equipment they'd discarded during the skirmish. As Alana was about to set off, Trent took her hand to stop her.

"I owe you big time when we get out of here."

Alana nodded. "Yeah, you do. And I won't let you forget that. If you do, I'll come looking for you." A small smile crossed her lips, then she slung the Stinger over her shoulder. Trent slipped his backpack on and grunted from the weight. Either he had grown weaker, or Alana had slipped some extra things in there. He found his rifle and followed her.

For an hour, maybe more, they descended the silent, dark passages with only their flashlights stretching through the gloom. Occasionally, they came across other passages joining theirs, but the new tunnels always led upward as the main avenue continued steeply down.

Conversation had been negligible, neither wanting to attract unwelcome attention with small talk. It was broken only by occasional meaningful glances, which motivated them both onward. The temperature increased every few minutes, making each step more of an effort.

Alana was the first to break the somber atmosphere. "How far down are we?"

Trent checked the app on his phone. "I think we must be almost two miles down. It can't be much further."

A sharp beeping sound suddenly came from his belt. He unclipped the gas detector. A red and green light on the display alternated with a rhythmic electronic beep. He killed the audio alarm.

"How bad is it?" Alana asked nervously.

"We've hit a gas pocket. It's not poisonous, but possibly highly flammable. Just don't start smoking."

Alana cocked her head. "Do you feel that?"

Trent looked at her with a frown before sensing it, too. "A breeze." It felt like somebody had left an oven door open. "I thought the shafts were for ventilation." He held up the detector. "This proves my point." He indicated down the tunnel. "Let's continue. If the air tastes odd, don't inhale and back away until I can check it out."

Alana nodded, hoisted the launcher in anticipation. Trent tapped her on the shoulder and shook his head.

"Don't even think of using that. One little spark and this whole tunnel will explode."

Alana seemed about to argue before hanging the Stinger back on her shoulder with an air of irritation.

The tunnel gently spiraled down before a wash of air let them know they'd stepped into a larger area. Nervously, Alana opened her backpack and retrieved two small night-vision goggles with SWAT branded on the side.

"We should turn the flashlights off from this point on."

Trent stretched the tight rubber strap around his head and felt the cold metal press against his forehead.

"I see nothing," he grumbled.

"Hold on." Alana powered hers up before activating the switch on the side of Trent's.

Trent blinked as a green wash filled his world. As his eyes adjusted, he tried to ignore the fact that it felt as if he'd entered a video game. He didn't dare tell Alana that, in case it branded him any geekier in her eyes.

"It's like being in a video game," Alana said with a note of glee.

They edged further down the spiral, a giant helter-skelter carved in the stone, then emerged into a vast space. The image in the goggles glowed brighter as they compensated for the low illumination filling the cavern.

Ahead was the imposing structure of the mothership. There was no mistaking it. The size of it took their breath away. They had approached it from behind. The four massive cylindrical engines towered overhead, gently throbbing with an intense blue light.

Two Deros scuttled across the cavern and entered the craft along a sloped entrance ramp, passing another exiting Dero which was heading straight towards them.

Alana groped for the Stinger, but Trent restrained her, and silently tapped his belt loop where the LEDs on the sniffer were going crazy. She looked pleadingly at him. Trent risked a look – and was relieved to see the Dero had veered away, vanishing from his line of sight.

"It's gone," whispered Trent. "The gas levels in here are explosive. Maybe it's residual from the engine, but we must be careful."

"Okay, okay, but what now?"

"I guess the Ops team would head inside the ship." He'd expected her to refuse, to question the logic of going any deeper. Instead, she nodded.

"Good idea. There could be a command bridge or something. If we find a way to sabotage the engines, this thing won't be moving anytime soon."

Alana studied the craft. What she initially thought was a smooth, flowing surface, she now realized, was a patchwork of plates and vents that only gave a sleek appearance. She was no expert, but the ship seemed to have the aerodynamics of a cow, and she mused how it could possibly have gotten here.

Trent seemed to read her thoughts. "It doesn't look at all like I imagined an alien spaceship."

"If it can't fly," she whispered, "it makes me wonder where these things came from."

Trent was struck by that thought. Aliens had been the wild, but logical, assumption. But if they had no way to get here in the first place...

"Maybe they've been here far longer than us? How many eons has this thing been under the earth? It could have crashed millions of years ago. Or have these creatures always been among us; evolving under the earth, away from prying eyes?"

"That's seriously screwing around with my head."

"There have always been people talking about a hollow earth–"

He trailed off, becoming aware of a deep buzzing noise to the left.

"Trent, where did that Dero go?"

Trent risked a peek around the outcrop and felt his blood run cold. "Holy shit... we're in trouble."

"What is it?"

When he didn't answer, Alana chanced a look herself. Only twenty feet away stood the Dero, its drill arms half embedded in the wall, which it bored into, dust issuing from the hole. Beyond it was a line of Deros – hundreds of them - all mining the wall.

"I didn't think there'd be so many," Alana said despondently, aware they only had one missile left.

"Let's just hope there are none left inside."

"I guess they are all creatures, like that slug we found."

"That's not something I want to think about. Let's just figure out how to get inside."

"Trent... I don't think the Deros are our worst problem."

Trent tore his eyes from the line of machines and looked at her incredulously. "Alana, this couldn't be any worse."

Then he saw what she was looking at: a lone Dero walking around the far side of the ship, away from the others. It appeared to be approaching something hanging from the wall. His enhanced night vision just picked out the figure of a Marine hanging from a rope. At the top of the cliff, he saw another team member crouched at the edge, taking the weight of the rope. Standing next to him was the unmistakable figure of the Major leveling, a missile launcher at the Dero.

Joseph felt every sinew in his body tighten as the Dero approached. He settled the launcher on his shoulder, slowly and with a minimum of movement. So far, the Dero hadn't seen the humans, although it slowed and cocked its head as though searching for something. Perhaps it had picked up their brief radio contact.

Lieutenant Mitchell was hanging from the wall eight feet in front and above the machine - but it did not appear to notice him. From Joseph's vantage point, he could see Gordon, Blake, and Douglas just yards from the machine, concealed by the claw-like rocky outcrop.

Joseph wondered why the Dero had not seen them. Perhaps its vision systems in the depths were based on something else. Then he heard Richards grunt from the effort of holding Lieutenant Mitchell with a broken leg. The Dero's head shot up in his direction – and all hell broke loose.

THIRTY-THREE

ALANA WATCHED in shock as the hanging Marine released his harness and dropped like a stone. His impact with the ground was blocked by a rock ridge. The Dero spurred itself forward in pursuit just as Major Joseph fired.

The missile struck the lone Dero in a farrago of flame and noise – and pandemonium struck. The Deros against the far wall broke rank, running in every direction before zeroing in on their burning comrade.

Alana's night-vision goggles were knocked from her head by Trent's elbow – and seconds later, the entire cavern blossomed with a blinding, burning bright light.

Major Joseph had enough presence of mind to look away as the Dero exploded with a violent fireball that rolled up the cliff face, forcing him and Richards back. They shielded themselves from the wave of heat. When he risked a look, he found his night-vision goggles were nothing more than a blinding white screen. He pulled them off and was amazed to see the entire cavern had lit up like daylight.

Flames engulfed Richards. He was out of Joseph's reach,

and his damaged leg caused him to stumble over the cliff edge. Joseph bolted forward to see him crash into the wreckage of the burning Dero below.

There was no time to mourn his friend. He squinted up at the ceiling to see the source of the light. The entire roof was covered in rolling blue flames like an inverted ocean. The mile-long gas pocket blazed with intense ferocity, casting long, dark shadows around the rest of the cavern.

Looking back down, he saw the men had vanished, although he could hear Blake's voice yelling over the intercom, too distorted to understand, but that meant at least some were alive.

The entire wall of Deros had broken away to deal with the intruders. Now most of them collided with others, blinded by the intense light. Several Deros had evidently been crossing the cavern by the roof - as they now hung upside down and were wreathed in flames. One by one, they lost their footing and fell the two-hundred-eighty foot drop to the cavern floor below, exploding on impact. Several bounced off the mothership and tumbled down the side - legs flailing until they smashed in a crumpled heap on the floor below. Armor shattered and the gastropod inside splattered across the rock.

While there was chaos, the Major had a chance. They still had their mission to accomplish, down to the last man. He clipped the nylon rope to his harness, primed his FN-SCARS automatic, before taking a running jump into the infernal landscape below.

Trent couldn't believe his luck as the cavern erupted in a massive gas fireball. Sheer thermodynamic fortune alone forced the conflagration through the ventilation tunnels all around, sucking the flames towards the roof to form the boiling sea of flames.

When the burning Marine fell from the high tunnel, Trent could not tear his eyes away as he followed the man's kicking body all the way down until he slammed into the burning husk of the Dero.

His head snapped up when he saw movement above and Major Joseph dove off the ledge, attached to the descent rope. He admired the man's indestructible nature, but it made him worry how he could possibly stop the Major from accomplishing his mission. These thoughts were disrupted as Alana pulled on his arm.

"It's now or never!" She sprinted across the open ground towards the mothership. The Deros around them were colliding together, some running in circles, others were motionless. How long they would be out of action was anybody's guess, but Alana was right.

Trent heaved his pack across his back and ran after her. By the time they reached the bottom of an access ramp sloping into the craft, he heard multiple cracks of gunfire behind them.

Lieutenant Mitchell used his Camillus Marine Combat Knife to sever the rope tangled around his legs. He dropped eight feet when Richards released the rope – both him and the warhead in the pouch hanging around his waist. He'd landed hard and busted a rib against the warhead. Mitchell wasn't concerned the weapon had cracked open. It would take more than a fall to do that, but now, every time he inhaled, it sent ripples of pain through his chest.

Douglas' voice roared over his headset, instructing the team to run for the ship. A quick check showed the Deros were milling in confusion. It was just the chance he needed.

There was no sign of his rifle, and he felt naked without protection. He hauled the warhead pack over his shoulder as he made for the nearest ramp. Gordon dodged in front of him, finger on the trigger to take down anything in their way. Uranium-tipped slugs penetrated the Dero's armor in a series of dull thuds, but none returned fire.

The ramp was yards away as a Dero staggered across their path as if dazed. It saw the two men and swayed in their direction - all four arms raised for the kill — just as Gordon's magazine ran dry. Both men dodged sideways, the Dero side-stepping to block their path.

Tracer bullets suddenly sliced through the air from the side, ripping the Dero's head apart. Sparks and ooze seeped from the machine as it shuddered violently; its arms flopped lifelessly to its sides. A quick check revealed Blake with the PSA-13, laying suppressing fire from the vantage of a tall boulder.

Mitchell's legs screamed as he pounded up the sharp slope. Every breath was like a knife in his side, but he could do nothing other than try to block the pain. He paused before entering the craft, Gordon overtaking him. Blake was still picking off the Deros one at a time, and he saw Major Adams leap from the tunnel mouth: limbs splayed star-like as he fell.

Mitchell readjusted the straps on the warhead harness and turned to follow Gordon into the craft. It was a short hexagonal passage — and Gordon was blocking the way forward with a blood-curdling scream. The Marine had blindly run into the gaping vertical maul of the most hideous freak of nature Mitchell had ever seen.

Slime dripped from the six tentacles embracing Gordon as they pulled him into the vertical mouth. The scimitar shaped teeth gouged his body, severing his arms.

Mitchell was too stunned to move as blood cascaded from Gordon's stumps. His screams rose in pitch as he tried to break loose from the monster. Bones cracked as he was yanked into the mouth, his body folding like a cheap doll. The creature twisted to face Mitchell; its body undulating on a trail of slime that crackled like wet flesh.

Mitchell pushed himself against the wall, noticing Gordon's discarded rifle. He reached for it – but the beast was closing the gap. It bellowed, a noise like hailstones bouncing on a roof. Mitchell could see Gordon's convulsing body still inside the mouth, flesh burning as digestive acids splashed over him.

A flailing tentacle wrapped around Mitchell's arm, pulling his hand away from the rifle. There was a thunder of gunfire that almost deafened Mitchell, and the top of the creature's head, crowned by unblinking eyes, exploded in a shower of mucus as Lieutenant Blake powered up the ramp, the powerful PSA-13 blazing. More holes ruptured across the creature before it dropped like a wet sack.

Horrified, Blake stared at the beast. Its mouth was partially open, and Gordon's crushed body jerked in a pool of acid. With one eye melted, he could only see with the remaining one that blinked uncontrollably. His mouth moved, but not a sound came out.

Mitchell grimly snatched Gordon's own rifle and planted a single bullet in his friend's forehead. No amount of training could prepare for that. Tears rolled down his cheeks. Blake's firm hand on his shoulder assured him he'd done the right thing.

Only when the gunfire outside started again did they notice there had been a lull in activity. They peered down the ramp to see Major Joseph and Lieutenant Douglas taking refuge behind boulders as the Deros organized themselves to regroup.

Alana guessed it was pure luck that they had not been spotted as they raced across open ground on the opposite side of the craft from the Marines. The heavy gunfire assured her the Deros were still very much active.

Since the rolling flames on the ceiling were still burning, she figured Trent's advice about not using firepower was now null and void, and she gripped the Stinger reverently with both hands as they reached the ramp.

The slope was at a smooth sixty-degrees, forcing them both to scramble on all fours. Halfway up, they were already a good forty feet from the ground, and Alana silently thanked God she didn't suffer from vertigo. Trent, on the other hand, stayed as close to the center as possible and stared at nothing but the ramp in front of him. It was fortunate timing that Alana looked up to see a Dero appear in the entrance ahead. It stopped short in surprise at seeing the humans.

The plasma arms locked forward as Alana raised the Stinger and fired. The missile completed its short cruise – obliterating the Dero. Alana and Trent hit the deck as debris flew over them. The impact flipped the burning Dero in the air – and it crashed back onto the ramp, now rolling like a boulder towards them.

"Trent!" shrieked Alana as she rolled aside.

Trent looked up just in time and tilted to the side as the burning wreckage passed within an inch as it tumbled down the ramp. His eyes bugged as he peered over the edge of the ramp to the ground below. Any further, and he would have rolled off the side. As a child, he'd had trouble with the garden slide. This was just an amplification of that nightmare.

He pulled himself back to the safe middle of the ramp - and was alarmed to see Alana had vanished... almost. Her fingers poked over the ramp's edge. Trent crawled across and braced himself as he peered over the edge.

Alana hung at an awkward angle, legs scrambling to find purchase. Her Stinger launcher lay forty feet below on the rocks below, smashed in half.

Alana looked up and forced a smile, "Trent, now would be a good time for help."

Trent fought a brief wave of vertigo. He puffed his cheeks, trying to gain confidence. After all he'd been through, a mere fatal fall should be nothing.

"I can't hold on much longer." Alana's voice was measured and calm.

Trent wiped his sweaty palms on his jeans and reached over the edge without looking. He spread his body across the ramp to prevent himself from being pulled over and searched blindly for her arm. He snagged her wrist and gripped as hard as he could.

"You got me!"

Trent grunted as he pulled her up. Alana used her other hand to lever herself up, her boots swinging until one caught the lip of the ramp. With Trent anchoring her, she rolled back to safety.

"Jesus, Trent, you know how to give a girl a complex about her weight."

With that, she raced up the rest of the ramp. Trent groaned and followed her inside the ship.

THIRTY-FOUR

THE COUNTDOWN just turned to fifteen minutes, and General Carver heard a technician's redundant confirmation of the event.

From the corner of his eye, he saw Spontain shuffle towards him. His face was pale, and he couldn't meet the General's gaze.

"I've been called away. I want you to keep me constantly updated while I'm in the air."

A sneer spread across Carver's face. He was surprised to find his thoughts rebel against the ingrained track made by years of obeying orders.

"Leaving the sinking ship?"

Spontain was stunned by the truthful response. "Pardon?"

"Cast the dice, then leave the table like a true Washington shit master." Rage swelled as Carver spat the words. "All my life I've followed orders from imbeciles like you, and now I find myself carrying out the most ludicrous of all. Launching a nuclear strike on home turf."

"May I remind you I am the Secretary of Homeland Security!"

"Believe me, if nobody in this room lives through the next few minutes, then neither will you."

Spontain puffed his cheeks, searching for an appropriate response - but words failed him. He spun on his heels and marched from the control center. At the door, he spun to wave an admonishing finger at Carver.

"When this is over, I'll have you court-martialed for your insubordination." But he was talking to Carver's back.

Spontain hurried to his waiting Bell chopper, which idled with blurring rotors, ready to leap into the sky. It was the fastest transport he could muster in the short time he decided to bail out. The President had ordered him to stay and watch over the operation. He just hadn't clarified *how near* he had to be to do so.

On a monitor, Carver watched the chopper rise from the park. He put on his headset and keyed a direct channel to a gunship still in the air.

By God, he would remain true to his word.

"Follow discreetly and be ready to bring the chopper down on my command."

The pilot's response was a monotone "Confirmed."

For a moment, Carver reveled in the freedom his spirit felt by the probability of his impending death, before realizing another minute had shaved off the clock.

* * *

IT WAS a beautiful summer's day with his wife's deep blue eyes staring full of love straight into his soul. It was a moment he came back to time and time again when an operation went awry.

In the time it took to open his eyes, Major Joseph Adams had traveled from Heaven to Hell.

The crushing reality of being trapped two miles underground, with a sea of blue flames rolling above his head and an army of mechanical aliens around him, was brought into sharp relief.

"I can cover you," said Lieutenant Douglas, close to his ear.

This simple sentence registered in Joseph's consciousness that this man would die to protect him, and he felt a surge of pride for his unit mixed with despair that they *would* probably shortly die.

Joseph glanced over the rock to see at least forty Deros cautiously advancing. He touched the small throat mic, reminding himself that the Deros seemed attracted only when Lieutenant Richards had made a sound. He spoke as quietly as possible.

"Mitchell, status?"

Mitchell's response was only audible in Joseph's earbud. "Gordon down, Blake with me. We're in the craft and see you with Douglas. Advise on Richards."

"Richards is down." The news that they were in the craft was all he wanted to hear right now. "Package status?"

"Still ticking."

The fact they didn't know when the detonation would be just added to the chaotic turn the mission had taken. It was irrelevant. There would be no way to outrun a nuclear blast. Not even one underground. He found he was staring at the rolling flames overhead and was struck by an idea.

"Mitchell, how many flashers do you have?"

While he waited for a response, he checked his own belt and Douglas's.

"Five between us," came Mitchell's reply.

Joseph took the flash grenades from Douglas' belt, and with two in each hand, readied them.

"Okay, both you and Blake throw as many as you can to the foot of the ramp. On my mark."

"Copy."

Joseph nudged Douglas and indicated with his head towards the ship. "When these go off, don't look, just run."

Mitchell's voice crackled over the headset. "Ready."

Joseph tensed. "On my mark, three..."

Douglas rose into a crouch, heaving the weight of the PSA-13 with him. He positioned himself to slide down the shallowest slope of the boulder.

"Two..."

Joseph readied himself to pull the pins from one set of grenades so he could quickly prime the other set before throwing them.

"One – mark!"

All four pins pulled in less than half a second. Joseph tossed them at the Deros. He heard multiple clanks as the other marine's grenades skittered across the floor. At the last moment, Joseph shielded his eyes in the crook of his elbow.

BOOM! The cavern erupted like a supernova as the nine grenades detonated almost simultaneously. It was a pure light, so bright that Joseph could still see it through his shielded eyes. He booted Lieutenant Douglas down the slope and pursued him. They landed on their feet and raced towards the craft. Around them, the Deros were either stationary or milling in confusion. Joseph was quick on his feet - but Douglas fell behind due to the weight of the PSA-13.

Joseph reached the foot of the ramp before the white spots that marred his vision finally vanished. He saw Douglas lagging behind.

"Douglas, come on!" bellowed Joseph as he raced up the ramp.

Even though his eyes were tightly closed, Douglas' vision had suffered from the flashes. He veered too close to a rocky outcrop, snagging the spinal cord connecting his headset to the gun. The helmet was yanked from his head with enough force to spin him around. He tripped onto his back and found himself pinned by the bulky PSA-13.

Pounding up the ramp, Joseph reached the two men inside the craft. He turned to see Douglas struggling on the ground. His immediate reaction was to rush back to aid his friend, but Blake's arm restrained him.

"No!"

Just as the words were spoken, several of the Deros unleashed a barrage of heat rays in random directions – but all thankfully away from the ship.

The first volley turned a portion of wall, approximately the size of a house, into molten rock, turning it into a dark black stain as it cooled with a deep cracking sound.

Douglas was on his feet as the second barrage of heat-blasts obliterated the rock they had been on - momentarily turning the surrounding ground into liquid. The heat-rays jolted left and caught Douglas. He was vaporized in an instant.

Joseph felt some relief that two blinded Deros were caught in the stray fire – instantly exploding under their companions' onslaught.

Blake hammered a hexagonal control button at head height next to the door. The portal spiraled shut, blocking sight of another volcanic blast destroying the ground at the foot of the ramp.

For good measure, he put a bullet in the button, hoping he'd trapped the Deros outside... and trying to overlook the fact they were all now trapped *inside*.

* * *

A DULL, red light permeated the corridor. It took Alana several seconds to readjust. The corridor itself was hexagonal, with wavy metal grating along the floor and walls. Passageways branched at acute angles rather than perpendicular, and ahead the corridor branched on three axes - up, down, and spiraled straight ahead. The unusual angles and curves had an unsettling effect on their sense of balance, teetering them to the side like a crooked corridor in a carnival haunted house.

"Okay," said Alana, as she took the safety off the M27. "We're here. Any more details on how we stop this mess?"

Trent tried to visualize where on the ship they could be. Possibly on the mid to lower-aft deck.

"I figured we find the bridge and press the big red stop button."

Alana looked at him incredulously. "That's your scientific master plan?"

Trent reached for his backpack and took out a package wrapped in cloth. He carefully unfolded the fabric.

"I also thought that hitting it with several pounds of high explosive might do something."

"C-4! Where did you get that?"

"It's amazing what you can purchase over the Internet with a credit card."

"You've got to be kidding me."

"We use small quantities to help blast holes when burying sensors in the rock. Schofield found a cheap place that supplied building materials. So, we ordered a little extra."

Alana smiled. "You are a man of many surprises."

"That was a veiled compliment, right?"

"Which way?"

Trent replaced the explosives in his backpack. With no guidance on how the creatures thought, he could only assume the bridge would be at the front of the ship.

"At a guess, up and forward. This way."

He flipped the safety off his own M27 and pressed forward. For the first time since this nightmare had begun, he felt a tremor of optimism.

THIRTY-FIVE

JOSEPH'S initial revulsion at the sight of the creature with Gordon's mangled body inside faded when he noted the bullet hole in the marine's skull. He hoped he'd have the courage to put a friend out of his misery.

He changed the magazine on his FN-SCARS and edged around the bloated monstrosity. Several yards in, they came to an intersection where the grating beneath his feet was still absorbing the creature's slime trail.

"Mitchell, how's our nuke?"

Mitchell gently placed the cradle on the floor and examined the warhead. The small LED pulsed rhythmically. No clock, no dramatic countdown. Just a single pulsing point of light. Was it an optical illusion, or was it beating faster?

"I can't see any way of disarming it. There are anti-tamper mechanisms in place to stop just such an event. I can try to decrypt the override code, but that's a million-to-one shot."

Joseph nodded. "Good odds for us right now."

Mitchell lost no time in connecting an adapted cell

phone to a data port hidden in the warhead. A line of numbers scanned across the screen as it crunched powerful algorithms. Eventually, "NO ACCESS" flashed on the screen. Mitchell let out a heavy sigh.

"Worth trying again?"

Mitchell shrugged. "I can leave it running. After all, people win the lottery every week."

Joseph punched the wall in frustration. "Great! That's just fucking terrific! Those damn assholes! Are you telling me that this thing could go off any second?"

Mitchell nodded, oddly calm.

Blake started to laugh, propelled by sheer nerves. "Least it'll be quick. I always wanted to be right in the middle of the action. Careful what you wish for, huh, Sire?"

Joseph nodded, collected his thoughts. "Okay, we still have a mission, and there is just as much probability that this thing will blow an hour from now as there is in two seconds' time, right?"

Mitchell counted two seconds under his breath before forcing a grin. "Did I ever tell you that it was your optimism that got me through Myanmar?" The reference made them all smile, even if the memory was a grim one.

* * *

TRENT AND ALANA made rapid progress up the decks without running into another creature. He hoped they were all busy with the marines outside. It was several minutes before they came across the first door blocking the corridor. It looked relatively simple to open, with a hexagonal control mounted on the wall. They were approximately above mid-deck halfway along the ship - at least, that's what Trent figured – and onward was the only option they had. Yet they hesitated, anxious about what lay beyond.

Alana raised her rifle. "You open it. I'll shoot whatever's on the other side."

Trent nodded tersely. "Good plan."

He pressed himself against the wall. Alana raised the M27 against her shoulder and sighted down the barrel. She nodded to Trent, who inhaled deeply before punching the control.

The door spiraled open with a whoosh, and Trent braced himself for the gunfire that never came. He readied his rifle at his waist, as he'd seen in so many movies, and took a step through the door.

The room beyond was massive. Trent's nerves jangled when he saw *hundreds* of Deros, but kept his cool when he saw they were empty exosuits hung from the walls, open like metal flowers. They sat in rows of twenty-five, towering five layers up. The entire setup reminded Trent of an aircraft carrier.

Alana followed, sweeping the room with the rifle as she looked around. "My God. It's a hangar."

Trent noticed the bottom rows against the walls were empty. "If they're the machines outside, I wonder who owns the rest of them?"

Alana did a quick calculation in her head. "This is not good."

"Maybe... if they've been down here for so long, that's all that's left of them."

He examined the interior of the nearest suits. He was surprised they had a new car smell. An assortment of monitor screens and dials lined the interior, placed high in the curved head section. Much further down, levers and curling joysticks looked more like a jumbled mass of branches than efficient controls.

"Trent!"

Alana's voice had an edge that immediately got his attention. He didn't even turn before he heard the distinctive Dero cry.

Through the door they had entered, he could see three slugs rapidly approaching down the corridor. Their tentacles flailed, the deadly barbed one poised to stab forward. There were more behind.

"Close the door!" snapped Trent.

Alana let off a short burst, hitting the lead creatures as she struck the door control with her palm. The portal spiraled shut.

Trent rushed for the opposite exit. "Can you lock the door?"

Alana quickly studied the smooth, blank control. "I don't know."

Trent was already running for the far door. He opened it - instantly firing a burst into the corridor beyond. But it was empty and stretched gently upward.

"Come on, let's go!"

Alana turned with fearful eyes. "Trent, I can't lock this!"

"Run!"

"Trent!" Alana looked imploringly at him, then the door spiraled open, and Trent glimpsed pulsing vile flesh and a serrated vertical slit of mouth. Alana fired a burst point-blank. The creature let out an enraged cry that was silenced as she punched the door control, closing it again.

Trent motioned to her. "Come on! You can't do that all day!"

Alana looked at him with soft eyes. "Trent, you need time to set the C-4."

The door briefly opened, and Alana immediately closed it.

Trent crossed back to her. "What are you trying to say?"

"We both knew this was probably a one-way trip. And at least I can do something useful here." She didn't even look up as the door opened, and she immediately closed it again, silencing the clicking wails of frustration beyond.

Trent ran a finger down her cheek. "I never wanted to be a hero."

She smiled softly. "The way you've performed down here, I could tell."

"I always planned on getting out of here alive."

She shook her head, thumping the door control with perfect timing just as it opened a fraction once more.

"Alana, we can figure this out–"

He was cut short as Alana yanked his head forward, and he felt her tongue press against his mouth. He'd barely had time to appreciate the kiss before she shoved him away - sealing the door once more.

"I'll cover you for as long as I can. Don't look back, Trent."

He paused as the door began to open a fraction, and a barbed tentacle poked through. Alana squeezed off a few rounds and closed the door, severing the limb that flapped on the floor like a fish.

Emotions washed through Trent. A tidal wave of loss. But instead of self-pity, he was hit with a spike of anger. These creatures had steadily taken everything from him. He owed it to Walt, Catherine, Alana – the whole city – to make them pay.

He stepped through the far door, giving one last look at Alana before it spiraled closed, separating them just as he heard her squeeze another off another burst of gunfire.

* * *

LIEUTENANT BLAKE FOUND the new corridor appeared to take them to the highest level, as far as he could judge. Another identical six-sided long corridor extended in front of them. Nothing needed to be said as the remnants of the team jogged towards the front of the craft.

One hand gripped his rifle, the other his last flash grenade. If they met any creatures, he didn't want to waste time with a firefight. For the first time, things seemed to run in their favor. Mitchell had confirmed the pulsing LED on the warhead was blinking faster as his hacking software continued its assault on the bomb's software.

The way ahead was sealed by a door. Joseph estimated they must now be at the front of the craft and hoped they had to go no further.

Mitchell kept back as Joseph and Blake took position on either side of the doorway. Joseph tapped the door control, and the portal spun open. Mitchell had just enough time to see a large, curved room beyond. A slug twisted around to face the intruders with a dry gargle - as Joseph popped the flash grenade and tossed it inside, hammering the door closed.

Just before the room was sealed, the grenade discharged, and they heard a shriek like fingernails across a blackboard before the Major reopened the door and they charged into the room, guns blazing.

THIRTY-SIX

ALANA KNEW she could not keep the game up for much longer before one of them tired, or the creatures found another way in. At least it was buying Trent time. What she didn't expect was for the door to suddenly buckle, smoke rising from the surface. She darted for cover behind a rack of Dero suits as the entire door became semi-molten and a familiar mechanical Dero stalked inside, plasma-arms glowing hot. Behind, a phalanx of slugs waited cautiously as the exosuit scanned the room.

Alana's mind raced. She was hopelessly outgunned, and hiding places were thin on the ground. She shouldered her M27 and deftly climbed up the side of a rack holding the Dero exosuits, taking cover on the second tier. So far, she hadn't been spotted.

She watched the Dero prowl the room. The creatures near the door gained confidence as they entered. She also noted, with some satisfaction, that a dead slug torn apart by bullets was slumped in the corridor.

It was only a matter of time before they looked up. Her mind fondly fell back to Ed. Only a few days ago, they'd been sharing a burger at In 'n' Out and speculating on future vacation plans as she shepherded another call from her mom to voicemail.

She slowly shifted position, moving inside an exosuit for cover. Lying among the nest of control levers, she was hidden from view, but still trapped.

Crouching on her knees, her eyes strayed towards two hefty control levers mounted horizontally on the floor and very distinct from the others. A wild thought occurred to her.

* * *

THE FIRST SLUG was blown away over a bank of controls, bubbling black bile across the displays. The second flailed wildly as it was blinded. Blake finished it off by nearly severing its head with concentrated gunfire.

Joseph quickly scanned the bridge, satisfied there were no other creatures, before taking stock of his surroundings.

It was undoubtedly the bridge. An enormous dome looked out onto a grand 180-degree view. Rising in front of the dome was the massive circular collar that surrounded the craft's nose. He could just see a series of massive fluctuating orbs - house-sized versions of the Dero's plasma-arms, attached to the collar that revolved three hundred and sixty degrees as it bored through the earth.

The bridge itself was tiered with a series of ramps and connected to another two entrances. Command desks were covered in hexagonal buttons marked with bumps and notches like braille. Levers and joysticks followed the same design ethos as those inside the Dero armor. Screens were curved like ovals of obsidian, positioned at the creature's head height. None of it was operable by a single human.

"Blake, cover those doors. Mitchell, the bridge is yours."

Mitchell removed the warhead from its cradle and carefully placed it on a control bank. Then he turned his attention to the program, trying a brute force attack on the bomb's interface.

Blake was moving between the two doors when he suddenly noticed a concealed ramp running down to a fourth door, where a gibbering slug was concealed in the shadows. It hissed at him, and two powerful barbed tentacles thrust into his chest. He was lifted into the air, firing wildly. His shots hit random controls and screens, forcing the others to hide behind the desks.

Joseph fired at the beast, trying to avoid hitting Blake, whose finger was stuck on the trigger. Stray fire caught Mitchell unawares, pulverizing his head as he knelt next to the warhead.

Joseph dropped as Blake's wild fire raked across the desk in front of him.

The monster flexed its barbed limbs and effortlessly heaved Blake apart with a fleshy crunch. His mangled halves thudded against control panels.

Joseph watched the creature turn towards him. He saw Mitchell's butchered remains, his skull cleaved in two. He was slumped over the live warhead, his brainpan gushing across the floor.

Now Major Joseph Adams was alone.

Trapped and alone. There was only one way out of this.

With a bellow from the pit of his stomach, and powered

by hatred he had never felt before, Joseph rolled from his hiding place and marched towards the rampaging horror as he emptied his entire clip.

* * *

THE DERO STALKED across the hangar as it searched for Alana. By some inaudible cue, eleven other slugs moved inside and spread out. By the time the last slug had entered the chamber, it had just enough time to register a hissing noise - before an exosuit leapt from its mounting on the second row, crushing the creature as it landed, the suit's flexible legs easily absorbing the impact. The other slugs scattered on trails of slime.

Inside the suit, Alana was bucked from the impact - but kept her footing as she stood inside the torso section that was too big for her. She looked like a child commandeering a tank.

Her feet were wedged against two pedal controls that behaved similarly to an automobile, and she figured the slugs controlled them with their body weight. Her arms were inside a slender set of restraints, akin to what she had seen used to control remote robotic arms. Through a set of grayscale blob-like screens that depicted the world like a fly's multifaceted point of view, she saw her own suit's plasma-arms wave like a drunkard.

The Dero across the hangar barely had time to turn before she used all her strength to squeeze two control levers together – a feat easier to accomplish with tentacles rather than fingers. The entire exo-frame rocked as the plasma-arms volleyed - the focused heat-ray combusted half the startled slugs and blew apart a restraining girder supporting a rack against the opposite wall.

Alana sidestepped as the entire rack toppled down, a wall of empty Dero suits crushing the remaining slugs. Then the entire structure pirouetted in slow motion and fell towards her. She braced herself for the impact - but was saved as the top edge of the falling rack lodged against the wall and formed a roof of exosuits, precariously hanging from hydraulic hooks.

The falling armor buffeted the Dero near the door, but it remained standing. It turned to Alana and charged with its drill arms forward, the wicked bits shimmering in the red light as they powered up.

Alana snarled and put all her weight on one of the foot pedals, making the suit lurch forward at speed. Both machines charged together like knights on horseback.

***

TRENT FELT numb as he raced from the hangar. The image of Alana's soft brown eyes imploring him to go haunted him. She had sacrificed her life for him, but he felt nothing but anger.

After following a long, upward sloping corridor and wrestling with his conscience about returning and attempting a heroic rescue, which he knew was impossible, Trent now faced another door. He surmised that the Deros only used doors for rooms and not for sectioning corridors. He tensed himself for what lay beyond.

The door opened with a faint whir and Trent fell backwards as a slug powered through. He blindly fired the M27, and the beast flopped lifelessly to the ground.

Trent's pride was dashed when he saw the creature was dead. That meant the marines must have gotten here first — and they were trained killers.

* * *

THE IMPACT PUSHED Alana on her butt, and she slid the length of the exosuit as the machines collided, sliding into the rear housing that protected the creature's body. She crawled to the main controls as the suit shook from the impact of the attacking Dero's whirling drills. She hooked her arms back into the plasma-arm straps and studied the monitor screens.

The Dero was locked against her in a tight embrace. One drill-arm was pushing into the torso like a stomach punch. She could hear the strain of the material as the drill bit.

Alana tried to swing the plasma-arms but met resistance. Her opponent must have pinned them down. She grunted as she put all her weight into moving a single plasma arm and was surprised when it suddenly swung free. On the monitor screens, she saw the other Dero had recoiled backward from the impact.

It revved the drills threateningly, positioning them over its head, akin to a scorpion's deadly tail.

Alana quickly maneuvered both plasma-arms forward and pulled hard on the triggers as the Dero rushed her.

The heat ray blast rocked her suit backwards. She obviously had misjudged the suit's stance as it toppled end-over-end, rolling like a pinball across the hangar. However, her shot was on target. The blast enveloped the Dero, and it exploded in a massive conflagration that caused the jammed exosuit rack above it to shake loose and topple down with a mighty rumble.

Alana rolled hard against the door she had entered through - the collapsing rack narrowly avoiding crushing her. Inside the suit, she lay spread-eagled, holding on for dear life as she pitched wildly around.

* * *

TRENT SAW TWO DEAD MARINES. He recognized one, although he couldn't remember the name, and did not want to look at the other, whose face lay in two halves across the bridge. One thing was for sure; neither marine was Major Adams - who Trent last saw swan dive from the cavern to his certain demise. It was a shame, as Trent had warmed to the Major during their brief meeting and sensed he was a man of intuition rather than one who blindly followed orders. He was drawn to a device resting on a desk next to the dead marine. Even without radiation symbols on the side, the small conical warhead was instantly recognizable. The single blinking light was not what Trent had expected. Next to it, a phone was connected, a series of codes flashing across the screen.

Trent edged closer. It was stupid to be so cautious. If it was about to blow, it wouldn't matter where he was, yet animal caution made him wary. There were no visible seams. No wires to pull. No obvious way to disarm it.

Those dumb bastards. Why hadn't they listened? Trent had almost known he'd have to try and stop the detonation. It was a practicality he'd ignored, and now, at the last hurdle, it was evidently impossible.

Trent raised the M27 to rifle-butt the warhead in the

desperate hope of breaking *something* open. Instead, he found himself yanked to the floor, the breath knocked out of him.

The rifle fell from his grasp as he felt his arm crack. There was a brief shot of pain, and then it went numb. He was roughly flipped over and stared into the wan face of Major Joseph Adams.

Joseph was enraged, but also shocked. "What the hell are you doing here?"

Trent gasped as the marine applied pressure. "Trying to stop you from using the warhead. Remember what I said? A blast from this depth is going to trigger a wave of fault lines and the whole goddamn seaboard will collapse. The science hasn't changed since you've been down here, Major. You're going to murder millions of people."

"I have my orders."

"Orders can be wrong."

"They were made by top men, Professor. People cleverer than us. The risks must be acceptable, otherwise they wouldn't have endorsed the plan."

"Are you nuts?" Spittle formed at Trent's mouth. "You seriously believe that?"

"I follow orders to protect my country."

"No, Major, you're destroying it. Why the hell would I come all the way down here to stop you? I'm a freaking seismologist. A nobody!"

Joseph released the pressure on Trent's neck and shook his head. "Even if you're right, there is nothing we can do. This warhead is from the Excalibur. It was activated remotely. We've been trying to stop it to give us a fighting chance of getting out of here. You can see how well that went. In a couple of minutes, this conversation will be terminally over. You might as well relax and accept it."

Trent wasn't paying attention. Joseph had relaxed enough to allow Trent minimal arm movements, obviously not regarding him as much of a threat. He noticed a red swelling in the Major's leg, a neat bullet entrance wound pulsing with a little blood.

Using the last reserves of strength, Trent punched out, one hand striking Joseph's windpipe – cutting him off mid-sentence. The other rammed his thumb as far as he could into the wound.

Joseph rolled off him in sheer pain.

Trent scrambled across the floor for the M27. His finger wrapped around the barrel as he felt Joseph grip his foot and drag him backwards.

Joseph unsheathed a wicked-looking knife. "You bastard!"

Trent arced the rifle around in a powerful batter's swing - the butt crumpled the marine's nose. Joseph released his grip but ignored the bloodied mess as he rose to his knees. Trent tried to hit him again with the rifle - but the Marine easily caught the weapon and yanked it from his hands.

Nimbly flipping it over, Joseph leveled it at Trent.

"Sorry, Professor. This operation must succeed. If I'm wrong, I'll see you a little further down."

Trent closed his eyes. A sudden rush of blood pounded in his ears, and his world slowed to a crawl.

His eyes flicked open a lifetime later when there was no impact. Joseph was examining the jammed weapon. He didn't wear the expression of a madman, but one of despair as he stared beyond Trent.

Time seemed to stretch further as Trent followed his

gaze – to see a mechanical Dero enter the bridge. Its drill-arms wound up with a high-pitched screech as Joseph cleared the jam and unleashed a stream of bullets. Trent threw himself over a control panel for cover.

The Dero lunged and speared Joseph through the chest with a spine-splitting crack. Blood frothed on his lips as he twitched and jerked. Servos whined as the Dero reversed the thrust and hurled the body across the bridge.

Too weak to move, Trent just watched as the machine wheeled to face him, stepping menacingly toward him with the drill arms poised to strike.

Then they suddenly powered down.

Trent blinked in surprise as the whole machine became limp. With a hiss, the exosuit unfolded open, and Trent pressed himself against the wall, bracing himself for the horror inside.

Trent blinked.

The horror was a petite, cute brunette covered in welts and bruises, and wearing a grim expression.

"Alana?"

"What are you sitting around for? I thought you wanted to blow this party?"

Trent's smile faltered, and he shook his head.

"What's wrong?"

He pointed to the warhead. "The nuke's primed to detonate at any moment."

"Can you disarm it?"

Trent chuckled. "I missed that class in high school. Can you?"

"What about the C_4?"

"I just have a feeling all that will do is dent the case." He let out a long sigh. His eyes focused on the solitary blinking red light on the warhead. He just shook his head, his shoulders finally relaxing, as he accepted the inevitable. He looked at Joseph's body slumped across the wall and felt guilty. They were technically on the same side, and yet it had come to this.

But Alana was unperturbed. "I think you're wrong. Out of the way."

Trent took cover behind the suit as Alana resealed the exosuit. Servos wheezed to life as it took on a more formidable stance. She maneuvered the machine with impressive skill to face the nuke.

Trent didn't get her plan. With a hesitant shudder, Alana raised the plasma-arms to focus on it.

Trent's mouth dropped open when he understood what she was about to do. He had a fraction of a second to throw his arms defensively across his face as the heat-blast removed half the control panels - vaporizing the warhead shell and components inside in an instant before they reached critical mass. The deck floor turned into a puddle of molten metal. It gave way through to the deck below with a crash. The liquefied radioactive warhead components welded uselessly to the surface.

Trent risked a peep over the lip at the mass below as it cooled with a loud plinking sound. Alana unfolded the Dero and jumped out triumphantly.

"Not bad," said Trent begrudgingly.

"Female thinking," Alana quipped back. "Now let's plant those charges and get out of here before the cavalry arrives."

"Whose cavalry?"

"Either. I'm tired of them both."

Trent set to work molding the plastic explosive over

every available surface. He primed the detonation for four minutes, although he still didn't know how they were going to get out. He'd placed all his faith in Alana, who impatiently guarded the door.

Two minutes later, the charges were planted and primed. Alana motioned to him. "Now get inside."

Trent stared uncomprehendingly at the exosuit. "What?"

"Jeez, for a scientist, you are the dumbest person I have ever met. We're not gonna walk through those masses outside. Get in!"

They both turned as they heard a faint gibbering cry and spotted five creatures rushing down the corridor towards them.

Trent didn't miss a beat as he clambered into the exosuit. Alana ushered him into the aft section as she climbed aboard, hot on his heels.

"Hold on to anything you can. This is gonna be rough."

Trent groped at niches on the floor. Alana knelt for the handles fixed on the floor and heaved them with a grunt. The suit immediately sealed over with a dull thud, isolating the gibbering hordes outside as the slugs entered the room.

Alana placed her feet in oversized stirrups; her arms gripped a pair of levers more at home on a steam train than advanced alien technology. With a grunt, she turned the suit around from the advancing creatures to face the exterior dome canopy.

"Hold on!" she screamed as she put all her weight on the speed control. The exosuit bucked forward.

From his position in the back, Trent could just see the exterior monitors in front of Alana. It took a second for his eyes to comprehend the multi-faceted view - and the fact that they were racing straight for the glass dome.

"Here we go!" grunted Alana as she shifted her body weight to move the plasma-arms forward, almost outstretched - then at the very last moment, she squeezed the bulky alien trigger.

The creatures watched helplessly as their prey blasted the canopy window apart in a perfect hole of bubbling glass - before jumping out a hundred and fifty feet above the ground - on a direct collision course with the solid rock face.

But before the suit impacted against the coarse rock, Alana fired again. The intense heat ray liquefied the rock enough for the suit to land in a newly formed tunnel. She kept the pressure on the volcanic beams as they melted the earth away while they powered upwards.

From inside, they watched the monitors as the rock surface bubbled in front of them. The exosuit ploughed through the stone like a comet traversing deep space. Alana kept the speed on.

"You know where you're going?"

"Up."

It was difficult to judge the direction with no reference point and indecipherable displays. The constant jarring of the machine pushed Trent firmly back, but he figured they must be nearly vertical.

From the refuge of the exosuit and the solid earth around them, they neither saw nor felt the effects of the explosives on the ship's bridge.

The creatures were obliterated as the remaining control panels exploded in a successive conflagration that crippled the craft. The rest of the observation dome shattered as shrapnel brutally struck it. The plasma-collar that surrounded the ship faltered, the fluctuating orbs shattering in a rainbow of light, as an unexpected energy surge pulsed through the mothership, leaving it stranded like a dead whale while fire rampaged uncontrolled through the foredecks.

* * *

THE GIRL from Ipanema played across the Beverly Center mall public address speakers as somebody's idea of a joke. After several days of chaos, consumerism was once more finding its feet in downtown LA, and the mall was full of people eager to stock up for disaster even at this early hour.

A little boy stared at the polished tiled floor, which appeared to shimmer. A gleeful laugh escaped his lips. His mother looked at him with a warm smile; laughter was something she hadn't heard for several days.

"What is it, honey?"

"The floor's turning to water!"

The mother giggled too until she followed the boy's gaze and saw the stone was glowing cherry-red.

"Oh my God!"

She pulled her son backwards by his collar - just as the ground exploded. Shoppers on the mezzanine watched as a plume of heated detritus shot straight up in a cloud of smoke and steam. Then a nightmarish mechanical Dero climbed from the pit.

Screams cascaded through the mall as people fled for cover. Water from a fractured pipe sprayed the area, turning into steam as it met the hot concrete. The woman shielded her face. When she looked up, her son was no longer with her.

"Nathan!"

With dread, she saw her boy staring fixedly at the giant

Dero. It approached him, plasma-arms pulsing like angry fireflies.

By the time she screamed and raced for him, the boy laughed again. She gripped him around the waist, but then froze in astonishment as the Dero unfolded - revealing two people. Both bore bloodied scars, but were laughing heartily as they jumped from the machine, collapsing on the floor, giddy from being alive.

They rolled into each other's arms and then kissed, long and deep, as the spectators watched in confusion.

EPILOGUE

DEEP BELOW THE EARTH, the threat now lay neutralized. Neutralized, but not defeated. The win for General Carver had come at a high price. He didn't care that Spontain was taking all the credit. It was irrelevant when the handful of right people knew the truth.

In a dark office deep within the bowels of the Pentagon, the small team running the Majestic files began coordinating the clearup deep below the earth. Already, an effective misinformation campaign was underway to detract from the truth, and the public, always desperate for normality, was eating it up.

Carver knew that was the way these things always played out.

It took almost a week to coordinate Army Engineers to descend and sift through the wreckage to discover the origin of these creatures. Trent was in his lab with Schofield, musing over his several dates with Alana since they'd surfaced. There was certainly mutual attraction there, but without the ever-present sense of threat, it seemed a little too normal. Maybe they weren't such a good match, or perhaps their combined loss was making them more guarded than ever.

That's why he was surprised when she entered the lab and gave him a casual greeting, as if they'd been friends forever. Even more surprising was General Carver, dressed in golfing slacks and a loud red polo shirt. Schofield's elation at the company was crushed when the General asked for them to be left alone.

Alana sat on the edge of a desk and folded her arms, her head cocked inquisitively to the side as Trent finally spoke up.

"I'm sorry for the loss of your–"

Carver held up his hand to stop him. They had both spent two horrible days being debriefed and hadn't glossed over the raw truth. Trent had expected they'd be arrested for murdering the Major. Instead, he was just ticked-off as another casualty.

"You did what you thought was right. And you were. The lives saved outweigh the losses. That's not exactly why I'm here."

Trent looked at Alana. If she knew anything, she had a perfect poker face.

"You're aware of Majestic clearance." Trent nodded, remembering the dire threats if he ever dared to speak of it. "We're a small, highly funded operation that relies on a network of operatives from all disciplines. I'd like you to join."

"Me?"

"Well, both of you." He waved a finger between them. "It seems with you two, the sum of the parts is much bigger than what you can accomplish alone."

"Well, I don't know if..."

"Let me make this clear. It's a one-time offer. There are far too many things happening in the world for me to pander to anybody's fragile ego."

"What exactly will we be doing?"

"Things you never thought possible."

Trent's brow furrowed. He hated cryptic answers. He looked at Alana, who gave the faintest hint of a smile.

Carver looked between them. "She wouldn't give me an answer until I asked you. So, are you ready to have your eyes opened about what's really going on out there?"

Trent met Alana's unflinching gaze and took a deep breath before he responded...

ALSO BY ANDY BRIGGS

CHEM

Majestic Files 2

Not all conspiracy theories are wrong…

Aircraft vapor trails slice through the skies around the world. A harmless side effect to international travel. Until aircraft investigator Sam Dwyer discovers something bolted to the wing of a fatal crash. Something that shouldn't be there…

He stumbles into a global conspiracy to lace the skies with chemtrails – chemicals designed to alter the population's behavior.

It's an intricate plot with global ramifications – and it's happening in plain sight!

With his life on the line, Dwyer races to expose the syndicate behind it. But their resources are vast. There is nowhere to hide...

PHANTOM LAND

Majestic Files 3

NIGHTMARES CAN'T BE CAGED...

Ghosts, wraiths, phantoms... science has just proved they are real animals from another dimension. So what better way to exploit the discovery...?

Las Vegas' new glittering jewel is a zoo with a difference. Come face-to-face with **specters**; watch **phantoms** soar through their enclosures; or dare to walk through the **banshee** tunnels. The world of the supernatural has been contained so you can confront your darkest fears...

It's a popular attraction – until a radical group of animal extremists try to liberate the beasts during the unveiling of the new star exhibit: An Angel of Death... and hell is unleashed.

Lowly zookeeper, Wes Talasky becomes the last line of defense. Forced to face his darkest fears so he can save the children of the woman he loves...

Blending science and horror into a rip-roaring adventure!

POINT NEMO

Majestic Files 4

A LONELY PLACE TO DIE...

Point Nemo - the most **remote location** on the planet...

Deep below the waves it's known as the **satellite graveyard**...

...And something **terrifying is stirring**...

A group of scientists have been gathered to investigate a mysterious find. A threat that may not be from this world. A threat that could destroy life as we know it...

Now the world's superpowers are descending on Point Nemo in a race to claim it as their own.

A rip-roaring adventure!

TRIGGER EFFECT

COMING SOON!

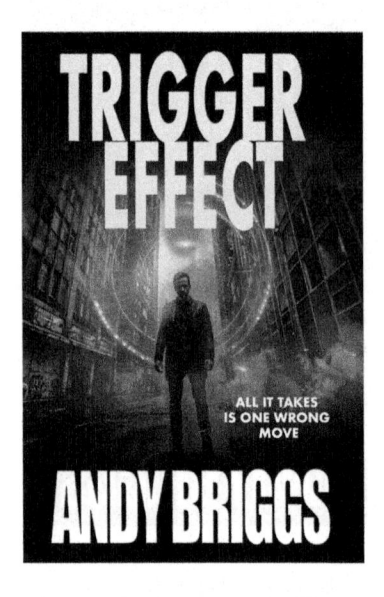

An explosive new thriller!

When White House press journalist, Tom Miller, gets bumped in the street, he is injected with something that slowly grows inside him like a tumor: an experimental bio-bomb.

It's inert... except for a long list of trigger effects that detonate it, all induced by the technological world around us.

All Miller has to do to survive is avoid everything...

Except he's discovered a list of other carriers... all headed towards a world summit. Now Miller is in a race against time – and the technological world - to stop the assassination and save his own life in the process...

Printed in Great Britain
by Amazon